PRELUDE TO ETERNITY

Borgo Press Books by BRIAN STABLEFORD

PRELUDE TO ETERNITY

A ROMANCE OF THE FIRST TIME MACHINE

by

Brian Stableford

THE BORGO PRESS

An Imprint of Wildside Press LLC

MMIX

CONTENTS

For Jane,

The Mistress of my Maze

ACKNOWLEDGMENTS

This story could not have been composed without the assistance of inspiration and crucial exemplars provided by numerous individuals, most importantly Dedalus, Plato, Pietro Locatelli, Heinrich von Biber, John Dee, Voltaire, Anton Mesmer, Richard Trevithick, Félix Bodin, Thomas Love Peacock, H. G. Wells, and A. E. van Vogt.

PRELUDE TO ETERNITY

CHAPTER ONE

THE LEVIATHAN OF STEEL AND STEAM

It took Michael Laurel a full five minutes to make his way along the platform at King's Cross Station in order to join the admirers ogling the steam-belching steel Leviathan that was England's most recent candidate to be the Seventh Wonder of the Modern World. It was reputed to be a prodigy, and a monster: a dragon such as the world had never seen, even in the Age of Myth and Magic.

When he finally arrived within sight of the locomotive, though, he was a trifle disappointed. It was certainly large and loud. It had the promised doorway to its infernal heart, into which the stoker would soon be shoveling coal at a furious rate. It had the promised sweat of steam oozing and belching from various narrow orifices. It had the promised smokestack generously distributing a fine fog of sooty particles. It was freshly painted in the claret-and-gold livery of the Academy. To Michael's eyes, however, trained to the study and reproduction of fruit and flowers, cloudy skies and expressive human faces, it lacked something.

He could not quite decide, at first, what to call the mysterious something that the locomotive lacked. It was not beauty, although the machine did have a certain irredeemable ugliness about its undeniable grandeur. Nor was it sublimity, although there was certainly a raw brutality about its innate power. Nor was it humanity, although there had been much talk in the coffee-shops where "Bohemian" artists and writers liked to congregate of the essential "soullessness" of the new generation of machines that was "despoiling the bosom of Nature". Indeed, it seemed to Michael, although it was merely a whimsical intuition, that the machine had far more humanity than most of the people he knew, and that machinery in general was more fully and more fervently ensouled than the quiet rural world of trees, meadows and streams—which, as a city-born and city-bred individual, he had never quite taken to his heart, although he liked to paint it well enough.

No, he finally decided, what the locomotive lacked, was not beauty, nor sublimity, nor humanity. What it lacked was *mystery*. Like all the products of modern technology, it was defiantly unmagical. It was the product of mathematical planning and precision workmanship. Nothing in its design and construction had been left to chance; there was no margin of hazard within which it might remain tantalizingly undefinable. In spite of its reputation, it was not a dragon at all, in the true sense of the word.

Michael knew that he ought to be grateful for the mathematical exactitude of the locomotive's planning and the scrupulous organization of its many parts. He was, after all, going to entrust his life to the monster, which was scheduled to reach the previously-unimaginable speed of sixty miles per hour on the fastest stretches of the brand new track laid between London and York. Indeed, he *was* grateful, in a dutiful sort of way—but his gratitude was tempered by the essential Romanticism of his temperament, which was inflamed at present by virtue of the fact that he was in love.

He sighed automatically as he remembered yet again—although it was impossible for him actually to forget it—that he was in love.

Sir Richard Trevithick sighed too, emitting a long hiss of steam through one of the more discreet of its many orifices.

"*There* she goes!" said the engineer, in a tone of smug satisfaction, pretending to address the stoker, although he was really playing to the packed grandstand. "Ain't she a beauty?"

Michael knew that engineers always called their beloved machines "she", even when the Academy had decided, in its wisdom to name them after males. Dick Trevithick might have been the proud father of the new wave of industrial revolution precipitated by the Cornish Engine, but the finest of his children would always be reckoned daughters, or mistresses, by the men who nurtured and guided them: the supposed masters who were, in reality, their faithful and adoring servants.

Michael knew that only a tiny minority of the excited people gathered on the platform to ogle the *Sir Richard Trevithick* actually had tickets to travel on the train. The others were ostensibly there to "see off" the lucky ones, although they had actually turned out to gawk at the locomotive, much as they turned up at Ascot or Henley to gawk at the season's fresh crop of debutantes, squired by the sons of the Admiralty and the Academy. Locomotives were, however, a trifle more democratic than the daughters of the aristocracy. Anyone could ride in the carriages they pulled—although some, admittedly, had to travel second class while others traveled first.

In spite of that democracy, and the unmagicality of which Michael might have been the only person present to be perversely aware, the members of the crowd were enraptured by the prideful Behemoth. Although nine days had passed since the engine had made its first timetabled journey from York to London and back again, without once breaking down—let alone blowing up, as several pessimists had loudly forecast—it was still seen as something fabulous, and as a glorious presentiment of the Age of Achievement to come.

Michael had taken off his hat in order to mop his brow with his handkerchief, so his hands and mind were fully occupied when a flabby hand suddenly slapped him on the back and the cheerful voice of Quentin Hope boomed in his ear. "Glorious sight, eh, Laurel! Makes one proud to be British, doesn't it?"

Michael could only stare forlornly at the hand that Hope extended to him in the wake of this enthusiastic greeting, although it occurred to him a few seconds later that it would have been simple enough to pop the handkerchief into the hat and extend his own to meet it. *For a man with the skilled and steady hand of a painter*, Michael thought, as he blushed in embarrassment, simultaneously trying to replace the hat on his head and the handkerchief in his pocket, *I really can be a remarkably clumsy oaf at times*.

Hope—a plump, pink-complexioned and ostentatiously jovial man who could easily have sat for a portrait of John Bull—merely laughed at his victim's confusion. He raised the unshaken hand to pat the artist on the shoulder, almost as if that were what he had intended all along. "Have you seen Jim Escott?" he asked, referring to his invariable traveling-companion, with whom he had been conducting a fervent running argument that was said to have extended over thirty years, every since the fateful day when the two of them had met in the junior common room on their first day at Eton.

Michael shook his head.

"No?" said Hope. "Can't say I'm surprised. How could the fellow stand here, confronted with this magnificent machine, and continue to contend that progress is an illusion? He'll be cowering in the carriage, I dare say, terrified of getting flecks of soot on his Savile Row suit. Your paints, canvases and easel safely stashed in the luggage van, are they, Laurel?"

Michael contrived a nod of the head. He had to admit, as he continued to stare at the steam locomotive, that Hope had a point. The *Trevithick* might not be magical, but it really did seem to be a perfect embodiment of the idea of progress, and a clear demonstration of its reality. However appropriate to its description borrowed terms like monster, Leviathan and Behemoth might be, the simple truth was that its mundane solidity, power and precision put every magical dragon of myth and legend to shame, demonstrating beyond the shadow of a doubt that the sure hand of the mechanic was nowadays mightier by far than the frothy mind of the fabulist.

Michael also had to admit, though, that the thought of entrusting his personal safety to the brutality of the locomotive terrified him. Had he had a choice, he would never have agreed to take his life in his hands by traveling in such a fashion—but he had not had a choice, because Cecilia had written to him to say that he "simply must" take the train. Even if, as seemed probable, she had intended the words *simply must* merely as an expression of enthusiasm, he was obliged to construe it as a command, because he was in love with her, and this was the first time that he had been invited to Langstrade Hall, her father's country residence, in order to meet her parents.

Michael had first been introduced to the Langstrades six months before, and had now seen Cecilia on seven precious occasions, but it had required patient planning on her part to persuade her father to issue such an invitation to him—not, alas, as a formally-recognized and officially-sanctioned suitor, but merely as a hopefully-soon-to-be-fashionable painter. He had not even been commissioned to paint a portrait of Cecilia, although he dearly hoped that his remit might be broadened out once he actually reached Langstrade; thus far, his mission was simply to paint the recently-completed edifice in the extensively-remodeled grounds that everyone in London Society liked to call "the Langstrade Folly".

"What wouldn't I have given to be on the engine's first scheduled journey last week, with the First Sea Lord and half the Admiralty, and the entire Privy Council of the Academy in tow?" Quentin Hope said, with an ostentatious sigh matched by a further hiss of steam. "The tenth round trip has a certain cachet of its own, though. It'll be something to tell our grandchildren, eh, Laurel? There'll be railways all over England by that time—probably all over the world—and you and I will be able to say that we were present at the beginning, if not on the Glorious Tuesday itself. We're still pioneers, aren't we?"

Hope sighed again, more profoundly this time. Yet again, *Sir Richard Trevithick* hissed fervently in excessive sympathy—reminding Michael, just for a moment, of his mother. The artist had to shake his head to clear it of that perverse thought, and Hope mistook the gesture.

"You don't agree?" he said. "Come on, Lad! I know you're an artist, and supposed to believe in all that Romantic fiddle-faddle about the loveliness of Mother Nature, but you're young, damn it! What are you, twenty-three, twenty-four? I suppose that makes you a child of the eighteenth century, but only just! You're a son of the Age of Steam, the Era of Progress! You must look to the future, my boy, as a wonderland of opportunity—and I shall make it my business this weekend to see that you do! Escott will fight me all the way, of course, and so will that old fool Carp, but Langstrade's in my camp, and so is Marlstone. They're both lunatics, admittedly, but they're lunatics on the side of the angels. Stick with me, young Laurel, and I'll show you the way the world's going, or my name's not Hope!"

The last remark was a quip that Quentin Hope produced so often that even Michael, who hardly knew the man, had overheard it half a dozen times before. Michael hastened to assure the optimist that his gesture had not been intended as a denial, and that he was indeed looking forward to telling his wonderstruck grandchildren that he had traveled from London to York on a train pulled by the *Sir Richard Trevithick* on the afternoon of Thursday the fifteenth of August 1822, a mere nine days after her first scheduled round trip.

Instead of rejoicing in this news, however, Hope sighed again. This time, the locomotive was not sympathetic.

Michael guessed that the third sigh had been occasioned by the fact that the older man might be beginning to wonder whether he would ever have the opportunity to dandle awestruck grandchildren on his own knees, in order that he could replicate the proud boast in question before an appropriate audience. Although it was by no means uncommon for gentlemen who had turned forty to marry, it was rare for those who delayed marriage so long to live to a sufficiently ripe old age to see their own grandchildren learn to walk. Michael hoped to be married long before he turned thirty, although he was quite convinced that, if fate were sufficiently cruel to prevent him from marrying Cecilia Langstrade, he would die a bachelor—quite probably of a broken heart.

He was distracted from this tender thought by the sight of a man elbowing his way urgently through the crowd, red-faced and perspiring in spite of his near-spectral thinness, which contrasted strongly with Hope's healthy rotundity. James Escott, it seemed, was not lurking in the first-class carriage reserved for the inner circle of Lord

Langstrade's weekend guests, avoiding soot and his rival's lyrical speeches on the modern wonders of steel, steam and telegraphy.

"There you are, Hope!" the thin man said, extending his hand as he arrived. "Good to see you, Laurel!" he added, swiftly.

This time, Michael had had time to prepare himself. His hat was safely ensconced on his head and his handkerchief had been discreetly retired to his trouser pocket. As soon as Escott released Hope's hand, Michael took his, and gripped it with what he hoped might pass for manly firmness.

"We'll have to hurry," Escott said, swiftly, obviously intent on interrupting Hope's anticipated eulogy. "The guard will be calling 'All Aboard' at any moment, and we're in the carriage next to the guard's van, right at the back. It was hardly worth the trouble of coming all the way up here, but I knew you'd be rooted to the spot, staring at the engine like some mesmerized somniloquist, and I knew that you'd be sure to miss the train if I didn't shepherd you aboard." He glanced at Michael as he added: "These starry-eyed optimists are all the same, Laurel. Heads in the clouds. No practicality. You'll join us, of course?"

"I only bought a second-class ticket," Michael admitted, blushing deeply. "I'll find a seat closer to the engine."

"Nonsense!" said Escott. "We have a spare seat in our reserved carriage—Sir Geoffrey Chatham has been detained in London, and won't be able to make the party at all. Signor Monticarlo and his daughter are there, and Lady Phythian arrived half an hour in advance, as usual, but there's one seat to spare now. We can't offer it to Carp, even if we wanted to, because he'll be traveling with his somniloquist."

"To be frank," Hope put in, "you'd be doing us a favor—raising the intellectual average, so to speak. I say nothing against Monticarlo, mind; he's a clever fellow, in his way, and his English is good when he plucks up the courage to use it, but he's not a great conversationalist. Lady Phythian, on the other hand, is an utter wet blanket—always treats Escott and myself as if we were a pair of naughty boys squabbling over our toys. It's a long way to York, and even a steam locomotive can't do the trip in the blink of an eye. Besides, I've promised to indoctrinate you in the philosophy of progress, and there's no better place to start than a railway carriage."

"And I can provide you with the necessary intellectual balance," Escott said, "to make sure that you're not blinded by the glare of Hope's rose-tinted spectacles. But we have to hurry, Hope, or we'll never get back to the carriage in time."

Michael was still hesitant, unsure as to what the rules of etiquette required or permitted him to say in response to the unexpected invitation.

"I can make sure you sit next to the lovely Carmela, if you like," Hope said. "She's said to be very artistic, and she makes up for the fact that she's reluctant to risk her English by smiling a lot."

Michael blushed yet again, this time in pure confusion. He had no idea whether Hope was simply trying to be kind, or whether he really did want the option of having someone else other than Escott to listen to him while he rode his favorite hobby-horse, but the one thing he did know was that he definitely did not want to arrive at Langstrade Hall in close company with a smiling Carmela Monticarlo, amid a drizzle of suggestive remarks about how well they had got on during the four-and-a-half-hour train journey and the subsequent ride in a hired diligence.

"Hope's right, for once in his life," Escott put in, his voice full of urgency. "If we're to have any decent conversation on the journey, we really do need a decent substitute for Chatham. Oblige us, please."

"But I only have a second-class ticket!" Michael protested, feebly, as Hope and Escott each took one of his arms and began to hustle him along the platform toward the rear of the train. "Won't I get into trouble if the guard catches me in a first-class compartment?"

"Not at all," Hope assured him, accelerating his pace. "The entire compartment's reserved; the seat's booked and paid for. Lord Langstrade would never forgive us if we allowed one of his guests to travel second-class while we had a seat to spare."

"Even a painter," Escott added, a trifle mischievously, as he lengthened his stride in order to keep pace with the scurrying optimist, "who's only been invited to immortalize his Folly. I'll wager that you'd rather be painting Miss Cecilia's portrait!"

Michael couldn't help noticing that this off-hand remark provoked a sharp glance of disapproval from Quentin Hope. He suffered a momentary stab of panic as he wondered whether the renowned optimist might be entertaining hopes in regard to Lord Langstrade's daughter.

It was not impossible, Michael supposed, that Hope might take advantage of the weekend to ask Langstrade for Cecilia's hand—and what Langstrade's response might be was anybody's guess, given that he had obviously inherited his father's legendary eccentricity. Who else but a Langstrade, after all, would have invited a little-known portrait-painter all the way to the wilds of Yorkshire to paint a mock-Medieval Keep in the heart of a Maze, designed according to a plan that had supposedly been drawn up by Dedalus himself?

"Isn't Gregory Marlstone traveling on the train?" Michael asked, although he cursed himself silently as soon as the words had spilled from his mouth. For one thing, the remark was bound to sound somewhat ungrateful, in view of the two men's generosity in offering to pluck him out of second-class chaos into first-class comfort, and the urgency with which they were exercising their invitation. For another, if there was the slightest possibility that Hope might be a rival for Cecilia's hand—if not her affection—then he certainly ought to seize the opportunity to confirm or falsify the hypothesis.

"Marlstone set off five days ago with six assistants and half a dozen carts," Escott told him. He had to pause thereafter when the cry of "All aboard!" was raised and echoed all along the platform, accompanied by a blast on the station-manager's whistle, but as soon as the thin man could make himself heard again, he continued: "Anyone else would have sent the equipment on ahead and followed at his leisure, but Marlstone won't let the components of his precious time machine out of his sight, all the more so since the fiascos at Horton Lacey and Chatsworth. If all has gone well with the convoy, he'll be there ahead of us, but my guess is that he'll have got bogged down somewhere in the Midlands, and probably won't arrive until Sunday. By the time he's got his blessed machine set up, the rest of us will be on our way home."

In spite of the difficulties of shoving their way through the crowd, Hope and Escott had succeeded in reaching the carriage containing their reserved compartment without ever letting go of Michael's captive arms. They literally lifted him off the ground in order to deposit him in the carriage, somewhat to the surprise and alarm of Lady Phythian, who had taken advantage of her early arrival to claim a window seat. The famous violinist Signor Monticarlo and his daughter Carmela had taken the two opposed seats on the far side of the carriage, next to the door to the corridor. Michael had been introduced to all of them at one time or another, but knew them even more slightly that he knew Hope and Escott.

The virtuoso and the two ladies did not seem unduly surprised to see Michael, obviously having no inkling of the ignominy of the second-class ticket, but they did not seem unduly delighted either. They greeted him politely, but rather coolly; when Hope propelled him toward the vacant seat between the two ladies, both of them seemed to Michael's anxious eyes to be a trifle disappointed that Hope had not taken the seat himself. In fact, the optimist took the spare window seat, while his meager companion took the seat opposite Michael.

Now that the carriage was fully-loaded it seemed rather cramped, largely because the luggage racks were full to overflowing and several items of luggage had had to be accommodated on the floor or on the passengers' laps. Signor Monticarlo, a short and delicate man with an abundance of sleek black hair and a moustache, was clutching one of his violin-cases. In spite of the capacious bandage she was sporting on her wrist, Carmela, who was a little taller and wirier than her father, was cradling another. Lady Phythian, who seemed rather large by comparison with the two Italians, had a proportionately enormous handbag on her lap. Michael had to maneuver his way to his seat with some skill, and felt that he was easing himself into a narrow gap as he sat down. Compared to conditions in a second-class compartment, however, the plushness and softness of the seats were sheer luxury.

Michael resolved to accept the inevitable with a good grace, sit back, and do his level best to enjoy the hectic journey to come.

CHAPTER TWO

THE BEGINNING OF THE JOURNEY

"Well," said Quentin Hope, as the train drew away from the platform, while the crowd left behind cheered and waved, "here we are in the very bosom of a mechanical miracle, participating in the latest glory of English science. Long live the First Sea Lord and the President of the Academy!"

""If ever there were a Ship of Fools...," Escott began, pitching straight in with evident relish—but he was immediately interrupted by Lady Phythian, who had obviously been present at more than one of Hope and Escott's showpiece arguments and was nursing a faint hope of being able to derail this one.

"I must be mad to have let young Langstrade talk me into this," the dowager pronounced, striking a melodramatic pose. "At my age, given my delicate health, the excessive speed is sure to prove fatal!"

Lady Phythian certainly did not seem to be in delicate health, in Michael's non-expert opinion. She was short of stature, but her embonpoint was robust, and her lungs were obviously in very good order indeed. In truth, she was not so very old, although she gave an impression of antiquity. She was probably no more than sixty, if that, but widowhood had conferred a particular stamp of authority upon her attitude and manner as well as her perceived status. As daughters and wives, however rich or aristocratic, Englishwomen were necessarily subservient, but if and when they became widows they acquired an independent authority that was somehow beyond challenge. Michael's mother had responded to her own widowhood by assuming an exaggerated concern for his well-being, but Lady Phythian had given birth to two sons and a daughter, and had married them all off successfully, so her widowhood had given her a far more general imperiousness reminiscent of the mythical Britannia in whose name the Admiralty ruled the waves.

Michael knew, by virtue of society chatter, that Lady Phythian had been relatively humbly born, as Ariadne Potts, but that she took great pride in the facts that her grandmother had been an Asherson, and that her husband, the late Viscount Phythian, had been a cousin of the Lowthers—a family that included the Earls of Lonsdale as well as several baronets of no particular significance. She had once been the evident social superior of her close friend Millicent Houghton, although the latter had overtaken her when her husband, Harold Langstrade, had been elevated to the peerage as the first Earl of Langstrade, reconnecting his surname to the Yorkshire village from which his ancestors supposedly hailed, and whose ancient manor he had bought from the Lords Office. Michael was not at all surprised, therefore, that Lady Phythian seemed to be looking down at him as he sat by her side, even though he was a head taller than she was. There was no hostility or contempt in her gaze when she deigned to turn in his direction, though; she was evidently reserving her judgment as to whether he was to be placed in the same "naughty boy" category to which she had long ago consigned Hope and Escott.

Michael guessed that the dowager's objection to high-speed travel was more a matter of conformity to expectation than genuine terror. He knew that there were legions of diehard conservatives in the land, who swore that nothing on Earth would ever tempt them to step aboard a carriage pulled by a steam locomotive. Such people were wont to opine that the human body had not been designed—whether by God or Evolution—to withstand the stresses of movement at such terrifying velocities, and that, in any case, such a mode of transportation had none of the camaraderie, romance and history of a journey by road. No one in his right mind, such skeptics stoutly maintained, wanted to live life at such an insane pace that a journey that had always taken at least two days was now crammed into a mere four and a half hours. He suspected, however, that Lady Phythian was not of that company. There was a slight twinkle in her eye when she made her dramatic gesture, and she pronounced her complaint as if she were reciting a line in a play.

"Reassure yourself, Lady Phythian," said Hope, serenely. "Destiny is on our side. The Commonwealth has long enjoyed the Empire of the Oceans, and now it has the means to exercise the same authority on land. Just as John Dee's telescope and Cornelius Drebbel's submarine paved the way for England to rule the waves, Dick Trevithick's Cornish Engines will make us masters of the Earth's surface, and its bowels too!"

Lady Phythian frowned at the use of the word "bowels" in a mixed carriage, but she was insufficiently quick off the mark to seize the initiative again by means of a further melodramatic pronouncement. Escott was not about to be forestalled for a second time.

"Steam will be the nation's ruin," Hope's rival stated, sententiously. "Using powerful engines to pump water out of mines will only encourage miners to dig deeper, so that the inevitable collapses will be all the more disastrous when they occur. Using those same engines to power mills has already thrown tens of thousands of craftsmen out of work, and reduced the remaining mill-workers to mere mechanical hands, rude slaves of machinery. The displaced and dispossessed will accumulate into a revolutionary rabble the likes of which England has not seen since the monarchy was toppled. Locomotives are direly dangerous even now, while they run on tracks and carry goods and innocent passengers, but when they're adapted for use in war—their engines fitted with cannon and their carriages filled with artillerists—they'll be so destructive that indiscriminate mechanized massacre will become routine. Enjoy your mechanical honeymoon, Hope—it can't and won't last."

"The days of warfare are numbered, Escott," Hope affirmed, confidently. "The Pax Romana was a feeble affair compared to the Pax Anglica. The world has never seen an alliance like that between the First Sea Lord and the President of the Academy, and their association will make certain that social progress advances hand in hand with technological progress. We are privileged to be alive at the dawn of the Euchronian Era, and hands that are idle today, or reduced to mindlessly repetitive labor because their old skills have become redundant, will not need the Devil to find them clever work. The march of science will do that, infallibly and triumphantly. Future generations of laborers will not be akin to slaves, even in careless metaphor; they will be true collaborators with machinery, participating in a marvelous complementarity of skills. Steam is brute force, but electricity is art, and electricity will be the foundation of the next technological revolution—as witness the telegraphic systems that control the signals distributed along the railway."

Michael observed that the Monticarlos had already lost the thread of the argument; although they both spoke conversational English with commendable fluency, and hardly any accent, the terms in which Hope and Escott were pontificating were too esoteric to be easily comprehensible. Carmela whispered something to her father in Italian, as if to start up a second, rival conversation, but the violinist frowned at her and shook his head, instructing her not to be impolite.

Having heard such exchanges a dozen times before, Lady Phythian obviously had no desire to listen to another, but it seemed that she had already despaired of any possibility of controlling such disobedient individuals. For the moment, she contented herself with making her disinterest in the argument manifest, turning away from Michael and Hope alike to gaze loftily out of the widow, as if she were indeed Britannia reviewing her estates.

Michael was now convinced that Hope and Escott had only been eager to invite him to join them in their carriage in order that they might obtain a relatively fresh audience for their eternal quarrel rather than to invite any contribution to their discussion, but he did not hold it against them. The same chatter that had informed him so fully of Lady Phythian's history and character had filled in their background for him. They had gone on from Eton to Balliol, and then—having come into their respective inheritances within a matter of months—had set out to make the Grand Tour together. Instead of following the customary route to Italy, however, they had decided to design their own itinerary, which would take them to even remoter cradles of civilization: to Greece, to Egypt, and finally to Crete, where they had spent a full year exploring the ruins of Knossos, the ancient capital in the vicinity of Makro Teikho, whose recently-excavated remains had become a playground for the assiduous antiquarians of England and the German States. It was there that they had met the present Earl of Langstrade, who had then been known as "young Harry Langstrade" to distinguish him from his father—who had only recently become "Old Harry Langstrade of Langstrade" instead of mere "Old Harry Langstrade"—and who had not yet met his wife-to-be, Emily Hale.

According to the gossip, it was the Grand Tour that had completed the opposition between the two traveling companions, perfecting its universality. It had been the three years of their "educational odyssey" that had extended Hope's innate optimism into a wholehearted philosophy of progress, and Escott's natural pessimism into quasi-apocalyptic gloom. It had also stretched Hope's Whig sympathies into near-radical enthusiasm for political reform and Utopian—or, as he preferred to call it, Euchronian—social planning, while elaborating Escott's Toryism into a near-mystical appreciation of the lost glories of the past. It had even been their years in and around the Mediterranean, so it was said, that had made Hope so plump and Escott so thin, because the former had thrived on native diets they had encountered there, whereas the latter had never been able to reconcile his stomach to their unfamiliarity.

Some people professed surprised that the two men had remained friends once they had returned to England to enjoy life as consummate *amateurs*, but they had always represented themselves as inevitable dialectical elements of a greater unity, like the north and south poles of a magnet. Now that he was able to listen to them holding forth at close range, as it were, Michael was able to appreciate the truth of that judgment. Had only one of them been present, his ideas would have been mere philosophical pontifications, overblown and essentially tedious, but because they were together, their contrasted ideas obtained a kind of vibrancy from a cut-and-thrust combat that was almost akin to music in its rhythm and resonance. Instead of being tedious, they seemed alive and electric, spitting sparks at one another like the various kinds of apparatus that had been built and exhibited to demonstrate the telegraphic principle.

For the moment, however, Michael was glad that the duty the two men had sought to impose upon him by means of their invitation was not particularly burdensome. Although he continued to lend a reverent ear to the erratic course of their flamboyant dispute, the painter soon allowed his attention to wander. His eyes strayed to the window, while his mind relaxed into a pleasant reverie, the principal image of which was Cecilia Langstrade's lovely face. How he longed to paint her cornflower-blue eyes and silky blonde hair! How he longed, in fact, to reach a far greater intimacy with that face than mere paint could ever permit!

Michael did not have the faintest idea what the probability was that he would ever achieve that kind of intimacy. That Cecilia liked him a great deal he had no doubt, but they had only met on formal social occasions, surrounded by crowds, and the letters they had exchanged had so far been rather tentative in their affectionate tone. He was very hopeful that the weekend house-party at Langstrade Hall would give him more than one opportunity to speak to her in private, far more confidentially than the formality of a letter would allow, and he was also very hopeful that such circumstances would confirm and enhance her manifest regard for him—but the small steps he might be able to take between a Thursday evening and a Tuesday morning were a long way short of the social ground that he would eventually have to cover if their relationship were to mature.

In theory, differences in social status were far less important nowadays than they had been in his late father's day—and if Mr. Hope could be believed, the erosion of that importance could only accelerate in future—but the fact remained that the Langstrades were now fully-fledged members of the aristocracy, while the Laurels were not. Horatio Laurel's highly distinguished naval career had won him sufficient social status to launch Michael into Society—in which circles a painter had to move if he were to have any chance of making a living—but could not give him "quality". The Langstrades' elevation to the aristocracy had, by contrast, provided the family with an inalienable certificate of quality, and the fact that it was recent inevitably served to make the present Earl even more conscious of that status that he would have been had he been the thirty-second instead of the second. The fact that the first Earl had insisted on regarding the entitlement as a re-elevation rather than a simple promotion, and as a long-belated recognition of an ancient due, was a further complication. Michael had no idea how the second Earl might react to the possibility of acquiring a mere painter as a son-in-law, even if Cecilia could be completely won over to the prospect.

The first Earl of Langstrade had been appointed to the peerage at the behest of the Academy, for his contributions to industry. He had been one of the pioneers of mechanization in textile manufacture even before the advent of steam engines, and had become famous in political circles for his stout resistance to Richard Arkwright's monopolistic maneuvers—a resistance that had become known as the Second War of the Roses, even though Arkwright's enterprise was based in Derbyshire rather than Lancashire. The first Earl had, however, always been insistent that his family had been aristocrats long before the Norman Conquest or the "Saxon Tyranny" that had preceded it. He claimed to be a direct descendant of Celtic Longstrides, who had fought for centuries to keep the Viking invaders of his beloved dales at bay before being trapped between two implacable forces in the series of contests that had divided England between Norse and Germanic invaders.

Indeed, Old Harry's antiquarian fantasies had extended far beyond that, asserting that the settlers in Britain who had become the Celts had been the descendants of Cretans who had escaped the catastrophic destruction of the Minoan civilization in the volcanic upheaval that had been responsible for the mythical Deluge, and that the Longstrides were the descendants of the greatest of all the ancient world's engineers: Dedalus. In Old Harry's contention, the revolution he had helped to bring about in the textile industry had been an extrapolation of family tradition, the modern mechanical loom being merely "a recapitulation of the Labyrinthine principle".

The only item of "evidence" supporting the first Earl's insistence on linking the Langstrades and the probably-imaginary Longstrides with Dedalus was a diagram of a maze inscribed on a piece of parchment that had been found in the ruins of Cribden Abbey, which had once occupied the site on which Langstrade Hall now stood. Just as the old hall had replaced the Abbey, Old Harry had insisted, the Abbey had replaced a pagan place of worship, whose central feature must have been the maze described on the parchment. Although the first Earl had been able to confirm, during his sojourn in the ruins of Knossos, that the design on the parchment bore no significant resemblance to the design of the actual Cretan Labyrinth, parts of which had now been excavated, he had merely concluded that the Cretan Labyrinth had been Dedalus' first draft, and that the engineer had spent the time in which he had been imprisoned in his own construction by the tyrant Minos dreaming of the new design that he had carried away to England when the volcanic eruption set him free.

The second Earl had inherited his father's eccentricity along with his wealth, and had thought it his filial duty to complete the grand plans that the first Earl had made, perhaps more in hope than expectation. Michael knew that he ought to be grateful for that, given that it was the expression of Lord Langstrade's whim that had generated his commission to paint "Harold Longstride's Keep", but he couldn't help feeling slightly uneasy about it. The instructions he had received were detailed, and there seemed to be an awful possibility that his picture would somehow fail to meet the Earl's expectations. He had been told that he must establish the perspective of the Keep very carefully, taking in both the immediate background of the wall of the reconstructed Maze and the more distant background of Bancroft Scar, positioning a symbolic yew tree within the field of view with the utmost care.

According to what Old Harry had passed off as a family legend, scrupulously handed down over the generations, the mighty Harold Longstride had once emerged from behind a yew tree to surprise and confront Emund Snurlson, the leader of a host of Viking marauders, on a late summer's day corresponding to the modern August seventeenth, in the year that would now be reckoned as 822 A.D. In consequence of his victory in the ensuing single combat—in which, for some unaccountable reason, Snurlson's followers had not intervened—the Vikings had retreated and their heroic conqueror had built the "original keep", in order that the Norsemen should never conquer the shallow valley in which his lands were situated.

Almost everyone except the present Lord Langstrade and his dutiful mother—including his wife and daughter—believed that the legends of Harold Longstride and the Dedalus Maze were the pure stuff of dreams, but that did not matter to Michael. It was in expectation of celebrating the millennial anniversary of Harold's supposed duel with Emund Snurlson that the new Keep—or the Folly—and its surrounding Maze had been built over the course of the last seven years; Michael, like Signor Monticarlo, Augustus Carp and Gregory Marlstone, had been invited to Langstrade Hall in order to provide an apt commemoration of the occasion. Lady Phythian had been included in the party because she, like the absentee Geoffrey Chatham, had long been a regular visitor to the Hall, while Hope and Escott had been preferred to the present Earl's other acquaintances because of their auspicious meeting in the ruins of Knossos.

Michael was able to take some comfort in the fact that he seemed, at present, to be the only intended contributor to the supposedly-momentous occasion whose contribution seemed fully assured. Gregory Marlstone's time machine had already failed to function twice at more widely-advertised and much better-attended exhibitions, and the London newspapers had turned against him in no uncertain terms, branding him a philosophical failure and freely referring to his third intended trial, even in advance, as "the folly in the Folly". Augustus Carp's reputation as a mesmerist had also taken a severe knock since he had suffered the sudden loss of his long-time somniloquist, a woman of delicate constitution carried off by the influenza; the replacement he had recently recruited was said to be mediocre at best. To cap it all, Carmela Monticarlo—who usually accompanied her father on the piano when he played sonatas—had sprained her wrist badly, forcing the violinist to restrict his intended program to solo pieces, in the performance of which he was reputed to be far outshone by his more famous contemporary, Signor Paganini.

Taking everything into consideration, Michael thought, as he stared out of the window of the carriage, looking over Lady Phythian's bulky shoulder, his performance with the brush ought to be the most reliable on offer—but that had to be balanced against the fact that he was far less famous in his own field than any of the other three "performers" was in his, and none of them had the burden of anxiety that arose from being hopelessly in love with his host's daughter.

CHAPTER THREE

LADY PHYTHIAN AND THE LANGSTRADE GHOSTS

"I don't agree that the current vogue for Medievalism, of which Langstrade provides a prime example, is inherently anti-progressive," Quentin Hope said to his loyal adversary—presumably in the response to the suggestion that it was, although Michael had not returned his attention to the argument in time to catch Escott's last remark. "Progressiveness doesn't require the past to be forgotten—quite the contrary. Without a keen awareness of the past, progress couldn't be perceived, let alone properly measured and appreciated, and it's entirely right that we should loyally celebrate centenaries and millennia of every sort, including imaginary ones. Centenary and millennial celebrations are inherently comparative, forcing us to observe and calculate how far we have come in the interim. It's entirely justifiable for the present Earl of Langstrade, as the heir to an industrial fortune forged in loudly-clattering automated mills and secured by democratic hegemony, to set himself up in contradictory juxtaposition with the legendary Harold Longstride, a pre-feudal chieftain for whom life was little more than eternal agricultural labor, punctuated by occasional bloody struggles against violent marauders."

"Langstrade's not interested in drawing comparisons to demonstrate the superiority of modern civilization over ancient barbarity," Escott retorted, scornfully. "His interest in the past is a purely nostalgic one, which represents a calculated antithesis to the mechanized source of his fortune and status. He's trying to identify himself with the imaginary Harold Longstride, who was invented by his father for precisely that Romantic purpose. The reason that Langstrade is so insistent that his fictitious ancestor still haunts the grounds of the Hall, along with his retinue—even though the modern building bears not the slightest resemblance to whatever might have stood there in the ninth century, and in spite of the fact that no presently-discernible trace of any keep existed before the foundations of the Folly were laid—is that aristocratic privilege is based in the prestige of the past, and requires endorsement by it. The imaginary ghost of Harold Longstride is a quasi-paternal figure, symbolic of an imagined heritage, and his actual non-existence is testimony to the force of the longing that Langstrade experiences to turn his back on the bewildering present and the prospect of an even stranger future: a longing for continuity, stability and an end to the madness of *progress*."

"I beg your pardon, Mr. Escott," Lady Phythian put in, sharply, "but the ghosts of Langstrade are certainly not non-existent, any more than they are *quasi-paternal*. As you know perfectly well, I have seen the phenomenon with my own eyes, on more than one occasion, and the number of other witnesses, in the course of the last twenty years, must run into the hundreds."

"With all due respect, Lady Phythian," said Hope, his voice dripping skepticism in spite of his conscientious attempt to feign a polite and placatory tone, "you can't be sure that what you saw was Harold Longstride and his retinue tracking Emund Snurlson, as the more credulous witnesses to the *phenomenon* contend."

"*I* never claimed that the apparition was Harold Longstride and his retinue tracking Emund Snurlson," the dowager replied, tartly. "That was Old Harry's interpretation, and it is not for me to question his opinion, but I had no way of attributing any particular identity to the apparition myself. I never had the slightest doubt, however, that what I saw and felt was supernatural in origin. Over the years, in fact, I am convinced that I have got to know it very well, and can certainly feel its presence whenever it is manifest—but I am still uncertain as to whether it is the spirit of a human being, or several spirits of several human beings. I am hoping that Dr. Carp might provide some illumination on that point, although his present somniloquist is something of a disappointment.

"The mere shadow of her predecessor, no doubt," Escott suggested, merrily. In spite of his deep interest in the mysteries of the past, Michael concluded, the pessimist was obviously a Sadducee when it came to apparitions of the dead and other spiritual entities.

"I know that you have never seen any apparition when you have visited Langstrade in the past, Mr. Escott," Lady Phythian said, sternly, "but that does not give you the right to disparage those who have. I'm no somniloquist myself, but I *am* sensitive to such otherworldly manifestations in my own fashion. I must insist on the absolute reality of the Langstrade ghosts, although I reserve my judgment as to the nature and identity of the spiritual entities in question."

"That's very wise as well as conscientious, Lady Phythian," Hope was quick to put in. "Progress in the nascent science of psychognosis has been slow, I fear, compared to recent progress in mechanics, despite the best efforts of men like Dr. Carp, but people with open minds hope and expect that the situation will improve dramatically as time goes by. Your attitude does you credit, as does your insistence."

The dowager did not seem particularly grateful for this intervention, and obviously suspected that Hope was insincere. Michael had the same suspicion.

"We're being a trifle rude, I fear," Escott countered. "We have three people with us who have not visited the Hall before, and even if Mr. Laurel has heard tales of the ghost, Signor Monticarlo and Signorina Carmela surely have not. Perhaps, Lady Phythian, you'd care to explain to them what it is that you have seen?"

Lady Phythian looked at Signor Monticarlo. Obliged to respond—and perhaps grateful for an opportunity to make a contribution to the conversation at last—the violinist nodded his head. "*Si*, Milady," he said. "I will be most grateful—and Carmela too."

Carmela nodded in agreement, and smiled, but could not manage even the faintest of "*si*'s."

Lady Phythian nodded in her usual imperious fashion, then paused for effect before continuing, apparently slightly inflated by pride now that the distinguished violinist's handsome dark eyes were fixed upon her, full of respectful curiosity.

"I've known the dowager Lady Langstrade since she was Millicent Houghton," she said, "and I've been a frequent guest at the new Hall ever since the reconstruction rendered it fit to live in—at least once a year for nearly twenty years now, in good times and sad times alike. I'd heard vague tales of the ghost long before I ever got to see it, but they were generally regarded as servants' gossip in those days. Although the old manor house was called Langstrade Hall, no Langstrades had lived in it for centuries—it was even owned, for a while, by relatives of mine, the Ashersons—and all the ghost stories associated with it were old enough to be treated with contempt. The reconstruction of the new Hall seemed to change that, though. Perhaps the ancient ghosts were disturbed somehow, and prompted to walk again—but I make no claim as to that.

"The first time I experienced an apparition for myself was seventeen years ago, but it was so slight—the merest of suspect presences—that it was only in hindsight that I realized what it must have been. The first time I *saw* ghosts, clearly and unequivocally, was in 1811. It was late at night, in August, during a heat-wave. I was in my usual room—the Yellow Room, it's called now—which faces east. I couldn't sleep, and I got out of bed in order to go to the window, in the hope that I might catch a breeze by leaning out, since none seemed to be capable of making its way into the room. That was when I saw a group of uncanny lights, moving slowly and methodically over what was, in those days, a vast lawn...."

Escott opened his mouth as if to interrupt—presumably, Michael guessed, to inform the Monticarlos that the location in question was now the site of the Langstrade Maze—but Lady Phythian, intent on telling her story in her own way, silenced him with an irritated frown.

"I woke Millicent," the dowager continued, "who woke the late Lord Langstrade, who summoned his butler, Heatherington, and his gardener, Jefferies, in order to mount an investigation. We all went out together, taking courage from our numbers. All five of us saw the lights from a distance, as we approached and agreed that they were not natural, but by the time we reached the ground over which they were moving, they had vanished into thin air. Jefferies declared that they must have been swarms of fireflies engaged in mating dances, but no one else believed that ridiculous suggestion for a moment."

This time it was Hope who tried to interrupt, quite possibly to offer a learned discourse on the mating habits of fireflies, but again Lady Phythian refused to relinquish the floor.

"*That*," the story-teller continued, emphatically, "was only the first time I saw the ghosts. Nine years ago, in 1813, the event was repeated, almost exactly. This time, again from the window of the Yellow Room, I was able to count the lights—there were eight—and was able to discern that they were ghostly lanterns, held aloft by shadowy hands, moving in strange spirals around a region at the further end of the lawn. Again, Jefferies, having arrived at the spot after their disappearance, declared that they must have been fireflies—but this time, Millicent, Harry and I had got much closer before the lanterns winked out, and none of us was in any doubt that they really *were* ghostly lanterns. That was when Harry—Old Harry, that is, not the present Earl, who was left to sleep, much to his annoyance—guessed that the apparition must be taking place on the anniversary of Harold Longstride's combat with Emund Snurlson, and that the ghosts must be converging on the yew tree in the shadow of which the crucial fight to the death had taken place.

"The third time I saw the apparition, seven years ago, it was clearer still. This time, I was able to make out the silhouettes of the human figures carrying the lanterns. They were, alas, not pale and shiny, as ghosts are often said to be, but dark and fugitive. I am certain nevertheless that they constituted two groups of four, the second group seemingly tracking the first along their strangely convoluted spiral route—although both groups broke up before the second caught up with the first, and they were in complete disarray by the time they disappeared again."

Escott, despairing of being able to get a word in edgeways, caught Michael's eye and raised his eyebrows expressively, unnoticed by the story-teller.

"I saw the apparition one more, three years ago," Lady Phythian continued, as unstoppable as the *Sir Richard Trevithick*, which was now traveling through the northern hinterlands of Hertfordshire at full steam, "but, much to my disappointment, instead of becoming clearer once again, it had returned to its former vagueness. Mr. Hope and Mr. Escott have never seen the phantom lanterns, even though they have been guests on the anniversary, but they always sleep in the Rose Room and the Lilac Room, both of which face south, and on the one year that they consented to wait up all night in case the ghost put in an appearance—four years ago, if I remember rightly—the phenomenon did not appear. They doubtless believe that I imagined the whole thing, and that it is partly because of my overheated imagination that the present Lord Langstrade insisted on completing his father's plans for the Maze and the Keep, but I know full well that what Millicent, Harry and I saw was not natural, and that it really was connected to the Maze."

Signor Monticarlo looked puzzled, but was too polite to interrupt; he merely exchanged a glance with his daughter, who smiled at him tenderly. Lady Phythian took the hint, though, and elaborated her explanation.

"In addition to hearing tales of the ghost," she said, "I had long grown used to seeing the document on which the Langstrade Maze is designed. Whether it really is a copy of a design originally made by Dedalus of Knossos I have no idea, but I am certain in my own mind that there is something mysterious and magical about it. I feel it whenever I look at the diagram, in the same way that I often used to feel the presence of the Langstrade ghosts when sitting on the lawn where the Maze now stands, even in broad daylight. I have felt it even more strongly while exploring the maze itself, during the years when its hedges were not as intimidating as they are now.

"At any rate, the ghosts whose lanterns I saw were definitely *walking the maze*, even though construction of the present Maze had not yet begun when I first saw the apparition. They were heading from the periphery to the center: the location where the Keep and the yew tree now stand proud once again, in commemoration of the glorious summer of 822 A.D., when Harold Longstride defeated Emund Snurlson in single combat and blocked the progress of the Viking invasion—the renewals of which he succeeded in keeping at bay for the rest of his life, although his descendants could not, in the end, resist the incursions of Eric Bloodaxe."

Lady Phythian nodded her head as she drew to her conclusion, as if to imply that what she had said was more than sufficient to confound the most determined skeptic who ever drew breath.

"With all due respect, Lady Phythian," Quentin Hope said again, just as insincerely as the first time, "and without wishing to endorse the unreasonably stubborn skepticism of my friend Mr. Escott, I wonder whether we might be confusing causes and effects slightly. You claim that the ghosts, in appearing to simulate the movements of someone walking the Maze that Lord Langstrade subsequently constructed on their stamping-ground, were reproducing some past event or ritual—but I can't help suspecting that your seeing the ghosts, and your interpretation of their movements, might well have been partially responsible for the first Earl's decision to site the Maze there, and the second Earl's decision to complete his father's plan. After all, there was no previous connection, even in rumor, between the ghosts and the diagram, was there? They were two entirely separate components of the first Earl's imagined family history."

"I am by no means the only person to have seen the Langstrade ghosts move in that peculiar fashion," Lady Phythian said, stiffly. "I was not the first observer to connect the pattern with the Maze, but once the connection had been pointed out, I was able to see with my own eyes, and feel with my own heart, that it was true. The present Lord Langstrade has seen the phantom lanterns for himself, and so have his wife Emily and his daughter Cecilia. They have all confirmed that the lanterns' movements do correspond, very precisely, to the pattern of the Dedalus design."

"That tends to be the way with ghost sightings in Britain," Escott put in, as if to inform Signor Monticarlo of a relevant item of folkloristic analysis. "Each seer reproduces what previous seers have seen, although each one also tends to elaborate the pattern a little further. There is a kind of *feedback* process, by which the reported illusions not only sustain one another but collaborate in their own elaboration and sophistication. That's what Hope would call the fundamental *psychognosis* of the phenomenon—the phenomenon of ghost-seeing, that is, not the supposedly supernatural phenomenon itself."

Signor Monticarlo was manifestly mystified, the terms of this speech having far exceeded the competence of his English but he nodded anyway and said: "*Si.*"

"There was *no illusion* involved," Lady Phythian insisted, her voice becoming frosty in spite of the sultriness of the carriage, whose atmosphere was becoming rather oppressive. "What I saw was quite real."

Michael judged that the built-up tension was in need of relaxation. "Unlike Signor Monticarlo and his daughter," he said, "I'm vaguely familiar with the legends surrounding Langstrade Hall, but I really ought to obtain a fuller and more accurate account of them before I take on the task of painting the Keep. Would you be kind enough, Lady Phythian, to explain to us in a little more detail what you mean by the *Dedalus design*?"

"The original representation of the maze," Lady Phythian said, apparently glad to be able to say something that could not call her honesty or perspicacity into question, "or, at least, the oldest surviving representation, is a piece of parchment that now hangs over the mantelpiece in the large drawing-room, carefully framed and protected by glass. The old Hall was built in the ruins of a Cistercian abbey that had been built in the thirteenth century and destroyed during Henry VIII's abolition of the monasteries. The abbey had been reputed to have custody of several holy relics and a number of scriptural documents. The relics had all been stolen, along with their reliquaries, and the documents removed—with one exception, which had been hidden in a niche in the old crypt. When the crypt was converted into a cellar during the building of the old Hall, that surviving parchment was unearthed."

The dowager hesitated briefly, presumably because she was about to move back into the realm of rumor and fancy, but soon took the plunge. "The diagram on the parchment was thought at first to be a sketch for one of the mazes that decorate the floors of so many Gothic churches, but the diggers working on the new Hall's foundations also found evidence of a stone maze that far antedated the Abbey and must have been prehistoric. There were not enough stones left to allow the design or precise extent of the prehistoric maze to be calculated, but there was sufficient similarity to encourage the conclusion that the design antedated the Abbey too. The parchment itself must be Medieval, but what it represents is apparently much older than the thirteenth century—or, indeed, the ninth.

"The former Lord Langstrade came to believe that the design depicted in the document was a representation of a maze designed to fulfill some magical or mystical purpose, connected to the first settlement of the valley by refugees from Minoan Crete, including the great engineer Dedalus, whose escape from imprisonment before the catastrophe that destroyed Knossos is plaintively symbolized in the myth of his manufacture of wings and the subsequent death of Icarus. I believe that Harry once considered recreating the Maze in the same local sandstone of which the Keep at its center was to be—and is—constructed, but the cost of construction would have been prohibitive, so his son contented himself with hawthorn hedges. The central hexagonal space is some fifty yards across in the actual version, and the distance between the two outer hedges is almost twice that; the total length of all the hedges is, I believe, more than a mile."

"Why did Lord Langstrade build the Maze around the Keep?" Michael asked, helpfully. "Does he imagine that Harold Longstride built his own Keep within a maze that was still present in his own day, or merely that he was aware that a maze had once existed there?"

"Harold Longstride would presumably have been aware that there had once been a stone maze on the site where he built *his* Keep," Lady Phythian opined, cautiously, "even if it had been broken up long before his own era. Legend would have told him as much."

"In respectful recognition of his own legendary status, no doubt," Escott murmured, so softly that Michael was not sure that anyone but he had heard the remark.

Carmela Monticarlo spoke in English for the first time, to say: "I hope that I shall see the ghost. I should like to see a ghost."

"Unfortunately, my dear young lady," said Escott, in his normal voice, "you might have to go into the Maze to do that, since the hedges have now grown so tall as to cut off the view from the first-floor, where I have stood by a window more than once by night, in the hope of catching a glimpse of phantom lights—in vain, alas."

"I look forward to seeing the design," Michael said, thoughtfully. "Indeed, I shall need to consult it very carefully, since I shall have to get to the heart of the Maze in order to set up my easel there."

"Don't worry about that," said Escott, with a mischievous sideways glance at Hope. "I'm sure that Miss Cecilia will be only too pleased to guide you, as she has previously consented to guide Hope and myself—not only into the heart of the maze, but out again, when you need release."

CHAPTER FOUR

SIGNOR MONTICARLO AND
THE *CAPRICCI ENIGMATI*

When the educational discussion of ghosts and the Langstrade Maze had concluded, Hope and Escott resumed their debate about progress almost seamlessly, as if the change of subject had been as good as a rest, giving them time to recharge their argumentative Voltaic piles.

Hope argued that any reasonable man ought to accept that technological and social progress were inextricably linked, marching forward in step, and cited as proof the fact that England, which had been in the forefront of technological progress for more than two centuries, had also maintained its position in the vanguard of social progress, having been the first major European nation to dispose of its monarchy. Indeed, he went further than that, arguing that the Glorious Revolution of 1642 could not have been wholly successful had it not been for the previous scientific and technological advances made by the members of John Dee's secret college, nor maintained in their absence.

The emergence of the ruling triumvirate comprising the First Sea Lord, the President of the Academy and the Leader of the Commons was, Hope contended, entirely dependent on the technological advantages that Dee had been able to donate to the Navy and the transformation of the esoteric college into a publicly accountable and meritocratic Academy. Without such balancing factors in place, he suggested, Oliver Cromwell might easily have made himself king, or might have been deposed by a Restoration, rather than paving the way for True Democracy.

Escott, by contrast, maintained that the Revolution, whose gloriousness he begged leave to doubt, had been based in religion rather than politics, and that its true parents had been Protestantism and Puritanism. He did admit that John Dee had played a crucial role in laying its groundwork, but as a protestant rather than a mathematician. According to him, democracy had no advantages over monarchy, because the essential function of government—the extortion of the many for the benefit of the few—remained exactly the same, and always would. Technology, in this view, was merely an aspect of the instrumentality of this extortion; although it seemed to be improving continually, as the power and cleverness of machines advanced, all that really changed was the intricacy of methods of political exploitation, which were bound eventually to reach a genuinely revolutionary breaking-point.

Even if England's apparent stranglehold on naval traffic—the Empire of the Oceans—were genuinely unbreakable, Escott claimed, the seeds of the nation's destruction had already been sown in its native soil, where the First Sea Lord was nowadays no more than a figurehead. The only way the nation could be saved and perpetuated, in his view, was by a reversion to Medieval values and a system of craftsmen's guilds, supported by a rigid imperial hierarchy.

Michael listened to all this intellectualizing rather diffidently, not caring much which of the two philosophical combatants might be right, if either of them were. It all seemed rather abstract to him, totally irrelevant to his personal concerns and problems—although he felt slightly ashamed of himself for thinking so, given that it made him seem a trifle small-minded. His eyes continually drifted to the window, in search of the peaceful green landscapes of rural England. Somewhat to his annoyance, though, his gaze was continually trapped by the telegraph poles that flitted past the fast-moving window with metronomic regularity—an effect that was curiously mesmeric.

Michael had only been subjected to intense mesmeric treatment once, at the age of thirteen, when his mother had summoned a Mesmerist in a desperate attempt to prevent him scarring himself by scratching the spots of a pox. The treatment had worked, after a fashion—he had, at least, avoided serious scarring—but the Mesmerist had pronounced him a difficult subject and recommended that he stick to Paracelsian therapies in future. He did not fall into a trance now, but he was annoyed by the fact that the poles, working in collaboration with their fellow symbol of the triumphs of modern technology, the *Sir Richard Trevithick*, seemed to be exerting a more tangible force on his resistant consciousness than the doctor had. Eventually, he had to redirect his gaze into the carriage again, settling it briefly on Signor Monticarlo because he feared catching the eye of the smiling Carmela.

Signor Monticarlo, who had been twiddling his moustache absent-mindedly, shifted uncomfortably when Michael looked directly at him, and attempted to join in with Hope and Escott's debate, albeit rather tentatively. He offered the polite suggestion that art often flourished under tyranny, offering the Italian city states of the Renaissance as his primary examples. This opinion was hotly denied by both Hope and Escott, who both lamented what the Roman Empire had done to the intellectual legacy of the democratic Athenians, and proclaimed that the genius of men like John Milton and Jonathan Swift could never have thrived in England under a monarchy, in which political situation both men would undoubtedly have been summarily dispatched to the gallows.

In the meantime, Carmela Monticarlo continued smiling—particularly, it seemed to Michael, at him, to whose presence she seemed to have warmed, gradually but considerably, if only because the two mature Englishmen seemed so disagreeable.

In an attempt to calm things down, and also to deflect Carmela's attention, Michael asked Signor Monticarlo what he intended to play during the recital arranged for the following night.

"Because I am compelled to set aside my usual program," the violinist said, picking his words carefully, "I shall try something new—something no one has ever attempted before. Have you, by any chance, heard of my compatriot, Niccolò Paganini?"

"I've heard the name," Michael admitted.

"I can't understand why he's so famous," Lady Phythian put in, obligingly. "I heard him play once, but I didn't like it at all. The scales and arpeggios were far too rapid, and his violin was out of tune. He's overrated, in my opinion."

If the dowager expected this dismissal to delight Signor Monticarlo, she was mistaken. "Paganini is a genius," the violinist stated, flatly. "I cannot match him. He has extraordinarily long fingers, so he can play notes that no one else can. I cannot hope to emulate him, but I share his interest in *scordatura*, and I shall try to make a more modest demonstration of its virtues."

"*Scordatura* involves unorthodox tunings of the violin," supplied Hope, ever eager to show off his erudition.

"*Si*," said Signor Monticarlo, curtly, evidently no more delighted to be interrupted while telling his story than Lady Phythian had been while telling hers. "Paganini's *Capriccio in A minor*, which no one else can play, is based on one of the Rosary Sonatas of the Bohemian composer Heinrich von Biber. There are fifteen in all, each one employing a different tuning of the violin. Five celebrate the joyful mysteries, five the sorrowful mysteries, and a further six pieces—five sonatas and a *passacaglia*—celebrate the glorious mysteries. Paganini's A-minor *capriccio* is based on von Biber's A-minor sonata, celebrating *The Coronation of the Virgin Mary as the Queen of Heaven*."

"And that's what you're going to play tomorrow?" Escott asked.

"No," said the violinist. "What I shall play tomorrow, along with a solo violin piece by Bach, is two pieces by Pietro Locatelli, whose *capricci enigmati* were also inspired by von Biber's sonatas, and are intermediate between them and Paganini's *capricci*. They were published in 1730, but shunned by musicians of the day and forgotten until Paganini revived them, prior to composing his own adaptations. One I shall play as published, the other in a fashion that has never been heard before."

"You mean that it's your own variation?" Hope enquired.

"In a manner of speaking. I think that Locatelli might have been playing a game or a trick in the published version, adding an extra enigma to his caprice—or there might conceivably have been a misprint. I shall alter the *scordatura*—the tuning of violin, as Mr. Hope says—in the way that ought, in my opinion, to have been specified, but was not. I believe that I might be first to play the piece in public as it was really intended to be played. It is possible that even Locatelli never played it in public himself, given the great unpopularity of the sequence in his own day. It is risky, I know, but Carmela cannot play, and Paganini has made *capricci* popular again, so I feel that I must risk it now, or never. It is something that I have wanted to do for a long time. I hope you will all be tolerant of my whim." He looked anxiously at Lady Phythian as he pronounced the last sentence, but he had lost her attention long before and she was staring out of the window again, watching the wilds of Cambridgeshire go by.

"That's fascinating," Michael said, generously. "I shall look forward to it greatly."

"Thank you," the violinist said, with more relief than genuine gratitude—but Carmela Monticarlo smiled at him again, more dazzlingly than before, and Michael blushed deeply, somewhat to James Escott's amusement and Quentin Hope's ironic delight.

Almost as soon as Signor Monticarlo, having ridden his hobbyhorse to exhaustion, had fallen silent again, Hope and Escott resumed their contest. Having killed off the topic of progress for the time being, they launched into a debate about mazes and labyrinths.

Hope generously took time out to explain to Michael that a labyrinth, technically speaking, was a "unicursal" design in which there were no branches, so that anyone walking a labyrinth was bound to end up at the center, albeit by a tortuously roundabout route, while a maze was "multicursal", thus creating the possibility that someone who kept taking wrong turnings might get lost indefinitely.

"One has to bear in mind, of course," Hope added, "that *the* Labyrinth—the one that Dedalus allegedly built in Crete for King Minos, was actually a multicursal maze, not a labyrinth in the stricter sense of the term. The Greeks mislabeled it, although they knew perfectly well what the difference was, as Plato makes clear in the *Euthydemus*, where Socrates likens logic to a labyrinth, in which the conclusion is always certain even though it seems to be the result of a roundabout process."

"Except, of course," Escott was quick to put in—as Hope must have known that he would—"that Dedalus didn't build the Labyrinth for Minos at all. In fact, he built it for Ariadne. The Greek myth of Theseus misrepresents the situation horribly, but that's of late origin. Homer makes it perfectly clear in the *Iliad*, when he describes Achilles' shield, which bore the design of the Labyrinth, and states in so many words that the Labyrinth was constructed for Ariadne. If that were not enough, when Hope and I were exploring the ruins of Knossos we found inscriptions to the same effect, which identified Ariadne explicitly as the Mistress of the Labyrinth."

"Leading us to conclude," Hope put in, "that Minos' daughter Ariadne—like yourself, Lady Phythian—was named after a more prestigious figure, presumably a goddess. Minos' daughter was probably a priestess as well as a princess, whose duties included *dancing the Labyrinth*, according to a prescribed ritual."

"Which would imply that Dedalus was a priest rather than an engineer," Escott said, taking up the thread again. "Just as the fact that Achilles' shield bore a Labyrinth design proves that the Cretan Labyrinth—and ancient mazes in general—were magical in purpose, intended as protective devices. Unfortunately the Cretan Labyrinth seems to have failed in its purpose, since the entire Minoan civilization was destroyed in an enormous catastrophe."

"Actually, it proves no such thing," Hope objected, "since Achilles was naturally invulnerable—save for his heel—and had no need of protective magic in his shield. And although Minos' daughter was, by virtue of her sex, the person who had to perform the maze ritual intended to evoke her namesake, the Mistress of the Labyrinth, it was undoubtedly Minos who commissioned his high priest, Dedalus, to construct the Labyrinth."

"Where did the Minotaur fit in?" Michael asked, innocently.

"He probably didn't, in any literal sense," Hope opined, "although the Greek emphasis on his role in the myth has given rise to the popular idea that mazes were intended as traps for monsters and demons rather than—or as well as—tracks for ritual processions and dances. That idea is also supported by folklore from elsewhere that often sets dragons in the heart of mazes, but the Minotaur doesn't seem to me to be a mere variant of a dragon. Personally, I suspect that Minos put about the story of Pasiphaë's passion for a bull and subsequent motherhood of a monster in order to pay her back for poisoning some of his younger paramours. Then he used the myth of the Minotaur as a pretext for denying his priestesses—including his wife and daughter—access to the Labyrinth, where they might have used that privacy to hatch plots to threaten his increasingly tyrannical authority. It was presumably the same motive that led him to imprison the architect of the Labyrinth within it. While Escott and I were exploring, we actually found a subterranean cell with a curious high-walled roof-garden; we had no way of knowing whether that might actually have been Dedalus' prison, but Old Harry Langstrade was very excited by it. At any rate, the volcanic eruption rendered the political issues surrounding Minos' despotic tendencies redundant. The catastrophic destruction of the entire Cretan culture set the progress of civilization back by hundreds of years, until Athens...."

"Rose up to continue the tortured rigmarole of Hope's vapid fancy," Escott said, waspishly. "In fact—to get back to your original question, Laurel—the real key to the Minotaur's supposed dual nature lies in the fact that the previous king of Crete, Asterius, had adopted Minos after he had allegedly been sired on Europa by the god Zeus, in the guise of a bull—so it was Minos himself who was accused, in vulgar parlance, of being a human/taurean hybrid when his reign became excessively cruel. The Minotaur was merely a symbol, invented to describe his monstrousness, but it was a particularly potent image in combination with the Labyrinth, partly because it did recall previous folklore placing dragons in the hearts of mazes. Mazes were associated throughout the ancient world with dragons and their mundane kin, as evidenced by Herodotus' description of the Egyptian City of Crocodiles, in which mummified kings were laid to rest amid mummified crocodiles. Hope and I searched for the lost city while we were in Egypt, but never found it. In any case, the mysterious Mistress of the Labyrinth was probably more closely analogous to Circe than to Athene, and that may be why Pasiphaë is sometimes represented in Greek myth as kin to Circe...."

At this point, Michael followed Lady Phythian's example and tuned out again, returning his gaze to the flickering telegraph-poles in spite of their seeming mesmeric threat, and consenting to drift into a light doze. While the conversation remained in such ostentatiously esoteric intellectual territory he deliberately reduced it to a mere buzz in his ears, akin to that of an irritating fly. He found, after a while, that he could ignore the telegraph poles too, by focusing his eyes on more distant points in the landscape—church steeples and belfries proved particularly useful—and tracking them as they retreated, relative to the speeding train, at a far more leisurely pace, as if they too were making a polite withdrawal from an arena of conflict that they found uncomfortable.

Michael did not consider himself to be stupid, or ignorant, but he always felt uncomfortable in the presence of naked erudition. He had not had the privilege of a university education, let alone of taking an exotic Grand Tour, and he knew that he would be at something of a disadvantage among the company assembled at Langstrade Hall, not only with respect to Hope and Escott but Gregory Marlstone, who had been studying natural philosophy at Corpus Christi while Hope and Escott were Classical scholars at Balliol. On the other hand, the present Lord Langstrade had apparently been a very undistinguished scholar at Merton, and had gone straight into the family business thereafter, while Marlstone had done likewise, following in his own father's footsteps as a builder of church clocks, before his eventual inheritance had allowed him to divert his attention to the more esoteric mysteries of Time.

Michael had never met Marlstone, and only knew of him by virtue of newspaper reportage of the failed experiments at Horton Lacey and Chatsworth. Apparently, the would-be inventor had not inherited his father's money until 1819, and it was only then that he had been able to interest himself in John Dee's speculative attempts to develop a theory of time. Marlstone was said to have demonstrated some of his own theories experimentally, but only on a very small scale and in private. His attempts to replicate his laboratory results on a much grander scale had gone sadly awry, occasioning much mockery from the hard-headed physicists who refused to believe in the possibility of perpetual motion machines and similarly paradoxical endeavors.

Annoyed by this derision, Marlstone had apparently hunted high and low for a location more conducive to the functioning of his apparatus, whose failure he attributed to "quasi-acoustic feedback in the temporal field" resulting from the architectural design of the structures in which he had conducted his full-scale demonstrations.

Apparently, the dimensions of the Langstrade Keep, although a trifle cramped, would be much more conducive to the establishment and maintenance of a stable "temporal field"—unless of course, Marlstone really was the kind of moonstruck fantasist that most people now took him for. At any rate, Marlstone's enthusiasm for the potential location had found a resonant echo in Lord Langstrade's enthusiasm for the tantalizing possibility that Marlstone's endeavors held out: the possibility of seeing through time. Although Marlstone only claimed successes in his private laboratory extending over a matter of minutes, and was reluctant to promise that his large-scale apparatus might be capable of providing views extending over years, let alone decades, Lord Langstrade was enthusiastic to see the principle demonstrated, in order that further progress in chronovisual technology might one day enable him to look back across a thousand years and more, in order to witness Harold Longstride's combat with Emund Snurlson for himself.

In spite of his recent vicissitudes, however, Michael suspected that Marlstone might look down on him in much the same way that Hope and Escott obviously did, considering him a shallow recorder of the world's contents rather than an educated analyst of their nature and meaning. What chance did a mere painter have, he could not help wondering, of comparing with such men as Marlstone and Hope in the eyes of his host?—as he would presumably need to do if he were ever to obtain approval for the marriage he hoped to make.

Lady Phythian was drawn back into Hope and Escott's discussion again when it turned to matters of psychognosis, by which time the *Sir Richard Trevithick* was streaking through Lincolnshire. Escott, as might be expected, was scathing about the potential of the supposed new science, while Hope was far more hopeful that it might eventually generate a theory of the mind of Newtonian elegance and subtlety. Both men, however, were agreed on rejecting present-day Mesmerism as mostly poppycock, and its supposed practitioners—including, by implication, Augustus Carp—as self-deluding fools or mere charlatans. Lady Phythian objected to this characterization, insisting that Dr. Carp was an exceedingly wise man, who had used his undoubted psychic gifts to provided solace to many a widow—herself included—and would doubtless continue to do so if only he could find a more adequate replacement for his late and much-lamented somniloquist.

"I don't doubt that somniloquists really do hear voices, Lady Phythian" Hope opined, "but we shall not be able to make any true progress in psychognosis until we abandon the fantasy that those voices emanate from the spirits of the dead. I don't doubt that Dr.

Carp's last somniloquist was able to supply you with a measure of solace following your husband's death, probably spiced with a healthy dose of commonsensical advice, but the voice that bid her do so came from within, not from the realm of the afterlife."

"Hope is, as usual, half right," Escott judged. "The voices somniloquists appear to transmit cannot emanate from the afterlife, but their origin in the mysterious depths of the human mind gives them no better access to wisdom, even of a commonsensical kind. In fact, the murky depths of the human mind are essentially chaotic, and their produce is essentially subversive and capricious. There is no possibility for progress there, but only one more proof that the idea of progress is a myth. What underlies the superficial order of the world is a deadly confusion, whose volcanic eruptions will always destroy the petty achievements of our constructive consciousness, and betray our fondest illusions of future happiness."

Once again, as he completed this florid speech, Escott caught Michael's eye and raised his eyebrows in a quasi-conspiratorial manner, but the gesture left Michael at a loss. He did not know whether the thin man was soliciting his agreement, taking it for granted, or signaling that he did not really mean a single word of what he said.

"What do you think, Laurel?" Hope suddenly demanded, although he could not have seen the raised eyebrows.

"I don't know," Michael admitted, trying not to stammer. "Perhaps I'll be able to form a better judgment when I've seen Dr. Carp in action. He's due to entrance his somniloquist tomorrow night, I believe, immediately after Signor Monticarlo's recital?"

Signor Monticarlo obligingly nodded in confirmation of Michael's presumption, but seemed pained at the thought that his pioneering revelation of a new variation of a Pietro Locatelli *capriccio* was to be followed by a display of Mesmeric somniloquism. Lady Phythian nodded too, with far greater conviction. Carmela Monticarlo smiled.

"Very wise, Laurel," said Escott. "Keep your powder dry. Don't fire until you have the bird in your sights."

"For a man who's never yet hit a bird in flight," Hope put in, "Mr. Escott is very free with his sporting metaphors—but he's right about your being wise to reserve judgment, Laurel. You might learn a great deal this weekend, if you're lucky. When the Sir Richard Trevithick carries us home again on Tuesday, we might all be a little wiser. I certainly hope so."

CHAPTER FIVE

THE DISPIRITED MESMERIST

By the time the *Sir Richard Trevithick* pulled into York station, dead on time, having failed to come off the rails yet again, Hope and Escott had tired somewhat of their perpetual performance, and had lapsed into a sort of weary torpor. No one had attempted to take on the burden of keeping the conversation going, so the last few miles had been covered in near-funereal silence.

Rather than continue their journey immediately in the hired diligence that was waiting for them in the station forecourt, the company decided—with not a single dissenting voice—to take an early dinner. They voted to take temporary refuge in a Coaching Inn that was situated less than a hundred yards from the railway station, set back slightly from the road. It seemed rather as if the august institution were staring at its new neighbor, obliquely and resentfully, from what would henceforth be the wrong side of the dusty highway.

While his companions from the carriage made ready to execute this plan, Michael went to collect his bags and equipment from the luggage van. Those of his traveling companions who had left trunks there were content to rely on the labels they bore to ensure that they were transferred to the diligence. The only person who joined him was Augustus Carp, to whom he had just been introduced for the first time.

Carp was considerably older than Hope, Escott or Monticarlo, or even Lady Phythian; Michael judged that he must be at least seventy, even if the snowy whiteness of his hair was slightly deceptive. Michael had expected the celebrated Mesmerist to have strikingly penetrative eyes, but Carp's gaze actually seemed quite meek, and his dull pupils did not give the least hint of any capacity for flashing fire.

"Have you been to Langstrade Hall before, Mr. Laurel?" Carp asked him, by way of making polite conversation, while the porters were busy unloading the luggage van.

"This is my first time," Michael admitted, "but I hope it won't be the last."

"It's my first time too," Carp said, dolefully. "I've visited many places in Yorkshire, but never Langstrade. I wish I might share your hope, but when one reaches my age, the likelihood that everything one does is being done for the last time becomes difficult to dispute."

"Mastery of animal magnetism does not confer exceptional longevity, then?" Michael observed, a trifle mischievously—then cursed himself immediately for having allowed a little of Escott's subversive personality to rub off on him during the train journey.

Carp did not take seem to take offense. "Only to a small degree, I fear," he said, with a faint sigh. "The effects of magnetism have kept me healthy and alert in the meantime, though, and have given me many other privileges denied to the ignorant and the contemptuous."

Michael assumed that the old man was referring to the conversations he supposedly held with the dead via his somniloquist. He had also been introduced to the woman currently playing that role: a buxom Frenchwoman named Jeanne Evredon, not much older than Carmela Monticarlo, to whose reluctant care the old man had confided his ward before coming to supervise the transfer of his luggage.

Michael's equipment was unloaded first, and Michael had to leave the old man alone temporarily in order that he might transfer the fragile items to the diligence personally. He took great care to check that the tools of his trade were safely stowed on top of the coach. By the time he was satisfied, Augustus Carp had finished supervising the securing of his own trunks to the postilion's station, and the two were able to walk to the Inn together.

The low ceiling of the inn's dining-room was stained yellow between its oaken beams by tobacco-smoke, and the walls were hung with a random admixture of horse-brasses and prints reproducing badly-painted hunting-scenes or steeplechases. There was a strong odor typical of such institutions, which Michael always took care to think of as the odor of oxtail soup, although he knew that it was really the olfactory ambience of human body-odor.

The Minotaur's refuge would doubtless have emitted a more intense version of the same odor, he thought. *But one always gets used to it after ten minutes or so—unless, of course, mine host takes it into his head to serve oxtail soup.*

Fortunately, this being Yorkshire, the innkeeper's wife was busy serving plates loaded with mutton chops, potatoes and Yorkshire pudding to all the diners.

Their companions had secured a trestle-table long enough to accommodate the entire party, but the two seats still vacant were positioned at one corner, between Mademoiselle Evredon and Lady Phythian. Politely standing aside to let the Mesmerist sit next to his protégée—although Carp hesitated before accepting the invitation—Michael sat down between the old man and the dowager.

Revived by the change of scene, Hope and Escott had begun holding forth again, but the size and shape of the table were such that other conversations could be comfortably undertaken in parallel. Lady Phythian did not seem ill-disposed toward Michael any longer, having obviously found his relative quietness and amiability a welcome contrast to Hope and Escott's warmongering in the railway-carriage, but she did not seem inclined to talk to him either, evidently preferring to cultivate the acquaintance of her other neighbor, Signor Monticarlo. Michael had no alternative but to resume his interrupted conversation with Augustus Carp, but he did not mind that; he was still curious to know more about the vocation of Mesmerism.

"It must be uncommon, Mr. Laurel," Carp suggested, before Michael could frame a question of his own, "for you to receive a commission to paint a building like Langstrade Keep. Recently-elevated aristocrats often have their brand new stately homes painted, I believe, but not their Follies."

"Do you consider the Keep to be a Folly, then, Dr. Carp?" Michael asked. "Hope and Escott do, of course, but I thought that you might be more sympathetic to Lord Langstrade's…eccentricities."

"I have long since learned to keep an open mind," Carp replied, with another sigh, "and I would not be so impolite as to say so to Lord Langstrade, but yes, I do consider the Keep to be a Folly, and I fear that the likelihood of my satisfying his lordship's expectations is far less than the likelihood of you completing the commission that he has imposed on you. If Jeanne were actually able to contact the spirit of Harold Longstride, I would be utterly amazed."

"But Lady Phythian is convinced that there really are ghosts haunting Langstrade," Michael told him. "She was telling us during the journey that she has seen them several times over, albeit in the grounds rather than in the Hall itself."

"There are ghosts everywhere," Carp said, morosely, "but they rarely turn out to be the shades we expect and desire them to be. Revenants have their own reasons for visiting the mundane world, and our ability to fathom those reasons is far more limited than we might wish. Thanks to the great Anton Mesmer, we have recently opened up channels of communication with the dead, but the inhabitants of the afterlife have, alas, proved no more reliable as helpers and informants than the present inhabitants of the mundane world."

"Well," said Michael, feeling obliged to attempt a compensatory cheerfulness, "for what it may be worth, I think that you have more chance of achieving some effect, even if your success seems less than total to Lord Langstrade, than Gregory Marlstone has of breaching the boundaries of time and allowing us to see into the past—not that we'll be able to see very much, since we'll be enclosed by tall hawthorn hedges."

"That is exactly the point, as I understand it," Carp suggested. "Because the hedges are recently-grown, and the Keep recently-built, he hopes that we might be able to see them shrink and expand, perhaps even to vanish and let us watch the Hall in the process of construction. I haven't discussed the matter with Marlstone personally, mind—but that's the inference I draw."

"You're probably right," Michael conceded, readily enough. "In that respect too, the Keep and its environs might be reckoned a particularly suitable location for his third full-scale trial. Will it be suitable, do you think, for your own endeavors?"

"Marlstone and I have the same objective, even if our instruments are very different," Carp observed, reflectively. "We both aspire to cross commonplace boundaries, and rumor has it that he also expects to make contact with phantoms if he should ever succeed in getting his apparatus to work. I too am dependent on an instrument whose unreliability can be frustrating—but if there are phantoms at Langstrade, as I'm assured that there are, I certainly hope that I might be able to make contact with them, and perhaps elicit some explanation of their presence." He glanced sideways as he spoke at Mademoiselle Evredon, who blushed slightly at the reference to her unreliability, but pretended not to have heard it because she was concentrating on whatever Hope was saying. Michael winced on her behalf, and dropped his fork, which clattered embarrassingly on the table-top.

"Personally," Carp continued, "I wish Mr. Marlstone every success. If his machine really can permit people in the present to catch glimpses of people in the past or the future, if only as silent phantoms, that would be a wonder to outshine all the others that we have recently seen. It might change the world far more profoundly than the steam engine."

"If we were to receive news from the future rather than the past, it surely would," Michael reflected. "If we were able to discover to-day what we would otherwise not discover for a hundred years... well, that way lies paradox."

"Only logic fears paradoxes," Carp said, in a rather mechanical fashion, as if quoting a saw. "We should be braver, if we are not to be prisoners of our own intellectual inventions."

"That's a nice thought," Michael said. "Even so, if Marlstone ever does get his time machine to work, there might be hazards involved, just as there must be in your work. If you or he can obtain accurate knowledge of the world to come, or transmit information from the present into the past, it seems to me that history itself must be at risk. The world would be in danger of dissolving into the kind of chaos that could only gladden the heart of a woemonger like Mr. Escott."

Carp was wise enough to appreciate that this was as much a challenge to the pretensions of Mesmerism as a comment on the potential dangers of chronovisual technology, but he did not take offence.

"People did wax lyrical about the potential dangers of animal magnetism when somniloquists first began claiming that they could obtain visions of the future," Carp admitted, gloomily, "but the utility of such visions has proved to be little greater than that of the enigmatic pronunciations of the pythoness of Delphi. When there is truth in what such visions offer, it tends to be cloaked in sufficient mystery to prevent the whole truth from being perceived until after the event, when rational reaction can no longer be effective."

"If you'll forgive me saying so, Dr. Carp," Michael said, "you sound a trifle disenchanted with your science."

"I have reached an age at which it is difficult to preserve a sense of enchantment," Carp told him. "To tell the truth, I suspect that tomorrow night's *séance* might be the last I shall ever hold, not merely at Langstrade but anywhere. Perhaps I should have retired when I lost my previous somniloquist, with whom I had built up a fine and irreplaceable *rapport*, but one is always tempted to continue one's life's work a little too long...not that you need to think of such things, Mr. Laurel given that you're at the very beginning of your own life and career. For you, this weekend will be a stepping-stone to success, and you are fully entitled to rejoice in that. Forgive my bad mood—comfortable as the railway train is, at least by comparison with the mail-coach, I found the experience of traveling in it rather stressful."

Michael did his best to reassure the old man by telling him that he was looking forward very eagerly to seeing a demonstration of somniloquism for the first time, but his efforts seemed to be in vain.

"You must forgive Dr. Carp," Mademoiselle Evredon eventually put in. "I am the one who has vexed him. He is disappointed in me." Like Carmela Monticarlo, she spoke English fluently, with only a hint of an accent, but she spoke relatively slowly, choosing her words with care.

"I have no right to be disappointed, my dear," Carp was quick to say. "You are in no way responsible for what happens while you are entranced. Your own personality is set aside, and the part of your brain that takes over the control of your voice is very different from the part that comprises your waking personality. I should not chide you for what you cannot help."

"Perhaps it's simply a matter of settling into a new partnership," Michael suggested. "With luck, tomorrow night's *séance* might cement the relationship and produce revelations that will restore your enthusiasm, Dr. Carp."

"Well," said the Mesmerist, making an obvious effort to rally his spirits, "we must certainly hope so. I would certainly like to repay Lady Langstrade's faith in me, if I can—and as you say, Mr. Laurel, the Hall certainly does seem to be haunted. If we can, indeed, produce revelations that might be of some use to the Earl, or to anyone else in the audience, that would be very gratifying. It is, after all, an auspicious occasion, even if it is one that has been invented by legend-making rather than occasioned by an actual event. Perhaps, if we cannot contact Harold Longstride, we might be able to contact Emund Snurlson, of whose real existence history seems reasonably certain."

The dinner was over soon enough, Yorkshire coaching inns having no inclination toward sweet desserts. As the inn offered surroundings in which few diners would be tempted to linger, the travelers immediately made preparations to continue their journey. As they got up from the table and began making token protests against Hope's insistence on settling the entire bill himself, Jeanne Evredon slid close to Michael and said: "Thank you for that, Mr. Laurel. Dr. Carp was in need of a boost to his morale, and I think you have provided it."

Michael attempted to insist that he had done nothing at all, but that only made the somniloquist smile at his modesty—and Michael could not help noticing that Carmela Monticarlo, who was watching them, lost her own smile in response. He was so embarrassed by that occurrence that he stubbed his toe on the table-leg as he moved away, and limped all the way back to the diligence.

CHAPTER SIX

THE POTENTIAL COMPLEXITIES OF TRAVELING IN TIME

The late summer sun had not yet set as the passengers made arrangements to take their places in the diligence. The three ladies were, of course, entitled to three of the seats inside by virtue of their sex, and Carp and Monticarlo were entitled to two of the remaining three by virtue of their age, but when those five had been loaded there was very little room left for anyone at all to take the sixth seat, because the luggage had overflowed the roof and several of the smaller bags had had to be stowed inside.

"You'll be much better off with Escott and myself in the coupé, Laurel," Quentin Hope suggested. "There'll be more amusing conversation there, I dare say, than there will inside. It'll be a warm evening, even when night falls completely—the sky's clear and there's a three-quarter moon—so you've nothing to fear from the weather, and the wind is a blessing in August, rather than the deadly curse it becomes once winter sets in."

"It's always a pleasure to hear philosophers like yourself and Mr. Escott displaying your wisdom," Michael replied, deciding that the coupé did, indeed, seem the preferable alternative and accepting the stirrup that Escott made with his hands in order to provide him with an upward boost. "I lost the thread of your debate at dinner, I fear, but I'm sure I'll pick it up again soon enough."

"We should have saved you a seat between us," Escott said, as Hope gave him a similar boost. "but we didn't think of it. Carp's not a bad old stick, though, in spite of his delusions. Did he regale you with tales of his exploits as a youth, when he was employed in James Graham's Temple of Health and Hygiene and knew the Duchess of Devonshire?"

"Alas, no," Michael said.

Hope accepted a boost from the obliging coachman, who then showed surprising agility in climbing up to his own seat. "Must be saving the juicy stuff for Langstrade's dinner-table," Hope opined, as he clambered past his companions in order to sit down on the far side of the coupé's bench, thus placing Michael in the middle. "You and I had better be careful that we don't run out of conversation before we arrive, Jim—things will be direly dull if we're all talked out."

They both laughed, utterly fearless of any such peril.

"If you wouldn't mind," Michael said, as the coachman used his long whip to tickle the rumps of the four horses tethered to the diligence and set the rig in motion, "I'd be glad to know a little more about Gregory Marlstone's time machine, if you're in a position to enlighten me beyond what I've read in the newspapers. Dr. Carp says that Marlstone and he have the same objective, although their instruments are very different, but I wasn't quite sure what he was trying to imply."

"Carp would say that," Hope declared. "He's interpreting the matter from his own standpoint—but Marlstone might take offence if you start talking to him about ghosts, so you'd best be careful when you meet him."

"*If* you meet him," Escott corrected. "Until I see him, I'll persist in picturing him bogged down in the Midlands. Hope's right, though—for once. Marlstone doesn't like the images that his machine is supposed to produce being described as *ghosts*, even though he thinks that they'll be intangible and inaudible, and in spite of the fact that he hopes, eventually, to offer us glimpses of people now dead."

"Why won't we be able to hear through time as well as see through it?" Michael asked,

"For the same reason that we won't be able to touch through time," Hope told him. "Marlstone doesn't believe that any *physical* displacement of matter by means of a time machine like his is possible—not yet, at any rate—and sound consists of vibrations in matter."

"Why *not yet?*" Michael queried.

"What Hope means," Escott put in, "is that, according to Marlstone's theory of time, the transportation of matter through time would require two time machines—one to transmit and one to receive. Once his first machine is working properly—if he ever does succeed in getting it to work properly—he intends to build a second, which might then allow material objects to be transported. Or, of course, it might not, depending on the correctness of his theory." Escott obviously thought that *might not* was the likelier alternative, but that was entirely in character.

"But in what sense would the objects be transported *through time*," Michael asked, "if both machines exist at the same time."

"Simultaneous transport *is* travel in time," Hope told him, "but that's not the point. Once the second machine is in working order, according to Marlstone's theory, the first wouldn't simply be able to transport matter to it *now*, but also to its future situation—or *vice versa*. It's all hypothetical, of course. Material displacement might simply be impossible, as Escott says. Indeed, *any* sort of temporal displacement beyond the stately march measured by our chronometers might simply be impossible, although I certainly hope that Marlstone's right about the bounds of reality being less disobliging."

"You might well be wondering, of course," Escott hastened to say, "why the first time machine, if Marlstone ever does get it to work, couldn't just transport material objects to its own future self, if any such transfer were possible at all, but apparently there's some reason why that's not practicable. There really would need to be two distinct machines in order to attempt physical displacement. Marlstone babbles on about a *law of conservation of non-identity*."

"You might also be wondering," Hope was quick to add, "why Marlstone's machine, if it were ever to succeed in doing anything, couldn't simply transmit material objects to machines in the future that haven't yet been constructed but eventually will be, and receive material objects in the same way, but Marlstone reckons that there's a problem there too, arising from what he calls *complementary attunement* and difficulties in overcoming *intertemporal gravity*. The fellow might simply be talking through his hat, of course—he's crazier than Langstrade, in many people's opinion—but he's no fool."

Michael thought about that for a moment, enjoying the play of the wind of the vehicle's progress upon his face—which did, indeed, produce a welcome relief from the somnolent heaviness of the sultry evening air. Then he decided to set aside the elements of the argument that he could not comprehend and return to simpler matters. "I see," he lied. "But if sound can't be displaced in time because it consists of physical vibrations, why does Marlstone think that light can be transmitted? Isn't light a matter of vibrations in the ether, or of exceedingly tiny material particles?"

"That's a good question" Hope said, seemingly sincere in the compliment. "You might be right, of course, and seeing through time might prove to be just as impractical as leaping back and forth between the centuries, but Marlstone seems to have observed visual phenomena during this small-scale tests, so he's convinced that there must be something special about light particles or the luminiferous ether that supports their vibrations. He rabbits on occasionally about the particulate nature of time, the harmonic subvibrations of the temporal ether and similar philosophical fancies but I'm not sure that his heart's really in it. I think he's prepared to accept the apparent fact, for now, and see how far such visions can be taken before attempting a fuller explanation. If his experience thus far is anything to go by, of course, then they probably can't be taken very far at all—maybe no further than a trivial optical illusion."

"Actually," Escott said. "I don't think Hope's explaining this very well—perhaps because he doesn't really understand it. As I see it, Marlstone thinks that the primary influence of the time machine—and perhaps the only one—isn't on matter but on mind. His time machine isn't like a railway carriage in which one can sit, able to look out and watch the past or the future go by; it's more like a magnet, which produces a field around it, which has the effect that people standing within the field—which is where all Lord Langstrade's guests will be standing on Saturday, if Marlstone has his way—will be able to *reach out* with their minds, to the extent that the field's intensity will permit. If they really are able to see their surroundings as those surroundings once were, or will be, they won't really be *seeing* them in the same straightforward way that their eyes transmit sensory information via the optic nerves; it'll be more like a vision conjured up by the imagination—a dream, if you like, but an *accurate* dream."

"In a dream, though, you *can* hear people speak and touch them," Michael pointed out.

"Well, yes—but what they say, and any apparent touch sensations, are products of the dreamer's imagination. As I understand it, Marlstone thinks that the way his time-field will operate on the imagination will impart true visual information, but not true auditory or palpatory information. That's where his notion of the essential harmonics of the temporal ether comes in. The idea is that the time-field works in a fashion analogous to the luminiferous ether, not sound-bearing media or tangible matter. As Hope says, though, it might all be complete rubbish. Marlstone's supposed sophistication of Dee's theory might be so much nonsense, like phlogiston theory."

"Mind you," Hope said, "if there's anything in it at all, Saturday's experiment might just provide us with an explanation of Lady Phythian's apparitions. If Marlstone does get his machine to work within the Keep, you see, and some or all of us are able to make use of its field to *reach out* into the past or future, those of us who reach out into the past, traveling distances in some way proportional to the intensity of the field at the point at which we're standing, might *become* the ghosts that have been seen on the site of the Maze. I'm assuming, of course, that the field works both ways, allowing Lady Phythian and others to reach out from the past just as easily as it will allow us to reach out from the present."

"Not that it's at all likely, mind," Escott put in, "given that Lady Phythian's ghosts seemed to be going into the maze rather than out of it, and we'll already be in the central arena when Marstione's time-field takes effect. *If* it takes effect."

Michael took another moment to think about the new possibilities his companions had raised. There was a certain delightful irony about the proposal that the second Earl of Langstrade and the guests that he had invited to help him celebrate the millennium of Harold Longstride's supposed combat with Emund Snurlson might actually *become* the "ghosts" that Lady Phythian and others had mistaken for the shades of Harold Longstride and his companions.

He shielded his eyes against the blood red glare of the sun, which was setting almost directly ahead of the diligence's course, amid the smoky haze that rose up from the land every day now that the harvest had begun and the stubble was being burned in the fields as the crops were cleared. Then another thought occurred to him. "If people living in the past or the future will be able to *reach into* the present, in the same way that we'll be able to reach out of it," he said, pensively, surely *some* sort of communication will be possible, even if we have to use sign language—or signaling lanterns."

"Good idea!" said Hope. "Perhaps the moving lanterns that Lady Phythian saw weren't walking or dancing the maze at all, but were merely trying to make some sort of message comprehensible by means of a code."

"Do you understand any codes of that sort, Hope?" Escott asked him. "I don't, and I cannot imagine that Carp or Monticarlo does—but I suppose Marlstone might. How about you, Laurel? Your father was a naval man, wasn't he? Did he teach you to read flags while he dandled you on his knee as an infant?"

Michael shook his head. Precisely because his father had been a naval man, away at sea for ten months a year, there had been precious few occasions for such dandling—which made it all the more unfair that his father had accused him, contemptuously, of being a "mummy's boy" when he had told him of his decision to train as a painter rather than a sailor.

"Mind you," Escott went on, "it might be more interesting, if the damn thing does turn out to work, not to bother *reaching out* with our own minds at all, but simply to wait and see who—or what—might reach out to us. The people of the future will have the advantage—which Lady Phythian and her fellow ghost-seers did not—of knowing exactly when and where Marlstone's experiment took place, and whether it was successful or not. If there's anything they want to communicate to us, they'll surely be able to find a better way than waving lanterns around. Putting up posters on the inner walls of the Maze might do the trick."

"That's typical of you, Jim," Hope observed. "Given the chance to look into the future for yourself, and see what progress might bring, you'd prefer to remain in the present, and see what—if anything—might come to you. You'd be just as delighted to see Harold Longstride peering myopically out of the year 822, I dare say, as you would be to glimpse your descendants from 2822, who'll have taken progress to a much further extreme and become godlike in their abilities."

"Lord Langstrade's the only one likely to be nursing faint hopes of catching a fleeting glimpse of Harold Longstride some day," Escott retorted, evidently stung by Hope's sarcasm, "not merely because the fellow never existed, but because Marlstone doesn't dare claim that he'll ever be able to generate a temporal field capable of extending vision over a thousand years. He refuses to offer estimates, claiming that once he's got the machine working he'll have to calibrate it, but he's only prepared to speculate about months— years, at the most—even when he's off on one of his hypothetical flights of fancy. On that sort of basis, the only people likely to be around in a future from which it's practicable to send messages back to us are…well, *us*. Our future selves, that is."

"Would minds reaching out from the past or future be limited to the present moment while the machine is actually in operation?" Michael asked, hopeful that he wasn't being too naïve. "If they could somehow *fall short* or *overshoot* within the field, they might be responsible for Lady Phythian's apparition, rather than us…us as of this Saturday, that is"

"That's an interesting suggestion," Hope conceded. "If Marlstone's field is to extend in time as well as space when it's switched on, past and future moments might be theoretically accessible from all points within it…within a limited range, of course. Months, as Escott says, or maybe years…."

"If that were the case," Escott was quick to deduce, "then the field must already be in existence, if Marlstone's machine is actually going to work, and must have been in existence, albeit with ever-decreasing intensity, for some considerable time. If so, it's no wonder Lady Phythian thought she could sense the field's presence even when she couldn't actually see anything. If so, in fact, the three of us ought be able to nip into the heart of the maze as soon as we get to Langstrade, and start *reaching out* without even waiting for Marlstone to throw the switch. And if we can't do that, we'll know that the machine isn't going to work, so we won't have to bother turning up to the scheduled demonstration on Saturday."

"It might be worth a try," Hope agreed, although he couldn't suppress a chuckle as he contemplated the apparent absurdity. "But if we fail, it won't necessarily mean that the time machine won't work at all—it might only mean that there's a flaw in the particular hypothesis we've just been extrapolating. Perhaps the field won't extend in time as well as space, or perhaps it will only extend forwards not backwards...."

"In which case," Escott concluded, "we'd be back to square one in the matter of explaining Lady Phythian's ghosts, if the time machine can provide an explanation at all."

"That's Socratic logic for you," said Hope, blithely. "An authentic Labyrinth, in the strict sense of the word. You go round and round and round and—*hey presto!*—you find yourself back at square one. If and when the machine actually works, I suppose we'll find out soon enough what its capabilities are, so we might just as well wait and see—but it's fun to speculate, isn't it, Laurel?"

"I suppose so," Michael answered, dutifully, although he felt that his head was spinning. All the possibilities that his companions seemed to see so readily, and in which they were capable of taking such manifest delight, picked up his own stray thoughts like a dizzying whirlwind.

There were no telegraph poles beside the road along which they were traveling—although Michael suspected that there soon might be, as the network gradually extended adventitious nerves from the central spinal column provided by the London-to-York railway and its signaling systems—but the slow retreat of the landscape, as the gently-rocking diligence hastened forward, still had a slightly mesmeric effect on his weary brain. Dusk was falling now that the sun had sunk into a cloudy lake of blood, and fugitive candlelight was beginning to appear in the windows of the farmhouses and cottages that were scattered at intervals by the roadside, nestling amid the spinneys and the hedgerows. The travelers were still in the heart of the Vale of York, of which Langstrade's so-called dale was a sloping extension between half-hearted hills, but the silhouettes of loftier moors were looming ever higher on the northern and western horizons: monstrous lumpen shadows gradually but inexorably encroaching upon a sky that would soon be spangled with stars.

The diligence lurched as it passed over a slightly humpbacked bridge.

"Was that the Nidd we just went over?" Escott asked, trying to peer around the edge of the vehicle into the gathering gloom behind. "We're making good time, if so."

"We're on the old Roman road," Hope reminded him. "It's still as good as ever. It's a pity we can't follow it all the way to Knaresborough before turning off on to mere cart tracks, but the road through Arkendale and Staveley is sound enough at this time of year. After that, we'll just have to trust to luck."

"Langstrade's no more than twenty-five miles from York, is it?" Michael said. "Surely it won't take us longer than two hours to get there."

Hope and Escott exchanged a glance, but the moonlight wasn't quite bright enough to show Michael their expressions. "He's a city boy," Escott said, as if that explained everything. To Michael, he said: "Twenty-five miles is a mere bagatelle, if you're traveling on an express train, or even if you've got four fine horses pulling a light carriage along an old Roman road—but our carriage isn't light, our horses aren't first rate, and the road will get a lot worse when we take a turn toward Arkendale. We'll have to make a stop somewhere, hopefully to change the horses—if we can only water them and let them rest, that'll add a further hour on to the journey—and by the time we get to within five miles of Langstrade, even if they've been changed for better animals, they'll be making such heavy weather of the uphill haulage that they'll be walking a good deal slower than we could. Better reckon on four hours, to be on the safe side."

"It'll be enough, at any rate, to make even Escott yearn for the speed of a railway locomotive," Hope added.

"I wouldn't go that far," Escott told him. "The weather's good, the company's good—thanks to you, Laurel—and the road hasn't become bumpy yet. Even the most pleasant of journeys tends to be exhausting—but think how grateful we'll be to sink into our beds when we finally arrive!"

"For a sophisticated pessimist, Jim," Hope opined, "you have an authentic talent for searching out primitive crumbs of comfort."

CHAPTER SEVEN

A Warm Welcome at Langstrade Hall

James Escott turned out—not for the first time, Michael sur-mised—to be a trifle *too* pessimistic. After changing horses in Ark-endale—which required so little time that the passengers on the dili-gence hardly had time to stretch their legs before climbing aboard again—the heavily-loaded vehicle made short work of the next stage of the journey, and the horses were still fresh enough to tackle the slopes beyond Staveley with a will. The party arrived at Langstrade Hall shortly after ten o'clock. The night was bright, as Hope had promised, and still warm; the only exceptional discomfort the trav-elers had suffered was the acrid dust projected into the air by the burning of stubble, which had been particularly irritating in the ex-posed coupé. Michael's nose had been running for some time, and he had had to make frequent use of his handkerchief, but the embar-rassment had been lessened by the fact that Hope and Escott had fared no better.

The current Lord and Lady Langstrade came out with the dowager Lady Langstrade, Cecilia and a clutch of valets to meet the coach. Grooms uncoupled the weary horses and led them away to the stables, while the valets set about the Herculean task of unload-ing the vehicle, and then sorting out the luggage and distributing its various components to various bedrooms within the Hall. The moon was descending into the west by now, as the sun had done long be-fore, but it had not yet sunk so low in the sky that the bulk of the Hall interrupted the play of its light on the battlements of the Keep or the crowns of the tall hedges of the surrounding maze.

Michael was, inevitably, the last person to be greeted by his hosts, but there was nothing cursory about the way that Lord Lang-strade shook his hand and bade him welcome—or, more importantly, about the way in which Cecilia smiled at him. The Earl straightened up immediately thereafter and informed his guests that cocoa would be served in the large drawing-room, followed by brandy in the smoking-room, should any of the gentlemen prefer not to retire along with the ladies. First of all, however, Michael was shown up to his room—which was called the Red Room, to distinguish it from the other guest bedrooms, although it had very little red in its décor—in order that he might wash and change out of his traveling clothes.

He took his time over his ablutions, fearful of attracting attention to himself if he should chance to be the first one down, but then had difficult locating a servant to direct him to the large drawing-room. He would have been the last to arrive had not Augustus Carp and his somniloquist been delayed by a quarrel, the muffled progress of which Michael overheard through the door of the Violet Room, situated at the opposite end of the corridor from his own, close to the stair-head.

The first thing he noticed, on entering the large drawing-room, was the presence of a burly stranger with bushy eyebrows seated in a vast leather-clad armchair. Because Lord Langstrade was in conversation with Signor Monticarlo, while their respective daughters dutifully danced attendance upon them, and both Lady Langstrades had been buttonholed by Lady Phythian, Escott and Hope were able to swoop upon their new friend and bear him away in the direction of the stranger.

"My dear Marlstone," said Hope, "may I introduce the celebrated artist Michael Laurel, with whom we had an extremely interesting conversation on the intricacies of time travel in the diligence. Laurel, this is Gregory Marlstone, who was fortunate enough to arrive without incident this morning, and has spent the day tirelessly transporting all his equipment into the Keep, ready for assembly tomorrow."

Marlstone stood up and shook Laurel's hand gravely. "I'm delighted to meet you, sir," Marlstone said. "Any man capable of taking an intelligent interest in the subject of time travel is very welcome at my demonstration. I hope to show you something on Saturday that will reward your interest lavishly."

"I'm exceedingly glad to meet you, sir," Michael replied, loyally, "and I look forward to your demonstration with great excitement."

"Mr. Laurel was wondering in the diligence about the range of the time-field you intend to produce, Marlstone," Escott said, mischievously, "and whether it will extend in time as well as space—

and whether, if so, it will extend backwards as well as forwards. I fear that Hope and I were unable to enlighten him, as we were slightly uncertain about the modifications you've made to John Dee's theory of time—especially the precise relevance of the law of conservation of non-identity, the practicalities of complementary attunement and the effects of intertemporal gravity. Perhaps you'd care to explain it to him."

Marlstone looked at Escott suspiciously, as if he were afraid that he might be the butt of some subtle mockery—an entirely justified anxiety, in Michael's estimation—and shook his head slowly. "It's far too late to embark upon a lengthy explanation now," he pronounced, perhaps a trifle regretfully, "especially in view of the fact that you've all been traveling all day and can hardly be at your intellectual peak. I hope to make time tomorrow evening to offer a full explanation of my modifications to Dee's theories, and of the nature of my project, to all interested parties. I shall try to answer any and all questions that might arise then."

"I hope there'll be time," Hope said, smiling broadly. "After all, we have to fit in Dr. Carp's experiment in somniloquism and Signor Monticarlo's violin recital too. It's going to be a very busy evening."

Marlstone had frowned slightly at the mention of Carp's name, and the frown deepened further as he saw the man himself come through the drawing-room's open double doors, followed, a few steps behind, by the red-faced Jeanne Evredon. Hope and Escott saw the frown deepen too, and Michael judged from the sly glance they exchanged that the two pranksters had immediately come to a mutual decision that they ought to effect an introduction between the manufacturer of time machines who disliked the term "ghost" and the conjuror of spirits who loved it. Since Marlstone was far too large to be easily moved, they rushed off together to collect the more maneuverable Carp.

Fortunately, Carp's belated appearance had also prompted the butler, Heatherington, to signal the maids that the cocoa should be served, and because Marlstone's armchair happened to be situated next to the sideboard on which the crockery had been set, Michael and the inventor were among the first to be awarded their cups.

Michael was thirsty, and glad of the relief in more ways than one—so glad, in fact, that he scalded his tongue and the roof of his mouth endeavoring to take too hasty a gulp. He blinked furiously, turning away from his companion in order to conceal his distress—and found himself looking straight at Cecilia, who had given her father the slip.

"I don't believe you've ever seen the drawing of the Langstrade Maze, Mr. Laurel," she said, in a honeyed tone that was music to his ears. "Might I show it to you—if Mr. Marlstone doesn't mind my interrupting?"

Marlstone seemed to be on the point of saying that he would rather like another look at the famous diagram himself—presumably in order to avoid being pitted against Augustus Carp while Hope and Escott looked on, eager to nurture their mutual embarrassment—but he thought better of it and nodded graciously.

Gratefully, Michael followed Cecilia to the mantelpiece, where she gestured expansively with her arm in order to make it obvious to any chance onlooker that she was merely discharging her obligation as a hostess and could not possibly be suspected of having any other motive for separating the young man from his male companions. In support of the pretence, Michael studied the framed diagram intently, confident that his artist's eye would enable him not only to memorize the design but also—when the time came—to navigate his way through the network of hedges without going astray.

"It's believed to be very old," Cecilia told him, speaking a little more loudly than was strictly necessary. "It's reputed to have a religious or magical significance, although no one knows exactly what it is. It's something to do with Dedalus of Knossos, I understand, and the legacy he left to the Celtic druids." She dropped her voice to a virtual whisper to add: "I'm extremely glad to see you, Mr. Laurel. I've been making conversation with that dreadful Mr. Marlstone for nearly an hour, while mother and father were busy fluttering around making arrangements for everyone's arrival."

Somewhat at a loss for words, Michael found himself mumbling: "Is he dreadful, then?"

"Perfectly," Cecilia assured him. "He scowls all the time, almost as if he can't help it. I could almost have been glad to see Mr. Hope."

Michael was nonplussed by the *almost*, the precise significance of which eluded him, but he thought was safe to say: "I've been in the company of Mr. Hope and Mr. Escott for several hours, almost solidly, and it's a great pleasure to find gentler company here. I hope you're keeping well, Miss Langstrade."

"You've been in the company of Signorina Monticarlo too," Cecilia observed, in a neutral tone. "Don't you find her charming?"

"I've hardly exchanged two words with her," Michael hastened to say. "I sat in the coupé of the diligence, while she was inside, and I was in conversation with Dr. Carp all through dinner in York. She *is* rather charming, I suppose, although her charms inevitably pale in present company."

"Mademoiselle Evredon seems quite charming too," Cecilia observed, deliberately misunderstanding his perfectly clear meaning. "She's a little out of sorts, though, if I'm not mistaken."

"I overheard Dr. Carp quarreling with her when I passed the Violet Room on my way down," Michael told her, confidentially. "I gather that their recent demonstrations have gone badly, and even though he's trying hard not to blame her, he feels that she's not quite delivering the goods the way his previous somniloquist used to do."

"He's in the Blue Room, of course," Cecilia observed. "Mother and Father had a long discussion about the propriety of putting them in rooms with a connecting door; it's not as if they were father and daughter, after all. The rules of etiquette don't seem to say anything about the proprieties pertaining to the relationship between a Mesmerist and his somniloquist."

"How unfortunate," Michael murmured. From the corner of his eye, he watched Hope and Escott attempting to stir up trouble between Marlstone and Carp. They did not seem to be succeeding; Marlstone and Carp seemed to be making every effort to chat politely and pleasantly, probably being equally determined to deny Hope and Escott the pleasure of setting them at odds. He was still trying hard to think of a means of paying Cecilia another compliment when they were interrupted by Lady Phythian, who had probably been dispatched by one or both of the Lady Langstrades to make sure that nothing untoward was going on.

"I told Mr. Laurel all about the Maze on the train," the widow informed Cecilia. "The ghosts too. Well, Mr. Laurel, what do you think of our *Dedalus design*?"

"It's very interesting, Lady Phythian," Michael said. "Most intriguing."

"Do you think the ghosts might appear tonight, Cecilia?" Lady Phythian enquired. "I'm in the Yellow Room, as usual—the same room from which I've seen them so many times before—but that fearful hedge wasn't there when I first saw them, and it used to be quite discreet. It's exceedingly tall now, isn't it?"

"It has to be tall," Cecilia told her, "in order to make it easy for people to get lost. If they could look over the tops of the hedges, it would be easier to map out a route to the center. It has to be thorny too, to discourage people from taking illegitimate short cuts. Jefferies has done a magnificent job training and shaping it, over the years. I'm sorry if you find that it blocks your view of any supernatural events, although we've been rather hoping that Harold Longstride's shade might prefer to patrol the battlements now that we've rebuilt his Keep. In any case, the anniversary isn't until Saturday, so the ghosts might not appear until tomorrow night, at the earliest."

"The Keep is very tall too," Lady Phythian observed. "You could use it as a bell-tower, if you wished—although I suppose you don't really need one, being in ready earshot of Cribden Church."

"Father would never stand for that," Cecilia replied, shaking her head as if the very idea were horrifying. "It's supposed to be a military installation, not a religious one. He's very insistent that the Langstrade Maze isn't the same sort of maze that you find on the floors of churches, symbolizing the difficulty of the path to Heaven, but is more closely akin to prehistoric mazes, which were presumed to have magical properties."

"Or to house dragons," Lady Phythian put in. "Mr. Marlstone's fearful machine will serve that function, I suppose."

"Oh, Father doesn't mind letting Mr. Marlstone install his time machine in the Keep," Cecilia assured her guest, silkily. "Mr. Marlstone has urged him not to expect too much, but Father can't let go of the frail hope that he might one day be able to obtain proof that Harold Longstride really did exist, and that there really was a Keep erected there a thousand years ago. Mind you, I think he'd settle for evidence that his Keep will still be there a thousand years in the future."

"A glimpse of the future might be a very reassuring thing," Michael murmured, pensively, thinking about his possible future with Cecilia, and how wonderful it would be to obtain a sign that it might come to pass. The flirtatious attention that Cecilia was paying him now seemed to indicate the satisfactory extent of her attraction to him, but he was as fearful of reading too much into her words as he was of assuming that her father would bow to her sentiments in the matter of making a suitable marriage.

"A glimpse of the future might also be a very alarming thing," Lady Phythian said, in flat contradiction to Cecilia's judgment. Michael forgave her, on the grounds that the dowager must be only too well aware that the future could not hold a great deal of promise for a woman of her age. After a pause, the old lady added: "I do hope that Mademoiselle Evredon is not going to *play the oracle*. I prefer it when somniloquists restrict themselves to facilitating conversations between the living and the dead."

"Have you seen a great many somniloquists, Lady Phythian?" Cecilia asked, innocently.

"Not so very many," the dowager told her, primly and rather defensively. "I do remember Dr. Carp's previous assistant, though. She was very good. It's such a shame that she died so suddenly. Influenza is a terrible scourge, especially for those of delicate constitution. I live in mortal fear of it myself."

"Indeed it is," Cecilia agreed. "I expect that Dr. Carp was heartbroken. He seems a trifle distraught even now."

That was certainly true, Michael observed, although whether the distress in question was due to Hope and Escott's continuing attempts to set the Mesmerist at odds with Gregory Marlstone or to his recent altercation with Mademoiselle Evredon was anyone's guess. While he was pondering the enigma, Michael finished off his cocoa, which had cooled sufficiently to be very welcome in his mouth and stomach alike.

"I expect that you gentlemen will be repairing to the smoking room any minute for a glass of brandy," Lady Phythian observed, with an envious sigh.

"I'm rather tired," Michael said. "I expect that I'll go straight up to bed once the ladies retire."

"Indeed you will not, Mr. Laurel" Cecilia said, very firmly indeed. "You will converse with Father and his friends, as a good guest should. I'm sure that you want to make a good impression. Don't you agree, Lady Phythian?"

Lady Phythian was clearly unsure as to what she was being invited to agree to, or why, but she murmured faint assent.

"Mr. Laurel is a painter," Cecilia continued, still addressing herself to the dowager, almost as if Michael were not there—although he felt sure that her remarks were primarily addressed to him. "He has a clever hand for portraiture. You should commission him to paint you, for the edification of future generations of Phythians, Pottses, and Ashersons. I hope that Mother might persuade Father to commission a portrait of her, or even the whole family—including Jack and the dogs, of course."

"I shall be interested to see what Mr. Laurel makes of the Keep," the dowager said, dryly. "Always provided that he can find his way through the Maze."

"I'm sure that we could find him a guide," Cecilia replied, "if there were any danger of his getting lost. It won't be necessary, though. My mother, attentive as ever to the needs of her guests, had one of her maids make a dozen copies of the diagram, which she intends to supply to all the guests, in order to help them navigate."

"That won't be enough to prevent people from getting lost," Lady Phythian said, with a faint snort of derision. "I speak from experience. Maps are fine things when you know where you are, but when you don't…."

"Lady Phythian is being too modest," Cecilia said to Michael. "Like her namesake, Ariadne, she is quite at home in the Maze. She has watched it grow up year by year, and she never fails to spend time there when she visits, in order to commune with her ghosts."

"The coincidence of names has been pointed out far too often to be amusing any longer," Lady Phythian said, seemingly a trifle nettled. "Nor are they *my* ghosts. You have a better claim to their ownership than I do."

"I fear not," Cecilia said. "Although I can find my way through it with perfect accuracy nowadays, I would never aspire to the title of Mistress of the Labyrinth. I haven't an atom of magic in me."

Lady Phythian did not contradict her—which seemed to Michel to be a little ungracious, although he dared not do so himself lest he overstep the ever-inconvenient bounds of etiquette. Michael also refrained from saying that he would not need a copy of the diagram, now that he had seen the original, because he felt that any such remark might too easily have been mistaken, even by Cecilia, for vulgar boasting.

Their conversation was interrupted again, then, this time by Augustus Carp, who seemed to have been driven to desperate measures to escape the clutches of Hope and Escott. "Please excuse me, Lady Phythian, Miss Langstrade," he said, "but I wonder if I might borrow Mr. Laurel for a moment."

"There you are, Lady Phythian," Cecilia observed, coquettishly. "Mr. Carp is about to commission a portrait—perhaps a commemorative image of him placing Mademoiselle Evredon in a trance."

Carp seemed utterly bewildered for a moment, and then leaned forward conspiratorially, to say: "I'm afraid not, Miss Langstrade. To tell the truth, I was beginning to feel a trifle browbeaten in the abrasive company of Mr. Marlstone, Mr. Hope and Mr. Escott—although I must admit that Mr. Marlstone had some very interesting speculations to offer on the nature of time and the possibilities of time travel, when prompted. I was fortunate enough to have a rather pleasant conversation with Mr. Laurel at dinner, and I had hoped to take refuge in a renewal, if you don't mind."

The last thing Michael wanted was to be dragged away to some corner in order that Carp might use him as a shield against less-than-polite society, so he intervened by saying: "Have you seen the parchment containing the diagram of the Langstrade Maze, Dr. Carp? It really is a most intriguing document. I'm sure that a knowledgeable man like you might have some interesting observations to make regarding its possible origins and mystical significance."

Carp evidently realized that there was a certain safety to be obtained in that fashion, so he obligingly stepped right up to the mantelpiece and thrust his face forward in order to study the framed parchment at close range. "Now that *is* interesting," he said. "I wonder if it might be worth trying an experiment tomorrow. If we were to allow Jeanne to handle it while entranced, she might be able to pick up some interesting impressions from it. She might be able to cast some light on its origins and significance."

"What a good idea, Dr. Carp," Cecilia said. "Don't you think so, Lady Phythian?"

"I do," said the dowager, who obviously felt that handling mysterious documents left over from the distant past might be safer than prompting the somniloquist to "play the oracle" in a futuristic sense.

"I wonder which hypothesis you favor regarding the original function of prehistoric mazes, Dr. Carp," Cecilia continued, evidently seeking to give the old man a chance to show off. "Were they intended as tracks for religious processions and dances, do you think, or were they intended as traps for demons and dragons?"

Carp considered the question for a suitable interval, but then replied, with undue wariness: "I'm not really in a position to make an informed decision. Which hypothesis do you favor, Mr. Laurel?"

"I have no idea," Michael said, blithely. "I'm only an artist, after all—I'm concerned with visual and imaginative impressions rather than historical speculations. I hope the Langstrade Maze doesn't end up trapping a dragon or a Minotaur, though. I'd much rather think of it as a guide to the dancing footsteps of some modern Ariadne, offering up a rhythmic prayer to the mysterious Mistress of the Labyrinth. Did the Druids believe in a Mistress of the Labyrinth too, do you think?"

"Druids?" Carp parried, still very wary. "What do Druids have to do with the matter?"

"The Druids were my suggestion, I'm afraid," Cecilia put in, her tone replete with a feminine innocence that was somewhat contrived. "Father's convinced that the parchment, or at least the design copied on it, is pre-Christian. The Celts who were living here before the first Christian missionaries arrived had Druid priests, didn't they? Sacred sickles, mistletoe and wicker men—that sort of thing."

"We know almost nothing about Druidism, I'm afraid," Carp said, apparently finding a foothold on firmer intellectual ground at last, "except for a few lines penned by disapproving Romans, who can hardly be counted as reliable witnesses. What Julius Caesar wrote about them in the *Gallic Wars* is mostly idle hearsay. If the Langstrade Maze has anything to do with Celtic religion, I fear that there's nothing in the literature to offer us a clue as to what the connection might have been."

"In that case," Lady Phythian suggested, "any enlightenment that your somniloquist might be able to provide would be doubly welcome." She did not sound overly confident.

And completely unverifiable, Michael thought. *So go ahead and improvise to your heart's content, Dr. Carp—if you can persuade Mademoiselle Evredon to go along with it.* Carp's expression suggested that he was no more confident of the prospect of obtaining useful enlightenment from his forthcoming *séance* than Lady Phythian, and Michael felt a generous impulse bidding him to help the old man out. He did not have the opportunity to say anything supportive, though, because Lord Langstrade touched him on the arm at that moment.

"I believe the ladies are retiring now," the Earl said. "Would you and Dr. Carp care to join me in the smoking-room for a nightcap, Mr. Laurel?"

"Certainly, Milord," Michael said, having received his orders and being determined to obey them as heroically as Theseus *en route* to confront the Minotaur in the Cretan Labyrinth, confident that he would be able to emerge again thereafter, guided by Ariadne's indicative thread.

Dr. Carp's antiquity gave the Mesmerist a legitimate opportunity to decline, however, and he seized it. "I do apologize, Lord Langstrade," he said, "but traveling is very wearying at my age, even with the aid of the railway. I shall go straight to bed, if you don't mind."

"Not at all, not at all, Doctor," said the Earl, breezily. "We'll see you at breakfast. Come along, Laurel—let's leave Dr. Carp and the ladies to their much needed rest. Have you met Marlstone?"

"Yes, indeed," said Michael, as he turned to follow the Earl, after having bowed politely to Lady Phythian, bowed a little more than politely to Cecilia, and nodded to Carp. "A fascinating man— I'm looking forward to his demonstration, and I certainly hope that he'll succeed in breaching the barriers of time at his third attempt. I'm very grateful to you for inviting me, and giving me the opportunity to witness such an historic endeavor."

"Which you'll doubtless be able to preserve for posterity, by means of sketches," Langstrade said. "That's in addition to your landscape of the Keep and its surrounds, of course. I'm assuming that if Marlstone does manage to produce any worthwhile phenomena, you'll be very enthusiastic to record what you see."

"Very enthusiastic," Michael assured him, carefully refraining from any speculation about what he might or might not be fortunate enough to see. "I'll be sure to take my sketch-book into the Maze as well as my canvases, so that I'll be ready for anything when Saturday comes."

"That's the ticket," said the Earl. "I knew I could rely on you—Cecilia told me so."

"She's too kind," Michael murmured, hoping that his tone did not betray his true sentiments too openly

CHAPTER EIGHT

A DISCUSSION IN THE SMOKING-ROOM

Hope and Escott were already in the smoking-room—which a proprietor with slightly different tastes might have preferred to call the library, as the space was clearly doing double duty. They seemed to be waiting to welcome Michael yet again, in his capacity as a fresh and reasonably obliging audience for their wit and wisdom. Like Dr. Carp before him, Marlstone also seemed glad to see Michael come in, although Michael deduced that the pleasure was symptomatic of the expectation that he might provide some relief from Hope and Escott's incessant banter. Signor Monticarlo seemed utterly indifferent to his presence, being far more interested in twiddling his moustache, but Michael did not take offence. The violinist was obviously very nervous in this strange social environment, and Michael was certainly able to sympathize with that.

While Heatherington poured five generous glasses of brandy, Langstrade said: "Well, Mr. Laurel—what do you think of the restoration of the Hall and the grounds, from an artistic point of view?"

"I'll have a better idea about the landscaping of the grounds when I see them in daylight," Michael said, thinking that he ought to be judicious in his flattery "but the Hall is very tastefully done. The drawing-room is pleasantly furnished and artistically decorated, the bedrooms well-appointed, and the overall design very neat. I like the wide corridors and the large windows, and the décor in here is perfect for a smoking-room. Your father obviously went to some trouble to fill out the bookshelves with well-bound volumes."

"York's a fine place for buying good-looking books," Langstrade assured him. "You could still buy them at a guinea a yard, all novels excluded, in those days—although the books in the alcove, relating to the theory and practice of antiquarianism, were far more carefully selected. We need more art-works, though. No family portraits accumulated over generations, you see. Father was a trifle troubled by the apparent dishonesty of buying pictures of other people's ancestors to make up the deficit. He preferred landscapes, but the ones he acquired are too uniform in their dreariness for my taste. Too many trees, too many cows and too much cloudy sky. I like historical paintings myself—battles on land and sea, with a deal of *action* in them. Hunting scenes, too. A few works of those sorts would look very fine in here and along the upper corridors, don't you think?"

"There are some very fine historical painters in France," Michael observed, judiciously, "but the English school has always been stronger in landscape painting and portraiture. Some of my peers do very fine hunting scenes, although I must confess that I don't feel that I've yet mastered the difficult skill of painting galloping horses."

"It's not too late to start building a collection of family portraits, Langstrade," Quentin Hope put in. "You should take advantage of Laurel—he's an up-and-coming man, even if he's not just being modest when he claims to be a duffer with horses. You should certainly commission a new picture of your wife, while she's still in her prime, and one of your daughter, while she's still in the full flush of youth—and one of yourself, of course, in your business suit, surrounded by subtle emblems of your trade, with your son and your dogs to either side. Laurel will know how to plan the composition, won't you, Laurel?"

"If Lord Langstrade is interested in work of that sort," Michael said, judiciously, "I'd be very grateful for any work he cared to put my way, and he would be guaranteed my most careful attention."

"Let's see how the picture of the Keep works out," said the Earl, cautiously. "One can judge a man more accurately when he's done his stuff, eh, Marlstone?"

Marlstone's heavy brows twitched at that, as the builder of time machines tried to work out whether he was being insulted, challenged or merely invited to endorse an anodyne comment. "I'll be interested to see Mr. Laurel's work myself," he said, in the end. "Especially any drawings he is able make of the phenomena that result from the time machine's operation."

"Your daughter's reputed to be artistic, isn't she, Signor Monticarlo?" Escott said to the violinist. "We ought to arm her with a sketchpad as well, just in case."

"Carmela dabbles in water-colors," Signor Monticarlo admitted, "but she has sprained her wrist rather badly, and is no more able to hold a pencil than to serve as my accompanist."

"Perhaps she'd make a good medium," Hope suggested. "Dr. Carp seems to have fallen out with his current somniloquist."

Signor Monticarlo was evidently less than delighted with that suggestion, but said nothing.

"Did Carp tell you why he and his assistant had quarreled while he was taking to you by the fireplace, Laurel?" Escott enquired.

"I'm afraid not," Michael replied. "We were talking about the maze. He suggested that Lord Langstrade might care to take the document out of its protective frame and let Mademoiselle Evredon handle it tomorrow night, in the hope that she might be able to pick up some impressions from it."

"Good idea," said Hope, but, having glanced at Lord Langstrade, hurriedly added: "Unless, of course, it's too delicate to be handled."

"Might shed some light on the enigma, though," Escott put in, in loyal support of his great rival.

"I must admit," Langstrade said, "that I'm more hopeful that Mr. Marlstone will eventually be able to shed light on the history of Langstrade than I am of Mr. Carp. Emily was the one who wanted to bring Carp here—probably because her mother and Lady Phythian put her up to it. Not that I've anything against the man, mind. I'm sure there must be something in this mesmerism business—I'm just not sure what it is. I take it all with a pinch of salt."

"Quite right," said Hope. Escott and Marlstone nodded in support. Signor Monticarlo shook his head, but the meaning of the gesture was far from obvious.

"Dr. Carp seems slightly disillusioned with the revelations of Mesmeric somniloquism himself," Michael told them. "At dinner in York, he was lamenting the fact that the spirits of the dead seem no more obliging or honest, in general, than the living."

"That's probably why he's annoyed with his new telegraphic connection to the other world," Escott suggested. "She's obviously been channeling bad advice. People always blame the messenger—especially when those who are really to blame are inconveniently out of reach. The problem with mediumistic communication is that it's purely verbal, and most verbal communication is inherently deceptive."

"But seeing is believing," Hope promptly put in, "and if Mr. Marlstone's demonstration is successful, we'll be able to *see* the dead and the not-yet-born going about their business, but won't be able to hear them tell us any lies—isn't that so, Marlstone?"

"I can't be certain until the field is actually operative," Marlstone replied, a trifle grudgingly, "but I hope to open a window into time that will allow us to see into the past and the future. The logic of the situation suggests, however, that any people we are likely to glimpse will be our past and future selves—and the likelihood is that they will, indeed, be mute."

"How disappointing!" Escott remarked. "I was hoping for something a little more spectacular, as well as more informative. I must confess that I was a little confused when you were trying to explain your theory of time to Carp in the drawing-room, and I don't quite see why you can't attempt to link your machine up to some future machine, in order to achieve a more substantial kind of time travel. You have, after all, taken the trouble to ensure that noon on Saturday is a particularly suitable moment in terms of temporal harmonics."

Marlstone frowned at that; the ease with which his features slipped into the expression suggested that he had been doing a lot of frowning recently. "I don't believe you understand how difficult it would be, Mr. Escott, to establish metaphasic hypersynchrony between two machines situated at widely-spaced points on the intertemporal gravity continuum, even with the aid of a powerful natural harmonic. One would need a machine far more sophisticated than mine, and a skill in operating it that I can hardly hope to acquire in decades, even if Saturday's experiment turns out to be successful. I certainly hope to build further machines, if my present one works, but the prospect of establishing metaphasic synchronicity between any two of them within my lifetime presently seems very remote indeed."

"What on Earth is *metaphasic hypersynchronicity*?" Lord Langstrade complained. "I didn't understand a word of what you just said."

A quick glance around assured Michael that none of the other listeners was any wiser than Lord Langstrade—and he had his doubts as to whether Marlstone really knew what he was talking about himself.

"It's too late at night to begin a full explanation of Dee-Marlstone time theory," Marlstone said, more resentfully than apologetically. "I hope to find time tomorrow evening to explain the principles of my machine to any interested parties. Briefly, though, if you imagine ordinary synchrony as a matter of setting two clocks so that they provide the same temporal indications, then hypersynchronicity is a matter of setting two time machines so that they provide complementary temporal distortions—*complementary attunement*, I call it. The metaphasic aspect comes into it because the dimension of time is not continuous and linear, as is commonly believed, but discontinuous and disposed in such a way that certain points in time are, so to speak, *in harmony* with one another—not unlike corresponding notes in different octaves of the musical scale, the octaves being, in this instance, the relevant temporal phases. As well as providing complementary temporal distortions, therefore, time machines facilitating physical displacement—including the displacement of sound—would need to be placed in a particular locational relationship within the temporal dimension. Even if the hypersynchronicity could be successfully established, there's still the matter of intertemporal gravity to be taken into account, and conservation of non-identity always has to be respected, so transmitting sound-waves through time—let alone material objects—is likely to be far more complicated than it might seem at first thought."

"Of course," said Escott, with delicate sarcasm. "It's so obvious when you put it like that."

"I still didn't understand a word of it," Lord Langstrade confessed. "Did you, Laurel?"

Michael felt a sudden flash of panic. Cecilia had commanded him to be here in order that he might make a good impression. He had vaguely hoped to do so by passing more-or-less unnoticed, but he felt that a pitfall trap had just opened up in front of him, which might not be easy to avoid.

"Not exactly, sir," he confessed, "but if I've grasped the essentials correctly, what Mr. Marlstone is saying is that if time machines are to work together—as they must in order for any transfer of goods or sound to take place, in much the same way that telegraphic communication requires a transmitter and a receiver—then they need to be *in tune*, like the instruments in an orchestra. You understand what I mean, don't you, Signor Monticarlo."

The Italian might not have followed what Michael was saying, but he understood an appeal for help when he heard one, and he was too much of a gentleman to ignore it. "*Si,*" he said, loyally, "I can—how do you say it?—*grasp the principle. Scordatura* would complicate the issue, but perhaps time machines are less capricious than violins?" In his turn, the violinist looked back at Michael, hopeful of some recognition of his modest joke.

Michael laughed, dutifully. "Very good, Signor Monticarlo," he said. "Do you think, Mr. Marlstone, that one might be able to obtain *scordatura* effects from cleverly-tuned time machines?"

"I haven't the slightest idea," the inventor confessed, warily, without going so far as to admit that he had no idea what *scordatura* meant.

"Well," said Langstrade, "if even you don't know, the rest of us can certainly forget all about it. Anyway, all we really need to know, if I'm not mistaken, is that we can expect to see through time on Saturday, even if all we can see is ourselves."

"According to my theory," Marlstone agreed, "we ought to be able to see *something* when the machine become fully operational at noon on Saturday, although…." He hesitated.

"Although?" queried Hope.

"I knew there'd be a *but*," Escott added, with a sigh. "There's always a *but*."

Marlstone scowled. His physiognomy seemed to have been expressly designed to facilitate scowling and frowning, and as an artist, Michael judged the scowl to be a very effective expression of feeling. "*Although*," the inventor continued, emphatically, "it must be admitted that there's a strong possibility of distortion. Vision through time might well be subject to effects that alter the imagery in a manner that I'm not yet in a position to specify."

Hope turned to Michael, in all apparent innocence, and said: "You seem to understand all this better than I do, Laurel, so perhaps you can explain to us in layman's terms what Marlstone's getting at?"

Having avoided the pitfall once, Michael now felt that he was teetering on the brink—and that the smiling Hope was more than willing to give him a push, perhaps purely for the sake of his own amusement, and perhaps because he had a reason for wanting Michael to come a cropper in front of Lord Langstrade.

"I'm just an artist," he said, speaking slowly to give himself time to think, although he feared that he might be building up a greater sense of expectation, "not a scientist like Mr. Marlstone, but I do have some understanding of visual distortion. We're used to the simple distortions created by prisms, lenses and curved mirrors, of course, but if you and Mr. Escott were right in what you were saying earlier, in the coupé of the diligence, about displacements in time being responsible for the various sorts of apparitions we mistake for ghosts, then something more awkward and profound might well be going on. I'm just an artist, as I say, so what springs to my mind is the idea that the images we'll see when Mr. Marlstone's time machine is put into operation might be more akin to *sketches* of the past than complete and colorful visual images. It's a crude analogy, of course. Does that seem reasonable to you, Mr. Marlstone?"

"Yes, it does," said Marlstone, grudgingly, presumably because he wanted to put Hope's nose out of joint rather than because he felt any particular affection for Michael or because what Michael had said really did sound reasonable to him. "I try not to make too much use of analogies, though. The language of mathematics is so much more secure."

"But we don't all speak it, alas," observed Escott, "So it's good to have alternative viewpoints, don't you think?"

"It's always as well to have a good balance of minds at a house party," said Lord Langstrade, peering at the empty brandy decanter. "That's the art of being a good host. You need a little luck too, of course, for things to go well." Michael presumed that he was thinking about Carmela Monticarlo's accident and Augustus Carp's disappointment with his new somniloquist.

"Oh, we'll be lucky," Hope put in. "My presence is always a lucky charm—don't you think so, Jim?"

Escott gave the impression that nothing was further from his mind. "There's no such thing as luck, alas," he aid. "There's merely the blind operation of chance. Of all the superstitions of the ancients, belief in luck—faith in a magical ability to defy the calculus of probability, that is—was the most desperate."

Langstrade suppressed a frown, obviously having had no intention of setting Hope and Escott off again.

"The trouble with pessimists," Hope said, serenely, "is that they think *luck*'s a dirty word, because they think all luck all bad. I don't—and I wish Lord Langstrade, and Mr. Marlstone, all the luck in the world with regard to the weekend's endeavors."

Heatherington had stepped forward, ready to fill the decanter again if need be, but the Earl shook his head. He had obviously had enough intertemporal gravity for one evening. He stubbed out his cigar expressively.

Obedient to the rules of etiquette, his guests did likewise, and drained their glasses.

"Well, chaps," Langstrade continued, "Mr. Marlstone's absolutely right about one thing: it really is too late at night for delving into such deep and intricate mysteries. I don't know about you, but I'm ready for my bed now. I look forward to resuming our discussions tomorrow. A cold breakfast will be set out by six, and the hot dishes will be added by seven, but you mustn't feel any compulsion to be punctual. Don't feel obliged to follow me up now, either, but I've had a busy day and I fear that I must bid you good night."

The principles of etiquette, of course, made it absolutely compulsory for all the guests to follow their host's example, and there was an immediate hectic flurry of goodnights directed in every direction, muttered more in confusion than harmony, but effective nevertheless.

Within a matter of minutes, Michael was back in the safe seclusion of the Red Room. He was far too tired to attempt any conscientious reappraisal of the day's achievements—or, indeed, to do anything else except collapse into bed and dream about Cecilia.

CHAPTER NINE

IN THE HEART OF THE MAZE

Michael got up at five-thirty the next morning, intent on catching the early light. He expected to be the first one down to breakfast, when the last chime of six had hardly died away, and he did find the breakfast-room empty, save for the inevitable servants, but when he made a semi-apologetic comment to Heatherington about his excessive promptitude, the butler told him that Mr. Marlstone had made a special arrangement to have coffee, toast and hard-boiled eggs served in his room, and had already gone to work in the Keep.

Michael wondered whether it might be possible to put in a special order himself for a couple of soft-boiled eggs, but his courage failed him and he settled for bread and marmalade with a glass of milk. The freshness of the produce made up for the poverty of choice. While he ate he studied the paintings on the dining-room walls, and concluded that Lord Langstrade had been absolutely right about his father's taste in landscapes. He did not know whether to be glad that the standard he would have to surpass was so low, or worried lest his own painting be considered out of keeping with those among which it would supposedly be hung.

No one else appeared while he was eating, and less than a quarter of an hour had passed when Michael set down his napkin and got up from the table. Heatherington immediately hurried to his side, clutching a piece of paper.

"Lady Langstrade asked me to make sure that every guest should have one of these, sir," the butler said.

Michael took the paper automatically, not realizing until he had looked down at it that it was a map of the Langstrade Maze. Although he had no need of it, it would have been more trouble to hand it back than to keep it, so he thanked Heatherington, folded it up, and slipped it into his waistcoat pocket. Then he went back up-stairs to collect his equipment.

A few minutes later, having donned his smock, he staggered out of the side door of the Hall, clutching his easel and a bag containing two ready-stretched and primed canvases, a sketch-book, an abun-dance of charcoal, numerous brushes, several lead tubes stuffed with variously-colored oil paints—which he had carefully mixed himself before leaving London—and a palette.

As he had anticipated, the Maze gave him no trouble at all, and he did not have to take the map out of his pocket at all. His memory had retained a perfect visual image of the layout of the hedges, and he had already worked out the system of turns that would take him to the center with the least possible delay. His path required him to spiral more than half way around the center of the maze five times over, but that did not seem unduly excessive, in a seven-ring maze, and his tread was perfectly resolute.

The approximately-rectangular central clearing at the heart of the maze seemed narrower and more crowded than he had antici-pated. As Lady Phythian had vaguely indicated on the train, the space within the innermost hedge measured some fifty yards across, but the bulk of the Keep made the remaining rectangle of lawn very much smaller. The façade of the Keep facing the only exit from the Maze into the central arena was only forty feet broad, but the edifice was surrounded by a moat that added a further five feet all round.

Fortunately, the building was not as deep as it was broad, and it was set back toward the hedge that had no exit, so there was a mar-gin of about twenty-five yards between the Keep's only door and the exit from the maze. Even so, the Keep seemed to loom up to an alarming height, and Michael immediately began to wonder whether it might not be far more convenient to obtain a much longer perspec-tive, perhaps by building a platform somewhere within the maze that would allow him to look over its hedges. Unfortunately, a platform tall enough to let him see the whole of the doorway—not to mention the entirety of the yew-tree that was growing to the right of the door and obviously predated everything else in the vicinity by several decades—would have been uncomfortably vertiginous as well as impractical, so he had no alternative but to make the best of his less-than-desirable proximity.

After comparing several candidate positions, and studying the Keep at closer range—which revealed that the moat was almost empty of water, thanks to the recent lack of rain, although it retained a thick layer of fetid mud—Michael eventually set up his easel to the left of the exit from the maze, so that he was at an angle of about thirty-five degrees from the yew tree, relative to the parallel lines of the innermost hedge and the Keep's façade.

He placed one of the canvases on the easel, selected a piece of charcoal and took a deep breath by way of mental preparation. Then he studied the façade of the Keep carefully, noting the exact height of the loophole-like windows that were its only source of daylight, and the angles they made with the top of the arched doorway and the crenellations of the fake battlements. The resultant diagram imprinted itself in his mind just as the diagram of the Maze had done, and his hand transferred the key points to the canvas as charcoal strokes positioned with perfect accuracy.

If only I were capable of such precision in everyday matters, Michael thought. *When I'm in society, though, or going about my domestic occupations, I'm no more than an unskillful sketch of my real self—assuming that the artist is my real self.*

He had hardly begun to fill in the principal lines connecting the key points, providing the outlines of the Keep, the yew, the opposite faced of the hedge and the distant scar, when Gregory Marlstone suddenly emerged from the building's dark interior.

Marlstone set himself squarely upon the little drawbridge that spanned the empty moat in front of the door, almost as if he were getting ready to defend the edifice against some marauding horde, and stared at the painter for a few seconds before advancing across the lawn to speak to him.

"Lord Langstrade assured me that I was to have exclusive use of the Keep today, Mr. Laurel." Marlstone said.

"And so you may, sir," Michael assured him. "I shall not need to come any closer than my present position in order to execute my commission."

Marlstone appeared to be making an effort not to scowl, although the alignment of his features was unsympathetic to the process of repression. "Do you intend to remain here very long?" he asked.

"For as long as the daylight lasts," Michael told him. "I shall take an hour's break to let the initial washes dry—which will give me time for a spot of lunch—but I have a lot of work to do today, and I need to take full advantage of the clear skies.

"That won't be possible, I'm afraid," Marlstone said.

"I, too, am working at Lord Langstrade's request," Michael pointed out, although what he actually had in mind was Cecilia's irresistible command. He did not stop sketching while he engaged in the verbal combat.

"I have nothing against you, my dear fellow," Marlstone said, still striving for politeness and amiability. "Indeed, I suppose I owe you a small debt of gratitude for the assistance you attempted to render last night, when those clowns Hope and Escott were trying to provoke me, but I fear that I can't grant you more than two hours this morning, at the most. I must ask you to leave by nine-thirty. I need to be left alone for the remainder of the day."

"I have a deadline too, Mr. Marlstone," Michael told him, stubbornly. "Although I could, in principle, put the finishing touches to my painting in London, I really ought to make every effort to complete it within the next four days, before I catch the train to London on Tuesday morning. In order to have any chance of doing that, I need to make a very solid start today, on the painting as well as the sketching. Oil-paint takes time to dry, you see, and I shall need to apply it in several careful stages. I assure you that I shall not set foot in the F...the Keep, and will not disturb you in the least."

"You don't understand, Mr. Laurel," Marlstone informed him, flatly. "As soon as my assistants have completed the assembly of the machine's principal parts—which, with luck, will not take more than two hours—then I shall need to run a series of tests in preparation for tomorrow's demonstration. Although I shall not make any attempt to set up an extensive field until noon tomorrow, when the conditions will be most propitious, I shall have to establish a series of limited fields today, in order to bring the machine into readiness, and there may be some danger of...leakage."

"Leakage of what?" Michael enquired, innocently.

"What I mean," Marlstone said, making an obvious effort to find words that a mere artist might be able to comprehend, "is that the experimental time-fields set up momentarily within the Keep might, on occasion, extend beyond its walls, perhaps as far as your present position. Would it be possible, do you think, to make your preliminary sketches from outside the maze?"

"I'm afraid not," Michael said. "It's not just that I need to be able to see the doorway, the moat and the yew, but that I have to organize the composition relative to the background. Would it be possible for you to run your preliminary tests after dusk, when I shall be forced to retire to the Hall?"

"No, it wouldn't," Marlstone said, grimly, seemingly ruling out any possibility of negotiation on that score.

"In that case," Michael said, "might I not be allowed to take the risk of remaining here, assuming full responsibility for any danger I might run? Given that I shall certainly not impede your work in any way, I don't see how you could have any objection to that. You're obviously prepared to run the relevant risks yourself, and I'm inclined to trust your judgment, even though I don't have the least idea how your machine is supposed to work, let alone what side-effects it might produce. Give that the entire house-party will be here tomorrow, when you activate the machine at full power, and all the people then gathered here will be vulnerable to any perils your machine might produce, I really can't see that you can object to my solitary presence while you run your preliminary tests." He was still working away assiduously, although he knew that it was rather rude of him to continue the conversation while hardly sparing his interlocutor a sideways glance.

"A scientist has to be prepared to take risks in the course of experimentation," Marlstone said, loftily, "but he has no right to expose others to such risks until he is certain that he has done everything possible to minimize them. The whole point of choosing noon tomorrow for the demonstration is that it should be relatively easy to establish a secure and stable temporal field at that time, with a clearly-defined range in both duration and spatial area. The fields I shall establish today, in order to adjust the apparatus, will be very brief in duration, but also highly unstable. Unlikely as it is that they will obtain any significant resonance from other points in the temporal continuum, there is a small possibility that exotic mental and visual effects might be produced."

Michael's hand had begun to tremble slightly, under the strain of the dispute, and he had to step back from his canvas and take a firm grip on himself. "I quite understand, Mr. Marlstone," he said, "how important the success of your demonstration is, not merely to you but to science. By comparison, a landscape painting undertaken by an unknown artist must seem a very trivial matter—but in the context of my own life and hopes, this commission is not trivial at all. My entire future might depend on it. I'm more than willing to run the risk of a few *exotic mental and visual effects* in order to accomplish it swiftly and with maximum effect. If you're afraid that I might interfere with your work, or attempt to spy on it, you can always bolt the door of the Keep and raise the drawbridge."

Marlstone scowled so magnificently that Michael was tempted to take out his sketch-book and start drawing, in order to record the expression for posterity. "The door has no bolt and the drawbridge is a fake," the inventor stated. "There is no mechanism inside by means of which it can be taken up. Lord Langstrade, being concerned purely with appearances, evidently thought it an unnecessary expense."

"In that case," Michael said, "you'll have to be content with leaving the door on the latch and taking my word for it that I'll remain by my easel—but I *will* remain by my easel for as long as I think it necessary, whatever the risk. If you're prepared to accept that risk, so am I. Did you run your tests successfully before your attempted demonstrations at Horton Lacey and Chatsworth?"

Marlstone was slightly taken aback by that, but his reply was simple enough. "Yes, I did," he said.

"Well, you seem to have come through those experiences quite unscathed. What mental and visual effects did you experience?"

The inventor seemed a trifle reluctant to answer that question, but he relented soon enough, perhaps because he thought it his moral duty to warn Michael what might happen, and perhaps because he could not, in the end, resist the temptation to share his secret.

"I experienced a sort of vertigo," Marlstone admitted, "and a curious confusion of thought, almost as if I were no longer in sole possession of my own mind and body—although I can only suppose that the latter effect was an illusion caused by the temporal redistribution of my own personality. I suppose it wouldn't do any harm to obtain a second description of such phenomena, given that they must have a significant subjective element, and my own experience might not be typical. As to what I saw…well, I saw *myself*. That wasn't particularly surprising, given that I was alone when I conducted the tests, and that the only person I could possibly have seen, by gazing through time across an interval of a few minutes, was me. The images were odd, though: attenuated almost to the point of transparency and...." He hesitated, searching for an appropriate term.

"Sketchy," Michael supplied, remembering his improvisation of the previous evening.

"*Unsteady*," Marlstone concluded. "Other objects in the vicinity also became blurred, probably because of the superimposition of competing visual imagery from slightly different times."

"*Times* in the plural," Michael observed. "You didn't manage to stabilize the field, then?"

"That wasn't really the problem," Marlstone said, drawn into discussion in spite of a gathering impatience that was evidently urging to put an end to the confrontation. "In my judgment, the effect was due to…well, to extend the musical analogy we were using last night, I suppose one might liken them to *overtones*: the subsidiary elements making up a complex musical tone, and determining its quality. It's a crude analogy, but not inapt."

"I see," said Michael, feeling rather like the proverbial blind man who said "I see" when he couldn't see at all. "Did these *overtones* have anything to do with the fact that your demonstrations failed when you tried to increase the magnitude of the field?"

"I don't think so. I'm almost certain that the fault was in the regulatory apparatus maintaining the fundamental harmonic, which needs to be very precise if…well, extending the same crude analogy to rather absurd extremes, if the *resonance* between the machine and the intrinsic subvibrations of time is to be perfect and sustained. Otherwise, the necessary homeostasis—stabilizing feedback, in layman's parlance—can't be maintained and the whole ensemble becomes, as it were, *discordant*, not so say *cacophonous*. I've done everything possible since the last catastrophe to refine the mechanism—but in order to make quite sure of that, I need to extend the range of my preparatory tests today, making them more elaborate than before. You really would be well advised to leave, Mr. Laurel, when I send my assistants away. If all goes well, I suppose it might be safe for you to return later—at three o'clock, say—but if there's any hitch…." He trailed off.

"I must repeat," Michael said, "that I need to work to my own timetable—or, rather, the timetable dictated by the necessity of completing the painting in good time. That is what Ce…Lord Langstrade would wish me to do," Michael felt proud of his amazing steadfastness in the face of menaces and ominous warnings, which was quite uncharacteristic of his normal, rather timorous self. *What an enigmatic caprice love is!* he thought.

Marlstone allowed his physiognomy to express itself according to its natural bent, but hesitated over what to do next, first pursing his lips and then chewing them reflectively. "I've given you fair warning, have I not?" he said, finally. "You do understand that anything that might befall you is none of my responsibility?"

"Entirely mine," Michael agreed. "I shall simply have to hope that my surroundings do not become so blurred that I can no longer obtain an accurate representation of their contours."

"You might faint," Marlstone advised him, grudgingly.

"Did you faint during one of your earlier trials?" Michael queried.

"Briefly. You might also find that your thought-processes are disrupted to an extent that, in combination with visual distortions, might make it rather difficult for you to work efficiently."

It was Michael's turn to frown. "I'll do my best to cope with any disturbance," he said.

"If all goes well, there'll be no problem," Marlstone told him, "but as you pointed out, the entire house-party will be here at noon tomorrow. I need to be as certain as I can be that my machine is in perfect order, and that she can set up a safe and stable field at that time."

She? Michel thought, briefly bewildered—but then he remembered that the engineer in charge of the *Sir Richard Trevithick* had also referred to his machine, quite tenderly, as "she".

"I understand," Michael assured him. "If some unexpected disturbance does occur, better that it occurs today instead of tomorrow, just to the two of us. As you say, though, it might be helpful to obtain a second opinion regarding the nature of any disturbance that does occur. I'm only too happy to volunteer my services."

At that moment, Gregory Marlstone did not have the appearance of a man who attributed much weight to the opinions of others, but he did owe Michael a debt of gratitude, however small, and he was compelled to recognize that he could not force or persuade Michael to leave. "Very well, Mr. Laurel," he said, attempting to be gracious. "I accept your generous offer. I look forward to hearing your report—if, indeed, there is anything for you to report."

Marlstone made as if to turn on his heel and march back into the Keep, but he checked the movement as his gaze was attracted to something away to Michael's right. Michael resisted the temptation to turn his own head to follow the direction of the inventor's stare, concentrating hard on capturing the exact shape and dimensions of what his private thoughts still insisted on calling "the door to the Folly". It was not until he heard another voice calling his name that he started slightly and allowed his concentration to be broken.

Cecilia was wearing a pretty pale-blue dress. It was she who had called his name, and he had no doubt that it was she who had taken the initiative in coming to visit him after breakfast—but propriety had demanded that she could not do that without mounting a pretence that she merely intended to take a random stroll and inviting at least one other person to accompany her. Unfortunately, even if the initial invitation had been selective, it had obviously been passed on in a generous manner. Not only was Lord Langstrade walking by his daughter's side, but he had a very considerable company in his wake, comprising his wife—who was clutching the hand of an eleven-year-old boy—Mr. Escott, Mr. Hope, and Lady Phythian. Lord Langstrade seemed to be in a buoyant mood, to judge by the way he was swinging the sturdy walking-stick he was carrying in his right hand: a masterpiece in polished mahogany, with an ivory pommel shaped like the hilt of a dagger.

In spite of the unwelcome presence of this veritable crowd, Michael's heart leapt. There had been a slim chance, the previous evening, that the force of his desire might have led him to mistake mere friendly politeness for something more, but the fact that Cecilia had no sooner finished breakfast than she had been impelled to search him out, at whatever cost in terms of dragging excess baggage behind her, left no conceivable room for doubt as to the depth of her fondness. She loved him! The enigmatic caprice had taken her in its grip as firmly as it had seized him.

"You two haven't met my younger brother, Jack, I believe," Cecilia said, brightly. "Jack, this is Mr. Laurel, the painter, and Mr. Marlstone, the inventor.

Jack bowed, rather clownishly. He had a catapult stuck in the back pocket of his short trousers, whose elastic slingshot was dangling awkwardly down, like an ill-placed tail.

Michael was tongue-tied by the sight of Cecilia's warm smile, so Marlstone had no difficulty seizing the initiative. "I must protest, my lord," he said. "I specifically requested that I was to have the Keep to myself this morning, and you agreed that I should be left alone."

"Oh, absolutely!" Lord Langstrade replied, cheerily. "No one shall so much as set foot on the drawbridge, or they'll answer to me. Remember that, everyone! Mr. Marlstone is to have the Keep entirely to himself!"

"Perhaps I would have made myself clearer if I had said *the Keep and the Maze*," Marlstone said, regretfully.

"Mr. Marlstone is worried about leakage," Michael put in, making a sincere attempt to be helpful in spite of his emotional rapture. "Leakage and overtones, which might cause dizziness and confusion to anyone caught within the field of his apparatus. The effect might extend as far as my station, I fear—but I was just explaining that my task is of the highest importance, and that it would be a pleasure and a privilege to share his perils, minuscule as they might be."

"Bravo!" said Escott. "Stout fellow. Don't you think so, Hope?"

Hope, for once, made no reply. His physiognomy, unlike Marlstone's, was ill-designed for scowling, but Michael had no doubt that the famous optimist was not in a good mood. He had evidently perceived Michael's response to Cecilia's appearance, and had deduced the reason for Cecilia's desire to explore the Maze.

"Mr. Laurel has refused to retire to an adequate distance while I conduct the crucial trials of my time machine," Marlstone told Lord Langstrade. "Any risk will, indeed be minuscule, but I really do think it might be best if everyone else took care to remain outside the Maze until tomorrow's demonstration at noon."

"But won't the risks—whatever they might be—be even greater then?" Escott asked.

"I believe that they will be considerably less," Marlstone hastened to say. "At that particular moment, the range and power of the field ought to prohibit all short-range self-interference, thus dispelling confusion and making sure that if we are privileged to see our past and future selves, the images will be as clear and distinct as possible. I'll explain it all in greater detail in my lecture tonight."

"Lecture?" queried Lord Langstrade, letting the tip of his walking-stick fall to the ground and leaning on it, although he was not really in need of its support. "What lecture?"

"Mr. Hope and Mr. Escott asked me last evening to explain the theoretical principles of my time machine. The explanation need not be as formal as a lecture, of course...."

"I should hope not," Lord Langstrade said. "We've got a full evening's...er...entertainment ahead of us, and I'm not at all sure that we'll have time for a lecture."

Michael could not help wondering whether Dr. Carp would be content to have his own experiment classified as "entertainment", but he let the thought pass across his consciousness fleetingly, in order that he could focus once again on the firm confidence that Cecilia loved him, and that all was well with the world.

"We're in no particular hurry," Hope assured the Earl and Gregory Marlstone, having recovered his voice. "Tomorrow night, after the demonstration, might be a better time anyway. Mind you, Marlstone's got a point about being let alone. If he wants us out of range, I think we owe it to him to take ourselves out of range— everyone but Laurel, of course. Laurel has his work to do, and we shouldn't be interrupting him any more than we should be interrupting Marlstone. The rest of us really ought to take a turn through the rose-garden instead—don't you agree, Miss Cecilia?"

It was Michael's turn to frown. Hope seemed to be intent on separating him from Cecilia as soon as possible. He became suddenly certain that Hope really might take it into his head to ask Lord Langstrade for her hand before the house-party came to an end, and might well make his bid urgently, for fear of emergent competition. Unfortunately, he had already taken his stand, and could not possibly allow any of the newcomers to stay and share his "minuscule risk"—Cecilia least of all.

Lord Langstrade had been measuring the distance between Michael and the moat, holding up his walking stick as if it were a yardstick. "Seems a perfectly adequate margin to me, Marlstone," he opined, gruffly, "but if you want the entire Maze to yourself, I suppose you'd better have it—except for young Laurel, of course. He has a job to do, as he says, and if he's willing to remain...."

"I'm willing to allow him to do so," Marlstone agreed, bowing to the inevitable.

"How brave you are, Mr. Laurel!" Cecilia was quick to exclaim. "I shall feel so much safer tomorrow, when I have your assurance as well as Mr. Marlstone's that I shall not be in any danger within the time machine's field of influence."

"I don't doubt that we'll *all* be perfectly safe," Escott muttered, so softly that only Michael and Hope could hear him, "unless we're bored to death by the absence of any effect at all. The crowd at Chatsworth was exceedingly disappointed."

"Mr. Marlstone has certainly shown a wise discretion in opting to make his third experiment in the presence of such a small and select audience," Hope murmured in reply.

"I agree with Lord Langstrade," Lady Phythian declared, loudly. "Mr. Marlstone has his trials to conduct, and Mr. Laurel his sketches to make. The rest of us should be kind enough to leave them to it—provided that we can find our way out of the Maze, now that the hedges have grown so oppressively tall. Will you guide us again, Cecilia?"

"I can do it!" Jack proclaimed. "I know the way." His mother made a gesture instructing him to be quiet, but there was a certain pride in her expression.

Cecilia had made no move to set off, but Jack had no reason to linger. He grabbed his father's hand and set about dragging both his parents back into the gap in the hedge. Lord Langstrade allowed himself to be drawn, and Lady Phythian immediately followed the family group.

Hope extended his own arm to Cecilia. "May I?" he asked.

"Oh, I wouldn't dream of separating you from Mr. Escott," Cecilia replied. "You look so well together."

Escott guffawed, but Hope did not.

"If you take a break at lunch-time, Mr. Laurel," Cecilia said, as she set off on her own, leaving Hope and Escott stranded, "You'll probably find us picnicking on the front lawn, or in the rose-garden—it's far too stuffy indoors when the sun's like this." She did not even glance at Marlstone, who had already turned his back in order to return to the Keep.

"Unless, of course, you're dizzy and confused," said Hope to Laurel, taking up where Cecilia had left off. "We wouldn't want you making a fool of yourself, would we?"

"Of course we would," Escott put in, though not unkindly. "We love to see people making fools of themselves—but I think you're right, Laurel; the danger's probably minuscule. Lovely word, that."

"Only a pessimist could possibly think so," said Hope, with a sigh, reluctantly falling into step with his old friend as Escott moved away.

CHAPTER TEN

A PICNIC IN THE ROSE-GARDEN

After all the fuss that Marlstone had kicked up, which had seriously impeded the progress of his work of art, Michael was almost disappointed that he did not suffer the slightest side-effect of anything that happened inside the Keep before the distant bell of Cribden Church chimed twelve.

Marlstone's assistants had completed their work by nine-thirty, and had dutifully made their way back to the servants' quarters at the Hall. Michael heard periodic sounds of muffled cursing for a full hour thereafter while they failed to find their way out of the Maze, in spite of being equipped with one of Lady Langstrade's maps. They wandered past his station, separated by one, two or three hedges, at least half a dozen times, but they had obviously succeeded in making their escape in the end. Occasional clangs, creaks and clattering sounds emerged from the Keep thereafter, but Marlstone did not appear again, and time—at least so far as Michael could tell—remained completely undisturbed.

At noon, satisfied with his progress and having applied the first washes to the surfaces of his canvas representing the blue background of the sky, the black rock-faces of Bancroft Scar, the straw-colored stonework of the Keep and the greens of the hedges and lawns, Michael laid his palette down, appraised his work, and decided to take a lunch-break. He considered the possibility of knocking on the door of the Folly to enquire whether Marlstone wanted to accompany him, but decided that it was better to honor the inventor's request to be left alone. He took off his smock and hung it on the easel.

He walked into the Maze, confident that he could make his exit without taking a single wrong turn—and so he did, although his roundabout journey was not without incident. In the third of the seven rings he came across Jeanne Evredon, standing at a junction on her own, weeping quietly. He thought at first that she might have come into the Maze simply to obtain a little privacy while she wept for some reason of her own, but when she saw him coming along the path between the tall hedges she acquired such an expression of relief that he could not doubt that she was lost, and frustrated by her inability to find her way. She had a copy of the map in her hand, but she obviously could not work out exactly where she was, and thus could not determine which way she ought to turn.

"May I be of assistance, Mademoiselle," Laurel asked.

"You certainly may, Mr. Laurel," she said. "I began by trying to find my way to the center, but I confess now that I shall be only too glad to find the exit again."

"Mr. Marlstone asked Lord Langstrade to ensure that no one else came into the Maze today," Michael told her, as he offered her his arm. "Did the news of the prohibition not reach you?"

"Oh!" said the Frenchwoman, in evident surprise, as she took his arm and fell into step with him. "No, it did not. I only wish it had—but I confess that I have been avoiding the company of others all morning. News of all kinds has had a great deal of trouble in reaching me, of late." She sniffed as she came to that conclusion, but she had contrived to stop weeping, and she used her free hand to mop her cheeks with a handkerchief.

"I noticed that you seemed unhappy last night, at dinner," Michael admitted, trying his utmost to be tactful. "It must be very difficult for you, attempting to form a fruitful partnership with Dr. Carp, when he had become so used to working with his previous somniloquist."

"Oh, the fault is not Dr. Carp's," she said, woefully. "He's right to be disappointed in me—even to scold me, although I truly can't help my inadequacies."

"You mustn't lose heart," Michael told her. "I dare say that a soliloquist's gift is not unlike an artist's—a trifle unsteady and subject to occasional depletions. There have been times when I have almost convinced myself that I am devoid of talent, and should never have ventured to pick up a brush. The feeling passes, though, with the whims of circumstance."

"It's not my gift that I doubt," she told him, dolefully. "It's...well, I fear that I have somehow become the victim of some malicious agency in the world beyond."

Michael was so startled by that that he almost—but not quite—took a wrong turn. "An evil spirit, you mean?" he queried.

"I suppose so," she said. "Nothing human, at any rate. I have sensed its presence now for a fortnight and more, but it has been increasingly evident with every passing day…and night. On the train, yesterday, its imminence was so fearful that I wanted to abandon the journey and turn back. Had I been on the mail-coach, I would have disembarked at the next Coaching Inn and refused to go a single step further—but that terrible steam locomotive gave me no such option. I begged Dr. Carp to cancel the *séance*, but he would not hear of it. He promised me instead that it will be his last, but I can't believe that—and if it were true, it would only make me regret my treason more. I'm frightened, Mr. Laurel, I admit…and the fact that I have no idea what I'm frightened *of* makes the fear seem even worse. And then, to make things even worse, I tried to hide away from everything in the heart of the Maze and got lost. What a fool I am!"

Michael felt that that the young woman—who could not have been much older than himself—was being a trifle over-confidential, but he put that down to her emotional anguish and her French parentage. He felt sorry for her, and wanted to comfort her as best he could, but he could not help thinking that if anyone were to see the two of them arm in arm, the news might fly back to Cecilia within the blink of an eye. He suspected that Quentin Hope would be only too eager to pour oil on any flickering flame of jealousy that was thus inspired. He therefore stopped well short of the exit and released her, pretending that he was doing so in order to look her squarely in the face.

"You have nothing to fear, Mademoiselle Evredon," he said to her, trying to sound firm and compassionate at the same time. "Dr. Carp is a good man, and so is Lord Langstrade. If you really do not want to attempt a somniloquistic performance this evening, they should certainly be prepared to release you from the commitment, however reluctantly. If you would like me to speak to Dr. Carp in private on your behalf, I will do so."

It was at that exact moment, however, that he felt the first flicker of the confusion about which Gregory Marlstone had warned him. His head whirled, and it really did seem, for a second or two, that his head was crowded with many more minds than it was accustomed to contain. There was, however, nothing *alien* about the other presences that seemed to be gathered around him, interpenetrating his own personality. They were familiar, and friendly.

Because he was looking Jeanne Evredon straight in the eyes, he saw clear evidence of the confusion that passed through her mind too, and feared that she might faint, or scream, but she too seemed to find the confusion strangely comfortable—more comfortable, at any rate, than the anxious and tormented clarity that had preceded it.

"Why, Mr. Laurel," she said. "I do believe that you're a Mesmerist!"

"Oh no!" he was quick to say. "That wasn't me! That was...," he trailed off, unsure how to explain, or even whether he ought to try.

"You're too modest, Mr. Laurel," she said, "and very kind. Thank you for your guidance and support. I think we should part now, though—I don't want run the risk of our being seen emerging from the Maze together. I have my reputation to think of, you know."

"Yes, of course," Michael said, mechanically, lost in amazement.

"Would you mind waiting here for a few minutes?" she said. "I really am grateful—for everything—but...I'm sure you understand."

Michael was not at all sure that he did, but he had no objection at all to waiting behind the hedge while she ran to the exit and slipped through. He remembered what Marlstone had said about the side-effects of the time machine's trial being largely subjective, and wondered exactly what Jeanne Evredon thought that she had experienced. He soon put the thought aside, though. When he eventually emerged from the maze himself there was no sign of the somniloquist.

He hesitated as to whether he ought to return to the Red Room for a jacket, but decided that the weather was too hot; even his waistcoat, light as it was, seemed a trifle burdensome. From where he stood he had a clear view of the rose-garden, which with on the north side of the house, and could easily see over the hedge surrounding it, which was no more than waist-high except at the corners. The majority of the Hall's remaining guests were picnicking on the lawn between two of the rose-beds, sitting in a circle around a vast tablecloth laden with dishes. The bushes in the beds must have been a glorious sight in May and June, but the once-huge white flowers had lost almost all of their petals now, and the ones that remained were crumpled, browning at the edges.

Whereas the hedges of the Maze were pruned with military straightness and leveled off as if with a spirit-level, Jefferies had been given permission to express himself more artistically in the rose garden hedge, the four elevated corners of which had been trimmed to represent the heads of animal. Michael identified them as a hare, a duck, a polecat—or, more likely, a domestic ferret—and a roebuck. He made his way there at a leisurely pace, tilting his hat slightly to shield his eyes from the sun.

"How good it is to see you safe and sound, Mr. Laurel!" Escott called out to him as he approached, having evidently figured out that he could annoy Quentin Hope by treating Michael amicably. "I'm delighted to see you undisturbed by the trickery of time. How is the painting coming along?"

"Quite well, Mr. Escott," Michael told him, as he bowed and nodded to the various members of the assembled company. "I've applied the first washes, but I need them to dry at least partially before I begin more detailed work on the sky and the ground."

"I dare say that Almighty God said much the same thing on the first day of Creation," Hope observed, tartly, causing Lady Phythian and the elder Lady Langstrade to bristle at the mild blasphemy.

Hope, who was sitting to Cecilia's right, made no movement to clear a space for Michael, but Carmela Monticarlo, who was sitting on her other side, immediately moved to her own left—elbowing her father along in the process—in order that the newcomer might sit between the two young women. Cecilia briefly made as if to shift to her left in order to relocate the space, but thought better of it and allowed Michael to take the place that Carmela had cleared for him.

Although he had only had bread and conserves for breakfast, Michael was not at all displeased to find himself confronted with similar fare now. The late summer heat was beginning to become oppressive now that he had been outdoors for almost six hours, and he had no desire to eat anything hot. There were stone jugs of ginger beer nestling in baths of ice, ferried from an ice-house excavated close to the shore of Cribden Tarn, and he gratefully accept a tall glass filled to the brim with the cold liquid before reaching forward to put two bread rolls on a plate and cut himself a thick slice of Wensleydale cheese.

"We've been anxious that some error in Marlstone's speculative calculations might have resulted in your being hurled back to the Stone Age or forward to Hope's Euchronian Era, helpless to return to your own time," Escott told him, jokingly. "We hadn't realized, until we received Marlstone's instruction to stay away from the Keep at all costs, that his experiments were so dangerous. It confirms all my worst fears about the horrors of technology."

"Don't be silly, Escott," Hope instructed his friend, fractiously. "We all know perfectly well that physical transplantation in time is quite impossible—unless, of course, one has two machines established in metaphasic hypersynchronicity."

"Actually, Hope," Escott retorted, promptly, "I've been thinking about that. How do we know that there won't be a time machine ready and waiting somewhen in your dread technological empire of the future, carefully set up in metaphasic hypersynchronicity with exactly this point in space at noon tomorrow, based on the knowledge—carefully conserved by centuries of history—that the world's first time machine became fully operational at that exact moment in Lord Langstrade's replica Keep?"

"Do you think that's possible, Mr. Escott?" Lord Langstrade asked, anxiously. "Perhaps I ought to tell Marlstone that I've had second thoughts about letting him conduct his trial here—or, at least, about inviting my guests to witness it at close range?"

Michael knew full well that Escott was perfectly confident that his suggestion was quite impossible, because the pessimist had no faith whatsoever that Gregory Marlstone's time machine would ever work—but he also knew that a lack of sincere belief would not prevent Escott from indulging in a wild flight of fancy. Even Carmela Monticarlo, whose English was limited, knew what to expect by now. She leaned a little closer to Michael to say: "I too am glad to see you safe."

That brought an instant response from Cecilia, who was perfectly prepared to take advantage of her greater fluency in her native tongue. "I'm delighted to find that the echoes and resonances of Mr. Marlstone's apparatus have not caused you any distress or dyspepsia. Mr. Laurel," she said, in a calculatedly innocent tone. "I love the idea that time, like the Platonic spheres, is blessed with musical harmonies, don't you?"

"Oh, indeed I do," said Michael, quite careless of the fact that he had not the faintest idea what the musical analogies contained in Marlstone's talk of temporal harmonics were supposed to signify.

"*In fact*," Escott said, rather insistently, with the obvious intention of drowning out any rival conversation that might reduce the audience for his speculations, "I think there has to be a definite possibility that the world as we know it will end tomorrow, at noon."

As conversational stratagems went, that was an unqualified success. Even Hope seemed startled, and curious to know more.

"The argument is perfectly simple," Escott said, airily. "Let us assume, for the moment, that Marlstone's theory of time travel, however odd and vaguely-formulated it might be at present, is broadly correct. Suppose that two time machines, located at any two points in future history, really could permit the physical transfer of material objects when established in what he calls *metaphasic hypersynchronicity*. The immediate effect of any such linkage would be that all the technological resources of the more advanced society would immediately become available to the less advanced society—which would, inevitably, be eager to deploy them, even if they were not to be imposed by conquest. The result would be that the less advanced society would rapidly become a replica of the more advanced one, and that the margin of historical development between them—perhaps extending over hundreds, or even thousands, of years—would be eliminated. To put it simply, the future would invade and subsume the past, creating an interval of technological equality."

"An expansive Euchronia!" Mr. Hope exulted. "A Euchronia capable of extending its own social perfection *back in time*, as a gift to all the previous generations whose patient labor and dutiful accumulation of knowledge enabled its construction. What a wonderful thought!"

"On the contrary!" Escott objected. "It is the most terrifying prospect imaginable. The ultimate tyranny of vile machinery, having destroyed the glories of Nature in its own era, would reach out into the past with its avid and implacable steel hands, to crush the glories of Nature in the past. The establishment of a dehumanized, static society extending over centuries and millennia, from the moment that the very first time machine became operative until...well, unless time machines can somehow be *uninvented* once they have first been invented, until the very end of time. A dread empire indeed—a universal, unconquerable, *eternal* empire."

"My God!" said the younger Lady Langstrade, breaking the shocked silence that followed this judgment. "What an idea! Has Mr. Marlstone been warned about this?"

"Actually," Dr. Carp put in, "I believe Mr. Marlstone said something about the matter last evening, shortly after Mr. Hope and Mr. Escott introduced me to him. Perhaps that's what prompted Mr. Escott's nightmare—although I understood what Mr. Marlstone was saying rather differently."

If looks could have killed, Escott's arrest for the old man's murder would have been all but inevitable, but circumstances favored the pessimist, and Augustus Carp actually seemed to take heart from the expression on Escott's face.

"Do explain, Dr. Carp," Hope was quick to say. "I must say that, although I certainly didn't take the same dire inference as Escott from what Marlstone was saying, I'm not entirely clear as to his reasons for rejecting the idea that time machines, if ever they were successfully invented would enable the inhabitants of future eras to rewrite their own pasts, paradoxical as that might seem."

"So far as I was able to judge," the Mesmerist replied, doubtless obtaining confidence from that fact that Marlstone was not present, "the key to the enigma lies in the analogy Miss Langstrade drew a few minutes ago, between Mr. Marlstone's theory of temporary harmonics and Plato's theory of celestial harmonics. Like Plato and John Dee, Mr. Marlstone is an atomist rather than a plenarist in his philosophical conception of space, and he seems to go a little further than the modern fashion in applying the same framework of thought to time. His application of the Pythagorean notion of harmonics to time is not unlike Plato's notion of the organization of the solar system about a *spindle of necessity* imbued with the implacability of fate. Instead of conceiving of time by analogy with a flowing river, as so many philosophers do, Mr. Marlstone seems to imagine moments as discrete entities scattered within a temporal void, in much the same way that elementary particles of matter are supposedly scattered in a spatial void, like planets and stars. He does not think, though, that moments are subject to the same simple orbital patterns as the planets within the Platonic solar system; he believes, along with the famous Dr. Dee, that their arrangement is far more complicated—labyrinthine, in fact. His own work involves the most sophisticated techniques of modern mathematics, applying the insights of Lagrange's *Mécanique analytique* to the extrapolation of non-Euclidean geometries, in order to calculate the resonant coincidences."

Hope and Escott looked at the old man in frank amazement, open-mouthed. Michael suspected that they might be a little less eager in their attempts to make a fool of him from now on. He also suspected that Carp had been up half the night preparing that little speech, ready to spring it on Hope and Escott as soon as the opportunity presented itself.

"I do not understand this," Carmela Monticarlo whispered in Michael's ear.

Michael refrained from saying "Nor do I"—not because it was untrue, but because he thought Cecilia might take exception to any expression of sympathy directed toward the signorina, however slight.

"What on Earth is all that taradiddle supposed to mean, Dr. Carp?" Lord Langstrade demanded, coming to the rescue yet again, emphasizing his question by waving his trusty walking-stick as if to demand attention and discipline from a class of unruly schoolchildren.

"In layman's terms," the Mesmerist said, clearly enjoying his moment in the spotlight, and speaking as if it required a tremendous effort for a man of his great and esoteric wisdom to lower himself to the use of everyday terminology, "Mr. Marlstone conceives of time travel not as a means of moving smoothly back and forth along a time-*stream* but as a matter of leaping from one propitious moment to another. I say 'propitious' because he alleges that it is not practicable to move from any moment to any other, but only to move through rare and intricate sequences of particular moments, whose potential linkage he describes in terms analogous to those of musical harmonics but whose calculation requires very advanced mathematics.

"The discrete nature of these moments protects them, in his view, from the kind of alteration that Mr. Escott has described in such apocalyptic terms. Any substantial transfer of material objects, or even of valuable information, from a future moment to a past moment would not result in a consequent cascade of transformation through all the intervening moments, but rather in the generation of a *parallel* moment, by what might be thought of as a process of *intertemporal budding*.

"Once separated from its parent moment, that 'bud' would become the seed of an new sequence of moments extending, as it were, *sideways* into the temporal void, leaving the original momentary chain unaffected. It is, I admit, a strange notion, and I was unable to grasp it immediately when Mr. Marlstone attempted to explain it, in response to Hope and Escott's prompting. Having given it considerable thought, though, I believe that I have grasped the gist of it."

"What is a *gist*, please?" Carmela murmured in Michael's ear. This time, he might have felt obliged to answer, but Hope came to his rescue—unintentionally, of course—by loudly taking up the thread of the discourse, intent on repairing the damage done to his intellectual image by Carp's casual intervention.

"In that case, Dr. Carp," Hope said, insistently, "the kind of eternal Euchronian Empire that was earlier envisaged—which would, of course, be an Earthly paradise, not the awful tyranny fearfully envisaged by Mr. Escott—would indeed become a possibility, thanks to the successful invention of time machines, but it would exist as a *branch* of the initial historical sequence rather than the parent trunk. Seen from without, as it were, time would, in this conception, resemble a tree rather than a stream—or a multicursal maze rather than a unicursal labyrinth."

"You're quite right, Hope," Escott swiftly put in. "Not about your Euchronian nonsense, of course—soul-destroying mechanical tyranny would definitely be the order of the day—but about the ever-branching tree, or multicursal maze. If Carp is correct about the consequences of Marlstone's theory, there won't be just *one* dread empire of eternity, extending indefinitely into the temporal void. There'll be dozens, or hundreds, or as many as the human mind can imagine, each one corresponding to the invention of a time machine on the main branch—which, if such an invention is practical at all, will obviously keep happening, over and over again."

Carmela Monticarlo leaned over yet again to murmur in Michael's direction, but Cecilia was ready this time, and laid her own claim to his right ear before the signorina could attain his left. "But if time is due to branch tomorrow, Mr. Laurel" she said, in a confidential tone, "which branch will *we* be in?"

Michael couldn't help feeling that the entire hypothetical discussion might well be pointless, if Marlstone's machine failed yet again, as it very well might, but it was in full swing now and had developed its own momentum. While Hope, with long-practiced expertise, picked up the thread of the main argument from Escott, Michael started his own side-branch, glad that he had to lean a little closer to Cecilia in order to do so, and willing to ignore that slightly reproachful glance that Carmela directed at him—with some justification, given that he had refused to make a similar concession for her.

"If I understand Dr. Carp correctly," Michael whispered into his beloved's ear, "we would be 'budded' along with the particular momentary bubble of time in which we are contained. Different versions of ourselves would be *present*, as it were, in *both* branches of the growing tree of time—in the branch fated to be absorbed into Hope and Scott's empire of eternity *and* in the parent branch that Dr. Carp likened to Plato's spindle of necessity, in which...." He trailed off, having been struck by a sudden idea that took his breath away.

"You mustn't tease me like that, Mr. Laurel," Cecilia scolded, although she did not seem at all displeased. "It's most unfair."

"I wasn't teasing," Michael assured her, hearing the pitch of his voice rise in spite of his determination to keep it low. "I just thought...." He stopped again, this time because the sound of his voice had caused James Escott to stop in mid-flow and turn to look at him, a trifle petulantly.

Hope took advantage of the pause to say: "Well then, Mr. Laurel—what *did* you think?"

"It just occurred to me," Michael said, now addressing the whole group, "that if Dr. Carp is right, and time can indeed branch in the fashion that he indicates, then the result of what he calls 'budding' would be two parallel moments, in one of which the time machine had worked, and in the other of which it hadn't. If that's the case, not only might time branch tomorrow, but it might have branched twice already, when Mr. Marlstone conducted his trials at Horton Lacey and Chatsworth—and it might keep on branching, every time he or anybody else tries again, from now until…well, as Mr. Escott says, *the very end of time.*"

He wondered, then, whether the other presences he had briefly imagined to be sharing his mental space might have been parallel selves in the process of dissociation rather than slightly-displaced past and future selves—if, indeed, they had been anything other than a mundane unsteadiness of his own consciousness

"Very good!" Escott exclaimed, mockingly. "Bravo, Mr. Laurel! You've just proved, by the time-honored method of *reductio ad absurdum*, that—at least so far as we're concerned—there's no possibility at all of Marlstone's machine working tomorrow, or ever. I shall be more than glad to leave you the responsibility of telling him that, when you have the chance."

"That all depends what you mean by *we*." Michael said. "If it were true that the labyrinth of time could divide in this manner—and I hope with all my heart that it isn't—there would be other versions of ourselves existing in the parallel moments that have already branched off, and there'll be others in all the branches formed in the course of our lifetimes. And if you, rather than Mr. Hope, are correct about the nature of those empires of eternity, every single one of our *parallel selves* will be condemned to a kind of Hell…and I shall be more than glad to leave the responsibility of telling Mr. Marlstone *that* to you, Mr. Escott, when you have the chance."

At that, Quentin Hope burst out into such loud sustained laughter that he turned purple, and almost choked—which was not at all the kind of reaction that might have been expected from a man who had just been told that he might be spawning secondary versions of himself continually, every one of which might be able to live in the Earthly paradise of his own optimistic expectation.

CHAPTER ELEVEN

FURTHER UNCANNY RIPPLES IN TIME

When Michael arrived back in the center of the Maze, shortly after one o'clock, he felt an inevitable temptation to march over the drawbridge and thump the door with his fist, demanding that Marlstone come out and listen to all the fearful anxieties that had been raised at lunch—but he did no such thing.

The fact was that, as soon as the lunch was over, the whole edifice of speculation had come to seem more than a little absurd. It was, after all, based on Hope and Escott's irreverent extrapolations of what Augustus Carp had inferred from a few remarks that Marlstone had made the previous evening, regarding a theory that must be reckoned dubious, even if it really implied what Carp had deduced from it. That did not seem to be sufficient reason for violating Marlstone's strict injunction that he did not want anyone else to come near him while he made his preliminary trials. In consequence, Michael simply put on his smock, took up his palette again, squeezed various colors out of the lead tubes he had carefully loaded in London, and began to apply his brush to the background of his painting.

As usual, Michael was soon totally absorbed in his work, oblivious to everything external to the painting and the image that he was trying to reproduce. He was concentrating so fiercely that when he felt the first flicker of vertigo he simply blinked his eyes, held his brush in suspension for a second or two, and then carried on, without sparing any thought at all as to the possible causes of the disturbance. When he felt another, ten or twelve minutes afterwards, he did exactly the same thing. It was not until the third such interruption, which lasted slightly longer than its predecessors, that he finally thought to connect the phenomenon with his earlier discussion with Gregory Marlstone, and with his brief experience in the Maze. Even then, his initial reaction was to reject the hypothesis.

It's just the heat, he told himself, *glancing up and behind him at the blazing sun. I'm concentrating so hard that I'm losing my mental balance slightly. I mustn't start attributing it to the possible effects of Marlstone's machine, or I'll begin to imagine all sorts of weird and horrid possibilities.* Satisfied with this rebuttal, he took a step back to appraise his work, his gaze flickering back and forth between the developing image on the canvas and the stern stones of the actual keep. The high-set windows now seemed more reminiscent of the dark slits that the pupils of some nocturnal animals became in bright daylight, and he had the strange impression that the Keep was watching him, as if studying him with a painter's expert eye, in preparation for making a portrait of him.

Oddly enough, though, it was the image on the canvas, not his view of the actual Keep, that suddenly seemed to become *unsteady*, as if its expert gaze were wavering. Michael immediately appreciated Marlstone's difficulty in finding a word to describe the phenomenon, and the inventor's reasons for eventually settling on that particular adjective. It was not that the lines of his sketch began to blur or flicker, or that the colors he had so far applied changed their tone. He was not even tempted to believe, in fact, that the painting had suffered any objective alteration. He was perfectly certain that the effect originated from his own consciousness, and was confined there. If there had been anything actually to see, he would have been "seeing things", but he could not be sure that there was anything else involved but an exaggerated sense of the possibility that the painting *might* be other than it was: that the lines might have been drawn in slightly displaced positions, that the colors might have been applied so as to produce subtly different shades, and that the loophole-like windows might really be loopholes…or the eyes of some exotic nocturnal animal.

The only unsteadiness here, he thought, *is my own. I've lost a little confidence in the sureness of my hand and eye. It's my own actions and judgments that have somehow come to seem precarious and dubious. It's just a feeling, nothing more. I have such sensations all the time when I'm not painting—my perennial awareness of my own clumsiness. I'm just not used to them when I'm focused on my work. There's nothing supernatural about it.*

That seemed so reasonable that he was able to shrug his shoulder, and resume work—and for a quarter of an hour, the phenomenon did not recur. When it did, though, it seemed worse than before. This time, his head reeled as he stared at the painting, which had somehow come to seem very uncertain indeed. He had to look away—but that didn't help. This time, the Keep itself seemed slightly unsteady, and so did the thick, neatly-groomed greenery of the surrounding hedge. The loophole-eyes might have been those of some gigantic worm rearing up from the ooze of the moat…or some baleful dragon, resentful at being confined to the center of a maze.

Michael had always been aware that there were living things moving within the hedge—a few small birds and a host of insects— but he now acquired an exaggerated awareness of the movements that might be going on within it, and of the vegetal life that the hedge itself possessed. He felt that he could somehow sense the hedge growing, and not merely at the tips of its branches. He felt that he could sense the hedge growing *in every direction*, including previously unimaginable directions that could not be accommodated within the usual three dimensions of space. He became more aware than before of the hedge's thorniness, to the extent that the mere thought of its multitudinous thorns made his skin prickle. All that was trivial, however, compared to the sharp exaggeration of his awareness of the hedge's *maziness*.

Michael still had a diagrammatic image of the Langstrade Maze engraved in his memory. He was confident that he could walk it faultlessly, even in pitch darkness. He did not lost that confidence now—but he felt that, in addition to the particular configuration of the actual maze, he was simultaneously aware of thousands, or even millions, of alternative configurations: that he had not only internalized the design of the Langstrade Maze but every possible seven-ring maze that could have been constructed by the same hedges within the same geographical bounds—and that made the Maze, and everything it contained, including himself, seem very unsteady indeed. It was almost as if the Maze itself had come to life, and that it was *hungry*….

Don't look! he commanded himself, abruptly and urgently, even though he knew that the command made no sense. *Don't lose yourself! Don't let it suck you in! Think about Cecilia!*

It was the last of these commands, rather than any of the others, that he was able to obey. He thought about Cecilia: about her face, her eyes, her lips, and about her apparent eagerness to be in his company, her apparent determination to woo him as he hoped to woo her, to the absolute exclusion of Quentin Hope, Carmela Monticarlo and everyone else in the entire world.

The sensation of dire unease passed yet again. The life that had suddenly infused the Maze relaxed, becoming dormant if not actually inert.

Michael sneezed, and blinked furiously. His head seemed crowded again, overfull of thoughts—not only those he was thinking now, but all those he had thought before, at least in the last fortnight, and all those he had not yet thought, but would within some unspecifiable interval.

He made a sudden effort to grasp some of those future thoughts, in order to get a grip of the sensations attached to them—to see, as it were, what they were responding and reacting to—but he could not do it. The past and present kept getting in the way, causing his intention to stumble. He felt certain that the future was there, potentially graspable, even though temporally confused, but the fact that he could not do it, even to the extent of capturing a single image or idea, was deeply frustrating.

You clumsy oaf! he chided himself. *It's you that's confused, not the world. A better man could make use of this, and become a true seer.*

He began to feel horribly sick then, and felt sure that he was about to faint, as if under the onslaught of his own self-criticism. He seemed to crumple up rather than collapsing, though, and was able to control his fall sufficiently to ensure that he ended up in a sitting position, holding his palette and brush safely aloft, like trophies. His head cleared again, and he never actually lost consciousness. His smock was long enough to protect his trousers from grass stains—which was perhaps as well, given that he only had two pairs, the other being partnered with his dinner-jacket

As he came to his feet again—without much delay, albeit rather awkwardly—he saw the door to the Keep open, and saw someone step out. He knew that it was Gregory Marlstone—who else, after all could it possibly be? He could not *see* Gregory Marlstone, however. He saw a strange blur, vaguely human in shape but quite unidentifiable in individual terms.

It was not until this monster arrived within a couple of feet of him, and began staring him in the face, that the blur resolved, and became—inevitably—Gregory Marlstone.

"Thank God!" Marlstone said. "For a moment there, when you fell over, I thought I'd lost you. Are you all right, Laurel?"

"Fine," Michael replied, finding his voice a trifle thick. "Are you?"

"I think so. I did warn you, didn't I? I gave you fair warning that something of the sort might happen—not that I expected *that*."

Michael blinked, and tried to focus his eyes on his painting. It wasn't easy, but in the end, he satisfied himself that the painting was unscathed. "What was *that*, exactly?" he asked. "I felt the other ripples, of course—at least four of them, if I'm not mistaken, although I might have missed a couple while I was lunching in the rose-garden—but that last one certainly topped the rest."

"It certainly did," Marlstone admitted. "There's no way it should have been able to muster that sort of intensity. The field was highly unstable, of course, but the machine wasn't functioning at anything like full power, and if my previous measurements were correct, there isn't any natural harmonic moment that the machine could tune into within a hundred years, let alone a few minutes. It's almost as if it found something resonant *outside* time—something from which it could actually *draw power* to amplify its own."

"Dr. Carp was saying at lunch that your theory allows the possibility that on every occasion that a time machine operates, time might *branch*," Michael told him. "That time might not be a linear sequence, however intensively coiled into a unicursal labyrinth, but a multicursal maze, in which new openings produce parallel sequences."

"Ridiculous!" was Marlstone's almost-automatic response. "The fellow's completely misunderstood what I was trying to explain to him last night. I was talking about quasi-lateral *shifts*, not *branches*: the possibility that the induction of complex resonances between the discrete moments of the temporal sequence by virtue of time machines operating in series might distort the unicursal pattern, perhaps contriving a permanent alteration. There can't be more than one temporal sequence—that would imply that there was more than one universe. The Dee-Marlstone theory doesn't permit that."

"Perhaps the theory's wrong!" Michael objected, more emphatically than he intended.

Marlstone put his hands on his hips and scowled—but he repressed the angry riposte that had obviously sprung to his lips and collected himself. "Perhaps it is," he said, "since I can't explain what just happened. She shouldn't have been able to produce a pulse like that. In fact, *she* couldn't. Ergo, she must have been channeling it from somewhen else. Which implies that time, as we experience it, really might have an *outside* of some sort, with potential resonance points of its own, or…." He stopped.

"Or what?" Michael prompted.

Marlstone hesitated for a long time, but finally said: "Or there really is another time machine operating way down the line—in the far future, I mean—which has somehow contrived to string together a whole series of harmonically sensitive moments and feed its own power through the chain as far as the present. Except that it's impossible, because there's no such sequence of moments within the natural harmonic sequences…so that idea is just as silly as the idea that there's an outside to time—or, as you put it, that time is multicursal rather than unicursal."

He fell silent again. Michael looked at his brush and his palette, carefully applied one to the other, and then started spreading paint judiciously on to his canvas again, working patiently on the blue of the sky. After a few seconds, though, he stopped. "What about Signor Monticarlo's suggestion?" he said.

"What suggestion?" Marlstone asked.

"*Scordatura*," Michael said. "There's more than one way to tune a violin, and you can still make music with unorthodox tunings. Is there more than one way to tune a time machine, do you think?"

Marlstone did not reject the notion out of hand—he had, after all, argued himself into an impasse, and could not afford to ignore any potential exit. "I don't know," he said, finally. "It's a checkable hypothesis, though—I suppose I could try it out. Maybe if I tune the old girl differently, not even bothering to seek the natural harmony…if I could pick up some unanticipated resonances that way, and then, perhaps…."

Michael continued painting, while Marlstone lost himself in a speculative reverie. Again, it was Michael who eventually broke the silence. "Are you going ahead with the trial?" he asked.

Marlstone frowned. "I don't know," he said. "Maybe it would be best to call it off, at least until I can figure out what happened just now. On the other hand…." He waited for Michael to prompt him.

"On the other hand?" Michael queried, obligingly.

"We're all right, aren't we? No harm done."

"It would seem so," Michael admitted, "but…." He waited in his turn.

"But?" Marlstone promoted, returning the compliment.

"But we're not really sure how far the ripple extended, are we?" Michael asked. "In time, or in space. I can't help wondering…I had a brief conversation with Jeanne Evredon a little while ago, when she told me that something from outside the range of her normal experience has been trying very had to put her off coming here this weekend. I'm not at all sure that Carp will be able to persuade her to go ahead with tonight's planned *séance*, although I did seem to succeed in cheering her up slightly, more by luck than judgment. Signor Monticarlo has been forced to change his intended program because his daughter sprained her wrist. Now you're in two minds as to whether to go ahead with your demonstration. Coincidence, do you think?"

"I must assume so," Marlstone said, flatly. "The events seem quite unconnected to me. Have you felt any mysterious influence trying to keep you away from Langstrade, or from completing your assignment?"

"Quite the contrary," Michael assured him. "But I'm just a humble painter. You and Carp are both tampering, in your different ways, with time...rattling the chains of causality, as it were. If the ripple that disturbed us just now really did spread out much further than you could have anticipated, in time as well as space...who knows what other effects it might have had? Not on me, though—I'm just a painter."

"Yes, you are," Marlstone said, waspishly, "and you've been hanging around with Hope and Escott, who seem to have infected you with their perpetual intellectual mischief-making. Not that they're fools, mind—they might be able to make something of themselves if the could only direct their infernal curiosity and dia-bolical cleverness to better purposes than rooting around in the ruins of Knossos or combing the Egyptian desert for Herodotus' mythical City of Crocodiles. And I have to admit that you've given me some food for thought. I'll have to check this *scordatura* possibility out, even if it takes me all afternoon and all night. I really do need to be sure that tomorrow's demonstration won't put us in undue danger."

"Glad to be of assistance," Michael said, absent-mindedly, lean-ing even closer to his painting. When several moments had passed, though, he became peripherally aware of the fact that Marlstone had not moved, even to remove his hands from his hips or the scowl from his face.

"What did you feel, when the pulse hit?" Marlstone asked him. "What did you *see*?"

"I felt dizzy," Michael reported, still speaking mechanically. "Unsteady." He realized that Marlstone might imagine that his ear-lier warnings were being parodied, and cast around for something more helpful, or at least more detailed, to say. "It seemed that the hedge had come alive," he went on, with a slight quaver in his voice. "It *is* alive, of course, but it had previously seemed inert, a mere as-pect of the background. I suddenly became *aware* of its life, and very sharply aware of it...and the Maze seemed to take on a life of its own too, almost as if it were trying to reach out to me, to *con-sume* me...."

"Really?" queried Marlstone. "That's not what I experienced at all. I thought...well, as I told you before, I thought I saw *myself*. A replica of myself, at least. I thought, when I saw it before, that I was seeing a shadow cast through time—a faint image of what I had been doing a few moments before, or would be doing a few moments hence—but this time, it was as if my other self were actually trying to communicate with me, to tell me something."

"I got an impression not unlike that," Michael admitted.

"You saw a different version of me, who wanted to tell you something?"

"No, I became aware of the seeming presence of different versions of *me*, and I tried to exploit the opportunity to discover something—but I couldn't. Did your replica succeed in saying anything to you?"

"Nothing intelligible," Marlstone countered, after a slight hesitation.

"But it did say *something*?" Michael asked.

"I think so—and if only I could read lips, I might have been able to decipher what it was…but there was no sound."

"Ah," said Michael. "That part of your theory checks out, then. The time machine enables you to see the future, but not to hear it."

"Apparently so. The time-field cut out before the replica could find some other way of communicating its meaning. That's when the nausea hit me, and I almost fainted again. I needed a full five minutes to recover before I was able to come out to see whether you were all right."

"That's odd," Michael said. "Either I lost a couple of minutes somehow, or my vision wasn't simultaneous with yours—although I suppose it didn't actually conclude until you were right in front of me. Until then, all I could see was a blur. You were quite unrecognizable"

"But the time-field was cancelled some time before I came out," Marlstone objected.

"It might have been cancelled *in there*," Michael said, nodding in the direction of the Keep, "but not *out here*—unless, as I say, I lost several minutes completely."

"I suppose that's possible," Marlstone admitted. "Once the old girl starts tampering with time, all sorts of previous impossibilities might become possible: time seemingly stopping dead or speeding up…."

"Time branching out," Michel added. "Empires of eternity forming and dissolving."

Marlstone looked at him quizzically.

Michael grinned, wryly. "Idle conversation in the rose-garden," he explained. "Someone—if it wasn't Hope, to begin with, it must have been Escott—suggested that if two time machines could obtain metaphasic hypersynchronicity, the transfer of information and material from the future to the past would dissolve the intermediate history, by unifying the intervening technological progress, establishing an empire that would extend across the whole of future time: a Euchronian Empire, according to Hope, or Hell on Earth, according to Escott."

"The whole point about time being particulate, in the Dee-Marlstone theory," the inventor complained, "is that any communication between resonant points is confined to the elasticity of the moment, incapable of disturbing the continuity of temporal evolution. It's not, in principle, impossible for material objects or sound vibrations to be displaced in time, but their substance and solidity can only be transferred in the direction of intertemporal gravity...forwards, in vulgar parlance. Entities traveling against the grain of intertemporal gravity—backwards in time—could only be fleetingly and insubstantially manifest at their attempted destination, and the law of conservation of non-identity would ensure any threat to the established continuity resulted in a sort of instantaneous rebound. If that weren't the case, time—and the universe—would simply disintegrate. Its basic fabric has to be elastic, or we wouldn't be here at all. Nor would anything else, whether anyone ever invented a time machine or not, because of natural resonances in the intrinsic subvibrations.

"The overtones that I produce artificially are of course, merely replications and amplifications of temporal phenomena that already exist. How could it be otherwise? I certainly provoked that pulse we experienced just now, but there's a sense it which it had to be potentially present already, or the stimulus I provided would have been impotent. There's no need to worry about empires of eternity establishing themselves as a result of future time machines being attuned to their predecessors and facilitating intellectual invasion, or in the main sequence of time generating an infinite number of branches. My theory doesn't allow for either possibility, let alone require them as logical corollaries."

"Do you really think that time and the universe care about what your theory might or might not allow, Mr. Marlstone?" Michael enquired, in a mock-polite manner.

"Obviously not," Marlstone snapped back. "But at least I'm attempting to test my hypotheses, in order to discover what's possible and what's not. What do Hope and Escott ever do, besides babbling nonsense and making mischief? And what are you doing with *your* life, apart from painting pretty pictures?"

Michael winced slightly, and refrained from retorting: *Falling in love.*

Marlstone's scowl deepened even further, and he stared at the painter in a manner that was not far short of menacing. "If I find that I'm wrong," he said, sullenly, "then I shall have to refine my theory. Unfortunately, while there's ever only one way to be proved correct, there are a thousand ways to be proved wrong, so I really can't say what the consequences might be if I do happen to be wrong. When I know a little more than I do now, as a consequence of my empirical enquiries, I'll be able to decide whether or not to proceed tomorrow."

"That's very worthy of you, Mr. Marlstone," Michael said, in a placatory tone. "I'm sorry if I offended you. I really am trying to help."

The final remark acted as a trigger recalling Marlstone to his duty. He stood up straight, and shook himself slightly, as if shaking off the burden of the previous half hour's conversation. "I've got to get back to work," he said. "I'm glad you're all right, Laurel. I don't imagine that there'll be any more pulses as powerful as that one, but if there are…well, you'll know what to expect, won't you? If you don't want to take the risk…."

"Oh, I do," Michael assured him. "I know that curiosity kills cats, but I'm an artist, so I have at least nine lives to spare. If I find myself within reach of my future thoughts again, I'll try harder to grasp one. Good luck with your further enquiries." And with that, he leaned forward even more ostentatiously than before, applying paint to his canvas with even greater care. From the corner of his eye, though, he saw Gregory Marlstone stalk away, and disappear into the gloomy interior of the Folly.

CHAPTER TWELVE

THORNS IN THE MAZE

Michael felt a few more flutters of dizziness before the light began to fade, but he experienced no further hallucinations and shrugged off the trivial disturbances as if they were utterly significant—as, indeed, they seemed to be. As soon as the sun was low enough in the western sky for the hedge behind him to cast a shadow over his work—which happened some time before the sun would set over the moors on the horizon, as viewed from outside the Maze—he began to pack up his equipment. He set the canvas within a broad woodwork frame fitted with a clasp, in order that he could drape a cloth over it without any danger of smudging his work, and carried it to the gap in the hedge that led into the Maze with the utmost care.

As soon as he stepped across the threshold of the maze a sense of deep unease descended upon him and consumed him, as if it were devouring him body and soul. The sensation flooded the chambers of his heart and marrow of his bones—and yet, it seemed to be sourceless. It was quite unlike the flickering effects that had "leaked" from the Keep, and he was not at all certain whether he ought to interpret it as something that had been lying in ambush in the Maze, waiting for him to step inside, or whether he ought to consider it as something that had been lurking within *him*, waiting for exterior gloom before emerging to take possession of his mental empire.

He almost stopped and turned back, but realized immediately that he could not do that. The Maze surrounded the Keep on all sides; there was no other way out of that strange arena. Besides which, Cecilia had called him brave, and he could not possibly allow the accuracy of her judgment to become questionable. He knew that he not only had to walk on, steadfastly, taking the correct turnings until he emerged from the gap in the outermost hedge, but that he ought to exercise his bravery more fully. As well as enduring the ordeal, he ought to analyze the sensation, and try to figure out what was happening to him.

He had never been conscious of the thorns lurking in the hedges while walking the Maze before, but he could not help being aware of them now, even though he was in no danger of being pricked while he remained on his feet, upright and mobile. He did not feel that the thorny walls of the labyrinth were reaching out for him—he knew exactly where they were and how they were distributed, so they posed no material peril at all—but their presence remained ominous and oppressive.

In a sense, he realized, that was the whole problem. He knew exactly where he was, but there was something about his whereabouts—in the broadest possible meaning of the term—that had *lost its bearings*. It was Langstrade Maze, and perhaps the whole of Langstrade Hall and its grounds, that had somehow become unsteady in time and space, as if teetering on the brink of some unimaginable abyss. Like Lady Phythian before him, he had become sensitive to the everpresence of the Langstrade ghosts, or to the creative principle that was responsible for their periodic appearance.

He remembered what he had said to Hope and Escott about the possibility that the field of Marlstone's machine might extend in time as well as space, backwards as well as forwards, so that if the machine were actually destined to work when Marlstone activated it at noon on Saturday, then its effects ought to be evident already, and might well have been evident, albeit fugitively, for years, if not centuries. That, Michael now deduced, must be what had happened, perhaps as a result of this afternoon's anomalous pulse rather than the time machine's fully-powered operation on the morrow—unless, of course, the two events were really the *same* event, distributed through time by the mysterious processes of temporal resonance.

What actually seemed to have happened, though, was more complicated than the vague possibility that Michael had glimpsed in the course of the speculative conversation in question. He had been thinking then of images thrown back into time from the present, which might be mistaken for "ghosts"—but what seemed to have happened now was that the maze had somehow been "charged" with the leakage of Marlstone's temporal field, much as a lump of iron placed in a magnetic field inevitably became magnetized itself. Had the maze itself somehow become an extension of the time machine? Had it become a kind of time machine in its own right? Could it throw its own image backwards or forwards in time?

No sooner had he bravely contemplated that set of possibilities, however, than Michael wondered whether he might have got the whole argument backwards. What if it were not the Maze that had been "charged" but merely his own body and mind? What if the phenomena that he was currently experiencing were internal rather than external in origin? What if *he* had become an extension of Marlstone's time machine, or a time machine in his own right?

The second set of possibilities automatically generated a third. What if he and the maze had *both* been "charged", so that some strange form of resonance had been established between them? Indeed, had not some such resonance already been established, before he ever stepped into the maze? Had he not committed it to memory at first glance, so easily that it might already have been present in his mind, merely awaiting activation by the trigger of visual connection?

It had been reckless, Michael realized, to ignore Gregory Marlstone's warnings, and to insist on staying in the heart of the maze wile the time machine was tested. He had been foolish to dismiss the danger as "minuscule", on the grounds that Marlstone had obviously come through past tests unscathed and that no one really expected the time machine to work successfully at noon on Saturday, any more than it had done at Horton Lacey or Chatsworth. He had had no choice, though; Cecilia had expectations—indeed, it was obvious now that she had expectations far in advance of anything he had previously dared to hope for, and Cecilia's whim was irresistible, so far as he was concerned. His objective now was not to waste time regretting what had happened, but to do his level best to work out what its implications might be for the future.

Perhaps, as with a lump of common iron exposed to a magnetic field, the induced effect would simply wear off. On the other hand, it might well have presently-incalculable consequences on the following day, when Marlstone mounted his full-scale demonstration—in which case…well, as to what those consequences might be, Michael would simply have to wait and see, hoping all the while that they would not damage his prospects with Cecilia.

Michael was extremely glad when he emerged from the entrance on to the open lawn, and the feeling of unease simply melted away. As soon as he was out of the Maze, the sensation of oppression vanished, so completely that he immediately began to wonder how he could possibly have fallen prey to such a silly illusion. He felt perfectly secure again, not merely in space and time but also in himself…but he knew, somehow, that his security was an illusion, and that the abyss on whose edge everything was tottering had simply been hidden from his consciousness.

He took a deep breath and raised his face to the sky, closing his eyes momentarily against the sun's reddening glare. Like its counterpart on the previous day, the impending sunset was glorious, tinted by all the seasonal debris suspended in the humid atmosphere. Almost immediately, while he shaded his eyes, the red-gold disk slipped into partial eclipse behind the chimneys of the Hall, two of which were smoking in spite of the season. Dinner was doubtless in preparation on the vast kitchen range.

A good day's work, Michael thought. *And now to find Cecilia....*

That turned out to be easier to think than to achieve, however. When he had stowed his equipment away and returned to the ground floor of the Hall, Cecilia was nowhere to be found. The elder Lady Langstrade had apparently spirited her away, along with the younger Lady Langstrade, Lady Phythian and Carmela Monticarlo, to indulge in some mysterious feminine activity. The violinist was practicing in the Orange Room, while Augustus Carp and Jeanne Evredon could be heard arguing in the Violet Room, so the only people that Michael found when he pursued his search were Lord Langstrade, Hope and Escott, who were playing billiards in the so-called gun-room.

The gun-room did, indeed, contain a rack of double-barreled shotguns in a locked cabinet—ten in all, although there were brackets for twelve. There was also a pair of antique dueling pistols mounted above the mantelpiece. A second rack, this one not under lock and key, held half a dozen fencing swords—épées, so far as Michael's inexpert eye could judge—while a third held eight fishing-rods, a fourth eight billiard-cues, and a fifth no less than a dozen walking-sticks, with Lord Langstrade's ivory-hilted favorite taking pride of place. The billiard table itself, unlike most of the other equipment, showed unmistakable signs of relentless usage. Lord Langstrade was evidently good at the game, as he had racked up more than twice as many points than his current opponent, Hope.

Escott, who was watching the game in a desultory manner, his only interest in its result presumably being the mildly delightful inevitability of seeing his friend soundly thrashed, looked up gratefully when Michael appeared in the doorway. "There you are, Laurel!" he exclaimed, as if greeting a long-lost cousin. "Come in, come in! Is Marlstone not with you?"

"He's still hard at work in the Keep," Michael told him. "He was just lighting a lamp as I left, to judge by the glimmer in the windows—Heaven only knows how long he'll be slaving away." *And Heaven only knows*, he added, silently, *what he'll feel when he tries to make his way back through the labyrinth to the world of sanity, solidity and security.*

"We'll all be slaving away eternally, if Escott's judgment can be trusted and the world as we know it really does end tomorrow," Hope put in, so cheerfully that he evidently had as much confidence in Marlstone's failure as in Escott's error.

"He says that was all a misunderstanding of the implications of his theory," Michael told them. "Can't we discuss something else? I think I've had enough of Marlstone and his time machine for one day."

"Couldn't agree more, young fellow," Lord Langstrade agreed. "All that nonsense over lunch gave me indigestion. A few games of billiards settled my stomach, though. I'll play you next, if you like—these fellows are no good at all."

"I'm sure that I'm even worse, Milord," Michael assured him.

"Nonsense!" Langstrade proclaimed. "You're an artist—bound to have a good eye and a steady hand. With a little practice, you're sure to become a master of the art and tactics of the game."

"I'll be glad to play if you wish, Milord," Michael said, judiciously, not bothering to own up to the fact that when he did not have a paintbrush in his hand he tended to be rather clumsy, "but I'm afraid you'll beat me very easily—even more easily than you seem to be beating Mr. Hope."

Hope shot him a mildly resentful glance, but Lord Langstrade laughed merrily. "When it comes to cannons, he's no Tom Digges," he said. Fortunately, Michael was able to see the joke. Thomas Digges was not an expert billiard player but a sixteenth-century mathematician. He had been a member of John Dee's famous "secret college", along with his father Leonard, Walter Raleigh and such young hopefuls as Francis Bacon and Cornelius Drebbel. The college, whose secrets had long since been disclosed, had laid the foundations of the Academy, whose President was nowadays reckoned to be the most influential member of the Great Triumvirate, even though the First Sea Lord remained the Commonwealth's nominal head of state. Michael was a little vague as to what Tom Digges' particular contribution to England's swift technological advancement had been, but he knew that it had to do with ballistics, and hence with the artistry of cannon fire. He had no idea at all why scoring shots in billiards were known as "cannons" but he did know how such shots were made, at least in theory.

"How's the painting coming along?" Escott asked.

"Tolerably well," Michael conceded.

"Will we get to see it this evening?"

"Certainly not," Michael said. "I'll be back at work first thing tomorrow morning, so I suppose you can sneak a look at it then, if you insist—provided that Marlstone doesn't ban you all from the Maze again."

"Marlstone will have to find his way out if he's going to join us for dinner," Hope observed. "Perhaps you ought to send Cecilia to show him the way, Langstrade."

That casual remark sent a stab of panic into Michael's heart, even though he had no reason to think that Cecilia had anything to fear from a stroll through the maze. "He found his way in this morning, with the aid of Lady Langstrade's map," Michael pointed out. "He doesn't need a guide."

"He's a better man than me, then," Escott remarked. "It might be a good idea to send young Jack out there when the sun sets, though, just to make sure—if Marlstone lingers too long, the darkness might confuse him."

"Jack's a dab hand at finding his way through the maze," Langstrade admitted, with the air of a man damning with faint praise. "If only he showed some inclination toward more suitable achievements than killing rabbits with that damn catapult of his...but I have to admit that it puts him one up on me. I don't know why I've never got the hang of the damned thing—the map's been hanging on the drawing-room wall ever since the Hall was rebuilt, but I've never been able to figure out its twists and turns."

"We all have our different talents," Escott said, adding a hint of irony to the platitude, although it was not obvious what it was supposed to signify. "What's your sport, Laurel? Shooting, fishing, fencing or hunting rabbits with a catapult?"

Michael blushed. "I've never handled a gun, a rod or a sword," he admitted. He had handled a catapult more than once, during his childhood, but to mention that would have dignified Escott's feeble joke.

"Definitely a city boy," Escott said. "Hope and I have shot everything, in our time: grouse, pheasant, partridge, duck...."

"It would be more accurate, on Escott's part," Hope put in, "to say that we've shot *at* everything in our time—including each other. Fortunately—at least in the last instance—we've always missed."

"Why did you shoot at each other?" Michael asked.

"Oh, we haven't always been the urbane and amiable individuals we are now," Escott said. "We were quite hot-headed in our youth. Fortunately, I had the choice of weapons when Hope called me out, so I plumped for a pair of single-shot pistols, like the ones you see over the fireplace. Had Hope had his way, we'd have used swords like *those*"—he pointed to the épées—"and our incompetence would probably have led to one or both of us bleeding to death. Instead, we escaped without a scratch between us. We were lucky that we never picked a quarrel with Langstrade back then—he can shoot and fence as well as play billiards, you know."

"Don't you believe it, Mr. Laurel," Langstrade said. "The only member of the household who ever fires a gun these days is Jefferies—he has custody of the two that are missing from the cabinet—and he's a far better shot than I ever was. Father did hire a fencing-master for me once, when he was playing the part of Lord of the Manor to the full, but I only learned the basic moves. I never took part in a competition, let alone a duel."

"I'll wager that you played at being Harold Longstride on the site of the Keep, though," Hope suggested, slyly. "A boy, a fencing-foil and an imagination adds up to that sort of caper as inevitably as one, two and three adding up to six."

"I spent a lot more time fishing in Cribden Tarn," Langstrade replied, gruffly, having colored slightly as the gibe struck home. "Father acquired the fishing rights when he bought the Manor—it was just about the only privilege worth having that he got for his money. Langstrade was a rich estate when it was presented to one of Henry VIII's cronies, thanks to the plunder of Cribden Abbey, but it was subject to centuries of attrition thereafter. Apart from the Old Hall and the grounds—which were in a terrible state until Jefferies got a grip on them—the only land left was a handful of meadows where the local farmers graze sheep."

"If the Abbey and the village were both called Cribden," Michael asked, "why was the manor that replaced the Abbey called Langstrade?"

"The village had been known as Langstrade, or Longstride, long before the Abbey was built," the Earl explained. "The monks changed its name when they consolidated its tenancies with their own domain. Our family obviously took its name from the old village, but by the time the manor reverted to its former title after the abolition of the abbey, the Langstrades had been scattered far and wide."

"Expelled from their homeland by Norman scum after the Conquest," Escott put in.

"Or by Anglo-Saxon scum beforehand," Hope supplied.

"Or perhaps by Roman scum even before that," Escott added. "History is overfull of scum, alas."

"You can mock," Langstrade said, not uncheerfully, "but the glorious heritage of the Celtic Longstrides is back where it belongs now, in the hands of their legitimate heirs—along with the fishing-rights to Cribden Tarn, and a talent for billiards that neither of you will ever be able to match."

The final remark was occasioned by the fact that Hope had just gone down to ignominious defeat, yet again. The optimist handed his cue to Michael, with a florid bow, and the painter stepped forward to take his turn as a metaphorical lamb to the slaughter.

Michael had not yet put a point on the board when Hope and Escott abandoned him to his fate, excusing themselves on the grounds that they had to dress for dinner, even though there was still nearly an hour before the meal was due to be served. Michael was not entirely displeased to be left alone with the man whose daughter he hoped to marry, although he knew that the billiard game was bound to be an ordeal even worse than negotiating the mysteriously-charged maze. It was something he had to do, though; he had been ordered to make a good impression, and he was obliged do his best.

His expectation that he would turn out to be a complete duffer at billiards was fulfilled in no uncertain terms, but Lord Langstrade did not seem to mind that. Indeed, Lord Langstrade seemed to have such a great fondness for winning that he was prepared to forgive any amount of clumsiness in his opponents, generously distributing such comments as "Bad luck!" and "Next time!" as Michael fluffed shot after shot. Michael soon caught on to the fact that a willingness to be beaten with a good grace would not do his cause any harm, and began lavishing compliments upon his opponent's shots with such enthusiasm that Langstrade was soon basking smugly in a continuous glow of warm praise.

"My skill is merely a testament of the long hours I waste in here," the Earl observed, with conspicuously false modesty. "I'm not like Father, let alone that dour fellow Arkwright. He built *his* stately home on a hill overlooking his mills, you know, and still insists on working an eighteen-hour day, even though he's as rich as Croesus. I've always had other interests—cultural interests—and I like to think that I'm a man who knows when enough is enough, when it comes to hard work. I've done my fair share, you know, but there comes a time in a sane man's life when he wants to enjoy his hard-earned leisure."

"The greatest wisdom of all, Milord, is to be satisfied with sufficiency," Michael assured him, but then could not resist the impulse to break his own injunction by adding: "I think it's rather bold as well as very generous of you to give Marlstone another chance to demonstrate his machine, and to lend him your beloved Keep for that purpose."

Lord Langstrade blushed again at that—but not, for once, with pleasure. "To tell the truth," he said, "the damn thing doesn't have any other purpose—although you do get a fine view from the battlements, of Cribden, the Tarn and the moors on one side and Bancroft Scar on the other. When Marlstone told me that it was exactly the right height to try his machine, and that he was certain that its unique internal design would permit him to succeed where he had previously failed, I was actually quite glad to hear that someone thought the edifice good for something. Hope and Escott call it 'Langstrade's Folly', you know, behind my back—they think I don't know, but I do. Father designed it, of course, and I didn't have to build it…but it seemed like an appropriate gesture of gratitude, for all that he's done for Emily and me. I suppose its special suitability might be something akin to the acoustics of concert halls, since this business of breaking through the barriers of time seems to have something musical about it. Perhaps I should have shown it to Monticarlo, in case he wants to play his violin there rather than in the large drawing-room."

"I think Signor Monticarlo would prefer the drawing-room," Michael assured him. "It will be more comfortable for the audience, I'm sure."

"True," admitted the Earl. "Same goes for Carp, I dare say. Do you happen to know why he and that girl are at loggerheads?"

"I couldn't say, Milord," Michael said, choosing his words judiciously.

"Damn nuisance, whatever it is. They're discreet enough to keep the actual argument to their rooms, but there's a definite tension in the air. That sort of thing can ruin a house-party, according to Emily—especially a select gathering like this one, which became even more select when old Chatham cried off. Nothing upsets Hope and Escott, of course, but Signor Monticarlo and his daughter are sensitive, artistic types…as you are yourself, of course."

"I can assure you that I'm not in the least discomfited by any tension between Dr. Carp and his somniloquist," Michael said, still sticking to the letter of the truth. "I'm sure that they'll be able to resolve their difficulties before tonight's magnetization. Signor Monticarlo's violin recital will soothe the atmosphere in advance." While Michael was delivering this speech, Lord Langstrade accumulated enough points to win yet another frame by a crushing margin, so the painter tacked on a "Well played, Milord" to the end of it.

Lord Langstrade replaced his cue in the rack, a trifle reluctantly. "Well, I suppose we'd better go and dress for dinner," he said. "Emily doesn't like it when I'm late, and she's certain to put the blame on me if you're late too. You really do show promise, you know, Laurel—a little more practice, and you'd be able to take on Hope or Escott with a fair chance of success."

"It's very kind of you to say so, Milord," Michael said, humbly. "If it will help me to beat Mr. Hope, I'll be more than glad to play with you again."

CHAPTER THIRTEEN

THE *CAPRICCI* PERFORMED

The seating arrangements for dinner had evidently been carefully planned by the present Lady Langstrade, with the aid of judicious suggestions from her daughter. Michael found himself seated between Cecilia and Augustus Carp, directly opposite the empty chair that was reserved for Gregory Marlstone—who had apparently been delayed in the Keep for an indefinite time. Michael was, in consequence, well out of conversational range of Carmela Monticarlo and Quentin Hope, who had been seated together, bracketed by the two dowagers.

Escott, too, had been separated from his long-time sparring partner, set between Marlstone's chair and Signor Monticarlo's. *How different the occasion might have been*, Michael thought, idly, *if Hope had had the choice of weapons in their duel.*

Dr. Carp was subdued, like a man desperately attempting to conceal some secret misery, no more inclined to talk to Michael than he was to converse with his neighbor on the other side, the elder Lady Langstrade, although he was given no choice in the latter instance. The Mesmerist's diversion gave Cecilia a virtual license to monopolize Michael, of which she seemed determine to take full advantage. She chattered to him about art, music, books and society, evidently having stored up a great many views on all these topics, which she had kept in reserve for a suitable occasion.

Michael bathed in the torrent of opinion like a hot and thirsty traveler in the pure water of a mountain spring, agreeing with every judgment and relaxing luxuriously in the freedom from the necessity to devise any of his own. It was an easy metaphor to conceive, because the dining-room was, indeed, very hot and stuffy, and the male diners, clad in formal dinner-jackets, were suffering somewhat, although the ladies' evening gowns were much less oppressive. At any rate, Michael's slightly one-sided conversation with Cecilia made a striking contrast to his slightly one-sided conversations with Hope and Escott, or his slightly less one-sided conversation with Gregory Marlstone. He had never been happier in his life. Whenever he caught an oblique glance of James Escott's cadaverous face—which wore an expression even gloomier than usual, perhaps because Escott was slowly stifling in his dinner-jacket or because Hope was out of bantering range—Michael beamed munificently, as if he hoped to dispel that other man's deep-seated pessimism by the sheer force of his own example.

Such was the emotional delirium of the situation that Michael hardly noticed what he was eating, although he was certain that the pheasant and asparagus soup was excellent, the braised roe-deer venison with leeks and turnips exquisite, and the peach and raspberry meringue roulade divine. Given that he had the nectar of Cecilia's words and the ambrosia of her expression on which to nourish his soul, the mundane alimentation of his flesh seemed to be an exceedingly trivial matter. Had there been a thousand alternative selves competing for the imperium of his brain while time was knotted in confusion, they would all have been singing Cecilia's praises in perfect harmony, as sweetly as any Celestial Choir celebrating the Coronation of the Queen of Heaven.

The time to repair to the drawing-room for coffee, liqueurs and Signor Monticarlo's recital arrived far too quickly for Michael's liking, but that did not prevent him from racing upstairs to remove his dinner-jacket, replacing it with the waistcoat he had worn under his smock while painting. Most of the other male guests did the same, although Lord Langstrade was obliged to retain formal dress because he was the *soirée*'s host, and Signor Monticarlo because he had to perform on the violin. Augustus Carp did not have to follow suit because Mesmerism was so modern a pursuit that it was not subject to the awful weight of tradition. Like Michael, he came downstairs again wearing a sober grey waistcoat over his dress shirt—the same one that he had been wearing earlier in the day. Hope and Escott, inevitably, had put on fresh waistcoats; Hope's was salmon-pink, while Escott's was royal blue.

Cecilia had obviously had a hand in the seating arrangements for the concert and the *séance* as well as the dinner-table, for Michael found himself sitting on the extreme left of the second row, next to the empty fireplace and directly beneath the diagram of the Maze, with Cecilia to his right and Jack Langstrade between Cecilia and the aisle. On the further side of the aisle the empty chair reserved for Gregory Marlstone was set next to Lord Langstrade's chair, with Carmela Monticarlo on the far right.

The seats in the front row had been placed so that none was directly in front of any of those behind, so Jeanne Evredon, who was at the left-hand extremity of that row, was positioned at such an angle that Michael could see her in *profil perdu*. Augustus Carp was sitting next to her, with the elder Lady Langstrade to his right, while Lady Phythian, James Escott and Quentin Hope were on the far side of the aisle, in that order. As hostess, the younger Lady Langstrade had a chair positioned in advance of the front row, almost level with the musician's music-stand, so that she could make the formal introductions.

Michael's knowledge of music was limited, and his knowledge of violin music was even more restricted. He had often opined in the past that a man could only refine one of the five senses at some expense to the others, and that his assiduous development of a painter's eye had left his ears a trifle undeveloped, especially with respect to music—and most especially of all with respect to the music of stringed instruments unameliorated by a piano accompaniment. The closed grand piano pushed back into the corner behind the music-stand seemed rather sad to Michael's sympathetic eye, especially in juxtaposition with the thick bandage wrapped around Carmela Monticarlo's wrist.

Having drunk his coffee, however, Michael sat down to listen to Signor Monticarlo with only one significant expectation: that he would be able to spend a further hour sitting next to his beloved Cecilia, rejoicing in her proximity, while no one else would be able to bother, interrupt or undermine him.

"First of all," said the violinist, after bowing respectfully in response to Lady Langstrade's fulsome introduction, "I should like to play two pieces by my honorable compatriot Pietro Locatelli, written almost exactly a century ago. I shall play the first in his series of *capricci enigmati*—'enigmatic caprices' in English—exactly as it was published, but I shall introduce a small variation in the *scordatura*—the unorthodox tuning of the violin—required by the second, in order to correct an apparent error in the published version. I hope you will find it interesting. Afterwards, I shall play a sonata by Johann Sebastian Bach, at the request of Lady Langstrade, with apologies for the fact that the choice of such a piece was severely restricted by the lack of an accompanist."

Michael listened to the first few chords of the first *capriccio*, but quickly decided that it was too sophisticated a piece for his simple tastes. It was too rapid and too jerky, and seemed to be designed to show off the cleverness of the instrumentalist's fingers rather than provide aural pleasure for the audience. He did not mind at all, though, for he was perfectly happy to ignore the music and focus his attention on Cecilia—even though he noticed, when he glanced across the room, that Quentin Hope was now looking at him with frank hostility. The optimist had evidently come to the conclusion that Cecilia's manifest fondness for a younger and more romantically-inclined rival would almost certainly provide a fatal stumbling-block to his own covertly-nursed ambitions.

When the first *capriccio* reached its conclusion, Michael clapped politely along with everyone else, but a rapid glance around the room suggested that no one else had appreciated the piece much more than he had, with the inevitable exception of Carmela Monticarlo. Even Lady Langstrade, who obviously wanted the concert to go well, had to feign her moderate gratitude.

The violinist swiftly retuned his instrument, but Michael did not expect to be able to tell the difference once it launched into the second piece, which he imagined in advance as a virtual cacophony. He realized his mistake, though, as soon as the bow was first drawn across the strings. All of a sudden, it was as if he had been snatched back to the heart of the Langstrade Maze, at the very climax of his unsteadiness.

This time, Michael knew full well that it was his own body—or perhaps his soul—that had been mysteriously "charged", without his being fully aware of it. He was perfectly certain that Signor Monticarlo had not been significantly affected by anything that had occurred in the Keep, and that his violin had not been magically transformed into an angelic harp, so it followed logically that he was the one who had been "magnetized" by Marlstone's temporal trickery.

Had there been any doubt about the matter, a single glance around the faces of the audience reassured him completely. Although Lady Langstrade and Cecilia were doing their best once again to feign a kind of artistic rapture, and Carmela was responding with dutiful loyalty to her parent's genius, Lord Langstrade was obviously bored and his mother's thoughts were evidently elsewhere, as were Dr. Carp's. Hope and Escott were listening dutifully, but without any undue excitement. Jack, who had not yet been sent to bed, in order that he might enjoy a little cultural improvement, did not seem to be enjoying the privilege at all. Heatherington, stationed beside the door, seemed to be putting all his concentration into his conscientious imitation of a statue, and the various other servants scattered around the room seemed intent on enjoying the luxury of having nothing to do for a defined interval. Indeed, the only person who seemed to be responding spontaneously to the music, with as much alarm as Michael, was Jeanne Evredon.

As soon as he had framed that thought, Michael knew that *alarm*, and not *delight*, was the operative word. As the music gripped him, and overwhelmed him—much as the Maze had done while he made his way out of it earlier that afternoon—he did not feel the slightest pleasure, although he knew that an audience ought to take pleasure in music composed and played with flair and feeling. That the music was good, and the playing first-rate, he did not doubt; nor did he doubt that the composer's aim had been to produce a piece by means of which a violinist might move his hearers to pleasurable rapture—but that was by no means the sensation that was provoked in his own nerves and brain.

He felt unease. He felt alarm. He felt danger. He felt that he was hanging in some kind of balance, in the sway of some fateful machine, or some mechanical fate.

He felt, as the piece progressed, that he had somehow become lost, in spite of the fact that he had known while he sat beside Cecilia at dinner exactly where he was, and had felt that it was exactly the place that he wanted to be.

As his love for Cecilia had expanded in the knowledge that she obviously favored his attention and affection, Michael had felt, for the first time in his life, that he knew exactly who he was, and that he was exactly the person he wanted to be. Now, without any warning, all of that had somehow been cast into a strange kind of doubt, which was all the stranger because he had no idea what kind of doubt it was, or how it had come about that he had been cast into it.

The music carried him away. It transported him, although he did not move a muscle, and Cecilia did not seem to have the slightest awareness that anything was happening at all. He felt that he was being spread out, not in any of the dimensions of perceptible space, or even in time as he normally experienced and imagined it, but in some other dimension that did not share the scrupulous linearity of the spatial dimensions, nor the inexorable flow of experienced time, but was, instead, tangled and labyrinthine, and whose flux was utterly chaotic.

It's the Maze! he thought, suddenly, as the music continued to evolve. *It's the Maze! It didn't release me when I stepped out of it. I'm still in harmony with it, somehow, and so is the music—not by some freak of chance, but because the Maze is taking possession of the music, molding it to its own design. The Maze is reaching out through time, from this very moment, into the mind of the composer, and replicating itself in another form, laying foundations for today and tomorrow and...who can tell how many other tomorrows, or even how many other todays?*

Once he had realized that and put it into words, Michael was able to relax slightly. The unease and the alarm did not go away, but he felt that he now had a slightly better understanding of what they might signify. After all, if the music and the Maze were somehow the same, then he ought to be able to find his way through the music as easily as he had been able to find his way through the Maze.

For several minutes, he concentrated on trying to feel his way through the exotic contours of the music, translating its sonic imagery into visual imagery, or at least becoming aware of the resonance between the two.

So there is *a way that sound can be transmitted through time,* he thought, *albeit an indirect one. Like visual imagery, sound can be distilled into thought, and thought is transmissible. Perhaps it's only thought that can move through time. That would make sense, after all; the whole purpose of thought is surely to conquer and master time, by means of memory and foresight, history, hope and fear.*

He glanced sideways at Gregory Marlstone's empty chair, wondering whether the inventor would have been able to feel the maziness of the music too, had he been present. He could not quite believe it. In fact, he had a sudden image of Marlstone's ghost, shifting restlessly in the seat that he would have occupied, had it not been for the advent of the anomalous ripple in time. The incipient scowl on the ghost's face was surely symptomatic of ennui—but Marlstone was not really there, in the flesh or in any other form, and the vision faded away.

Michael glanced at Jeanne Evredon then, and immediately jumped to the opposite conclusion: that the impression she gave of having been gripped and devoured by the magic of the music was authentic, and akin to his own. She could hear what he could hear—but how? She had gone into the Maze that morning, and had certainly been in it when the first ripples had spread out from the Keep, but surely she had not been there in the afternoon, when the most powerful pulse had occurred?

It didn't make any difference, Michael thought. *She'd already been attuned.*

For a moment, he regretted hurrying past the doors of the Blue and Violet Rooms on more than one occasion, in order not to hear the raised voices within. He wished that he had paused instead, and placed his ear to the door, in order to discover exactly what it was that she and Dr. Carp were arguing about, and what the Mesmerist thought about her conviction that she was afflicted by an evil spirit.

Is it evil? he thought. *If it's merely the Maze…but perhaps it's not. Perhaps it's a dragon, or a Minotaur.*

That was no help, though. In spite of having asked Hope and Escott the question, Michael had no idea where the Minotaur fitted into his flight of fancy, if it fitted in at all, nor whether mazes really could contain and confine dragons.

What Jeanne Evredon had told him in the Maze offered a clearly legible clue to what was happening, though. Somehow she had anticipated this moment. Somehow, she had known that something was going to happen here at Langstrade that would change her—and she had been afraid. She had not wanted to come here, and she had not wanted to remain—but Carp had given her no choice. Carp had insisted, and because he was a Mesmerist, and she a mere somniloquist, she had been obliged to yield the point. She had protested, but she had been obliged to given in.

Michael could not believe for a moment that Augustus Carp wished his new assistant any harm, but the Mesmerist presumably felt very differently about the prospect of something happening here, especially if he had meant what he said about this being his last *séance*. Michael did not know whether the *séance* would actually go ahead, but he suspected that if it did, it might qualify as a breakthrough in the science of psychognosis to compare with the breakthrough that Gregory Marlstone was still hoping to make in physical science.

While these thoughts ran through Michael's head, Signor Monticarlo played on, and on. The musical maze did not lose its grip on him for an instant—but he no longer felt *lost*. Although he was by no means free of anxiety, he did not feel trapped. He felt that, although he was not entirely certain where he was, he now knew which way to go. Even though he could not see what was at the heart of the Maze, as yet, he was confident now that he could find his way there—and back again.

Eventually, the Italian paused in his playing for a second time, and lowered his instrument again. Everyone in the audience clapped politely and murmured approvingly, Michael included. As he applauded, though, Michael breathed a literal sigh of relief, and glanced around the room again. Little had changed, in the attitudes adopted and expressions worn by all but one of his neighbors. Lord Langstrade, the dowager Lady Langstrade and Jack were still concealing their boredom. Hope and Escott were still relaxed. Carmela was still adoring, the younger Lady Langstrade, Augustus Carp, Lady Phythian and Cecilia still striving heroically to surrender themselves to the genius of the music and its performance. Jeanne Evredon, by contrast, looked even more terrified than before.

Unlike Michael, the conclusion of the supernatural communion did not seem to have left the somniloquist relieved. It had, instead, confirmed her worst fears. She knew that whatever had begun had not concluded, and the urgency of her terror seemed to indicate that it was not the events of the morrow whose prospect was frightening her. Michael was tempted to lean forward and ask whether she was all right, if only to offer her the comfort of hearing a friendly voice, but did not dare give any attention to another woman while Cecilia was beside him. He was glad to observe, though, that Augustus Carp had become belatedly aware of his protégée's distress, and was now leaning toward her to take her hand and speak to her in a whisper. The manner in which she consented to be calmed, although the wildness in her eyes suggested that she was not much comforted, informed Michael that she had lost her contest with the Mesmerist yet again. She still had to make her own contribution to the party this evening, allowing herself to be put into a trance by the imperious magnetism of Augustus Carp's hands and eyes.

But we all have our parts to play, Michael inferred. *Some of us are more aware of that than others, perhaps because some parts are more crucial than others and perhaps because of the mere apparent order of events, but Gregory Marlstone's time-field has us all in its grip. Whether or not we have gone into the heart of the maze already, we shall all be in its toils tomorrow, when the crucial switch is thrown—and there is, in consequence, a sense in which we are already there, already enclosed, captured and overwhelmed...but* not *irredeemably trapped. There is a way out of this, for those who can find it—and to those who can find it, the duty falls of leading the others to the exit. This is not necessarily the end of the world as we know it. It is an opportunity as well as a threat. Every labyrinth awaits its Theseus, and Theseus will always triumph over the Minotaur, provided that he has the loving assistance of Ariadne.*

That was a fine thought, Michael judged, worthy of a hero and surely symptomatic of his own heroism—but as he looked again at the terror still written on Jeanne Evredon's face, his confidence could not help but falter.

That terror gradually ebbed away, though, as Signor Monticarlo's third piece continued. A sequence of covert glances informed Michael that the somniloquist was gradually recovering from her shock, perhaps beginning to convince herself that what she had just experienced had been some kind of waking dream, brought on by her own anxiety, and was not to be taken seriously.

When Michael looked back at Cecilia's face, however, he saw the ghost of a frown in her features. Covert as they were, his glances had not gone unnoticed, and they had been construed as a minuscule but tangible betrayal. It required no effort for Michael to smile adoringly, and emphasize with the full authority of his sadly unmagnetic eyes that hers was the only beauty in the world. He saw her smile in response, but he knew that there was still a slight hint of doubt in that smile, and more than a hint of criticism.

He knew that he would have to be very careful during the *séance* that was scheduled to follow the recital. He would have to keep his attention focused on the only thing that really mattered, compared to which such matters as the supernatural power of the Langstrade Maze and the possible end of the world as he knew it paled into utter insignificance. And that was what he resolved to do, as the gentler strains of the Bach sonata lulled him as well his companions, and helped him become fully aware and appreciative once again of the divine presence beside him.

CHAPTER FOURTEEN

Unexpected Somniloquistic Revelations

When Signor Monticelli put his violin down for the last time, and welcomed the loud applause of his audience with a sequence of bows, there was a general stir of movement. Many of the audience-members got to their feet and moved to the back of the room, to stretch their legs and exchange comments on what they had just experienced. The Mesmerist and his assistant got up together, leaving an empty space in front of Michael and Cecilia. Signor Monticarlo immediately came over to them, while Carmela collected his violin and two servants gathered up the music-stand.

"It was not a success," I fear, the virtuoso declared, looking Michael straight in the eyes.

"Oh, but it was magnificent," Cecilia protested.

"I thought the second piece very effective," Michael added.

"*Si*," said the violinist. "I observed that—but I think that you were the only person who really heard it."

"I'm sure that's not the case," Michael protested, but offered no other names.

"Mademoiselle Evredon, for one, seemed quite moved," Cecilia observed, obligingly, "and mother was quite delighted."

"Mademoiselle Evredon was terrified," Signor Monticarlo said, in a voice whose polite softness belied his meaning. "Do you know why that was, Mr. Laurel?"

"The exotic tuning of the instrument certainly had a rather disconcerting effect," Michael said, "but I think you are perfectly entitled to consider the intensity of her emotional reaction as a tribute to your playing, and your perception of the way in which the piece needed to be played. Perhaps she mistook the nature of her own reaction, and expressed as apparent terror something that was really more…primal."

"What do you mean, Mr. Laurel?" Cecilia asked, unsure as to whether she ought to take offense at the suggestion.

"I believe I understand what Mr. Laurel means, Miss Lang-strade," Monticarlo said, "and I thank him for it. He has the makings of a connoisseur." The little man reached into his pocket, and produced a visiting-card, which he handed to Michael. "That is my London address," he said. "You would be welcome to call, while we are still in residence there." Then he bowed and followed Carmela out of the room.

"What on Earth does he mean by that?" Cecilia asked, obviously suspecting that it was for Carmela's sake that the invitation had been issued.

"He's simply being polite," Michael told her, feeling guilty about the slight insincerity. "When we traveled up in the railway carriage I asked him about his music, merely by way of conversation, and he seems to have inferred that I have a genuine interest in his countryman, Signor Locatelli. I must admit that the second *capriccio* he played was like no other piece of music I have ever heard, and that it struck a chord within me." He hastened to add: "But I doubt that I shall take up his invitation. I shall be far too busy."

The music-stand had now been replaced by a stiff-backed but soft-cushioned chair with varnished wooden arms. Augustus Carp led his somniloquist to it, and propelled her into it with gentle but irresistible pressure. She seemed half asleep already, and Michael guessed that Carp had already employed his Mesmeric gift in order to calm her down and secure her acquiescence.

Once all the other members of the house-party had taken their seats again, after an interval of ten minutes, Lady Langstrade undertook the second formal introduction, presenting Carp and the somniloquist to the audience. Carp bowed solemnly, but Jeanne Evredon did not so much as nod her head.

The Mesmerist explained, more painstakingly than was necessary, that he was about to place his subject in a deep trance, in which condition she would lose her sense of self and would become a vehicle available to other voices. He asked his audience to regard the *séance* as an experiment in psychognosis rather than a theatrical performance or a purposeful exercise in communication.

"If anyone has questions that they want to address to the somniloquist, I shall be happy to relay them in due course," he said, "but I beg you to pose those questions in an orderly manner, and to be patient with my intermediation, in order to avoid confusion. I would like to think that any answers we obtain in the course of the *séance* will be honest and reliable, but I must warn you not to take that for granted. Psychognostic science is in its infancy, and we are still groping our way toward an understanding of the mysteries of the human mind, and the arcane of the universe to which the mind becomes responsive when it is in the somniloquistic state.

"Whether the voices that speak through the mouths of magnetized somniloquists really include the voices of souls that have departed this Earth, as many people believe, I do not know. The implications of their frequent claims to be spirits speaking from the afterlife are somewhat compromised by the fact that they often appear to tell lies or make mistakes. Nor can I explain why predictions of the future issued by the magnetized are so often unreliable, although I suspect that the principal reason is that the future is as yet unmade, and that any hand of fate working within its making is direly unsteady in its work, ever liable to be frustrated by the whims of chance. Whatever information Mademoiselle Evredon is able to communicate to us this evening must, in consequence, be treated with a degree of skepticism, no matter how insightful or pertinent it may seem."

Having thus done his duty, Carp proceeded with his subject's entrancement. Although he had only been working with Jeanne Evredon for a matter of weeks, he had obviously built up sufficient rapport with her to entrance her without difficulty, and he was merely completing a process already begun. The young Frenchwoman did not seem to offer any resistance to his sonorous commands, and relaxed very meekly into a state of torpor, slumping inertly against the supportive back of her chair.

"Can you tell me your name?" Carp asked the somniloquist, seeking to demonstrate that she was, indeed fully entranced.

"I have no name," the magnetized woman replied, according to a familiar formula.

"Do you know where you are?" Carps asked.

"Yes," she replied, unhelpfully.

Carp was neither astonished nor annoyed by the excessively literal reply. "Please tell us where you are," he instructed.

"Inside the Maze," the somniloquist replied, to everyone's surprise. Michael felt as if his heart had skipped a beat.

"Are you referring to the Langstrade Maze?" Carp asked, slightly puzzled.

"Yes."

"We are now in the drawing-room of Langstrade Hall, a hundred yards west of the Maze. Can you see that now?"

"We are inside the Maze," the somniloquist repeated.

Carp permitted himself a slight frown this time, but evidently thought it wise to let the matter lie. "Very well," he said. "Is there anyone who would like to address the company gathered here, employing your voice as a medium?"

"Yes." Even though the answer was monosyllabic, it seemed that the timbre of the somniloquist's voice had changed completely.

"Please state your name," said the Mesmerist.

"I am the Mistress of the Labyrinth," was the reply—rather paradoxically, it seemed, for the medium's voice had shifted toward the baritone spectrum of the vocal scale, and no longer had anything feminine about it.

"What is your name?" Carp asked again, evidently unsatisfied by a mere title.

"I have no name," the medium repeated, in her new voice. "I am the Mistress of the Labyrinth."

"What do you have to say to us?" Carp asked

"I apologize," the voice said. "It is necessary. Time is; time was; time is past."

Michael knew that he had heard those words—or something very similar—before, but he could not place the quotation.

"For what are you apologizing?" Carp asked. "Have you done harm to anyone here?"

"Not yet," was the reply to that.

Carp frowned again, but he appeared to be more intrigued than annoyed. "Do you intend to do harm to anyone here?"

"No. I shall protect everyone, to the best of my ability."

"But you expect harm to come to someone here?"

There was no answer to that; Michael deduced that the question had not been sufficiently imperative.

Carp rephrased the question. "Do you expect harm to come to anyone here?"

"There is a risk," the voice declared. "There is danger, which is of my making. I apologize for the danger. It is necessary."

"What kind of danger?" Carp demanded.

"The danger of becoming lost. The danger of injury. The danger of annihilation."

"And which of us is under threat?" Carp wanted to know.

"All of us," the voice replied.

Michael thought it significant that the voice had said "us" rather than "you", but Carp did not pick up on that point. Instead, the Mesmerist said: "From where does the threat emanate?"

"Everywhen," was the reply.

"What does that mean?" Carp asked.

"What it means," was the reply.

Carp collected himself briefly, then said: "Does the danger come from Gregory Marlstone's experiment in time-manipulation?"

There was no answer to that. Again, Carp tried rephrasing the question. "Will the danger be averted if Marlstone does not activate his time machine tomorrow?"

"No."

Carp frowned, and hesitated. Quentin Hope took advantage of the pause to say: "Ask the Mistress of the Labyrinth what the original purpose of prehistoric mazes was. Ask her whether they were intended to map out paths for ritual processions, or to trap demons."

Carp' frown depended, and he did not seem at all disposed to accede to this request—but the voice seemed to be unaware of the protocol of Mesmeric interrogations, and did not wait for the question to be relayed, as custom demanded. "Both," it answered.

Hope laughed. "Very diplomatic," he opined.

Lady Phythian raised her hand to attract the Mesmerist's attention. "Yes, Lady Phythian," Carp said, gladly.

"Would you ask the spirit, please, whether the Langstrade ghosts will walk tonight?" she asked.

This time, Carp was certainly about to relay the question, but once again, the voice did not wait. "Yes," it said.

"Will the ghost of Harold Longstride be among them?" Escott hastened to put in.

"Yes," the voice replied, unequivocally.

"Can you name the other ghosts that will walk tonight?" Hope asked.

"Yes," the voice replied. This time, a ripple of amusement ran through the audience.

Carp attempted to seize back the initiative. "Please state the names of the other ghosts that will haunt the grounds of Langstrade Hall tonight," he requested.

"The Earl of Langstrade," the voice stated, "Michael Laurel. Quentin Hope. James Escott. Gregory Marlstone. Lady Ariadne Phythian...."

By the time the voice reached the sixth name on its list, the audience had caught on to the fact that something odd was occurring—slightly belatedly, because the first name in the list could easily have referred to the first Earl rather than the present one. While a ripple of puzzlement replaced the ripple of amusement, the voice went on: "Cecilia Langstrade. Carmela Monticarlo. Pietro Locatelli. Emund Snurlson. Dedalus. Edward Kelley...."

Michael's impression was that the voice might well have continued, but Carp had become annoyed. "This is absurd," he said. "Several of the names you have listed are those of living people, and others are names of people who never existed. You are making fun of us, are you not?"

"No," replied the voice.

"But if Hope and I are right in our conjectures regarding the Langstrade ghosts," Escott said, as if he had just had a flash of inspiration, "then the names of living persons *would* be on the list, for what Lady Phythian saw would be images of ourselves displaced in time by Marlstone's machine. Pietro Locatelli's ghost has already walked this evening, after a fashion, thanks to Signor Monticarlo, while Emund Snurlson, Dedalus and Harold Longstride are everpresent, in spirit, in Lord Langstrade's thoughts and endeavors. The truly surprising name on the list is…."

"I must call for order, gentlemen!" Carp said, raising his voice to interrupt. "This is not an argument in a railway carriage or an idle discussion in a smoking-room. It is an experiment in Mesmerism—*my* experiment in Mesmerism, and perhaps my last. I must demand, with all due respect, that you let me conduct it in my own way—in the *appropriate* way."

"Well, get on with it then!" exclaimed Quentin Hope, rather rudely.

Carp pursed his lips, but he had obviously made up his mind to make a third attempt to discover the identity of the voice. "When you were alive," he asked, maintaining his voice at a level sufficient to drown out the whispers that were running through his audience, "what was your name?"

"I have no name," the voice repeated, in a curt fashion that seemed to Michael to be a trifle mulish.

"Are you, in fact, the spirit of a human being who once walked the Earth?" Carp asked.

"No."

"Then what are you?"

"The Mistress of the Labyrinth."

"Are you a demon?"

"No."

"A goddess?"

This time, the voice hesitated, although Jeanne Evredon's lips quivered, as if a reply might be trembling there.

Carp waited, expectantly, but Escott lost patience again: "Why should Edward Kelley haunt Langstrade?" he called out.

The mesmerist was obviously determined not to be put off again by Hope and Escott's interventions, and spoke very sharply as he said to the magnetized somniloquist: "You will respond to my voice, and my voice alone! Do you understand that?"

"Yes," said the somniloquist—although it was not obvious to Michael that the affirmative answer to the question implied consent to the instruction as well as a confirmation that the mysterious voice understood what had been said.

"Ask her the question, then!" cried Hope.

Carp gritted his teeth, but he evidently decided that the only way to retain control of the situation was to yield a little ground. "Why is Edward Kelley numbered among the ghosts of Langstrade?" he asked.

"Because he is ambitious to commune with angels," was the enigmatic reply.

Carp immediately rounded on Hope and Escott. "In my experience, he said, "it is rarely fruitful to ask somniloquists questions that begin with *why*. Whatever the voices may be, they seem to have notions of causality and motivation that differ significantly from ours."

"Ask her which angel Kelley is ambitious to commune with here," Escott shot back, unrepentantly.

Carp was visibly agitated now, but the question obviously intrigued him, and he relayed it obediently.

"Any that might care to reply," the voice riposted.

Carp did not wait for Escott to continue snapping at his heels. "Will anyone, in fact, reply to Kelley?" he asked.

"Yes."

"Who?"

"Michael Laurel and Quentin Hope."

That caused a stir. More heads turned toward Michael than toward Hope. The painter shrugged his shoulders slightly as he blushed, to signify that he did not understand the allegation any better than anyone else.

"Are Laurel and Hope angels, then?" asked Carp, impatiently.

"No," replied the voice.

"Does Edward Kelley take them for angels?"

"He will. He does. He did."

"This is getting us nowhere, I fear," Carp said, mopping his brown with his handkerchief. "If anyone except for Mr. Hope and Mr. Escott has a question to put to the voice, I beg him to do so now, for I fear that Mademoiselle Evredon may not be capable of sustaining her trance much longer. For her sake, I do not want to prolong the *séance* to the point at which she lapses into unconsciousness.

Lord Langstrade, do you have a question that you would like me to ask?"

"I do," said Lord Langstrade. "Would you kindly ask the spirit who devised the plan of the Langstrade maze, and when."

Carp relayed the question to his subject.

"Signor Monticarlo," was the bizarre reply, "less than an hour ago. Pietro Locatelli, a hundred years ago. Dedalus, three thousand five hundred years ago."

It was Signor Monticarlo's turn to look astonished and shrug his shoulders to express his complete lack of understanding. This time, however, Michael thought that he did have an inkling of the meaning of what the mysterious Mistress of the Labyrinth might mean. There was a sense in which the Locatelli capriccio corrected by Signor Monticarlo *was* the Maze, which now extended in time as well as space, thanks to the mysterious pulses emitted by Marlstone's time machine. If certain moments in time really were capable of harmonic resonance, then the idea of the music, if not the actual sound, might be transmissible through time, appearing more than once in the past, in the form of an instantaneous spark of inspiration. Given that he had been able to internalize the maze having only glanced at it, others cleverer than he must have the same ability.

"Lady Langstrade," Carp said, addressing his hostess rather than her mother. "Would you like to ask a question?"

"Yes," said the Earl's wife. "Would you ask the spirit, please, who killed Emund Snurlson in the year 822?"

Carp nodded, approving of the precision of the question. He repeated it.

"The second Earl of Langstrade," was the reply.

Hope burst out laughing yet again. "The fencing lessons didn't go to waste after all, Milord!" he said. "While you were playing on the lawn as a boy, your pretended thrusts must have extended back in time over a thousand years, propelled by a gust of wind from Marlstone's time machine!"

Exactly like the composition of the Langstrade Maze, Michael thought.

Lord Langstrade looked furious, but made no reply to Hope's gibe.

"Ask her whether the world as we know it is going to end tomorrow—just to set Escott's mind at rest," Hope continued, irrepressible in the wake of his jest. Almost everyone in the audience looked at him sharply, critical of his irreverence.

There was obviously no way that the Mesmerist was going to make any further concessions to his tormentor-in-chief, so the question remained conspicuously unrelayed. Indeed, Carp was fighting so hard to control himself that he did not even ask whether anyone else in the audience had a question to answer, and raised his arm as if to signal that he was bringing the *séance* to a close.

All of a sudden, though, Jeanne Evredon's voice changed again, as if the self-declared Mistress of the Labyrinth had been abruptly displaced by a very different spirit, and a voice that seemed to be masculine, in spite of being higher in pitch than the previous one, said: "Catastrophe is inevitable, but the world might yet be saved."

Carp spun around. "What catastrophe?" he demanded

"The invasion of the present by the future, and the past by the present," the voice replied—and then continued, of its own accord: "The world as *we* know it might be saved, but if heroic action fails, the Era of Change will commence, and its dread empire will not easily be set aside."

"Who is speaking?" Carp demanded, sharply.

"Michael Laurel," was the reply.

Michael felt his heart sink as his name was incongruously pronounced for the second time, feeling somewhat persecuted—but before the silent stares could become oppressive, the irritated Carp had launched himself back into the argumentative fray with a will.

"Is the gentleman sitting at the end of the second row, beside Miss Cecilia Langstrade, the person to whom you are referring?" the Mesmerist demanded.

"Not yet," was the bewilderingly equivocal answer.

Cecilia took it into her head then to come to the rescue then, although she must have known what a dire risk she was taking. "Dr. Carp," she said, "would you kindly ask your medium who I am fated to marry?"

A hush of a different sort fell upon the audience. Michael closed his eyes and prayed that the reply might be equally equivocal, if it was not to be in his favor. However unreliable the answer might be, in objective terms, he knew that it was bound to have an effect of some sort.

Carp made no attempt to soften the blow by means of tentative phraseology. "Who will Miss Cecilia Langstrade marry?" he asked, intemperately. The snap in his voice reflected his extreme irritation with the progress of the *séance*.

"Whomsoever she pleases, if she marries at all," came the reply, the voice resuming the baritone pitch of the Mistress of the Labyrinth. It was a better reply than Michael had dreaded, although it was by no means as explicit as he could have wished, and he could not help regretting the apparent displacement of the voice that had claimed to be his own.

"Who am *I* destined to marry?" Quentin Hope asked, waspishly.

"Whomsoever wishes to marry you," was the reply, which did not wait for any intermediation by the Mesmerist. This time, it was Escott who laughed aloud while others contented themselves with muted chuckles.

"If you will forgive me saying so," said Signor Monticarlo, speaking from the rear, "it seems rather eccentric to forsake questions about the possible imminent end of the world for questions regarding the romantic fortunes of various members of the company." His daughter looked at him with an expression that seemed slightly disappointed.

"That was not my doing, Signor," Carp said, flatly. "I will consent to relay one last question. Mr. Laurel, since the voice that was speaking through the medium of my somniloquist just now claimed to share your identity, albeit somewhat displaced in time, do *you* have any question that you would like me to put to the present voice?"

Michael was taken unawares by that question, but he only paused momentarily, suppressing the temptation to point out to the somniloquist that the voice claiming to be his own seemed to have handed responsibility back to another. "Yes," he said, hesitantly. "Will you ask the voice what it was that frightened Mademoiselle Evredon so terribly when Signor Monticarlo played his second piece this evening?"

Carp seemed almost as surprised by that question as Cecilia was, but he shrugged his shoulders, as if accepting defeat in his attempt to restore any vestige of continuity and order to the occasion. "What was it that frightened Mademoiselle Evredon during Signor Monticarlo's recital?" he asked, wearily.

Michael immediately regretted having asked the question, because the somniloquist shot to her feet, standing bolt upright as rigid as a ramrod. An expression of pure terror took possession of her features yet again.

"Because *I'm in the maze,*" she cried, her voice rising in a rapid crescendo to the pitch of a scream, "*and I can't get out!*" Then she collapsed and fell heavily to the floor, unconscious.

CHAPTER FIFTEEN

THE GHOST-HUNTING EXPEDITION

Like the good servant he was, Heatherington instantly ceased pretending to be a statue. Making quick hand-signals to the waiting servants, he sent willing helpers racing to the stricken woman's side. Augustus Carp made a quick examination, then asked the servants to pick his assistant up, carry her up to the Violet Room and put her to bed.

The Mesmerist turned to the audience, most of whom were glued to their seats by shock, and said, in a voice tremulous with strain: "I apologize, ladies and gentlemen. One never has any advance warning as to how somniloquistic *séances* might progress. I wish I could say that this was the first time that one of mine has produced such bizarre results, or degenerated into such disarray, but I cannot. Such things happen—and I must warn you again not to read too much into anything said here tonight. What it might mean, if it means anything at all, I cannot tell. Once again, I must apologize, and bid you goodnight." With that, he strode out of the room, hot on the heels of the servants carrying Mademoiselle Evredon, and practically ran up the stairs, overtaking them on the way, with the key to the Blue Room in his hand.

"That didn't go as I'd hoped," Cecilia Langstrade muttered, in a voice that she probably thought inaudible to everyone except Michael.

Jack Langstrade had, however, contrived to avoid being sent to bed during the intermission between the recital and the séance, and he heard the comment clearly enough. "Well *I* thought it was simply spiffing, Sis!" he opined.

Even if Gregory Marlstone had not been locked away in the Keep, trying hard to figure out how and why his time machine had malfunctioned earlier in the day, there would probably have been few volunteers to listen to his proposed lecture on the theory underpinning the construction of his time machine. Michael would have been very interested to hear it, even though he knew that it would be far beyond the grasp of his limited intellect, but he felt quite exhausted in the wake of the violin recital and the *séance*.

Lord Langstrade took control of the situation, exactly as a good host should, and opined that it would probably be best for the gentlemen to retire to the smoking room for a strong brandy or three, while the ladies took cocoa in the small drawing-room. The chorus of approval was distinctly muted, but no one raised any objection to what was, in the circumstances, virtually a command.

"If you don't mind, Milord," Signor Monticarlo said, making use of the only escape route available to him, "I am very tired following my performance. I shall wish you all goodnight."

Everyone wished the violinist goodnight—including Carmela, who did not accompany him upstairs, but followed the elder Lady Langstrade into the dining-room instead.

Michael was strongly tempted to follow the Italian's example, but he could not bear the thought of leaving Quentin Hope, James Escott and Lord Langstrade to talk about him behind his back—as they would be bound to do, given the extent to which his name had featured in Augustus Carp's *séance*—so he made a manful attempt to shrug off his feeling of exhaustion.

"And then there were four," said Escott, looking at Michael with an element of sly challenge in his gaze.

"I knew it was a mistake to invite that fellow Carp," Lord Langstrade opined. "You'd expect that a man of his experience could mount a better performance than that."

"I honestly believe that he was trying with all his might to do so," Escott said. "The fault, if there was one, lay with Mademoiselle Evredon's attempt to masquerade as the Mistress of the Labyrinth. I know that Hope and I have a reputation for mischief-making, but I suspect that young woman could give us a run for our money, and she was surely trying to do so. Perhaps she was trying to pay Carp back for the unkindness he has showed her in their recent quarrels. I suspect that he won't be working with her again."

"Once word of this evening's fiasco gets around," Hope opined, "he probably won't be working anywhere that people of our sort are likely to encounter him. That medium of his seems quite sweet on you, though, Laurel—almost as sweet as Carmela Monticarlo. You certainly have a way with the ladies." The optimist did not go so far as to add that he did not envy the woman unlucky enough to marry such an obvious libertine.

"I don't believe that her comments were a subtle way of expressing an attraction to me," Michael said, firmly. "Wherever her voices come from, I think they really were trying to say something meaningful about the Langstrade Maze and tomorrow's experiment. I have no idea who Edward Kelley is, though."

"Don't you?" Hope was quick to say. "If you'd gone to a decent public school you'd know. Educational standards obviously aren't what they used to be."

"That's a trifle harsh, Quentin," Escott chipped in. Turning to Michael, he explained: "Edward Kelley was a minor member of John Dee's secret college. He never produced any significant advances in mathematics, like Dee or the two Diggeses, or any notable invention, like Bacon or Drebbel, but he was as much a member of the inner circle as Raleigh. He was said to be Dee's skryer, but the secrecy of the college makes it difficult to be sure."

"What's a skryer?" Michael asked, figuring that it as better to confess his ignorance rather than take the risk of being caught out by Hope.

"A kind of seer," Escott replied, promptly. "A somniloquist, I suppose, although it was long before Mesmer's day, so that term hadn't yet acquired its modern meaning. He was said to be able to communicate with angels by means of a shiny black stone—a similar process, I presume, to that by which Mademoiselle Evredon communicates with her voices, except that the modern fashion is to identify such dubious informants as the voices of the spirits of the dead, rather than as angels."

"That explains, I suppose, why Edward Kelley might be reaching out with his mind in search of the voices of angels, even as far as present-day Langstrade," Michael conceded, "but I don't see how Mr. Hope and I can possibly be expected to answer his desire."

"We can't," Hope said, squarely. "You need to remember Carp's warning, Laurel, and take heed of it. These spirit-mimics invariably spout a good deal of nonsense, perhaps innocently and perhaps in the hope that absurdity will pass for enigmatic meaning. Don't bother your young head with trying to figure it out."

"You don't believe that the voice speaking through Mademoiselle Evredon really was an external agency of some sort?" Michael asked.

"Of course not," Hope replied. "When she—the Frenchwoman, that is—was tired of pretending to be the Mistress of the Labyrinth she claimed to be *you*, remember? Do you believe *that*?" He looked hard at Michel, then at the other members the company in turn. No one admitted to the belief that the spirit of Michael's future self really had spoken to them through the medium of Augustus Carp's somniloquist.

"All the same, though," Lord Langstrade said, "if she was trying to get back at Carp by chucking his prepared script out of the window, she certainly put a lot of rubbish in its place."

"She gave you credit for killing Emund Snurlson in Harold Longstride's stead," Hope reminded him. "You might be grateful for that."

"And we've been assured that the dread empire of eternity, or the so-called Era of Change, *might* still be averted, if we're heroic enough," Escott added, raising a quizzical eyebrow in Michael's direction. "I suppose we might be grateful for that news too, eh, Mr. Laurel? Your future self was doubtless trying to do us a good turn by letting us know. The world as we know it *can* still be saved from catastrophe, in order that it might go to Hell in its own sluggish way."

"Or gain the Earthly paradise by more laborious means," Hope countered, automatically.

"But for the time being," Michael said, quietly, "we're still in the Maze—and I'm not sure any more that even I can find my way out."

"But we're *not* in the Maze, are we?" said Lord Langstrade.

"No," said Escott, "but we jolly well ought to be, if we're supposed to be playing a heroic role. Indeed, we *have* to be, if we're to inject any meaning at all into the messages we've just received from the World Beyond."

"What do you mean?" asked the Earl.

"I mean that the ghosts are scheduled to walk tonight—and we're supposed to be among them. If images of us, refracted through time, really are among the many ghostly lights that Lady Phythian has seen over the years, then we really need to get out there, in order to project the images in question And we have good reason to do so, don't we? Even if we can't believe for a moment that the ghosts of Dedalus, Harold Longstride, Pietro Locatelli and Edward Kelley will be walking the maze in search of us, we can hardly resist the temptation to make certain, can we?"

"Ah!" said Langstrade, pensively.

"Signor Monticarlo seems to have gone to bed a trifle prematurely," Hope observed. "He's the one who would have wanted to see Locatelli. That's a pity."

"Not at all," said Escott, "since Lady Phythian's testimony has already told us that the eight lights she saw most distinctly consisted of two groups of four, one tracking the other. That's four real ghosts and the four of us, isn't it?"

"Actually…," Michael began, remembering that the mysterious voice had also named Lady Phythian, Lady Langstrade, Carmela and Cecilia among the ghosts in the maze—but Hope gave him no opportunity to finish.

"That's right!" the optimist said. "Lord Langstrade will certainly want to meet Dedalus and Harold Longstride, while Laurel and I seem to have a meeting scheduled with Kelley. We'll have to leave Locatelli to you, Escott—how's your Italian?"

"Better than Langstrade's ancient Greek and Celtic, I suspect," Escott retorted. "Are we on, then?"

"Absolutely!" said Hope. "As you say—no matter how absurd it all is, how could we possibly resist the temptation? And we do have a duty to the continuity of history to cast the shadows in time that Lady Phythian's been looking out for ever since she was Ariadne Potts. It's the least we can do, as gentlemen."

"You really want to go out to the Maze?" Lord Langstrade said, uncertainly. "In the dark?"

"We'll have to take lanterns with us, obviously," Escott said. "Lady Phythian was quite clear about the lanterns. If Mr. Laurel will deign to accompany us, we'll be in no danger of getting stuck. He got in and out all right today, twice over, thanks to his artistic sensibility. If he's nervy, though, you'll have to ask Heatherington to make up the party. There has to be four of us."

But we're already in the maze, Michael objected, silently, *and it's obviously much bigger and far more complicated than I thought. While it just consisted of hedges, however thorny, I knew my way around it, but now it's comprised of time and music, I'm not so sure.* Aloud, all he said was: "I wouldn't dream of staying behind."

That seemed to make Lord Langstrade's mind up. "All right," he said, "let's do it. I'll go tell Heatherington to find us some lanterns."

"What about guns?" Escott asked. "I know they're not supposed to be much use against ghosts, but given that we're solid enough…."

"No guns," said Hope, decisively. "Stumbling around the Maze in the dark, we're far more likely to shoot one another than anyone else, and I certainly don't want to be walking in front of Escott if he's got a loaded shotgun under his arm."

"I agree," Michael said, hastily. "No weapons. We're not looking for a fight."

"No guns, then," Lord Langstrade concluded.

"Are you going to change out of your dinner-jacket?" Escott asked the Earl

"It's not worth the bother," Langstrade opined. "It's probably getting cool outside by now—do you chaps want to put jackets on?"

Michael was as quick to reject this suggestion as Hope and Escott were.

"Fine," said Lord Langstrade, and rang the bell to summon Heatherington. "We need four lanterns," he instructed the butler. "I'll need my hat and my walking-stick, too—we're going out for a stroll."

Heatherington nodded his head, as meekly and emotionlessly as a well-disciplined somniloquist, and withdrew.

"We're not going to see anything, though," the Earl added, addressing his companions. He sounded less than completely convinced—unsurprisingly, in Michael's opinion, given that he had previously taken so much pleasure in the idea that his mock-ancestral manor might have a mock-ancestral ghost to go along with its mock-Medieval Keep and its mock-Medieval labyrinth.

"Well, that will be indicative too," Hope declared. "If I understand Francis Bacon's much-vaunted scientific method correctly—which, as an Eton and Balliol man, I surely do—then experiments that produce negative results are just as significant, in their way, as those which produce positive ones. If no ghosts walk, except for us, it will prove that Mademoiselle Evredon's entire performance was just so much hot air. We'll keep it to ourselves, though—I think we've done old Carp enough damage for one night."

"More than enough," Escott agreed. "We did have help, though—we couldn't have done quite as much without Mademoiselle Evredon's gnomic support."

"I never realized that the secret college had a somniloquist as well as all those pioneers of science and invention," Michael said, reflectively. "It puts a slightly different twist on England's Academic glory, don't you think?"

"Definitely not," Escott was quick to say. "Enthusiasts for science and technology like Hope inevitably like to think of Dee's gang as hard-headed theorists and inventors, but they never saw themselves that way. They were seekers after occult wisdom, and had no idea, in advance, where they might find it. Their experiments in supernatural communication, like Carp's experiments in psychognosis, were just as sincere as their ventures in mathematics and physics. Dee was an assiduous student of astrology and alchemy as well as astronomy and mathematics, as was every other Renaissance sage from Roger Bacon and Albertus Magnus onwards. He had no idea, to begin with, whether Kelley's skrying or Francis Bacon's chicken-stuffing was likely to produce the more interesting and valuable results—and we don't actually know for sure that it didn't. It's not impossible that all their triumphs were based on information dictated by Kelley's angels."

"Yes it is," Hope contradicted. "Utterly impossible—although I shall certainly be able to tell the college a thing or two, if I do happen to meet Kelley in the Maze tonight. I can't imagine why my name was coupled with Laurel's in that regard, though. What can he possibly have to teach the secret college? Its members already knew about oil-paints and perspective."

Michael did not rise to this bait.

Heatherington returned then. He silently handed a lantern to each of the four men, and then handed a broad-brimmed hat to Lord Langstrade, along with his stout ivory-handled walking-stick. When all these objects had been distributed, Heatherington bowed rather brusquely and withdrew. Michael took the inference that the servant disapproved strongly of the nocturnal expedition, but that wild horses could not have dragged a word of criticism from his taut lips.

"I'll wager that you never thought, when you were listening to Lady Phythian tell her story in the railway carriage yesterday," Escott said to Michael in a low voice, as they made their way on tiptoe to one of the Hall's side-doors—moving quietly for fear of disturbing the ladies in the dining room—"that within thirty-six hours you'd actually *become* one of her ghosts."

"If not two of them," Hope quipped.

"What's that supposed to mean?" whispered Lord Langstrade

"He's just showing off again," Escott said, softly. "Hope realizes—as I do myself, admittedly—that Marlstone's machine might perfectly well cast *two* images of the four of us into the past, originated from slightly different present moments, which will inevitably move in step, as if one were following the other. If so, alas, we won't meet any of the other ghosts within its bounds…but let's not prejudge the issue. You'll have to guide us through the maze, I suppose, Laurel…although we must remember to separate and drift apart when we reach the central arena, just as Lady Phythian observed."

"Must we?" Langstrade queried.

"Absolutely," said Hope, again. "Our duty as gentlemen, remember? History must be conserved. Otherwise, the whole thing might come apart. Wouldn't want that, would we?"

"No," said the Earl, unconvincingly, twirling his walking-stick. "I suppose not." By this time, they were outside, and the Earl had closed the door quietly behind them.

The trek across the lawn was completed in a few minutes, and the other three men then stood aside to let Michael take the lead as they went into the Maze. He felt responsibility descend upon him like an unseasonably thick cloak—although it might, he thought, on due reflection, be mere weariness.

"You're the one with Ariadne's thread graven in his memory, my young Theseus," Hope said, taking care to maintain a perfectly pleasant tone. "Watch out for the Minotaur, though—not to mention fire-breathing dragons and swarms of mating fireflies."

"If Mr. Marlstone's machine is the Minotaur," Michael riposted, as he led the party along the outer ring of the maze past the first seductive junction, which gave access to an impasse, "it's unlikely to do us any harm tonight. What worries me slightly more is the prospect of meeting the Mistress of the Labyrinth."

"What on Earth did the somniloquist mean by that?" Lord Langstrade asked. "I didn't understand it at all."

"Cretan myth is somewhat confused with respect to Dedalus' Labyrinth," Hope was quick to explain. "As well as the Minotaur, there was a mysterious female personage attached to it, sometimes referred to as the Mistress of the Labyrinth, sometimes simply as the Lady. Escott and I found evidence...."

"Oh, that's right!" Langstrade said, cutting him off. "I remember now. You went on about it for days on end when we were all in Crete."

"The Mistress of the Labyrinth was undoubtedly the prototype of the Christian Virgin, in her capacity as Queen of Heaven," Escott put in, thoughtfully. "That was the subject of Heinrich von Biber's sonata, remember—the one that Pietro Locatelli adapted, and which was in turn adapted by Niccolò Paganini."

"That's a patently false analogy," Hope said. "I don't say that Laurel is right to be *afraid* of meeting the Mistress of the Labyrinth, but any pagan goddess is likely to have been far more exacting of her worshippers than the meek mother of Christ."

"When Carp asked the voice whether she was a goddess," Lord Langstrade recalled, "she didn't reply...but she seemed to be about to say *something*. I must admit that I'm utterly at a loss when it comes to finding any sense in all this, and I don't know how you chaps can be so complacent about it all. Why did you ask that final question, Laurel? It took me completely by surprise."

"Yes," said Hope, interestedly. "Why did you? You were supposed to be asking a question of your future self, remember? It's almost as if you were deliberately trying to bring the somniloquist out of her trance."

"I asked the question because Signor Monticarlo had asked it of me before the *séance* began—and because I was curious to know the answer myself," Michael said, as he led the party from the fifth ring of the Maze into the fourth. "I wanted to know whether there was anything in the Maze to be frightened of—and, if so, what it is."

"And what made you think there might be?" Escott asked—but then stopped dead, causing Hope, who was behind him, to bump into him and curse.

"Can you hear that?" Escott asked.

"What?" asked Lord Langstrade. "Oh...."

Michael could hear it too: the sound of music, played on a seemingly distant violin. He recognized the piece.

"It's Monticarlo, practicing again," Hope said, dismissively. "A trifle antisocial, at this time of night."

Michael didn't bother to point out that the Orange Room, in which Signor Monticarlo was lodged, was on the far side of the Hall, nor that the music was not, in any case, coming from the direction of the Hall. Indeed, if it were emanating from any Earthly location, it could only be coming from the upper regions of the Keep. He could not imagine that Marlstone had a violin among his equipment, or that was likely to be playing it if he had, so he concluded, privately, that the music was in the heads of its listeners, composed of pure and mazy mental imagery.

He turned a corner into the third ring just then, and immediately turned again in order to follow a path parallel to the one the party had just been following, in the opposite direction. He had taken three strides before he looked back to check that his companions were following him, and when he saw that he was quite alone, he stopped dead.

"This is why I thought that there might be something frightening in the maze," he murmured, belatedly answering Escott's question. The music seemed to be worming its way into the depths of his mind now, although he knew that he could not really be *hearing* it at all, since sound could not be transmitted through time.

He went back to the gap in the hedge and stepped back through it, to see whether his three companions had somehow missed the turning and carried on straight ahead. There was no sign of their lanterns anywhere.

I knew the Maze had become more complicated than it was before, he said to himself, forming the words rather deliberately. *I couldn't be sure, of course, that it now extends in time as well as space, but that must surely be the case. Somehow I've taken a step that has taken me out of my own time. But isn't that supposed to be impossible, for physical objects? Always provided, of course, that I'm still a physical object.*

He reached up with his right hand, closed his fist and tapped himself on the forehead with his knuckles. He felt solid enough.

But that doesn't mean anything, he told himself, *if my hand and my head are made of the same stuff.* He reached out with his left hand, which was clutching the lantern, and thrust the lantern into the densely-clustered branches forming the wall of the Maze. The lantern vanished into it without meeting any resistance, its ghostly light eclipsed.

Even though he had been half-expecting that result, Michael felt his heart accelerate, and felt a wave of incipient panic.

Damnation! He thought. *I really am a ghost. I'm a phantom, blown away from the present by a gust of wind from Marlstone's time machine...except that it's much more complex than any mere gust of wind. That's what the music is: the thread extended by the Mistress of the Labyrinth to draw her victims through the maze in a solemn procession...or a crazy dance.*

He had no doubt, now, who the Mistress of the Labyrinth was, or that she really had spoken through the medium of the somniloquist. "She" was Marlstone's time machine, now moving by virtue of her own inertia, as powerfully and irresistibly as any Leviathan of Steel and Steam, along her own Labyrinthine track.

But from where, Michael wondered, was she drawing her power, if Marlstone had not yet engaged the full force of his own mysterious driving mechanism?

To make perfectly certain of his own insubstantiality, Michael stepped sideways and thrust the full length of his right arm into the hedge, bracing himself reflexively against the assault of the thorns. None came. His flesh met no more resistance than the stick.

Well, he thought, *if that's the case, there's no reason to take the roundabout route to the center, is there?*

Bracing himself again, he stepped clean through the hedge into the next ring of the Maze. It was easy. A dozen more strides took him through three more hedges and into a third pathway—but then he hesitated, sure that he ought to have arrived in the center by now, if he were only moving through space. He had not—and he paused to wonder whether his "short cuts" might only make it more difficult to find his way back to the present.

But what does it matter? he said, silently. *I'm trapped in the Maze regardless, until the Mistress of the Labyrinth consents to let me out. We all are, whether we know it or not, and we all have been, for quite some time. Marlstone's machine is already doing its work, extending its influence back from tomorrow noon into today, yesterday, and who knows how many other yesterdays? Hundreds of thousands, if the ghost of Harold Longstride really is haunting the Maze on the sixteenth of August 1822, in any more than a metaphorical sense.*

He stepped through yet another hedge. This time, the stride did take him into a central arena of sorts—but not the one with which he was familiar. He was, however, quite certain that it was the same location in purely geographical terms, even though there was not the slightest sign of the looming Keep. There *was* a yew tree, growing in a similar location to the symbolic yew tree he had included in his painting, and the particular shape of the black silhouette of Bancroft Scar was still recognizable to an artist's eyes, even by moonlight.

When he glanced behind, to estimate his exact position by means of the hedge, he was not surprised to see that the hedge was no longer there either. Nor was Langstrade Hall. Where the Hall had stood a few minutes ago—or *would stand*, a thousand years hence, or perhaps *had stood* a thousand years ago, there was nothing but a silent forest, whose tall trees obscured the low-lying place where the waters of Cribden Tarn might or might not have been. There was a three-quarter moon descending toward that western horizon, but he took no comfort from the familiarity of its partly-obscured face.

Michael Laurel knew that his ghost had traveled a great deal further than the mere minutes and hours with which Gregory Marlstone had ostensibly been juggling on the afternoon of Friday, August sixteenth, 1822—and although he had to suppose that an insubstantial ghost had nothing to fear from any physical threat, he was afraid. He was afraid that he was lost, and that he might never get back to his own time, his own body, and his own world—because he was afraid that none of those things still existed, or ever would, in any presently-meaningful sense.

CHAPTER SIXTEEN

THE GHOSTS IN LANGSTRADE MAZE

Michael walked toward the yew-tree, not for any particular reason, but simply because it was the only thing within walking distance that seemed half-familiar. In the distance, the horizon delineating where the starry sky met the Earth was undoubtedly comprised by the ridge of Bancroft Scar, but he could not see the face of the inland cliff, so he could not see whether the rocky protrusions and wooded clefts followed the same pattern as those in his painting. The stars were doubtless the same ones that shone on Langstrade Hall in the nineteenth century after the Nativity, but they too seemed lost in the remote regions of the Heavens, and did not offer Michel any impression of homeliness. The yew was all he had.

When he got closer to the tree, he perceived that it was very ancient. It was thick in the trunk and very gnarled, with as many dead branches as living ones, although the living ones carried summer foliage. There was something shining through the ragged bark, apparent from the heartwood of the trunk, at about head height. He mistook it at first for a pale lantern, although he realized as he drew closer that the gleam was purely reflective. The glimmer did not originate from his own ghost-lantern, however, but from the stars in the sky and the three-quarter moon that was behind him in the west.

The moon would have stood directly above the chimneys of Langstrade Hall, had there been a Hall, but the Hall was lost in time. The reflected light seemed just as coquettish as the moon's own face, with its teasing quarter-shadow. Pale as the reflected light was, Michael realized that the object secured within the trunk of the tree was actually black in color. It was smooth and polished, but jet black.

Michael recognized the substance, in spite of its anomalous location, as obsidian: a glassy substance produced, he seemed to remember, by volcanoes, valued by sculptors for its sinister charm but notoriously difficult to work. He realized that the block of obsidian must have been integrated into the tree-trunk by the artifice of human hands: that it had been deliberately set into the wood, in order that the tree would actually grow around it, over a period of decades, imprisoning it and enclosing it. He could only presume that it had been done for religious reasons, in connection with some kind of pagan belief. The action had been intended to make the tree something more than a tree, to fit it with a kind of beacon...or a kind of magical window.

The music of the maze was still playing in Michael's head, although his ears were inactive. He could not hear any of the sounds of the world into which he had come, because sound waves made no apparent impact on his eardrums—but he *could* hear the music, and he could also see. If light passed through his eyes as easily as sound passed through his ears, then there had to be some other conduit of sensation that substituted for sight: a *second sight*, akin to the special sensitivities of somniloquists.

When he arrived in the imperfect shade of the tree, he tried to peer into the obsidian window, fully expecting to see nothing but a void.

He saw a man staring back at him: a man with no ears.

Even more remarkably, the man with no ears seemed to see him, and started with alarm.

"Don't be afraid," Michael said, reflexively, forgetting that he could not make any sound in this world that was not his own.

The fact that he made no actual sound did not seem to make a difference to the magical stone, which evidently transmitted his meaning regardless, relaying it to the earless man's mind without the need of any physical transmission. The other started again, evidently finding it difficult to obey the instruction.

"My name is Michael Laurel," Michael said. "Will you tell me yours?"

The other's distant lips moved. "Edward Kelley," was the substitute for sound that seemed to slips into Michael's brain, borne by the fateful music, which seemed irredeemably eerie by virtue of the *scordatura* effect.

"Edward Kelley?" Michael repeated.

"Edward Kelley?" echoed another voice, which Michael took for an echo inside his own consciousness, until it added: "Did you say *Edward Kelley*, Laurel?"

Michael turned his head, and saw Quentin Hope standing behind him, the phantom light of his phantom lantern making his phantom salmon-pink waistcoat shine weirdly and garishly bright in a gloomy world devoid of any other color.

"Yes," Michael said. "We are, I think, on the far side of his black stone—the one with which John Dee's skryer sought to communicate with angels. The far side in temporal terms, that is—it's just an element in the Maze."

"Of course," said Hope—and smiled. It was a genuine smile of amusement, slightly supercilious.

"But why does he have no ears?" Michael asked. "That makes no sense."

"Kelley had a misspent youth," Hope told him, glad to be playing the educator again. "He was convicted of forging the coin of the realm and his ears were cut off as a punishment—a relative light punishment, in those days, for such a heinous crime. One presumes that he was only forging sixpences, not sovereigns." The optimist giggled cheerfully, enjoying himself thoroughly.

He thinks this is a dream, Michael realized. *He thinks that he is asleep, enjoying a lucid dream, in which the day's remarkable events are stirring his imagination. He thinks that he is safe, and that he knows what he is doing. He is his confident, optimistic self— perhaps even more so than he ever feels free to be in waking life, no matter how hard he pretends.*

The painter stepped aside, with a slight bow. "This is your destiny, Mr. Hope," he said, politely. "This is your moment: the moment when your intellect might change the course of history for the better. You may inform John Dee's secret college of all the things its members need to add to their own resources, in order to bring the great tide of progress to its flood."

"I know that," Hope replied, gaily. "I know exactly what to say. I'm an angel, after all. My name is Hope."

Hope stepped up to the mysterious telegraph set up by the Mistress of the Labyrinth, by means of surrogate human hands that had only the vaguest idea of what they were trying to achieve. Without wasting an instant, the philosopher of progress began to make his own contribution of wisdom to the mighty tide that Michael had mentioned: the tide that would ultimately produce the time machine herself.

What would Escott say now? Michael wondered. *Would this confirm or falsify his conviction that progress is a misfortunate or malevolent force, driving humankind to Hellish enslavement?* But Escott was not here; the Mistress of the Labyrinth had been careful to separate the two rivals, in order that their interminable argument could not spoil her scheme.

Michael had just begun to wonder what ultimate objective the Mistress of the Labyrinth might have, and whether it was likelier to result in Hope's Euchronium Millennium or Escott's perpetual infernal torment, when he was impelled by a sudden, urgent *arpeggio* to take a sideways step.

He found himself on a battlefield.

The battle—somewhat to Michael's relief—was over, but he was thankful nevertheless that he was a ghost, incapable of any olfactory sensation, for he knew that the stink of death must have been appalling. Corpses lay strewn around, and the warriors still standing all had blood on their blades and bludgeons. Not that any of them was actually *standing*, in the sense of standing still; they were all moving, no longer purposefully, in the sense of striking out with murderous intent, but restlessly, possessed by an agitation that would not let them be still. They must have been exhausted, Michael knew—just as he had been exhausted himself what had recently seemed a little while ago—but there was something in them that would not let them pause. It was not, in their case, the music of the Maze, but something incarnate in their flesh: the residue of a killing frenzy.

There had been a battle of sorts—there was not the slightest doubt about that—but, as Michael scanned the arena with his insubstantial gaze, he was left in no doubt that it had been a direly one-sided affair. It had, in essence, been a massacre, although the fallen men had made what efforts they could to defend themselves. Their "weapons" still lay beside them: *sticks and stones*, Michael could not help thinking, although those that had metal components were actually crude agricultural implements of various sorts: spades, pitchforks and hoes, he presumed. Most were just improvised clubs.

The weapons carried by the victors were little more sophisticated, in terms of workmanship, but at least they had been specifically designed for use as weapons: bronze swords and metal-headed maces. The victors had shields too, and armor of a patchy sort, including crude metal helmets to protect their skulls. They did not resemble the pictures of Vikings that Michael had seen in the books he had been given as a child, but he guessed readily enough that that was what they were. They were raiders who had crossed the North Sea to England in search of plunder. Settlers would doubtless come in their wake, but these were just killers hunting in a pack, intent on pillage.

They had already done the first part of their work, but they had not yet passed on to hunt down the women and children who had fled the hopeless conflict, because they had not yet been rallied by their chief. They were moving about randomly, aimlessly, because they could not help but move, in spite of their weariness. The dire excitement of the slaughter had not yet let them go. Some were mounting a pretense of looking for men among the fallen who had only been stunned or crippled, in order to finish them off, but it was only a pretense. If anything moved, they would doubtless react, but they were moving themselves simply because they could not rest.

It was not until Michael moved again himself that anyone saw him—and then the automatic reaction came into play: the impulse to charge and kill, with brutal determination…but as soon as that first response had been formed into an intention, it was betrayed by another.

The slayers could not only see Michael—they could see that he could not and did not belong to their world. They could see that he was a ghost, armed with a bizarre light. They were in no doubt about that, even though it seemed highly probable that none of them had ever seen a ghost before. They saw him with their second sight rather than their eyes, and that special kind of sensation already carried the knowledge of what he was. These were men who believed implicitly in ghosts, and dreaded their appearance. These were men saturated since early infancy with the conviction that the sight of ghosts boded ill.

Michael was surprised to find that his first reaction to that awareness, as he saw the terror in the expressions of the men who beheld him, was sheer exultation. He delighted in his unprecedented ability to serve as a figure of alarm, to strike terror into the hearts of individuals who were—in spite of their filthiness and obvious brutality—his fellow men. When they began to flee, he was ecstatic. He could have danced with joy—but that would not have been appropriate to his new role, so he stood his ground instead and raised his free arm, pointing his pale forefinger first at one warrior, and then another, as if he were Death personified, selecting those he intended to take and calculating the order and the means by which he would proceed.

The victors fled in disarray—but they were not so stupid to drop their weapons as they did so. They still intended to fight another day, if they were allowed the opportunity to do so.

Only one man stood his ground. He was evidently the leader—the one man forbidden by his status to flee. He was no less terrified than the others, but he had no license to run away. He was the chief, and had to take the responsibility of confronting Death.

Michael walked toward the man who had not fled. The other was standing in front of a yew-tree. It was not the same yew-tree as the one in which unknown hands had set a magic block of obsidian, but it must have been growing in the same general area, no more than five yards from the other. The ridge of Bancroft Scar still provided a stable background to the unsteady arena.

The Viking did not even back up against the trunk of the tree. He simply raised his sword-arm, and pointed his bloodstained blade at Michael, much as Michael was pointing his fateful finger at him, as if instructing him to return to the dread Underworld from which he had presumably emerged.

At least, Michael assumed that was what the barbarian's words were intended to mean—but all he "heard" was meaningless jabber. The spoken words were the only "sounds" he could hear, but their employment of an alternative kind of sensation could not make them meaningful.

Unlike Edward Kelley, Emund Snurlson was not English; even by supernatural means, he could not speak English. His thoughts were as incomprehensible as the futile vibrations his vocal cords were imparting to the dead air.

Michael stopped, not because he was intimidated by a sword that could not possibly hurt him, but because he did not know what to do next, since nothing he could say would be understood by the angry warrior.

Snurlson made as if to lunge forward with his weapon, but thought better of it. He looked at Michael curiously, as if he were suddenly uncertain as to exactly what it was the spirit might want with him. The Viking's eyes were blue, and his hair was blond. His face was dirty and pockmarked, his clothes were filthy and ragged, and the bronze of his armor was stained with verdigris, but the color of his eyes and hair, wanly revealed by the equivocal light of the three-quarter moon, were suddenly reminiscent of the color of Cecilia Langstrade's eyes and hair.

The Langstrades are not Celts at all, Michael thought, wanting to laugh but suppressing the impulse. *They're Vikings. In terms of blood and bone, if not ideas, they're descended from the victors, not the vanquished. But what does that matter, in the hard currency of legend? They are, in the ultimate analysis, what they believe themselves to be, and what they aspire to be, not what the long-forgotten play of circumstance dictated that their fleshy heritage should be.*

We are human, not yew-trees, and we can choose our past as well as our future.

Emund Snurlson took a step toward the ghost that doubtless seemed to him to be heralding his doom, and raised his sword in protest against the threat of destiny. Again he spoke—or, rather, shouted—but again the meaninglessness of the words made them a mere discordant accompaniment to the music of the maze: something that no longer belonged to the pattern, and required to be excised.

That was when the second Earl of Langstrade stepped out from behind the bole of the yew-tree, and shouted a challenge of his own to Emund Snurlson. Langstrade was a ghost, of course, and Emund Snurlson could not possibly have understood the words he used, but the Viking knew and understood a challenge when he heard one, even when it emerged from the World Beyond.

To Michael, Langstrade looked utterly absurd, with a felt hat perched on his head and clad in a dinner-jacket, wielding his polished walking-stick, but he knew that the strange costume would probably make the ghostly newcomer seem all the more imposing, and all the more threatening, to the ill-clad Viking.

Snurlson moved sideways, so that he could keep both ghosts in view, unwilling to turn his back on either of the emissaries of the dead, but he was careful to move to his left, in order that his right hand—the one in which he held his sword—was directed toward the newcomer rather than Michael. The Viking had realized instantly that the newcomer was the one he had to fear more: the one who was actively seeking to do him physical harm.

Langstrade put down his lantern, and took his walking-stick in both hands.

Then, with a wonderfully theatrical gesture, Lord Langstrade drew his hands apart, and the walking-stick divided into two parts. The lower part revealed itself to be a sheath, and the upper part as a long dagger, which gleamed so strangely in the light of the lowered lantern that it resembled a shaft of golden light.

Michael chided himself for not having guessed before that Langstrade's favorite stick was a swordstick.

Langstrade paused momentarily, for effect, and then assumed the stance that his fencing-master must have taught him when he was a child, with his legs braced, his left arm on his hip, and his right arm extended horizontally. The dinner-jacket cramped his style slightly, but the hat more than made up for that, giving him just a hint of the casual dash of a Royalist cavalier. The poniard previously concealed in the sword-stick was not nearly as long as an épée, so the gesture had a hint of incongruity about it—but Emund Snurlson did not know that. Emund Snurlson knew nothing of the sport of fencing, and the ghost's pantomime must have seemed terribly ominous to him.

Michael knew that the phantom be could not actually cut through the Viking's flesh, and he knew that Snurlson must, on some level, know that too—but there was no mistaking the naked terror in Snurlson's eyes.

The barbarian did not attempt to imitate Langstrade's stance, or this theatricality. He simply charged, probably understanding how absurd it was to charge a ghost, but acting under the compulsion to do *something*, and incapable of formulating any more rational action.

It was all over in a flash. The wild, ungainly sweep of Emund Snurlson's blade might have taken Langstrade's head off, if it had been sharp enough and if Langstrade had been made of flesh and blood, but it went straight through the phantom form. Langstrade's phantom blade also went clean through the Viking's torso, as he thrust with practiced ease, scrupulously maintaining the horizontal attitude of his blade. It could not do any more physical damage than Snurlson's blade. Snurlson, however, was not a ghost but a ghost-seer. Snurlson knew just enough of the supposed ways of ghosts to be terrified of them, even though his own notions of propriety commanded him not to flee from them, and he knew just enough of the ways of fate to be utterly convinced of his doom.

When the phantom blade went through Emund Snurlson's heart, therefore, that heart stopped. Emund Snurlson fell down dead, slain by the second Earl of Langstrade, reaching insubstantially across an interval of a thousand years.

Langstrade looked at Michael, and said: "Father would be so proud."

"Indeed he would," Michael told him, feeling that this was a perfect opportunity to curry favor, and make a good impression.

Langstrade glanced behind him. "I wonder how Father knew about the tree, though," he said.

"I expect that he dreamed it," Michael said. "Just as you must have dreamed this moment, perhaps a hundred times before."

Langstrade frowned, and returned the blade of his swordstick to its sheath. "Do you think so?" he said. "I can never remember my dreams for more than a few moments after waking."

"You'll remember this one, I suspect," Michael said. "So will I—at least, I hope so."

"Can you still hear that music?" Langstrade asked. "Monti-carlo's damned violin has put it into my head, and I can't get it out, even though it can't really be playing."

"I can hear it," Michael confirmed. "It *is* playing, and it won't be giving way to Johann Sebastian Bach any time soon. We're in the Maze, and we'll be here until the Mistress of the Labyrinth has finished with us."

A strange expression crossed Langstrade's face then. "I'm Har-old Longstride!" he exclaimed. "*I*'m Harold Longstride—but how will anyone ever know? There's no one here to witness my triumph but you, and you're a ghost from the future, as I am."

"It doesn't matter," Michael told him. "Even if all these fallen men really are dead, the tale will be told. When the men who ran away creep back, and find their leader slain by supernatural means, they'll be forced to invent an explanation. Even if they haven't actu-ally seen you—and it's more than probable that more than one of them is watching us now from the cover of some distant thicket—they'll be forced to invent you. It doesn't matter how you acquire your eventual name; you're a legendary figure now. You are, or will be, the *real*—the one and only—Harold Longstride."

"Well," said Langstrade, picking up his lantern, "I'm proud of myself, too. We'd better get back, don't you think? I'm afraid you'll have to show me the way—I'm lost. Can you do that?"

"Yes, I think I can, if I follow the music," Michael said. "I think the way out is in *this* direction."

His intuition was sound. He stepped out of Emund Snurlson's world as easily as he had stepped into it. Either he had made a false step in the dance of time, though, or the Mistress of the Labyrinth still had work for him to do. The maze into which he had stepped was not made of hawthorn but of stone—and when he stepped back again, automatically, intending to return to the battlefield where Harold Longstride, Second Earl of Langstrade, now stood alone and victorious, he remained in that markedly different arena.

CHAPTER SEVENTEEN

DEDALUS AND THE BRAZEN HEAD

There was still a yew-tree in the space, although it was definitely not the same one, and it was definitely not growing in the same narrow region. There was still a starry sky, albeit one reduced to a square patch by the high stone walls, but that too was not the same one, in terms of the particular pattern that the stars displayed at the zenith. The lofty moon was now full, and seemed unnaturally large and yellow, although its pock-marked face was quite familiar.

The stone walls of the enclosure seemed uncomfortably close, claustrophobic even to a ghostly consciousness. There was no exit—no horizontal exit, at any rate. There was something set in the flag-stoned floor that might have been a trap-door leading down into a cellar, or a vast subterranean complex. It was difficult to be sure because the trap-door was closed.

I expect that I could descend through it if I wished, closed or not, Michael thought. *The solidity of the Earth is not what maintains me on its surface. I expect that I could descend all the way to the Earth's core, if I wanted to, and could master the trick of it—but why should I, when gravity has no purchase on me, and nothing lies that way to interest a man who has no credence in a literal Hell?*

The simple fact was that he had no wish to explore the subter-rains of the maze in which he now found himself. What he wanted to do was to hold a conversation with the man who was sitting on a bench under the yew-tree. Had it been daylight, the boughs of the tree—which must have been very ancient, since some of its twisted boughs were dead while others were decked in summer foliage—would have shaded the bench from hot sunlight. Michael did not doubt that the sun would have been hot by day. Because it was the dead of night, however, the man on the bench was not in need of shade; he had probably come up from the depths to sit down there because he could not sleep, and he could not sleep, in all likelihood, because there was something on his mind.

The man under the tree had been sitting with his head balanced on his fists, while his elbows were balanced on his knees, but when he saw Michael, the prisoner lifted his head interestedly. He seemed glad of the company—even the company of a ghost, and perhaps *especially* the company of a ghost.

Unlike the ill-fated Emund Snurlson, Dedalus the Engineer was not in the least frightened by the appearance of a ghost—even a ghost as peculiar as Michael must have seemed. Michael had no doubt that this was a man who could have looked at a ghost clad in a dinner-jacket and armed with a swordstick, with an oversized hat on his head, and felt nothing but welcome curiosity.

For once in his life, Michael bitterly regretted never having been forced to study the Greek of the ancients. Dedalus, as a Cretan of the Minoan Era, belonged to a society that had become legendary before the Greeks learned to write, and surely would not have spoken the Greek of Pericles and Plato, but there would probably have been enough similarity between his language and theirs to permit the exchange of a few meaningful words.

I wish Escott were here, Michael thought, but then changed his mind. He did not wish that Escott were there. He wanted this moment for himself.

Dedalus spoke, his manner and the inflection of his virtual speech suggesting that he was asking a question: *who are you?* perhaps, or *why are you here?*"

"My name is Michael Laurel," Michael said. "I was sent by the Mistress of the Labyrinth. I don't…."

He stopped, feeling foolish. He had been about to say that he didn't know why he had been sent, but he did. He knew exactly why he had been sent, and why it didn't matter that he couldn't speak the language of the doomed Minoan Empire. Escott was quite unnecessary.

Michael took a piece of paper from his waistcoat pocket, glad for once in his life that he was too poor to possess a second waistcoat into which to change after dinner. He unfolded the phantom piece of paper, while Dedalus—who had never seen an actual piece of paper—looked on with interest. Then Michael displayed Lady Langstrade's map of the Langstrade Maze to the interested engineer.

Dedalus was an artist as well as an engineer. Michael had every confidence that the other would look at the ghostly map with an artist's gaze, akin to his own, and that it would be engraved on his memory within a matter of seconds.

"Can you hear the music?" Michael asked, although he knew perfectly well that Dedalus could not understand what he was saying. "Of course you can. Like Pietro Locatelli, you've always been on the brink of hearing it, waiting patiently for it to begin. You won't be able to build this one, I fear—not in Cretan stone, at any rate—but you'll be able to take the image in your head when you fly away. Not literally, alas—I'm presuming that the Greeks were no more scrupulous in their myth-making than any other Romanticists—but figuratively. You *will* escape; I'm sure of that."

Dedalus had memorized the plan of the maze, and was now looking up at the face of his ghostly visitor, with dark eyes that seemed even darker in the moon-shadow of the yew. He seemed to be intent on listening, even though he could not understand the words that Michael was speaking.

"If I were you," Michael said, as he folded up the piece of paper and returned it to his waistcoat pocket. "I'd be careful to take a souvenir with me when I finally obtained my release—a few seeds from the yew-tree, perhaps. I'd plant them when I finally reached the terminus of my flight. That way, there might be descendants of this very yew-tree growing in some distant corner of the world, retaining a symbol of your escape through the generations, for thousands of years."

Dedalus smiled, with simple pleasure rather than understanding. He set his head slightly to one side, as if to listen to distant strains of music.

"Me too," Michael said. "We're not the beginning and the end, though—we're just different aspects of the beginning. I can only hope that my beginning is as fruitful as yours, and I'm not at all sure that I can trust the Mistress of the Labyrinth, but what choice do I have? Give my regards to Theseus, if you ever get to meet him. I've got to go now—I'd like to get home before midnight chimes in Cribden church, because I have to make an early start tomorrow, on my painting of personified Folly. Unlike you, I can simply step through the wall of your prison."

That was what he did, hoping to find grasping, hawthorn hedges on the other side of the stone wall—and that was what he found. Indeed, he found himself inside a stout hedge, completely entombed in densely-packed and thorny branches. He had stepped through such hedges before, but always without pausing. Now he was suspended within one, and it was impossible not to feel trapped. He knew that it was absurd, but he felt panic rising within him, vertiginously. He was suddenly very conscious of the thorns projecting at every angle *within* his ghostly form, penetrating his sense of himself, if not his actual self, like so many daggers. He was conscious, too, of the fact that the hedge was *alive*.

This hedge, he realized, was different from the others. There was a sense in which this hedge was just as much a phantom as he was: a dream-hedge, capable of hurting him—if it so desired.

Emund Snurlson, he remembered, had been killed by a phantom blade. Immaterial as he was, the consciousness of matter could still harm him, if he allowed himself to give way to fear. If he allowed himself to become convinced that he was trapped, he *would* be trapped. What was worse, if the Mistress of the Labyrinth wanted to convince him of that fact, then he would not have the strength to resist her desire.

He was, however, still under orders to be brave. Emund Snurlson the Viking had only been forbidden to run away by his status as a chieftain; Michael Laurel the lover had been instructed by the object of his adoration to *be* brave.

In any case, was he not a hero now? Was he not a Theseus, who had discharged not one but three missions in the Maze, even if Hope had actually taken on the burden of informing the secret college and Lord Langstrade had slain Emund Snurlson. He had been their guide, a surrogate for the Mistress of the Maze—and he had given the Maze to Dedalus without requiring Escott to explain to the sage what he was doing. The Mistress of the Labyrinth could not possibly want to harm him—and had, indeed, made a formal promise to protect him, to the best of her ability. Real or virtual, this maze had no intention of hurting him.

Michael calmed his panic, and banished his impending dizziness. He swam through the broad hedge, and emerged into an alleyway in what felt like the Langstrade Maze. It could not actually be an alleyway in the Langstrade Maze, however, because no alleyway in the Langstrade Maze had been blocked in 1822 by a huge figure of a human head, seemingly forged in some coppery alloy akin to bronze or brass.

Michael did not need a map to discover where in the Maze he was, and how to find the exits; the music told him all that he needed to know. He knew perfectly well, simply by means of thinking rationally, that the giant head could not imprison him, because logic dictated that if it blocked the way to the external exit, then it could not possibly block the way to the internal one—and in any case, he could step through the hedges if he wanted to, for he was still a ghost and he had no fear of being trapped in a Maze that did not intend to hurt him.

Even so, Michael felt that the brazen head *was* blocking his progress: that it posed a sphinxian riddle that he needed to solve, if he were to succeed in returning to the actual Maze and the moment he had left behind: the moment he still thought of as *the present*.

The brazen head was the head of a man: a rather thin and fleshless man, to judge by its proportions and jutting contours. It was not until it raised its brazen eyelids, however that Michael realized whose head it was, at least in effigy.

The brazen eyes that looked at him were blank and uniform, but Michael did not doubt that the mind behind them could see him, and would understand him if he spoke. "Mr. Escott?" he said, sounding the syllables as a question rather than a statement more out of politeness than uncertainty.

"Laurel," the head replied, moving its brazen lips with difficulty. "I'm having the most frightful nightmare. Have you ever become conscious within the course of a dream, and felt that you absolutely had to move, in peril of your life, but could not find the strength in your limbs to lift a finger?"

"Yes," Michael said. "Everyone has dreams of that sort, I believe."

"Not quite like this one," Escott's effigy assured him. "When I have had such dreams before, it has always been a simple matter of physical movement, but this nightmare is lying upon me with far greater mass and ingenuity than that. I feel that I am stuck in time, Laurel, not only unable to move my limbs, but also unable to rejoin the fleeting moment. I have been *left behind*, Laurel. I am *stuck in the past*. I cannot get back *in time*. If you cannot help me, Laurel, than I shall die here. I shall be lost forever, and no one will ever know what became of me. I shall be a mystery."

"Then I must try to help you, Mr. Escott," Michael said, firmly. "Do you, perchance, have any idea as to how I might do that?"

"Alas, no," said Escott. "That is but one more facet of the nightmare: I know that I am direly in need of help, but I have no idea how that help might be rendered. It is an allegory of life, is it not? We go through life nursing yearnings that will not let us rest, but which we know not how to fulfill?"

"Do we?" Michael queried. He did not add: *But I have fulfilled mine—or will, if fate does not intervene to raise immovable obstacles between myself and Cecilia.*

"Yes we do," said the pessimist, with gloomy conviction. "It is the human condition, in a nutshell—a Shakespearean nutshell, where we might be able to imagine ourselves kings of infinite space, but in which *bad dreams* continually remind us of our narrow limitations. I have wasted my time, Laurel. For forty years and more, I have wasted my time and my luck. Had opportunity knocked, I would not have heard it. I have lived a life of idleness, if not of luxury, playing the scholarly amateur, perennially posing as an envious and sarcastic commentator on the endeavors of others. I have taken delight in misery, Laurel—including my own—and now I am condemned to this eternal punishment because of it. I have been captured by the Mistress of the Labyrinth, who is indeed more closely akin to Circe than to Athene, and she has turned me into a brazen dragon. I am gripped by a nightmare, and it will not let me go. I do not claim to deserve your help, Laurel, but I need it, and would be grateful for it. Can you help me?"

Michael felt sure that he could, if only he could figure out a way—but nothing came to mind. The *capriccio* was still playing in the depths of his consciousness, but it offered no clue. "You must help me to help you, if you can, Mr. Escott," he said. "You are, after all, a scholar. You know far more about the world's mysteries than I do, or ever shall. You must help me to figure out your own."

Escott's effigy tried to smile, but failed. "Alas," he said, "my knowledge of legendary brazen heads in somewhat limited. Apart from the fact that there was a giant man of bronze named Talos, the last survivor of an ancient race, who was charged with guiding the island of Crete, I know of only one other. Even Talos might not have existed, for some subversive antiquarians claim that he was merely a bronze bull cast for King Minos, who had an unusual fondness for such creatures until his wife was stricken by her unfortunate obsession. Hope and I have been to Crete, you know, and explored the remains of the Labyrinth that Dedalus built, and where he was imprisoned."

"I was in Crete myself just a little while ago," Michael said, pensively, "if only in spirit. What is the other legend?"

"One of the great scholars of the Middle Ages—some say Roger Bacon, others Albertus Magnus—is reputed to have forged a brazen head by alchemical means, to serve him as a oracle. He waited for a long time to hear it speak, and grew weary, so he went to bed, commanding a servant to wake him if the head should speak. The boy waited, and eventually the head said: 'Time is', but then fell silent again. After a moment's hesitation, the servant decided that it was not worth waking his master for the sake of such a small pronouncement. After a long interval, the head spoke again, saying: 'Time was', but then fell silent once again. After a moment's hesitation, the boy reached the same decision as before. After another long interval, the head said: 'Time is past.' This time, the servant ran to wake his master, but it was too late—when they returned, the head had exploded, and shattered into tiny pieces. I would not like to think that such a fate awaits me, but I fear it, Laurel. I fear that I might shatter into a million shards."

"Time is; time was; time is past," Michael repeated. "I knew I'd heard that somewhere before when the somniloquist pronounced the words. The Mistress of the Labyrinth said it, when she volunteered her apology. The legend is, I suppose, a parable of inevitability—but that cannot have been what *she* meant, for her entire *raison d'être* is to play fast and loose with supposed inevitability. She has sent me back through the maze to show its plan to Dedalus, to witness the slaying of Emund Snurlson and to introduce Hope to Edward Kelley, just as she had earlier sent Signor Monticarlo's music spiraling through the maze into the dreaming minds of Pietro Locatelli and Dedalus. All these things had already happened, but still she had to *make* them happen, else the world as it is would not be the world as we know it. Perhaps, Mr. Escott, we have unmade a world tonight—a world in which Gregory Marlstone's time machine could never have been invented—in order to preserve *the world as we know it*."

"You promised that the world as we know it might be saved," Escott reminded him, "while you were not yet your present self, or its ghost. You asked us for heroism. It seems that I have been unable to provide it, and perhaps I must pay the price. I congratulate you, though, on your achievements. At least it was you that the Mistress of the Labyrinth sent to inform me, not Hope. He's a fine fellow, and the best friend I have in the world, but he does take an unholy delight in gloating whenever he obtains the slightest advantage over me. How delighted he will be to have made his contribution to the tide of progress!"

"So he will," murmured Michael. "I dare say that he will ask for Miss Cecilia's hand in marriage while the wave of exultation bears him aloft, if we ever get back to 1822."

"Why should he not?" Escott asked, innocently. "Miss Cecilia is a lovely woman, and will make a fine wife for some lucky fellow."

"I know that," said Michael. He did not want to reveal the reason why he did not want Quentin Hope to do any such thing, even though he was more than half-convinced that no such proposal could ever be accepted. "The point is, Mr. Escott, to extract you from your nightmare, if it can be done, and we have wasted too much time already. Time is, was, and is past, and we do not want to miss the moment that we call the present, if we still have a chance of catching it. I think I know what needs to be done, but we shall have to work together, since neither of us can achieve it alone."

"What do you propose?" Escott's effigy asked.

"I propose to step through the brazen head," Michael told him. "As I do so, I shall attempt to gather you up and carry you out of it with me—but you must hold on to me tightly, Mr. Escott, and not let go, however dizzy or sick you might feel, just as I must hold on to you."

"Will that work?" asked the pessimist, dubiously.

"I hope so."

"Aren't you afraid that you might become trapped in my nightmare as well—gorgonized in time?"

"I wasn't quite as afraid of that," Michel said, a trifle waspishly, "as I am now that you've explicitly raised the possibility."

"I'm sorry," Escott said, contritely.

"Apology accepted," Michael said. So saying, he set down his ghost-lantern, rubbed his hands together, braced himself and hurled himself forward, setting off like a sprinter in a race.

It was like diving into an ice-cold pool of dark water, although that was obviously a reaction of his own mind rather than any physical property of the metal from which the effigy was forged. There was no human figure within the head, imprisoned there like Dedalus in his stone cage; Escott's consciousness had been dissolved and dissipated. It had not exploded and shattered, but it had certainly robbed of its fundamental integrity. The rescue was not a matter, for either of them, of grabbing on to one another with their arms, or catching hold of one another's clothing. In order to "gather Escott up" and "carry him out", Michael had to take possession of him in quite a different way—or, perhaps more accurately, to allow the other to take possession of him.

For one brief moment, Michael and Escott were not two phantoms but one; not two intellects, but one; not two wellsprings of emotion but one—and that, in itself, was a source of such panic and nausea as Michael had never known possible.

Michael had felt his mind crowded before, but only by other versions of himself—thoughts he had already entertained, or would entertain in a very short lapse of time. Even that had made him feel dizzy and sick—but sharing his mind with a different person entirely, a man with thoughts and feelings and ideas very different from his own, was a much more painful and dangerous experience, which threatened to blow his sense of identity to smithereens.

Had Escott been correct in his fear, and Michael had been trapped inside the head too, it would have been unbearable. The fusion would have destroyed them both—but Michael had made a decisive leap, and he was not about to stumble. As soon as the initial bound reached its terminus he launched himself into one more gigantic stride and burst out of the brazen head—like Athene from the head of Zeus, one of them could not help thinking—but with another soul contained within himself, which lost no time at all in wriggling out of him, desperate to be free.

Escott's reconstituted phantom collapsed, and lay supine on the grassy path between two tall hedges. Michael remained standing, though slightly annoyed that he could not lean on the hedge for support, and took a deep breath of whatever phantoms thrived on instead of air.

The lantern he had set down before jumping was still on the ground, five yards away. The obstacle had vanished. The maze was clear.

But how did there come to be an obstacle at all? Michael wondered. *It surely could not have been the Mistress of the Labyrinth who planted it, for it's entirely in her interests to let us move freely. Perhaps there is a Minotaur in the maze, after all—a monster intent on undoing her work. This business is not finished yet. Indeed, it will not even begin, in earnest, until noon tomorrow. All of this night's bold endeavors were mere groundwork—preparation for the challenge to come.*

Escott opened his phantom eyes, and sat up, still apparently marveling at the fact that he was free. He had lost his own lantern, though, and the blue satin of his waistcoat was ripped so badly that its solid equivalent, if it inherited the damage, would probably defy any attempt at repair.

"Are we home?" Escott asked. "Is this 1822?"

"I don't know," Michael told him. "If I'm not mistaken, I can see a distant glimmer lantern-light filtering through the hedges, which indicates that someone is moving along one of the parallel pathways—but I cannot tell how many lanterns there might be, or whether their light is real or phantom. Perhaps we have only to step through the hedges in order to rejoin our flesh and blood and permit the present moment to reaffirm its grip on our consciousness—but I'm a novice in this business, and I don't know anything for sure."

"But if we can rejoin our flesh and blood, it will all be over?" Escott said, with an altogether uncharacteristic surge of optimism.

"No," Michael told him, with doleful certainty. "The real catastrophe, I fear, is yet to arrive."

CHAPTER EIGHTEEN

FURTHER ENCOUNTERS
IN THE LANGSTRADE MAZE

Escott's ghost was not yet ready to resume its perambulations, so Michael stepped through the hedge on his own in order to discover what the filtered light was. It was the light of a single lantern: a material lantern, held aloft by a material person, who seemed all the more material by virtue of who she was.

"Lady Phythian?" he said, in frank astonishment.

The widow, who was still clad in her evening-dress, peered at him in frank disappointment. "Mr. Laurel?" he said. "I was looking for ghosts. Tonight, I thought, I would be bound to find one."

Michael thought for a moment that he might have returned to solidity without being aware of it as he stepped out of the hedge, so he thrust his lantern into the branches yet again, meeting no resistance. The phantom light was snuffed out.

"I am a ghost," he said, not to annoy Lady Phythian but to express his puzzlement. Then a thought occurred to him. "What year is this?" he asked, thinking that this might be one of the earlier years in which the ghost-seers had come in search of her fugitive phantoms. He realized even before she answered, however, that he was being foolish. Lady Phythian had not known his name prior to 1822, and would surely have mentioned a meeting like this one in the story she had told in the railway carriage.

"Don't be silly, Mr. Laurel," the widow retorted. "Where are the others?"

"I don't know," Michael told her. "Mr. Escott was close at hand a few moments ago, but the maze keeps shifting. It's a long time since I've seen Hope or Lord Langstrade." He had to suppress a giggle as he noticed the double meaning in his last remark."

"I meant the others with whom I came into the Maze," Lady Phythian said, irritated by his mistake. "Emily, Cecilia, and Signorina Monticarlo. We heard music. Emily said that it must by Signor Monticarlo's violin, but Carmela swore that she would know her father's playing anywhere, and that it must be the ghost of Pietro Locatelli. She seemed very frightened—we should not have brought her with us, I suppose, but Emily had decided that there ought to be four of us, and she did want to come. She told us on the train, if you remember, that she would like to see a ghost. I must have taken a wrong turn somehow, for we became separated. The Maze seems exceptionally confusing tonight, although I confess that I have never been entirely sure of myself while within it. Even Cecilia, who knows it so well, seemed uncertain of her direction."

"Cecilia is lost in the Maze?" Michael queried, feeling a sudden stab of alarm.

"Yes. I think it was Cecilia who first proposed to her mother that if the ghosts of Langstrade were actually images of real individuals, cast back in time by the effects of Mr. Marlstone's time machine, there ought to be four of us. Heatherington provided us with lanterns, although he clearly disapproved, and we set off bravely, as I have done before on many an occasion. I must confess, however, that my bravery has faltered slightly since I found myself alone. That has never happened before."

So there really were eight lanterns in the Maze, Michael thought, *divided into two groups of four, seemingly following one another as they progressed through the Maze. But what did the Mistress want with Cecilia, Lady Langstrade, and Carmela? What has she done with them? Or has the Minotaur caught and devoured them?* The idea of Cecilia gorgonized in bronze was too horrible to contemplate.

"Don't worry, Lady Phythian," he said. "I'll search for them, and I'll find them, with the music's aid. Can you find your way to the center?"

"I think so," the dowager replied. "If I can't, will you come back and find me too, Mr. Laurel?"

"Yes I will," Michael promised—and stepped back through the hedge from which he had emerged a few moments before, with only one thought in his mind: to find Cecilia. For the first time, he addressed the Mistress of the Labyrinth directly, and addressed her as if she really were a goddess and not a machine: "Please," he said, in an agonized whisper. "I've done your bidding—now take me to Cecilia, I beg you."

He stepped through another hedge, and found himself face to face with the object of his desire. Like Lady Phythian, she was made of flesh and blood, and seemed far more relieved than frightened by the sudden sight of him.

"Michael!" she said. "Thank God!"

He did not take the trouble to correct her. "Are you all right?" he asked her, urgently.

"Yes, of course," she said, "but how…." That, presumably, was when she realized what he was. After a brief and fearful pause, she added: "Are you dead, then?"

"I certainly hope not," he said, but swiftly added: "and I have no reason to think so. I have temporarily mislaid my flesh, it seems, but I believe that it is safe and sound—probably asleep, though fully charged with some kind of Mesmeric magnetism, and dreaming with more authenticity than it has ever dreamed before. Marlstone's time machine is gaining power, it seems, and reconstructing history to ensure her own invention—but what her further ambitions are, I have no idea, nor do I know what kind of climax she anticipates at noon tomorrow, when she is fully activated."

"Catastrophe is inevitable," Cecilia quoted, "but the world might yet be saved. The invasion of the present by the future, and the past by the present. The world as *we* know it might be saved, but if heroic action falls, the Era of Change will commence, and its dread empire will not easily be set aside. That's what your future self said in the *séance*. It was all real, wasn't it? Dr. Carp was angry, but that was just because he didn't realize what was happening. It was all real. It *is* real."

"Yes, it is—for the time being," Michael said. "The present has invaded the past…and the future, I suspect, has begun to invade the present, setting ghost-traps that might capture some of us and impede the progress of the rest. The Maze has become direly difficult, my love, and we shall not easily find our way through it, even with the aid of Ariadne's thread."

"My love?" she echoed. Her tone was unusually—and, indeed, uncannily—sober when she added: "Yes, I am your love, am I not? But we have not yet contrived to find a moment to ourselves alone, in the flesh—and if I were not convinced that this is some kind of waking dream, I would be terrified even by *that* thought, the most desirous of all."

"Do you know how to reach the center of the Maze?" Michael asked.

"Yes, of course," she replied. "It's through that gap just a few yards behind you. Someone must have got there ahead of us, for I can see the glimmer of at least one lantern."

"I have to go back," Michael said. "I promised Escott, and Lady Phythian, and must honor my word—but I will meet you there as soon as humanly possible."

"Humanly?" she challenged—but there was actually a chuckle in her supplementary voice, and a sparkle in her eye that might as easily have been a gleam of phantom light as a reflection from her lantern.

"Or superhumanly," he assured her. "I'm a hero now, and invulnerable to common harm."

"Be careful of your heel," she said. "Everyone has a weakness."

He was impatient not to delay any longer, and tried to step back into the hedge in order to return to Lady Phythian—but the music that had been enabling him to move, and assisting him to find his way, suddenly stopped. It did not seem to him that the *capriccio* had reached its end, but rather that Pietro Locatelli's ghost had been interrupted in its playing. Michael thought the latter more likely, for he felt that there were things still undone, preparations still unmade. He thought that he could sense the frustration of the Mistress of the Labyrinth, a hitch in her painstakingly-laid thread. Suddenly, the life of the Maze seemed discordant, as if some evil spirit that had been lurking within it had begun to breathe fire.

Instead of fulfilling his promises, as he yearned to do, Michael's consciousness was rudely precipitated back into his flesh.

It was a horrid sensation.

For a long moment, suspended somewhere between instantaneity and eternity, two variant consciousnesses battled for possession of the moist grey matter of his brain. They were both versions of himself, far less alien to one another than he and Escott had been when their ghosts had briefly fused, but they were nevertheless not the same, and their fusion was direly difficult. To call it nightmarish was an understatement, and the process flooded the fleshy host with dire alarm and awful sickness.

The body that was trying to contain that hellish combat collapsed unconscious, and would not consent to wake up again until the conflict was settled—but awaken it eventually did.

This happens every time I wake up, Michael reminded himself. *Every dream-self that forms in my sleep battles briefly for possession of my mind before I wake—but those dream-selves are easily banished, and mostly easily forgotten. This time, it is the dream-self that has prevailed. I am still, in greater part, the ghost I was, and the less adventurous individual that kept possession of my flesh has faded from memory. If only the process were not so cruelly exacting…and if it happened often, how could I help but go mad?*

Slowly, he sat up, and rubbed his sticky eyes.

He was in the Maze, exactly where he had just met Cecilia, a few yards from the gap that gave entry to the center. His lantern was set on the ground beside him. It was one of four. Three other men were sitting up, just as he was, in similar bewilderment.

"What was *that*?" Lord Langstrade demanded, looking down sorrowfully at his soiled dinner-jacket. "I've had the *strangest* dream—but I've never woken up feeling as bad as *this* before."

"Something knocked me down," said Quentin Hope. "A blast of wind, or a chord in that strange music—which has now fallen silent, I see. I've never experienced such shock, or such agony—but I don't seem to be injured."

Escott merely groaned, as if to imply that his own agony must have been far worse, since he could not even speak of it.

"Where are we?" Langstrade asked. "Are we lost?"

"No," Michael said. "We're not lost. We're only a few yards from the exit to the center. There's lantern-light visible, slanting obliquely through the gap. Let me go first, to see what there is to be seen—if the sight is too terrible to behold, the rest of you will be able to beat a retreat without confronting it."

"That's all very well," said Escott, gloomily, "but how shall we find our way out without you to guide us?"

"Trust yourselves," Michael advised them. Presumably, they did, because when he stood up and moved forward to cover the last few yards to the exit, none of his companions went with him.

There was a lantern set on the ground, no more than a dozen feet away from the exit. Three others were held aloft on the edge of the lawn, in front of the drawbridge to the Keep. Michael stepped forward into the gap, raising his own lantern above his head in order to increase his field of vision.

Someone immediately picked up the lantern that had been set down, and held it up so that her face was as fully illuminated is his.

"Michael?" said Cecilia. "Is it *really* you?" Her voice dropped to a whisper. "When you…when your *ghost* didn't come back, I was worried…."

"Yes, it's me," Michael said. "In the flesh."

The other three lanterns within the central area of the maze were being carried by the younger Lady Langstrade, Lady Phythian and Carmela Monticarlo. Evidently, Lady Phythian had found her own way to the center, and had been able to rejoin her companions.

"We were expecting ghosts from the distant past," Cecilia said, in a tone that held more disappointment than relief. "We were promised Harold Longstride, Edward Kelley and Pietro Locatelli, but we've seen no one unfamiliar, although we've heard the strains of a phantom violin."

"We had slightly more success," Michael told her. He raised his voice. "Come forward, Lord Langstrade, Hope and Escott—let us do what we must and scatter as we emerge, so that Lady Phythian might see us, more-or-less dimly, three, seven and eleven years ago. We ought to be grateful, I suppose, that we are now the shadow-casters, and no longer the fugitive shadows." *The past is in place now*, he thought, *but the battle to sustain it has not yet been joined.*

"How brave you are!" said Cecilia, as the other three maze-walkers emerged, breaking formation as they did so. "You must have thought that we were ghosts, and yet you came into the heart of the maze anyway!"

"How brave *you* are," Michael riposted. "You must have thought that *we* were ghosts, and yet you stood your ground as a sentry at the entrance to the maze, waiting to watch us emerge and challenge us."

Lady Phythian meanwhile, had turned to confront Hope and Escott, and to scold them like the naughty boys there were. "Did I not tell you, in the carriage, that there were eight lanterns, held aloft by human forms? Fireflies, indeed!"

"The fireflies were none of *our* invention, my dear lady," Hope reminded her. "We always knew that the suggestion was ridiculous."

Perfectly ridiculous, Michael thought.

The door of the Keep opened then, as the ladies must have been expecting it to do before Michael and his companions arrived, and Gregory Marlstone stepped out. He was no ghost, but he was no less terrible an apparition for that. His eyes were haggard, his features drawn, and his movements were oddly jerky, like those of a marionette impelled by invisible strings.

Michael noticed that there was a tray on the drawbridge just outside the door, which bore a small stack of empty plates and two stone jugs. Someone—presumably a servant, acting on the bidding of the ever-thoughtful Heatherington—had brought food and drink to the beleaguered inventor in order that he might not be driven mad while he worked by hunger and thirst. A suggestion of madness seemed to have attained him anyway, alas.

"You must all go away," Marlstone said. "Far away. The demonstration is cancelled. The problem now is not to start her working but to stop her. I've been trying all day to disengage the mechanism, but I can't do it. She keeps playing tricks with time, and everything I do is undone, everything I attempt anticipated, everything I think of falsified. She's running amok, and I'm helpless. You must all leave—in the diligence if you can. If you can reach York before morning, you must catch the train to London. You can't escape her reach entirely, but her power must diminish the further you are from the center of her field. You will doubtless be subject to any alterations she can induce in the past, but you might still escape the full intensity of her grip, if you flee. Go! Go *now*! I must stay, but I have a moral duty not to expose anyone else to the peril of my error. I must try to save the world, but you must save yourselves. Run, I implore you, as fast and far as you can."

"I think, Mr. Marlstone," Lord Langstrade said, steadily enough, "that you have had a nightmare. We have had strange dreams ourselves, but the ghostly music has stopped now, and the world has set itself to rights again. You ought to come back to the Hall with us, and get some sleep."

"You don't understand," Marlstone said. "The ripples have calmed, for the moment, but it's only a pause. Noon tomorrow has yet to arrive, and she no longer needs me to activate her field. She's in control now—and I have no idea what she intends to do, or why. Indeed, I doubt that she is capable of intention or motive. She's only a machine, after all. It's possible—probable, even—that she is being manipulated, guided by some other intelligence, elsewhen in time. I don't know how, because it shouldn't be possible, given the pitch of the fundamental and the temporal distribution of available resonance-points, but something has *got into her*—something terrible, I think. I have no idea what will happen at noon tomorrow, but I fear that it might destroy the world as we know it, once and forever."

"We've already discussed that at some length," Hope informed him, serenely, "but there's nothing to fear, provided that we put our faith in progress. If your dark mistress requires any further assistance to secure that progress, I shall be only too glad to help. Langstrade's right—you'd do better to go to bed and get a good night's sleep. Tomorrow might be a long and arduous day."

"As your hostess," Lady Langstrade put in, "I feel entitled to demand that you do as you're asked, Mr. Marlstone. This is my husband' party, after all—you're a guest, and have the obligations of a guest, just as we have the obligations of a host and hostess. Come back to the Hall, and start afresh in the morning, when you've rested and had breakfast."

Marlstone opened his mouth as if to reply in anger and anguish. What the inventor almost said, Michael felt certain, was: "You're all mad!" He did not pronounce the fatal words, though. He must have realized, just in time, that Lady Langstrade was absolutely right. He was a guest in her home, and he did have obligations under the rules of etiquette, just as she had—and without the rules of etiquette, civilization would collapse, just as surely as it would if the threads of Time were cut, and all its human marionettes simply collapsed. Besides which, any such remark would have been bound to smack of the pot calling the kettle black.

Carmela Monticarlo took a step forward on to the drawbridge, and smiled at the inventor. "Will you take my arm, Mr. Marlstone?" she asked. "Will you be kind to escort me through the Maze." It was the first slight slip she had made in her use of the English language, so far as Michael could recall.

It was the kind of request that a gentleman could not refuse. Meekly, Gregory Marlstone stepped forward. He was evidently exhausted, and befuddled by lack of sleep, but he understood the obligations that one fellow guest owed another, according to the code of politeness.

"That's right," said Lord Langstrade, approvingly, waving his walking-stick in the air. "Let's all get some sleep, and worry about the end of the world in the morning."

CHAPTER NINETEEN

THE MORNING AFTER THE NIGHT BEFORE

The next morning, Michael got up at five-thirty, washed and dressed, and went down to breakfast on the stroke of six. He found Gregory Marlstone already in the breakfast-room, standing up and haranguing Heatherington. The other guests were apparently still in bed.

"You *must* make absolutely certain that no one comes into the Maze this morning," the inventor was saying to the butler, insistently. "It's absolutely imperative that I be left alone while I make one last attempt to stop my time machine and prevent catastrophe. If you can, you must persuade the guests to leave, but the one thing you *must* do, even if you cannot do anything else, is to forbid them to come into the Maze."

"I fear, sir," the butler replied, his politeness so scrupulous as to be icy, "that I have no authority to forbid anyone to enter the Maze, or to go anywhere else in the grounds. Only Lord Langstrade can issue orders of that sort, and I can do no more than pass on your request, in order that he might decide for himself whether to act upon it."

"That's not good enough, you insufferable *machine*!" Marlstone complained.

"Let him alone, Mr. Marlstone," Michael said, as he sat down at the table and helped himself to bread and marmalade. "He's right, as you know perfectly well, and it's unworthy of you to rail at him like that."

Marlstone rounded on the newcomer. "What has it got to do with you?" he demanded, intemperately. "You're just some fool of a painter, who doesn't even know when he's sticking his head in a lion's mouth, and is too stupid to care!"

"Sit down and eat something," Michael retorted, mildly. "If you're going to spend the next six hours laboring like Hercules to save the world, you owe it to the world to keep your strength up. Thank you." The last two words were addressed to Heatherington, who had taken advantage of Marlstone's distraction to pour a cup of tea.

Marlstone looked for a moment as if he might explode, but he still had enough presence of mind to collect himself and sit down. Heatherington poured him a cup of tea as well, wearing a contemptuous expression on his face that spoke volumes.

"You intend to resume work on your painting, don't you?" the inventor said to Michael.

"Of course I do," Michael said. "It's what I came to do. Do you really think it will make an atom of difference whether I'm standing at my easel, playing billiards with Lord Langstrade or fleeing southwards in a railway carriage when the clock in Cribden Church strikes noon?"

Marlstone simply shook his head, and said: "You're a fool."

"No, Mr. Marlstone, I'm not," Michael said, placidly, in between mouthfuls. "I might not have had a university education, like you, Mr. Hope and Mr. Escott, but I'm not a fool. In fact, I think I understand the nature of time as well as you do, if not better, even though I don't know the first thing about the mathematics of metastatic hypersynchronicity, intertemporal gravity and the harmonics of the temporal ether, or the corollaries of the law of conservation of non-identity."

Marlstone was taken aback by Michael's apparent confidence, and narrowed his eyes suspiciously, as if he thought that Michael might be mocking him. "*What* do you understand?" he demanded, pugnaciously.

"I understand that the only moment that really exists is the present one," Michael said, speaking slowly, although he was not making it up as he went along. Indeed, the idea had emerged into his mind while he was still in the margins of sleep, and had gradually clarified itself while he washed and dressed, bringing with it the conviction of revelation. "Everything that moment contains is, of course, the product of the past, just as everything it portends is the substance of the future, in the same way that everything I am—just like every other human being—is the sum of all the accidents of happenstance that have befallen me and all the choices I've made, while everything I do is calculated to produce some future result. The fact remains, though, that everything there is, simply *is*, and is confined within the moment of the present: a single incessant instant of *becoming*, too brief to be measured and imperceptible in itself, because all that we can ever see, let alone remember, is the ghost that it leaves behind. That single, ever-changing moment is the summary of all past existence, and the prelude to eternity; that is its nature and its essence."

"Very poetic," said Marlstone, with a slight sneer. "Where did you read all that?"

"I didn't," Michael said. "I worked it out for myself." He suspected that he might be claiming a little too much credit, and that the revelation might have been a gift from the Mistress of the Labyrinth, but he still felt entitled to claim some of the credit for "working it out".

"But how does it help to solve the problem?" Marlstone wanted to know.

"I didn't say that it helped," Michael told him. "I just said that I understood something of the nature of time. I understand that the moment of becoming is evolving toward some kind of crisis, and that what happens when that crisis erupts will somehow redetermine all of the past that it seems to have left behind, and all of the future that it seems to imply. I don't know what will happen to us when the crisis comes, and I don't know if it's even possible for the human mind to imagine it, but I do believe that we needn't and mustn't panic, if we're to play a part in the reconfiguration of the future that the crisis will facilitate. We ought to stay calm, and sane, and polite—and do what we came here to do."

"In your case, paint a picture of the Keep?" Marlstone said, sarcastically.

"Exactly," Michael said.

"What I came here to do," Marlstone informed him, loftily, "is a great deal more difficult than that." He drained his tea-cup, although the care he had to take in order to leave the residual leaves behind undermined the gesture's capacity to emphasize his point.

"Perhaps it was," Michael agreed, mildly, politely refraining from any suggestion that Marlstone might have been a mere puppet, invented by the Mistress of the Labyrinth for the purpose of her own self-construction.

Marlstone buttered a slice of bread, and began spreading fish-paste on it. Then he asked Heatherington if he might have another cup of tea. The butler obliged, still radiating a controlled and implacable hostility.

Michael thought that the tacit peace treaty they had now established might extend as far as Marlstone walking through the Maze with him before they took up their respective stations of duty, but it did not. While he was donning his smock and picking up his equipment, Marlstone stalked off ahead of him, and Michael never caught him up. By the time Michael arrived in the center, the inventor had disappeared into the Keep.

Michael patiently set up his easel, positioned his canvas, deployed his paints on his palette, and set to work. He had not the slightest idea what part he would be fated to play in the settlement of eternity's affairs, so he simply did not bother to think about it. He focused all his attention on the two things that were of primary importance—the painting and his love for Cecilia—and he simply blanked everything else out.

It was a strategy that worked perfectly while he was still plying his brushes and undisturbed by any other human presence, but when he heard the Cribden Church clock chime nine he felt that he ought to take a short break to rest his eyes and arms. No sooner had he stopped work than Lord Langstrade emerged from the Maze and came to a halt in the open space, looking at him quizzically.

The Earl was alone—which seemed slightly surprising, given that he had not previously been confident of his ability to navigate the maze unaided.

After a brief pause, Langstrade strolled over to the easel. "Do you mind, Mr. Laurel?" he asked, indicating with a gesture that he was angling for permission to inspect the work in progress.

"Not at all, Milord," Michael replied, and moved aside briefly so that his employer could take up the position from which the landscape was intended to be viewed.

For a full two minutes the Earl's gaze moved alternately back and forth between the painting and the scene represented therein. Finally, he nodded his head. "It's very good," he said. "You've really captured the essence of the Keep—although I'm still in two minds about the yew-tree. I know the tree's symbolic, but still I don't quite understand what it's symbolic *of*."

"Continuity, Milord," Michael murmured. "The ancestor of that tree was here when Emund Snurlson was slain, and a remoter ancestor provided shade in the prison-space above the dark cell to which Dedalus was confined by the tyrant Minos."

Langstrade thought about that for two full minutes, before venturing a further question. "It *wasn't* just a dream, then?" he said. "You remember it too. We were really there."

"The entire past is a kind of dream from which the present moment is perennially waking, Milord," Michael told him, "but no—it wasn't *just* a dream. I was present when you slew Emund Snurlson with a phantom sword, and became the legendary Harold Long-stride."

"And that *is* how Snurlson died? Really and truly? In 822 A.D."

"Slain by a phantom blade, Milord. His heart stopped. It could not do otherwise. The Vikings never got this far inland again until Eric Bloodaxe founded a kingdom in York, a century later. Your strike changed the course of history, just like Dedalus' sighting of the map of the maze, and Hope's little chat with Edward Kelley though a black window in time. *We* changed history, both know-ingly and unknowingly—for it needed no conscious involvement for us to serve as Lady Phythian's ghosts, the manifestation of which provided us with the motive to come into the Maze in time to catch the tide."

"It's all rather paradoxical," Langstrade observed.

"As Dr. Carp once pointed out to me, only logic is afraid of paradoxes. We should be braver, if we aspire to be more than auto-mata driven by the despotism of cause, effect and the calculus of probability."

"Right," said Langstrade. "Jolly good. Has anything further happened this morning?"

"I haven't felt any more ripples," Michael told him, "but that doesn't mean that she isn't doing anything, it just means that she isn't doing anything that's manifest in the here and now. We still have an appointment with destiny at noon, and I don't doubt that she's still doing her utmost to prepare herself, and her instruments, as the moment evolves."

"Who's *she*, exactly?" asked Langstrade, warily.

"The Mistress of the Labyrinth. The time machine."

"And what does she want? What is she trying to achieve?"

"As Marlstone says, it's not obvious that she *wants* anything, or is capable of any motivation at all. In his way of seeing things, she's just a machine. On the other hand, when I was staring at the *Sir Richard Trevithick* on King's Cross Station yesterday, I couldn't help feeling that machines might have more soul and intelligence than we give them credit for—more, at any rate, than mere Nature. If there's some kind of contest between Nature and Mechanism to determine the direction of the evolving moment, as Romantic rheto-ric sometimes suggests, I'm not at all sure which side I ought to pre-fer. I don't have the kind of faith in progress that Hope has—or the faith in its illusory nature that Escott has, for that matter."

Langstrade chewed his lower lip momentarily, and then said: "Escott came to see me this morning. He asked for my permission to ask Cecilia to marry him."

Michael had thought himself beyond the reach of astonishment, but that news struck him like a punch in the gut. "*Escott* asked you for Cecilia's hand?" he gasped, suddenly winded. *The ungrateful swine!* he thought. *After I risked my life and sanity yanking him out of that bronze tomb, he promptly takes it into his head to try to break my heart!* He realized, though, that Escott had no way of knowing how he felt about Cecilia, even if the combative pessimist had noticed a certain tension between him and Hope, and that it must have been the experience of being entombed in such an extraordinary fashion that had woken Escott up from his long existential torpor and urged him to attempt a crucial change in his circumstances.

"It surprised me too," Langstrade admitted. "I was expecting Hope. In fact, he came along half an hour later with the same request. He flew into quite a rage when I told him that Escott had got in first, and swore that the fellow had only done it to spite him, to pay him out for that quarrel they once had, when they fought the duel he mentioned yesterday. He calmed down a little though, when I told him what I'd said to Escott."

Michael felt numb, and quite incapable of asking what it was that Langstrade had said to Escott—and, for that matter, to Hope—even though it was the most important question in the world.

Gregory Marlstone came out of the Keep then and strode over the drawbridge with a truly imperious air about him. He came to stand beside the easel, his scowling gaze alternating between Michael and Lord Langstrade, as if he were trying to make up his mind which one he ought to attack first. Eventually, though, he relaxed, and became defensive instead, although he did not sacrifice his characteristic scowl.

"I'm truly sorry, Milord" he said to Langstrade. "I never realized. I miscalculated badly. I thought the experiment was perfectly safe, because its temporal range was so restricted. I should have suspected, but I didn't realize that it was all connected: the Keep, the Maze, even Monticarlo's concert. I was blind. I'm sorry. I can't do anything about it now. You might think that I can simply refrain from setting the machine in operation, but I can't. It's already operating, already beyond control. We're just microscopic cogs in a catastrophic plan that extends backwards—and perhaps forwards too—across millennia."

"I know that," Langstrade replied, a trifle miserably. "I've already done my bit—my first bit, anyhow."

"Don't feel too badly about it, Mr. Marlstone," Michael said to the scowling man. "You might imagine that you invented the machine, but the reality is that the machine invented you. You're just as much a product of the dream-imagination as Harold Longstride. We all are."

That was a little too presumptuous for Marlstone's taste. He rounded on Michael angrily. "The only reason you think you're such an expert now," he said, "is because you happened to be standing here yesterday when the field emitted that pulse, and fell more completely under the machine's spell than anyone else—including me. I can't for the life of me figure out how to do it, but at least I know what it is that I need to do, and I'm still trying. I haven't the slightest idea what *you* might be able do, except for standing around spouting philosophical hot air and slapping paint on your pathetic scrap of canvas."

"That's a bit strong, Marlstone," Lord Langstrade said. "I don't like to hear my guests insulting one another like that."

"*Your* guests!" Marlstone hissed, seething like an overheated Cornish Engine. "Do you still imagine that you're the host of this catastrophe? You're a pawn too, as you just admitted. I built the machine, but you built the shell to house it. Whatever has gone wrong, it has as much to do with the design of your infernal Folly and this damnable Maze as with my mathematics and mechanics—but you were only the instrument that *she* employed to build them."

"We three ought not to quarrel," Michael said, swiftly. "We're all on the same side, after all."

"Are we?" Marlstone queried.

"I think so," Michael answered. "That's what the rules of etiquette require, at any rate. We're *all* fellow guests of Langstrade Hall. We have a duty to one another, and to tradition. If the words relayed by Mademoiselle Evredon from my future self can be taken at face value, the present is due to be invaded on the stroke of noon—by the equivalent of futuristic Viking marauders, I presume, intent on laying waste to everything before paving the way to Hope's Euchronia or Escott's Hell. Our duty is to stand together, to protect the ladies if we can, and to defend one another. I don't know how we might do that, or what obstacles we'll have to overcome—and we might stand no better chance than a rabble of Celtic peasants faced by Emund Snurlson's berserkers—but that's our objective. That's what we have to do, if it's humanly possible. According to my future self, it is. Whether he's reliable or not, I can't be sure—but who else am I to trust?"

Marlstone's scowl deepened impressively. "That's all very well," he said, bitterly, "but I still don't have a clue as to what we might hope to achieve, if and when everything starts to fall apart."

"Nor have I—yet," Michael said, meekly. It seemed a wiser course than making a more provocative answer.

Marlstone's bellicose pose relaxed slightly. "Of course not," he said. "I'm sorry—I've been slaving away for the best part of three hours, trying to stop the machine, but it frustrates my every move. I'm not even sure that's the right thing to do—perhaps she's the one thing standing between us and chaos. I don't know anything any more. The theory seemed so elegant, so perfect—but all I had to do was to look at my perfect equations, think for a moment, and ask myself: *what if there's more than one way to tune a time machine? What if there's more than one set of functional harmonies?* I never even thought of it—and now the world as we know it is about to collapse, and God only knows whether she'll be able to put it back together again, if she even wants to. She might fancy herself the Mistress of the Labyrinth, but she isn't really, any more than I am."

Michael stretched his arms, which now seemed sufficiently rested, then raised his palette and his brush, and resumed work on the body of the Keep, carefully delineating each individual slab of stone. He must have been doing that for three full minutes, while Marlstone and Lord Langstrade simply stood there, watching him, when he suddenly stopped, realizing that he had left an awful gap yawning in the continuity of his existence. He looked at Langstrade, but was still unable to frame the question.

"I told Escott and Hope exactly the same thing," Langstrade said, evidently reading Michael's expression. "I told them that Cecilia had ruled them both out, and that I had no intention of going against her wishes—ever."

Michael felt tears welling up in his eyes, even though he knew that the whole issue might be redundant if the world as he knew it really did come to an end in less than three hours' time. He blinked the inconvenient moisture away.

Langstrade looked at Marlstone, defensively. "I'm not really an aristocrat," he said, as if what he'd just done were something for which he needed to apologize. "I was nearly in my teens when Father got the Earldom. We were already rich, obviously, but...well, Father didn't shop around for a wife for me, as if I were just an instrument for forging social alliances, and I'm not going to shop around for a husband for Cecilia. She can make her own choice. Why not?"

"You'll get no argument from me on that score, Milord," Marlstone told him. "If I had a daughter, I certainly wouldn't want her to marry a pompous ass like Hope or a flippant ironist like Escott." The way he glanced at Michael suggested that he wouldn't have wanted his hypothetical daughter to marry an artist with philosophical delusions, either, but he still had sufficient reserves of politeness not to say so.

"Right," said the second Earl. "Mustn't idle around, though—Emily will be wondering where I am, and I've other guests to attend to. Until then…is there any point in saying *good luck*, or are we way beyond the reach of luck now?"

"We're never beyond the reach of *chance*," Marlstone said, presumably refusing to use the word *luck* because he was a scrupulous calculator of mathematical probabilities who thought the concept a superstitious illusion, "any more than we're beyond the reach of Fate. Paradoxical as it might seem, they co-exist. Maybe they wouldn't, in a universe in which time machines were impossible, but that's not the universe we're living in."

At least for now, Michael thought—but he said nothing aloud.

Lord Langstrade went back into the Maze, without any apparent fear of getting lost, and Marlstone went back over the fake drawbridge into the Keep, carefully closing the door behind him.

Michael continued to paint methodically and inexorably, while his heart gradually decelerated its racing pace. *Marlstone's right*, he thought. *I have no idea what's going to happen at noon, any more than he does, and I have no idea what I'm supposed to do afterwards. At least he knows what he wants to do, even though he has no idea how he's supposed to accomplish it. All I know—all I've known since I received the invitation that brought me here—is that I'm in love with Cecilia, and that she's in love with me. That's more than enough for me, but how can it be enough for the Mistress of the Labyrinth? The time machine must have brought me here for some other reason than that. After all, the time machine can't care whether or not I love Cecilia, can she? She has to be concerned with bigger issues than mere human affection. She's had to create the Maze, the Keep and the mechanical parts of her own body—not to mention founding the secret college along the way, perhaps just to make sure that we had a steam locomotive to bring us here….*

The painting took over again then, absorbing him so completely that he had no mental energy to spare for such idle speculations. He moved his eyes and his hand from the Keep to the tree, intent on placing every leaf correctly. It was, after all, a symbol, not only of the continuity of existence, but of the growth of character and possibility, of efflorescence and fruition, of sturdiness and endurance, of rootedness and ambition. He had a moral duty do it justice, if he could—and he still had more than two hours in hand before noon.

Ten o'clock had, however, already chimed when he was rudely jerked out of his reverie by the sound of a scream. It had come from somewhere inside the Maze, due west of his position. He had no doubt whatsoever that it was Cecilia's voice, and knew that she must have been on her way to see him, to bring him the glad news. He did not know whether she had been seized by a dragon or a Minotaur, or overtaken by some direr fate, but he knew that he had been wrong about the timing of the catastrophe. Like the events of last night, it had been impatient to begin; it had not waited for noon.

The time when heroism was to be required had arrived early.

CHAPTER TWENTY

BEYOND THE REACH OF HISTORY

Michael moved with a swiftness of which he had not thought himself capable, throwing aside his brush and palette and tearing off his smock as he raced into the Maze. Because he was only flesh and blood, he had no alternative but to follow the course of the path he had memorized, going back and forth and around and around in what seemed to be a deliberately perverse series of traps and delays. His course was unobstructed by any enormous heads, but he did have to hurdle two recumbent bodies, lying unconscious on the path. The first was Jack Langstrade, whose right hand was clutching the shaft of his catapult. The other was Jack's father, who lay upon his walking-stick. Under normal circumstances, Michael would never have passed them by without trying to render assistance, but the circumstances were far from normal.

Eventually, he reached a third prostrate body: Cecilia's. She was lying unconscious in the outermost ring, not far from the entrance. He picked her up and carried her out on to the lawn facing the Hall. He laid her down on the ground as tenderly as he could.

He rubbed her wrists and slapped her face very gently, hoping to restore the blood-flow to her brain. Her eyelids fluttered momentarily, and then opened to reveal her blue eyes, which stared into his face, blankly and uncomprehendingly. Michael supported her head with his left hand, while he opened the palm of his right hand in order to use it, very awkwardly, as a fan, directing a current of air into her face. "Cecilia, my love!" he exclaimed, in an agonized tone, throwing etiquette and discretion to the winds.

Whether it was his words, his hand-gestures or merely the support he was providing that did the trick, Cecilia seemed to return more fully to her senses. She opened her eyes much wider, and stared at him with more intelligence in her eyes. The expression that came into her face was not, however, a loving one.

She sat up. Immediately, she pulled way from Michael's tentative embrace, and looked wildly around. Her flickering gaze took in the expanse of lawn, the wings of Langstrade Hall, the ornamental hedge of the rose-garden, the driveway to the gate, the meadows in which cattle were silently grazing, the distant steeple of Cribden Church, the grey water of the tarn, and the horizon formed by the distant Pennines. Then her gaze settled on Michael's face again. It was still devoid of the slightest hint of love.

"When the hell *is* this?" she snarled, in a voice quite unlike her usual melodious trill.

"We're in the grounds of Langstrade Hall, my darling," Michael told her, thinking that she must have been severely disorientated by whatever crisis of identity had caused her to scream and swoon—although that did not render her casual blasphemy any less startling.

"Not *where*, you moron—*when*?" was her equally astonishing reply.

Michael's thoughts reeled dizzily from the shock of the insult, but he contrived to reply: "It's some time between ten and eleven o'clock on Saturday morning." The expression on her face told him, very clearly, that the information was insufficient. "August seventeenth, 1822," he added, automatically, before the realization fully sank in that the person looking at him through Cecilia's gorgeous blue eyes was not, in fact, Cecilia.

Twenty-four hours before, he would not even have been able to entertain such a thought, but now he leapt to the conclusion with almost no effort at all. He had been possessed himself, albeit as a ghost, and knew that it was possible.

"*What have you done with Cecilia?*" he spat out, with deadly hostility. "*Where is she?*"

Not-Cecilia's face took on an expression of extreme bewilderment. "1822?" she repeated, incredulously. "That's not...you can't mean 1822 *A.D.*?" Something in Michael's expression must have told her, then, that it might be wise to reply to his question, if not actually to answer it. "She'll be perfectly safe," was the countermove she came up with, "provided that nothing happens to me. Help me to keep this body safe, and you'll get her back soon enough. If not...."

Michael had never known that he was capable of such hatred as he felt at that moment—nor such frustration, for he realized that he could not attack the futuristic Viking who had stolen Cecilia's body in any fashion at all. Indeed, as the other had been so quick to say, he had to do everything possible to protect her from harm, if ever Cecilia were to resume control of her own flesh and blood.

"You have to help me," not-Cecilia said, in a voice heavily laden with menace. "You have to tell me what I need to know. If I can do what I need to do, I'll be gone in no time—back to my own cherished flesh. If not…." Again, the dire threat was left hanging, but there was a question in the flinty blue eyes.

"All right," Michael said, swiftly. "I'll help you."

"Okay," the Viking said, cryptically. "What do you mean by 1822?"

"What else could I possibly mean but 1822 A.D.?" Michael countered, genuinely nonplussed.

"Don't be stupid—that's minus 273 E.C. It would have been quite impossible to build any kind of time-bending apparatus then."

"It is, nevertheless, 1822 A.D.," Michael assured her, stiffly. "According to the father of the young woman whose body you have possessed, it's the thousandth anniversary of Harold Longstride's epic duel with Emund Snurlson—which is why Lord Langstrade gave Gregory Marlstone permission to test his time machine in the Keep." *More to the point*, he added, for his own secret edification, *it's the day that her father refused requests for her hand from James Escott and Quentin Hope, so that she might make her own choice of husband. I won't let you take her away from me.*

Not-Cecilia seemed to have stopped listening. She was looking down at her own body, stretching out her limbs for appraisal. She did not seem to like what she saw in the least. Her own body, Michael inferred, was probably a great deal more muscular, almost certainly male. Evidently, the Viking from the future had not been able to exercise much choice in the selection of a victim of possession. She looked up at Michael again, fearfully this time. Then she looked wildly around for a second time, and muttered: "Think, damn it!" as if exhorting herself to a vitally necessary effort.

Not-Cecilia's eyes followed the line of the hedge to either side, then flicked back to the House, as if searching for some proof that this could not be the year that Michael claimed. "It's impossible," she said, her blue eyes accusing him of lying. "There weren't any computers in minus 273 to make the calculations, and no nuclear reactors to power to a machine. Mind you, if the damn thing's been vamping from us it's probably been bleeding energy from every tuned-in time machine between the twenty-second and the fifty-fifth—but it would still need an initial impulse of its own to initiate the transition. That would have to be maintained for days, in local terns, if the void weren't to be warped into hopeless paradoxicality. Good God, were there even *steam engines* in minus 273?"

Michael was not at all sure about the propriety of giving information to the enemy—although he felt reasonably sure that the Viking, unlike the Mistress of the Labyrinth, really *was* an enemy—but he couldn't prevent himself from replying, with a certain injured pride in his tone: "We certainly do have steam engines in 1822, in wonderful abundance. You are in Yorkshire, Madam—the very cradle of the Industrial Revolution. I traveled here from London on Thursday, in a train pulled by the *Sir Richard Trevithick*, the steam locomotive reckoned to be the seventh wonder if the world."

In the distance, as if to add emphasis to his words, Cribden's church clock began, unhurriedly, to chime eleven.

Not-Cecilia stared at him. Michael had never seen Cecilia's cornflower-blue eyes so harsh and steely, and hoped never to see them so harsh and steely again. "You're lying!" she said. "You're trying to distract me, while the opposition puts the grabs on the machine. Railway locomotives weren't invented until Victoria's reign. George IV was still on the English throne in 1822."

"Don't be ridiculous," Michael said, reflexively. "There hasn't been a monarch in England since Charles I, and there's never been a King George at all."

The color seemed to drain out of not-Cecilia's face. "Oh, *luck!*" she said, making the word sound like the worst oath ever to be emitted by a mortal mouth. "I've been dropped into a bloody *alternate*! How the hell am I going to get out of *this*?" She started as she saw someone come out of the Hall, using the same side-door that Lord Langstrade's quartet of ghost-hunters had used the evening before.

The first person to make her exit was Lady Phythian. She was running, as if fleeing, at a surprisingly rapid pace. The second, a few moments later, was Quentin Hope. He was carrying a shotgun, and seemed to be about to raise it in order to fire at the unarmed dowager—but then he thought better of it, as the door that he had swung shut behind him suddenly exploded, a vast hole having blasted in the upper part of the batten by a gunshot. Hope set off running too. The door was kicked open again, and James Escott emerged, similarly equipped with a shotgun, one of the barrels of which was still smoking.

"Oh, *luck!*" not-Cecilia said, again. She dived into the gap in the hedge, pulling Michael after her, and hid behind the corner of the entrance to the Maze. "An alternate with *steam*-powered time machines," she muttered, hardly pausing in her train of thought. "Of all the hellish…well, impossible or not, it's got to be eternity-fodder now. Where *is* the bloody steam engine, then?"

"What steam engine?" Michael replied, innocently.

Not-Cecilia groaned again. "I haven't a lucky clue what a stream-powered time machine would look like, you stupid monkey-brain, but I'm damn sure I can't see any trace of one. Where's the lucky time-field being projected from?"

Michael couldn't help frowning at the flood of what was obviously intended to be extremely indelicate language, but he knew that this was no time to lose control of himself. Marlstone's time machine had already opened a substantial portal to invasion from the future, even though there had been more than an hour left before noon. The world as he had known it was, as anticipated, teetering on the brink of annihilation. The idle speculations floated in the rose-garden had not been so idle after all. It was, indeed, possible that the present day—or the morrow, at least—might be utterly transformed by an influx of wisdom and technology from future eras. But would that wisdom come from Hope's Euchronia or Escott's mechanized Inferno? And would it obliterate the interval of history between the two time machines, or merely start a new branch in the tree of time, as Carp had suggested? More to the point, was there still time to stop it happening, or control the outcome?

It must, Michael decided, be possible to control the outcome, because that must be exactly what the futuristic Viking wanted to do. Should he, therefore, tell her where Marlstone's time machine was, or should he do everything practicable to keep her away from the Keep?

"What the luck do I know about steam engines, anyway?" not-Cecilia muttered to herself, before pulling herself together. She took another peep around the corner, and Michael did likewise. Lady Phythian was fleeing across the lawn at an angle, and Hope was following her, but Escott seemed undecided as to whether to take another shot at Hope or let him go. Behind them, the younger Lady Langstrade and Carmela Monticarlo appeared at the side-door of the Hall. For a moment, it seemed that they were about to step through, but then Michael heard the very faint sound of a violin, carried across the lawn on a fugitive breath of breeze. Lady Langstrade and Carmela both looked around, then stepped back inside and closed the door

Not-Cecilia put her hands to her head, as if she had fallen victim to a sudden headache. "Come on!" she croaked, harshly, "*tell me!* If you ever want to be reunited with your lucky Cecilia, you've *got* to help me!" Her expression suddenly became deeply suspicious.

"Who the luck *are* you, anyway?" she snarled. "You can't really be a native, or you'd have been taken over, if not by one of ours, by one of *theirs*. You're messing with my head, aren't you? This isn't minus 273, and you're from somewhen downstream. What is it that you're trying to stop me figuring out?"

"The time machine is in the Folly," Michael said, quickly coming to a decision, although it seemed to him that he was merely casting a die and trusting to luck—the non-obscene kind of luck that was the only kind he knew.

"Folly?" echoed the visitor from the future. "What folly?"

"The Keep," Michael explained "It's supposed to be a replica of a ninth-century keep built by Harold Longstride to defend the dale against Viking invaders, following his victory over Emund Snurlson.

Non-Cecilia simply stared at him, utterly nonplussed. "It's powered by a nuclear reactor, isn't it?" she said. "Fission or fusion?"

Unable to answer this question, Michael simply stared at her. His thoughts, meanwhile, were running on apace. *This is how the invasion from the future works,* he told himself. *Cecilia, Lady Phythian, Hope and Escott—and probably others, including Jack and Langstrade, who are already in the Maze—have been dispossessed of their bodies by the Viking raiders from the future, and the Mistress of the Labyrinth will have to stop them getting to the Keep if she's to protect the time machine from being taken over and brought into full attunement with some future machine, or machines, so that the physical invasion can begin. But whose side should I be on? Which result will I prefer?*

Whoever was currently using Cecilia Langstrade's delectable body was still looking at Michael as if she were direly uncertain what manner of beast he was. "Are you going to tell me who you are?" she demanded. "I don't really care whether you're from anywhen downstream, provided that I can do what I need to do—but if you aren't going to help me, I might as well kill you now."

"I'll help you if I can," Michael said, quickly, feeling that his insincerity was forgivable in view of the threat of homicide, and deciding that he would be much better placed to employ delaying tactics if he were in close company with the advance guard of the invasion. "I'm not sure I'll be much use, though," he added, immediately getting started on the delaying tactics. "I'm just an artist, not a fighting man. What do you want me to do?"

As he was speaking, not-Cecilia leaned sideways in order to peer around the corner of the entrance to the maze yet again. She obviously did not want to confront Hope or Escott while they had guns and she had no weapon at all, and would probably have to be wary of confronting anyone at all, given the frailty of her stolen body. Obviously, the invaders from the future were not united among themselves,

"Which way's this Folly?" she demanded.

"It's in the center of the Maze," Michael told her. "I know the way."

The color had only just begun to return to not-Cecilia's face. Now it drained out again. "This is a *Maze?*" she queried. "Oh, *luck!* Do you know your way through it?"

Michael thought it best to be economical with the truth, while appearing to be doing his best to help, so he reached into his waist-coat pocket and pulled out the piece of paper that Heatherington had given him, a phantom version of which he had shown to the impris-oned Dedalus. "I've got a map," he said.

Not-Cecilia grabbed the paper, unfolded it, and stared at the diagram of the Langstrade Maze. Her pale face went paler, and her expression became tortured. "Where did you get this?" she spat at Michael. He presumed that she meant *you* in a broad sense, referring to everyone who had played a hand in the making of 1822 A.D., and suspected that she might not take it kindly if he simply said: *Heatherington gave it to me.*

"Legend has it that it was handed down by Dedalus, the builder of the Cretan Labyrinth," Michael explained, dutifully. "It's said that he escaped to England when a volcano destroyed Cretan civili-zation, and ended up here."

"Oh, *luck*," not-Cecilia said, yet again. "No wonder we couldn't get the worm through as anything more than the vaguest phantom— it was snared by a lucky Locatelli Maze! Hell, I'm probably all on my own, and so are the skippers that slipped through from down-stream. If this lucky body hadn't actually been *in* the maze…well, I have to play the hero now, or I'm well and truly screwed—and so are you, whoever you are, and your beloved Cecilia too, if we can't put a stop this in time. Opposition be damned! We have to work to-gether now, or we'll all be headed for oblivion in a shooting star!"

While she was speaking she turned the map around in her hands, as if trying to orientate herself with the aid of the map. She put her left hand to her temple, and muttered: "Something's trying to entrance me—but there was no mechanical mind control in minus 273! Even the psychognosis is anomalous! If this really is an alter-nate, freshly-woven from the ether, the operation must have been planned *way* downstream. If someone from beyond the Cee-Zee has contrived to implant a time machine all the way back in a ripple equivalent to minus 273, and steal enough power from machines tuned in to the Change War to get far enough into its own arrears to shunt them all off-track, and somehow to surround the seed-device with a Locatelli Maze, then the whole five-thousand-and-some is under attack. The entire house of cards could evaporate, or sclerotize. Who the luck *are* you, Mr. Artist?"

"I'm Michael Laurel," Michael replied—but for the first time in his life, he wondered whether he was telling the whole truth, and nothing but. *Of course I'm Michael Laurel*, he thought decisively, casting suspicion firmly aside—but he still wasn't entirely certain that he might not be someone else as well.

"When are you from?" not-Cecilia demanded, her voice a menacing whisper now.

"I was born just before the turn of the century," Michael told her.

The time-traveler's eyes bored into his, with attempted Mesmeric authority. "Well," she conceded, still whispering, "if you're lying, you're well-shielded. You still have to help me, though. I've *got* to get into that tower, and I can't afford to get into a brawl on the way. I've got to get hold of the reactor controls, and tune them into the thirty-third. If those idiots with popguns can just get their heads around the idea that we need to join forces for once...." In spite of her headache, she seemed to be thinking very hard indeed—almost as hard, in fact, as Michael. For the time being, however, she seemed to be just as much at a loss as he was when it came to formulating a plan of action.

I ought to try to get into the Keep too, Michael thought, *if only to find out what Marlstone, or not-Marlstone, is doing—but I can't afford to get trapped in a brawl either. So what the luck am I going to do?* "Am I correct in deducing," he said aloud, to the time-traveler, "that, so far as your history is aware, the first viable time machine won't be invented for another 273 years—which is to say, in 2095 A.D.?"

"We don't have any history," the invader replied, grimly. "History ended in year zero. What *we* have is a five-thousand-year-plus Era of Change, in which technological stability is complemented by total conflict."

"There's some kind of eternal Time War going on?" Michael asked, just to make sure.

"What else can you expect, in a world when everyone and anyone is likely to find, at a moment's notice, that the consciousness of everyone around him has just been displaced by skippers from further downstream, or upstream skippers fighting a rearguard action with stolen technics? It's not eternal—no skipper's ever come back from anywhen downstream of the fifty-fifth—but whether there's war or peace, history or eternity after that is anyone's guess. We thirty-thirders have always preferred to assume that it's the boundary of the Euchronian Eternity we've been trying to establish for three thousand years, although the diehard pessimists keep right on insisting that it must be the Ultimate End of the World, after which there'll be no time at all."

"So various time-travelers from the future are about to start fighting one another to the death for control of the Marlstone machine?" Michael said, trying to get it straight in his head. "But you've decided that you all need to combine forces against a greater threat?"

"If you're really a historical, you wouldn't understand," the fake Cecilia assured him. "If you're not, you already do. Anyway, I don't know the answer to the second question myself. I'm just a humble foot-skipper, and I seem to be on my own. The one thing I do know is that we have to get to the machine, and quickly."

"Why?" Michael demanded. He already had a vague idea, but he was direly in need of a little certainty in what was obviously an extremely confused situation.

"Because we have to disrupt the weaving of the alternate before the effect spreads too far downstream. Either we have to smash the machine—although that might not be possible, if it's cleverly designed—or we have to help the future operators to stabilize the tune it's playing, so that someone downstream can start shipping *materiel* through. If the thirty-thirders can't do it, better the bastards from some other resonance-point succeed than the roof of time falls in on all our heads, but if I can't get it across to those other idiots that there are bigger things at stake here than loot and flesh—even two hundred and seventy-three years of loot and billions of warm bodies—they'll just shoot this body down. If this really is a scheme hatched further downstream that any human mind has ever skipped, we have *got* to subvert it."

"Why?" Michael asked. "If it really is the work of people from an era of eternal peace and prosperity, surely you ought to welcome their endeavor?"

"Oh, I'm all in favor of the Euchronian Empire," not-Cecilia told him, "provided that it's *our* Euchronian Empire. What the luck do you think we're all fighting for? We have to move, though. The guys downstream must be trying everything humanly possible to tune in so that they can move apparatus through the focal point when the actual resonance-point arrives, but if the moment isn't seized, it'll be gone. If the chain's a six-pointer, it might take weeks, in real reckoning, for headquarters to set up a usable beachhead from the thirty-third, even if I can help out from this end, and I have to start before the local optimum arrives. Are you with me, or do I *really* have to kill you?"

Michael thought that he understood what was at stake. If the time-traveler actually contrived to take control of Marlstone's machine, and her masters "downstream" contrived to bring a sequence of their own machines into tune with it at the crucial moment, then the Era of Change would henceforth begin *today*—and history, as Michael and all his contemporaries knew it, would end, to be substituted by a war in which God only knew how many sides were hopping back and forth through the centuries, taking over people's bodies and identities willy-nilly, in vain attempts to dictate an ever-shifting pattern of events sprawling over more than five thousand years of un-history.

Perhaps, he thought, the best thing that he could do, in the circumstances, was to knock the time-traveler unconscious, if only to save Cecilia from being shot by Hope or Escott—but that would have meant hitting Cecilia, and that was something that he was very reluctant to do, even though Cecilia was definitely not herself at present. The second best thing he could do, obviously, was to continue to play along, at least for the time being, just in case she was capable of carrying through her threat to kill him.

The person employing Cecilia's delectable body, alas, was not as scrupulous as Michael was. She was obviously incapable of reading his mind, but she seemed to have figured out the cunning manner in which his thoughts were moving. While he stood there, dithering helplessly, and as someone's footfalls became audible on the other side of the hedge, not-Cecilia caught him square on the chin with an unexpected right hook, and Michael fell sideways into the hedge, momentarily stunned.

The thorns, which almost seemed to have been lying in wait for him, gripped him avidly, as if with a loving but savage embrace.

CHAPTER TWENTY-ONE

STORMING THE CITADEL

By virtue of fierce and painful struggle, Michael eventually managed to free himself from the thorns, although his only waistcoat and second-best trousers were ruined in the process, and the dizziness that had been afflicting him periodically for more than twenty-four hours had been excited once again by the after-effects of the unexpected punch.

Not-Cecilia had run into the Maze. She had dropped Michael's map, but that was presumably because she had no more need of it. She had referred to a "Locatelli Maze" as if it were something familiar. That element of the time machine's contrivance had evidently followed a conventional pattern.

Michael stood up straight, intending to go to the entrance of the maze and looked out—but he was too late. James Escott's slender form was already coming through it, shotgun at the ready.

"Don't shoot!" Michael cried. "I can help you!"

"Who the luck are you?" not-Escott snarled.

"Someone who knows what year it is and what's happening here," Michael snarled back. He hardly paused before adding: "It's minus 273, and someone from way downstream of the fifty-fifth has planted a time machine here, intending to blow the entire Era of Change into oblivion."

Escott's dark eyes fixed themselves on his, obviously attempting to exercise Mesmeric authority. Michael had no alternative but to stare back, meeting the challenge squarely.

"Okay," not-Escott said, presumably accepting temporary defeat. "I'm listening. Convince me you can help."

"The time machine's in the Keep in the center of the Maze," Michael said. "The machine's local manufacturer is in the Keep.

There are now three other people in the Maze, although two of them were unconscious last time I saw them. None of them has a gun, but if you want to get to the Keep in time to take a hand in this you'll need to hurry. You probably know how a Locatelli Maze is laid out, but I've been through it so many times it's virtually second nature. Follow me, and I'll get us to the center without delay—provided that we don't bump into any unexpected obstructions."

Not-Escott stared at him, incomprehension mingled with mistrust. The Viking decided soon enough, however, that he had nothing to lose. To hasten his decision further, more footfalls sounded outside the Maze, running along the hedge. "Go!" he said, abruptly.

Michael went, at a run. He fled through the Maze as fast as his legs could carry him, but he did not manage to catch up with not-Cecilia. Lord Langstrade and his son were no longer lying unconscious on the path, but there were no obstructions of any kind blocking the way.

When Michael eventually erupted into the central arena of the Maze, though, he stopped dead. Less that ten yards away, Lord Langstrade and Jack were squirming on the ground, seemingly engaged in a wrestling-match, in which the small boy seemed to be holding his own with surprising skill.

The fake Cecilia, moving surreptitiously, had obviously gone around the squabbling pair, and had almost managed to reach the nearer end of the drawbridge. As soon as Escott saw her, though, he raised his gun to his shoulder and shouted: "Stop!"

Not-Cecilia stopped—and so did the wrestlers. Langstrade and his son released one another and moved apart, then began to get to their feet, slowly.

Michael knew that Jack and the Earl had no way of knowing that Escott had already fired one shot, and they were presumably able to guess that the double-barreled weapon could be fired twice before needing to be re-loaded. They were very careful to make no hostile move.

Not-Cecilia paused momentarily, but she did know that the shotgun had already been fired, and her one and only priority was to get into the Folly, where Marlstone's time machine was. As soon as she set off to make a run for the doorway, though, someone emerged from the tower to take up a position on the drawbridge, blocking the entrance with his body. The person in question was inhabiting Gregory Marlstone's body, and the aggressive pose he struck was almost as familiar as the scowl he wore, but Michael was certain in his own mind that it was not the inventor at all. It had to be some time-displaced soul, opposed to the particular army in which Cecilia's possessor was in service as a humble foot-skipper.

Gregory Marlstone was a big man, and whoever was using his body now obviously appreciated that fact. He had a desperate gleam in his eyes. Given that the drawbridge was so narrow, it would not be easy for anyone to get past him—especially a delicate creature like Cecilia Langstrade. The fake Cecilia evidently realized that. She immediately drew herself up to the fullness of her meager height, and turned sideways so that she could address the three men at the entrance to the Maze as well as not-Marlstone. She began to harangue the entire company in a very insistent manner.

"There are bigger things at stake here than old feuds between the thirty-thirders, the thirty-sixers, and the forty-fivers, you idiots!" she shouted. "There's one thing we all want, and that's to widen the battlefield. This is minus 273, damn it—and it's a lucky alternate! There must have been some far-downstream jiggery-pokery involved in opening the door, but we can still out-maneuver the masterminds behind it, if we can just work together. We've got a chance to reclaim nearly three centuries for the Era of Change, but we have to help someone—*anyone*—downstream tune a big machine in before the local optimum arrives. If we can't do that, we have to smash this one before optimum and sever the link. If *any* operators downstream can tune in well enough to move some heavy apparatus through, we can all come out ahead in this affair—but if the way-downstreamers complete their own plan, we'll likely be blasted into oblivion. If we carry on trying to knock seven bells out of each other, we'll lose everything—but if we combine forces, we can change more history at a single stroke than anyone's ever changed before. Who's with me?"

Michael had never thought of Cecilia as a leader of men, but he had to admit that whoever was using her body just now might have given Joan of Arc a run for her money. There seemed to be at least three rival groups among the five Vikings currently present, but the revelation that they had somehow contrived to land in 1822 A.D.— and not the 1822 A.D. whose record was preserved by their own history—was evidently sufficient to make them rethink the causes of their rivalry.

Michael heard not-Escott, not-Langstrade and not-Jack utter a rapid collective mutter of disbelief, in which the word "impossible" featured more than once, but the former combatants took time out to look around: at the neatly-trimmed walls of the innermost hedge of the Maze, the distant cottages on the ridge above Bancroft Scar, and the sandstone walls of the Keep. The Keep was brand new, but it looked old—evidently old enough, in combination with everything else, to convince the visitors from the future that they really had been cast away in the remoter regions of history, before the Era of Change had previously begun.

Michael guessed that not-Langstrade, who was the first to call out "We're with you!" was one of not-Cecilia's fellow "thirty-thirders"—but the others didn't know that for sure, and not-Escott, who took up the cry immediately afterwards, must surely have been from another party.

"Okay," said Jack. Michael deduced that the word was some kind of expression of consent.

Marlstone, however, said nothing, and did not change his position or his attitude. Not-Cecilia could do nothing against him, given the delicacy of her frame, but not-Escott raised his gun, not-Langstrade raised his walking-stick—apparently not having realized that it was actually a swordstick—and Jack looked around for a pebble with which to load his catapult.

Then not-Lady Phythian suddenly erupted from the gap in the hedge, hotly pursued by not-Hope, and for a moment, it seemed that chaos might erupt again.

There was, at any rate, a pause as the two newcomers skidded to a halt and surveyed the scene in front of him.

"Don't shoot!" not-Langstrade shouted to not-Hope, urgently.

"It's okay," not-Jack shouted, presumably to not-Lady Phythian, almost simultaneously. "There's a truce! We've all formed an alliance against *him*!" His dirty forefinger pointed at not-Marlstone. "We have to storm the tower and take the machine!"

Michael, who had lived in London ever since leaving boarding-school, knew enough about mob psychology to understand how easily common causes could be adopted when the right spur was applied. He was not surprised to see the entire party unite spontaneously, and then surge forward to join not-Cecilia, who turned her attention back to the lone man on the drawbridge.

"What about you?" not-Cecilia demanded. "Are you with us?"

"It's no use," the man on the bridge replied, his voice overwrought. "You don't understand—the machine's untouchable. I can't even get up to the platform. Even if I could, I wouldn't even know how to begin to tune it. It has nothing in common with any time machine I ever saw—or that any of you ever saw. I can't believe that the fifty-oners can tune in to it, and if they can't, *your* people have very little chance indeed."

"In that case," not-Cecilia, was quick to declare, "we have to play the hero and smash it before the optimum. Whatever the risk—

even if we seven are trapped here—we have to smash it. If the way-downstreamers get their way...."

She stopped, evidently having become aware that she was losing her audience. Some of them, at least, had been in the palm of her hand a few moments before, but the word *trapped* had given them pause for thought.

"Let's see it," not-Cecilia demanded of not-Marlstone. "Let us all see what we're dealing with."

"No!" another voice shouted, urgently. Michael was surprised to find that it was his own. "Hold the drawbridge, Marlstone! Don't let them in!"

The man on the drawbridge probably had no idea who "Marlstone" was, and could not possibly know why the instruction had been shouted, or on whose authority, but he was in no doubt that the words had been addressed to him. He stood stock still, quite nonplussed—still serving, if only by virtue of his inertia, as an obstacle. Michael charged forward, as if coming to his aid.

No one else knew who he was either, or what his agenda was—including not-Cecilia. That didn't prevent her, though, from yelling: "Stop him!"

Not-Langstrade moved as if to intercept Michael's charge, but rather half-heartedly, not sure that he wanted to obey someone he had considered an enemy only a few moments before. Michael lowered his head and butted the Earl's body in the chest. The body fell backwards, and the walking-stick flew out of its hand. Michael changed direction just sufficiently to enable him to pick up the swordstick—to whose secret only he seemed presently privy—and continued in his course. Not-Cecilia seemed to consider trying to intercept him, but obviously thought better of it.

Michael bounded on to the drawbridge. Not-Marlstone finally moved, coming forward to meet him, with a scowl on his face that certainly did not advertise any friendly intent.

Michael tried to check his stride and draw the swordstick, but the maneuver went hopelessly wrong, His momentum caused him to stumble, and he lurched forwards, fighting with all his might simply to stay on his feet. He failed, and rolled over, cannoning into not-Marlstone's legs. Not-Marlstone, who had been moving forward, lost his own balance, tripped, and fell off the drawbridge into the muddy moat.

Michael completed his forward roll, more by luck than by judgment, and came to his feet again. He turned around immediately, and placed his back to the door of the Keep. Finally, he succeeded in drawing the blade of the swordstick, and extended it before him, in what he intended to be a threatening manner.

It was only then that he realized the blatant absurdity of striking any sort of fencing pose, when two of his opponents had shotguns, and one of them had two cartridges as yet undischarged.

Not-Hope and not-Escott immediately raised their weapons, but hesitated.

"Shoot him!" not-Cecilia screamed.

Both men fired, almost simultaneously.

The "skippers" controlling the bodies of the optimist and the pessimist might have been expert marksmen while safely embedded in their own flesh and equipped with familiar weapons, but neither of them had ever seen a double-barreled sporting-piece before today, and they were cursed with the native incompetence of their borrowed flesh. The guns leapt up in their unpracticed grip, and fired higher than intended. Michael was untouched by a single pellet, although the door above his head and the walls to either side were liberally peppered.

Not-Cecilia had obviously inherited the legendary fickleness of womanhood along with her borrowed flesh, for she immediately revised her earlier judgment and shouted "Don't shoot!" at not-Hope, who still had one shot in hand. When he looked at her with frank annoyance, she added, by way of explanation: "If the machine's way up in the top of the tower, and the big guy couldn't reach it, the only way to stop it is to shoot it. Have you got any more cartridges?"

Not-Hope and not-Escott exchanged guilty glances. They had obviously paused long enough in the gun-room, after smashing their way into the locker, to load the weapons, but they had been in too much of a hurry to fill their pockets with spare cartridges. They had only one shot left between them, and they dared not waste it on Michael.

I'm not Theseus after all, Michael thought, *but Horatius Cocles, who defended the bridge to Rome's main gate against an army. Was he killed or not? I can't remember. Hope would know, and Escott too—they're Eton men.*

In the meantime, the six-man "army" assembled on the grass closed ranks, while not-Marlstone—who obviously had to be counted as its seventh member now—stood up in the ditch, covered from head to toe in horrid slime. The other six gathered at the end of the drawbridge, but did not set foot on it, while Marlstone refrained from taking hold of the wooden platform, fearful of being stabbed.

"I'll get him," said not-Jack, who had found a pebble with which to load his catapult and was already stretching the elastic string.

Michael did not suppose that non-Jack was any more familiar with catapults than not-Hope and not-Escott had been with shotguns, and he knew from distant experience that they were notoriously inaccurate weapons, so he stood his ground like the hero he was—and then howled in pain as the missile grazed the top of his left ear before smashing into the wood of the door, with more than enough force to convince him that a direct hit might have killed him. He had reckoned without the boy's reflexes, trained by killing rabbits.

Fortunately, not-Jack needed time to fit another pebble into the cradle of his weapon and draw back the elastic. During that interval Michael reached behind him to clutch the door-handle, opened the door, and slipped inside, cursing the thrift that had forbidden the younger Lord Langstrade to equip his mock-Keep with a functional drawbridge, or even to put a bolt on the door.

He was immediately aware that the atmosphere within the Keep was intensely charged with some unspecifiable force. When he had felt something similar in the Maze he had not been sure whether it was actually the Maze or merely himself that was charged, but he was in no doubt now that he was inside the Keep, at the core of the temporal field, that the phenomenon was both objective and subjective. He was sure, too, that there was a world of difference between being "charged" and being "possessed". The Mistress of the Labyrinth—Marlstone's time machine—had not taken possession of him at all, and was not even crowding his head with alternative versions of himself, let alone any alien presence, but he was in no doubt that she had enhanced his own capacity somehow.

Unfortunately, that enhancement was no vulgar matter of mass or physical strength. Placing his back against the door in order as if to make a tokenistic—but obviously futile—barricade, Michael looked around to see if there was anything to hand that might serve the purpose better.

It was dark inside the building, in spite of the pairs of loophole-windows set high in each of the four walls, but there was enough light to enable him to make out something swinging from side to side in front of him. Michael realized, to his astonishment, that the swinging object was a pendulum bob. It was suspended by a cable from an axle fitted into the walls of the tower, beneath a platform accommodated in the space beneath its fake battlements. He could not quite make out the escapement mechanism to which the pendulum was presumably attached, nor the form of the machine that the escapement must be regulating, but he could see two other objects suspended in the gloom: two leaden weights whose gradual descent from a spindle set at a similarly great height must be powering the machinery regulated by the motion of the pendulum.

Gregory Marlstone's time machine, Michael realized, was not powered by steam. He recalled that Marlstone's father had been a manufacturer of clocks, of the gross kind accommodated within church towers. Marlstone's time machine—the mysterious Mistress of the Labyrinth—was powered by clockwork.

Rickety scaffolding set against the side-wall of the Keep to his right, equipped with a network of ladders, provided a route of sorts up to the platform where the time machine and it clockwork driving-mechanism were housed, but the light filtering through the loop-holes showed him that the ropes securing one of the ladders had come loose, and that the ladder was now dangling down, uselessly. The machine was inaccessible—from the floor of the Keep, at least. It was quite possible that seven Vikings working in association might be able to get the ladder back into place and hold it firm while one of them climbed up—but how could a mere foot-skipper be expected to render effective assistance to his allies downstream, when confronted with a clockwork-driven time machine and having no more than a few minutes in hand?

Michael felt a sudden urge to laugh, and actually opened his mouth in response—but then something heavy slammed into the batten of the door from the other side, and the reaction to the impact was communicated to his back with brutal force, causing his teeth to snap shut, trapping the tip of his tongue. He experienced a sharp stab of pain, and felt the taste of blood on his mouth. More blood was running down his right cheek, from the graze inflicted on his ear, but it was no more than a trickle. He had inflicted worse wounds on himself in the past, with pen-knives or mere sheets of paper.

Even a few minutes, he thought, might be time enough for one of the Vikings to smash the machine. There were bound to be tools of some kind on the platform, and not-Hope still had a cartridge in his shotgun.

He pressed himself backwards against the double-door of the Folly, bracing himself against the second impact that was sure to follow the first, although he was not optimistic about his ability to prevent one or other batten from being broken down.

Surely it must be noon by now, he thought. *It seems like an eternity since Cribden Church chimed eleven!*

Before the expected impact came, however, a temporal ripple ran through him—recognizable now—and he had to grit his teeth to fend off the associated wave of nausea and mental unsteadiness. Suddenly, it seemed that there was a direr enemy inside the Keep than those without: something invisible, writhing in the space beneath the sweeping pendulum like some kind of snake…or worm. Non-Cecilia had mentioned a worm, he recalled, and in Medieval terminology, "worm" was often used synonymously with "dragon". There was an evil spirit working against the Mistress of the Labyrinth, and had been since she had first become active—but as not-Cecilia had complained, it was the most fugitive of phantoms.

Fugitive or not, it still had some notion of what it was doing. Whether it was working by instinct or intelligence, it had a part to play.

Because it was invisible, Michael could only see where it was *not*: a void vacated by the dust-particles that otherwise filled the air with a faint haze, faintly illuminated by the shafts of summer sunlight slanting down through the loophole-windows.

The worm—the dragon at the heart of the Maze—was climbing up the pendulum-bob in a slow but smooth spiral. Its blind snout reached into the gloomy shadows where the escapement and the time machine were nestling.

A bolt of lightning—or something very similar—suddenly erupted out of the darkness at the top of the tower, blinding Michael's eyes. For several seconds, as the darkness resumed, everything was hopelessly confused—and then one of the battens of the door gave way behind him, sending him staggering forward into the path of the worm-burdened pendulum. Even though he could not see the bob, he evaded it somehow, feeling the wind of its passage as it swung past him, and he continued forwards, groping his way to the far wall, in order that he might use it for support.

Before his vision had cleared completely, other people rushed into the tower. He heard their footfalls pause, as if for dramatic effect. Then someone howled, apparently in wrath and disappointment. Evidently, the futuristic Vikings had never seen a clockwork time machine before, and were far from delighted to discover that such a thing was possible—except, of course, that it wasn't. The clockwork could only be providing the tiniest imaginable impulse to the Mistress, who was actually drawing her power across time, from a whole series of time machines located in various eras of the turbulent future, by means of a *scordatura* tuning that the operators of those time machines, like Gregory Marlstone, had never previously imagined to be possible.

But what now? Michael thought. *What NOW?*

Not-Hope raised his shotgun, aiming upwards into the gloom, and fired. The gunshot echoed eerily in the confined space, seemingly multiplied tenfold and amplified by the reverberation. If the pellets hit any part of the time machine, however, they did not seem to do any significant damage. Not-Hope cursed his incompetence, volubly.

Not-Jack raised the catapult above his head and fired a second pebble, which certainly hit something metallic before it rebounded and fell back to the floor, clattering as it skittered over the flagstones—but that shot, too, proved impotent.

The howl of anguish had died away by then, but it was suddenly replaced by a howl of joy, this time from more than one mouth, as the invisible worm reached out again, and lightning flashed in ready response—or, at least, *began* to flash. This time, it was quite obvious that the flash was not really lightning at all, for it was far too slow, far too *controlled*. It was not as bright, and did not blind him, although he had to shield his eyes with his free hand, but as Michael watched the uncanny light expand and swirl within the space through which the pendulum was swinging, he was overwhelmed by a dire sense of dread.

"The fifty-fivers have broken through!" not-Cecilia cried. "They've cracked the lucky harmonic. We've won!"

CHAPTER TWENTY-TWO

DANCING THE MAZE

Whatever the first lightning-bolt had been, Michael realized, it had been a horribly bad omen. It must, Michael deduced, have come from somewhere "downstream", signaling that the warriors from the Era of Change were on the brink of completing their attunement, with the aid of their ghostly worm. A cross-time connection had been established, in the very nick of time, and now the invasion would begin in earnest, materially.

Obviously, the Mistress of the Labyrinth had had her own reasons for wanting to keep the time machine going, while simultaneously trying to make sure that none of the ghostly mental missionaries dispatched into the present from the future—who had employed tactics far more ungentlemanly than those employed by the Mistress's own missionaries—could complete his allotted task. It was also obvious, though, that there had been a subtler race against time in progress, which had always been likely to be a close-run thing. Michael had to trust the intuition that told him that it was now one of the Armies of Change that was on the brink of victory: a victory that would be disastrous for the history that Michael knew, and whose future development he could not help but be anxious to protect. But what could he do about it, now that the battle was on the brink of being lost?

Somewhere in the remote distance, Michel heard the clock of Cribden Church begin to chime, and knew that it would chime twelve times—or that it would, at least, *try* to chime twelve times, like the heroic mechanical intelligence that it was.

Too late! he cried, silently—but somehow guessed, almost immediately, that it was *not* too late, and that the timing of the breakthrough had not merely been permitted but actually engineered by the Mistress of the Labyrinth. So, at least, he had to hope and believe.

The slowed-down lightning-flash suspended above his head seemed to dim, but that was only by comparison with a complementary swirl of light that suddenly emerged beneath his feet to fill the floor of the Keep—a floor that suddenly seemed very large indeed. Although the two floods of liquid light were not directly connected, there was some kind of mirror-relationship between them.

The Keep's seven invaders—or eight, counting the worm—looked down.

"Oh, *luck*!" said not-Cecilia.

The mud-stained not-Marlstone groaned: "I told you so!"

Both of them, along with the other five human-seeming time-travelers, had already turned in the direction of the door, as if intending to retreat, but it was a mere desperate reflex. There was no retreat. They were caught.

The new Labyrinth, Michael assumed, was drawing power through the door that had been opened in time, in far greater abundance than the Mistress had been able to steal before—and that flood would increase vastly as the twelve chimes of noon vibrated in the air above the dale.

The seven human figures that had burst through the door of the Keep with such bellicose fervor were writhing pathetically now, whipping the air with their arms as if trying to take off and fly, but all they achieved was to become unrecognizable humanoid blurs, while the new whirlpool of light consumed them. It was as if they were sinking, or *melting* into the mazy tide of luminosity rising from the floor—but Michael neither sank nor melted, and the worm clung to the pendulum cable.

Feeling the stone floor secure beneath his feet, Michael continued to lean his back against the wall of the Keep, with the splayed fingers of one hand in front of his eyes, and the other clutching the ivory hilt of Langstrade's swordstick.

The maze designed in liquid light on the floor of the Keep was very much larger and much more complicated than the one described by Dedalus, Pietro Locatelli and Signor Monticarlo, but it clearly bore a family resemblance to it. The other had been, as Locatelli had aptly titled it, a *capriccio*: one of a whole sequence of *capricci enigmati*. This one was far more than a *capriccio*, and far more than a sonata. The new Labyrinth, Michael judged, was not one of the six glorious mysteries known to Heinrich von Biber, but a kind of seventh wonder: not merely another bead on the chaplet of an existing temporal sequence, or a new branch on its rosary, but a whole new set of threads twisting through the ultimate void.

Michael had no way of knowing whether the new Labyrinth really was the master-plan of some unknown genius from the legendary far future that extended beyond the Era of Change, inaccessible and unknown to the masters of primitive time machines, or whether it was something spontaneous, arising miraculously from a soul that had become incarnate in Gregory Marlstone's time machine by virtue of a freak of chance, but he was no longer in any doubt as to whether the mysterious Mistress of the Labyrinth was capable of wanting anything. She was not only capable of wanting what *she* wanted, and wanting it very much; she was capable of wanting what *he* wanted, and of a determination to help him—not merely by way of a bargain, in compensation for the help that he was rendering her, but because she approved of what he wanted. Just as she had approved of what Quentin Hope had wanted, in respect of the broader philosophy of progress, the Mistress of the Labyrinth approved of Michael's art and Michael's love—and she was not the kind of Mistress to settle for anything less than *all* she ever wanted.

He could hear a violin playing, apparently very loudly, although the sound could only be making its way into the Keep through arcane material channels. This time, the music was not accompanying a ghostly displacement of Pietro Locatelli, originated a hundred years ago, but was being played in real time, by Signor Monticarlo. Dissatisfied with the previous evening's performance, Monticarlo had doubtless begun by merely practicing—but his practicing had turned into composition, and his composition—inspired, no doubt, by the Mistress of the Labyrinth—had acquired immediate perfection. The labyrinthine music had already trapped four times as many skippers as had contrived to escape its snare, and had also provided safe havens for the minds displaced by the skippers who had run into the Keep, in virtual brazen heads that were refuges rather than prisons—but there was still work to be done in that respect.

The new Maze had no center, but it included a vast series of cells set at the termini of various dead-end passages, marked with various symbols that were difficult for the human eye to clarify or identity, because they extended in more than three dimensions, but presented the virtual appearance of brazen masks. A few of these masked cells held prisoners, but they were widely scattered. Michael's painter's eye knew from their pattern that there were forty-two in all, but that the ones of most personal relevance to him fell into two groups of seven. Seven of the brazen masks had familiar features, while seven were Vikings.

Like many Mazes, this one had a puzzle innate within it. It only took Michael a few seconds to visualize the solution to the puzzle. At first glance, the task of reaching all fourteen of the critical points in the Maze, in exactly the right order, seemed terrifyingly difficult, all the more so as it was not at all obvious how he might move into or through the Maze from his present position. His artist's eye had sufficient aesthetic sensibility, however, to tell him how the Maze ought be negotiated in order to reach the prisoners he needed to reach, and how to deliver them to safety while leaving the remainder in the traps appropriate to their culpability—or, rather, how the Maze might be *danced* in order to achieve that end.

The Maze had to be danced, because it had to be sustained in its mysterious harmony while it was in musical formation, and that could only be done by dancing. The Mistress of the Maze was its primal dancer, its shaping force, its creative goddess. She had a purpose, and a jealous desire, whether or not they had been originated and assured by some higher identity, and the Maze was an expression of that purpose and desire. She had been dancing this Maze since the moment when it had first been imagined—which was, in one sense, the moment when Gregory Marlstone had envisaged his machine, long before he had constructed it and made it ready to be set in motion, but which was also, in another and perhaps more accurate sense, the origin of time itself.

Michael's mind filled with a musical dream, not unlike the one he had experienced the previous evening when, Signor Monticarlo and Pietro Locatelli had both played the Locatelli *capriccio*, but much more vivid and much more real. He had no option but to dance to the music of the new Maze, so he did.

The dancing he did was actually more like flying; in fact, he *literally* flew into the air that was enclosed within the Keep's propitious space. He flew like a windborne avenging angel, blade in hand.

The slow lightning above him—the breath of the insatiable, monstrous Era of Change—and the worm that had triggered it both recoiled before him. Within the heart of the fading thunderbolt he saw armies and artillery, and guessed that their potential firepower was sufficient to blast the world apart—but they were no more now than a lick of fiery breath, and the invisible worm was no more than an intimidated thread. There was no real combat, to speak of. Michael was a hero, after all, and he could fly—as Dedalus never truly had, in spite of the credit of legend. The worm tried to flee, and five thousand years of incessant warfare fled before it.

Instead of having to battle the retreating enemy, Michael was able to reach out as he danced in the air, to shuffle the faces behind the masks with delicate precision, taking seven displaced souls into his momentary possession, as he had been taught to do, and replacing them where they belonged. In order to do that, he had also to take seven unfamiliar souls into momentary possession, before casting them into a dark Underworld from which they would never return—but he was an angel, after all; it was the role he had to play, and it did not sicken or pain him. The wind of his passing was so awesome, as it swept through the contours of the maze, augmented with every turn, that it sent the souls of the damned tumbling helplessly through the alleyways of the Maze as they fell, one by one, into their cages of brass.

Michael had almost reached the exit of the new Maze when the lightning-flash suspended in the Keep suddenly began to expand again, and the worm turned. Precisely because the Mistress of the Labyrinth had concluded her own weaving, her enemies came into full possession of their own power once again. Michael screamed in rage and frustration, thinking that he might yet be shot down in flight, and that the world as he knew it might yet be doomed.

Then, still impelled by his whirlwind dance, he flew up into the air, and whirled the blade of the swordstick around with a single mighty sweep, slashing clean through the body of the invisible worm, and cutting clean through the cords sustaining the driving-weights of Marstone's clockwork time machine. Had the blade been mere matter, it would have passed harmlessly through the phantom worm, but it was *charged*, as he was *charged*, and it was deadly—as the worm had evidently been aware when it had tried to retreat.

The weights fell, and so did the two halves of the sundered, blasted worm.

The weights were only impelled by gravity, while the lightning was impelled by a much greater force, produced by sunbursts—but the weights had less than thirty feet to fall, and the lightning had centuries of intertemporal gravity to oppose. For one horrid moment, it seemed as if the lightning might win and reclaim its worm—but the vanishing labyrinth of light swallowed the broken worm like a hungry bird, and it was the weights that struck the floor first. The clockwork of the time machine, no longer guided by the pendulum, grated horribly as it suddenly seized up.

The grating sound turned into an oddly human screech, and Michael tumbled through the exit from the temporal maze at the very instant when its luminous threads folded up, and its awesome multicursal complexity collapsed into a mere unicursal labyrinth.

There was not so much as a sigh from the Mistress of the Maze as her soft voice, maternal warmth and measured presence vanished from the dark and sullen space, her elegant dance completed and all her monsters duly slain.

Michael was tempted to think, as he fell to his knees and clutched the pendulum-cord in order to support himself, that the whole of time was in the process of being healed, and that it might never be disturbed again, but he knew that any such conviction would be far too optimistic.

Some day—perhaps not for a hundred or a thousand years, but some day—someone else would invent a time machine, which might not be so generous, or so human, in its self-disposition. Then, the Era of Change would begin anew…or the Dread Empire of Eternity, or the Euchronian Millennium, or something else, depending on the whimsical collaboration of fate and luck.

Time travel, Michael understood, was not a wise thing to invent even once, and likely to be deadly if invented twice. Visitors from the future, even if they were unable to arrive in the flesh, were bound to cause trouble. From their own temporal viewpoint, they would change history simply by arriving, let alone by virtue of what they might do thereafter, with the information in their minds and any physical equipment they might contrive to transfer. Chaos was bound to ensue—and would not easily be resolved. It really did not matter overmuch whether the hypothetical spindle of necessity was imagined to be casting off new buds, or whether it was envisaged as tying itself in knots—the maziness of the temporal ether was equal to either interpretation, or either challenge—the real point was that the one and only moment of becoming would be become unsteady, troubled and corrupted by a dark malaise. The unicursality of logic would be replaced by a multicursality in which it was theoretically possible to be lost forever, and the music of time, dissolving into discord, might be replaced by an eternal and irredeemable cacophony.

Once a time machine had been invented, and had become available for resonant interaction with its future kin, the reimposition of unicursal order was bound to be a very costly business, and such order could only be provisional unless and until the time machine had been uninvented again—a task even more paradoxical, and thus even more difficult, than the original invention. Obviously, that process of uninvention required pivots of some sort: not only goddesses but heroes, prepared to fight the forces of confusion with their minds and their arms, and with resources of a far more fundamental sort.

Michael knew that he had succeeded in his own part of the ordeal far more by luck than by judgment—but he thought he understood, now why the inhabitants of the Era of Change thought luck obscene. The point was that he had succeeded, just as Signor Monti-carlo had succeeded, and the Mistress of the Labyrinth herself. It had all worked out, with the awkward precision of what Quentin Hope would doubtless have called, more accurately than he knew, a *deus ex machina*.

Cribden Church clock had completed the twelfth chime of noon, but it had left strange overtones vibrating in the empty air above Langstrade Hall. The clockwork mechanism powering Gregory Marlstone's time machine made a feeble attempted to extend its screech further, but the sound faded into cacophonous ignominy. The machine had stopped. The chain of moments that had briefly extended for thousands of years into the future was severed. History had resumed its course: the course that it had seemingly followed since the dawn of time—or would, at least, seem *from now onwards* to have followed since that pale and tentative dawn.

There were seven bodies lying inert on the floor of the Keep, with two shotguns and a catapult lying nearby. Michael dropped the poniard of Lord Langstrade's swordstick on the floor, and used the hand thus liberated to stop the swinging pendulum as he went past to kneel beside one of the supine forms.

Michael picked Cecilia up and carried her out of the Keep and across the drawbridge. He eventually set her down close to his easel, where his painting still rested serenely, unaffected by the entire adventure. He felt a strange sense of *déjà-vu* as he watched the eyelids open, and eyes whose blueness was exaggerated by the reflection of the summer sky stare up at him.

There was nothing steely about their gaze

"I seem to have fainted," Cecilia said, when Michael set her on her feet. "My head hurts terribly. I think I was coming to see you, but I seem to remember feeling faint almost as soon as I had set foot in the Maze. I had the most remarkable nightmare, in which I was imprisoned in a giant head of bronze, and it has left me with the most painful aftermath. Have I been poisoned?"

Michael offered her his arm, so that she might support herself, but she sat down on the grass instead, and put her aching head in her hands.

"Yes," Michael told her, as he sat down beside her, "You were poisoned, for an hour or two, but the Mistress of the Labyrinth protected you, while…." He left off there, unsure as to what he ought to tell her. Propriety instructed him to be silent, but she was, after all, his intended wife, from whom he ought to have no secrets.

"Your ear's bleeding," Cecilia told him. "Are you hurt?"

"It's just a scratch," he assured her.

"Were we inside the Keep?" Cecilia asked, apparently remembering, at least, where she had been when he had picked her up.

"Yes," Michael said.

"Is Mr. Marlstone still there?"

"Yes," Michael confirmed told her. "Nor is he alone. He's been poisoned too, as were your father and Jack, Mr. Hope, Mr. Escott and Lady Phythian—but it might have been a great deal worse, I think. The Langstrade Maze must have shaped and directed the field of the machine, in such a way that only a small contingent of Vikings contrived to get into the dale, and most of them fell prey to a Mesmeric spell woven by Signor Monticarlo's violin. Had you not actually been inside the Maze...." Again he trailed off—but Cecilia was not yet feeling well enough to give him her full attention, or to demanded further explanation of what he was saying.

"Everything's all right now, though," Michael went on. "I managed to cut the cords of the driving-mechanism and stop the machine, exactly when it needed to be stopped—to the very second. I can't claim the credit for that, though—the time machine was the expert in timing, as is only appropriate. I don't believe that Marlstone will have the audacity to attempt another trial—but if he insists, I doubt that he'll obtain any result at all, and will only make a fool of himself."

"I'm glad it's over," Cecilia said, trying to collect herself as her distress gradually eased. "I was afraid, when the machine threatened to run amok."

"So was I," Michael admitted, no longer feeling the need to be brave, or to pretend to have been brave. "It was a very frightening time."

"Will Mr. Marlstone be upset," she asked, "that so many people came into the Keep and disturbed his experiment?"

"I don't think so," Michael said. "At any rate, he can't complain, because I succeeded in doing what he tried to do and failed—and he'll have to change his clothes and take a bath before he does anything at all, because he fell into the moat and covered himself in mud. I'll tell him that my success in stopping the machine was pure luck, but he probably won't believe me. To a mathematician like him, *luck* is a dirty word."

"Was it *pure luck*?" Cecilia asked.

"In a way, yes—but it was also fate, and cunning design."

"Whose design? Yours?"

"I fear not—that particular design required far more cunning than any mere artist could provide, or even a clockmaker's son.

Such an accomplished designer, I suspect, will not be born for thousands of years…but eternity is a long time, and I don't doubt that she'll be born one day."

"A great inventor, no doubt?" she said, looking at him quizzically between her dainty fingers, which were still clutching her agonized head.

"Quite the contrary," Michael told her—but then he tired of speaking in riddles and stood up. He went to look at his painting, to make perfectly certain that it was making satisfactory progress, in spite of the time he had lost.

While he was appraising it with a critical eye, Jeanne Evredon came though the gap in the hedge from the Maze. "Lady Langstrade—Millicent, that is—has dispatched her daughter, Carmela and myself to search for eight lost souls," the somniloquist said. "We're picnicking in the rose-garden again, but there's no sign in the house of Lord Langstrade and Jack, or Mr. Hope and Mr. Escott, or even Lady Phythian. I hoped, at least to find Mr. Laurel and Mr. Marlstone here."

"Everyone's here," Michael told her. "Hope, Escott, Lady Phythian, Marlstone, Jack and his father are all in the Keep."

"Are they all right?" the somniloquist asked. "When noon chimed and no catastrophe occurred, we assumed that Mr. Marlstone's machine had failed again—but we did not know that so many people had ignored his Lordship's prohibition and come to witness the experiment. Did you know that you have blood on your cheek? You seem to have grazed your ear."

Michael felt a stab of conscience as he remembered that he had not paused to ascertain whether the other people lying in the Keep were still alive, only being able to think about Cecilia. Before he could rely, though, he saw Jack Langstrade emerge unsteadily through the broken doorway of the Keep, at the head of a strange procession. Mr. Hope and Mr. Escott were supporting one another, trying in vain to walk in step as they made their way over the drawbridge, and then came Lord Langstrade and Lady Phythian, the aristocrat nobly assisting the limping widow. No one was supporting Mr. Marlstone—he was far too muddy to encourage the slightest touch—but his was the strongest physique of all, and he strode over the drawbridge with a firm gait that was almost swaggering.

They were all groaning fearfully, wincing as the sun beamed its kindly light down upon their bare heads, and complaining loudly of having been poisoned. As soon as they saw Michael, Cecilia and the somniloquist waiting for them, they stopped complaining to one another and redirected their efforts, in quest of a better sympathy.

Unsurprisingly, Escott was complaining loudest of all, proclaiming that he had already had one such headache the previous night, before going to bed, and that a second one was adding injury to injury, and insult to insult. Lady Phythian was incapable of saying anything, and Marlstone was dumbfounded by the sorry condition of his clothing. Jack contented himself with moaning softly. Mr. Hope declared that he must have eaten something that disagreed with him, but Escott immediately retorted that it felt more as if something with which he had disagreed had eaten him. Both men announced that they had hurt their fingers and shoulders too. Lord Langstrade took time out from his own misery to opine that the injuries in question looked like the kind of injuries that a novice sportsman might suffer from firing a shotgun awkwardly."

"Speaking of shotguns," Cecilia said, "are those pellet-marks in the door of the Keep? And why has one of the battens been broken down?"

"Don't worry about it, my love," Michael said. "Let's go have lunch—your mother and grandmother will be annoyed with us if we delay any longer." He noticed that Jeanne Evredon had blushed when he spoke the words *my love*, and then smiled, as if she had just been let in on a secret.

"By the way," Michael said to the somniloquist, as the trio moved into the Maze without waiting for the others to catch up with them, "I have a message for my former self, which I'd like you to relay, if you can."

"I already have," the somniloquist reminded him. "I can still remember it, word for word. Are you the future self that sent the paradoxical message?"

"Yes I am," Michael confirmed. "Dr. Carp would be proud of me, I think, for I am no longer intimidated by logic."

"And I," she replied, "am no longer intimidated by Dr. Carp—or, for that matter, the Maze. I was lying down in my room a little while ago when Signor Monticarlo began to practice, and I was afraid that the terror I had felt the previous night might return, but it did not. Quite the reverse, in fact. I have no idea what piece it was he played, but it was the most remarkably calming music I have ever heard I my life, and I feel quite renewed. Miss Langstrade, may I borrow Mr. Laurel's spare arm, while he escorts us both to the rose-garden?"

"You may," said Cecilia, without the slightest hint of jealousy or resentment. She knew now, it seemed, that she no longer had any cause for anxiety in respect of the force and direction of Michael's affections.

CHAPTER TWENTY-THREE

THE COURSE OF HISTORY RESUMED

Michael cleaned up his face easily enough, and was only a little late joining the other picnickers, but by the time Gregory Marlstone had changed out of his muddy clothes and washed his face, lunch was almost over. "I fear," the inventor announced to the crowd sitting on the grass between the resplendent bushes, in a slightly peevish tone, "that my experiment has been a complete failure, for the third time—complicated, admittedly, by various unanticipated effects of a minor sort, but a failure nevertheless. I'm beginning to fear that I might never succeed. At any rate, there is no question of my attempting another demonstration in the near future. My entire theory is evidently in need of radical reconceptualization."

"I wouldn't say that it was a *complete* failure," Lord Langstrade informed him, judiciously exercising his rights and duties as a host, "but I must admit that the machine's operation left me feeling quite confused and rather nauseous. I rather wish that I hadn't attended the demonstration, and I can't quite remember why I did. You were right to forbid us it seems, and I, of one, wish that I had heeded your demand."

"I feel the same sensation of confusion and residual dyspepsia," Marlstone admitted, "but I'm not convinced that it has anything to do with my machine. It might have been something we ate."

"It certainly was not!" the younger Lady Langstrade retorted. Signor Monticarlo and Carmela are perfectly well, and so is Mademoiselle Evredon. Indeed, we all feel quite remarkably healthy—inspired, as it were, by the soothing music that Signor Monticarlo was playing in his room." She looked around for moral support, and the three guests she had named nodded vigorously. The elder Lady Langstrade also presented a personification of perfect health.

"I certainly don't think it was anything I ate," said Lady Phythian, loyally. "I suspect that I must have slipped into some sort of quasi-somniloquistic trance. I had a perfectly horrible nightmare."

"Is *that* what happened?" Escott said. "Damn it, Carp, have you been playing tricks on us? Was it you who gave us all this terrible headache with some magnetic jiggery-pokery?"

"Certainly not," the Mesmerist replied. "I too feel remarkably well—better than I have for years, in fact, and if there was any magnetic influence at work in the Hall this morning, it was a curative one. I wish I could claim credit for it, but I cannot. What was that piece you were playing, Signor Monticarlo? Bach, perhaps, or Beethoven?"

"I am flattered that you should think so," the virtuoso replied. "I was—what is the English word?—*improvising*. To tell the truth, I cannot remember exactly what notes I played or even how the violin was tuned...I wish that I had written the piece down, but I did not. I am only sorry that Mr. Laurel missed it—I feel sure that he would have appreciated it."

Michael could not see any way to explain that he had heard it, and had appreciated it, so he contented himself with saying: "I'm sure that I would, maestro."

Carmela Monticarlo smiled at him—but Cecilia did not seem to mind at all.

"Well, I think you're playing games with us, Carp," Escott insisted. "I think you decided to teach Hope and myself an unkind lesson, because we were less than reverent about your skills during your *séance*."

"Were you?" asked Carp, cheerfully feigning innocence. "I didn't notice." He no longer seemed in the least dispirited, and was darting occasional glances at Jeanne Evredon charged with the utmost benevolence.

"That could not explain," Lady Phythian put in, "why I feel as wretched as you do. Dr. Carp certainly has nothing against me."

"Nor me," said Jack Langstrade. "I thought his *séance* was spiffing, and said so—didn't I, Sis?"

Cecilia confirmed that this was true, but entered no plea on her own behalf. Lord Langstrade also rallied to the Mesmerist's support, insisting that their unfortunate malaise must have been a side-effect of the activation of Gregory Marlstone's machine.

"It's possible, of course, Mr. Marlstone," the Mesmerist said, with sly good humor, "that what you have in the Keep isn't really a time machine at all, but an unprecedentedly powerful generator of animal magnetism, which puts Anton Mesmer's modest inventions to shame."

"It is most certainly *not* possible," Marlstone informed Dr. Carp, frostily. "What I have in the Keep is most definitely a time machine, albeit one that has never quite contrived to work as it was intended to work, and perhaps never will."

"Amen to that," muttered Lord Langstrade.

"Do you really think that it might be possible to construct Mesmeric machines, Dr. Carp?" the younger Lady Langstrade asked. "Not merely somniloquistic machines, but machines that use the latent power of animal magnetism to cure injury and disease?"

"It's certainly possible, Milady," Carp opined, "but we have no way of knowing when it might become practicable. I'm sorry to hear Mr. Marlstone dismiss the possibility that his machine might have generated Mesmeric force, for that would surely have helped to explain all the strange dreams that so many of us seem to have experienced last night and this morning."

"So your future Mesmeric machinery will be able to generate and shape dreams, too?" Cecilia remarked. "How wonderful! Now that really is a Euchronian prospect—don't you agree, Mr. Hope?"

Hope, who seemed unusually subdued, perhaps because of his lingering headache, said: "I'm unconvinced. Such machines might, I suppose, have some curative value, if not oracular merit, but I would advise any would-be inventor to bear in mind the sad fate of Dr. Graham's Temples of Health and Hygiene. There's a thin line between scientific Mesmerism and quackery, which tempts the most scrupulous of us."

"Did you know, Mr. Hope," said Augustus Carp, responding promptly to the deliberate cue, "that I worked in one of Graham's so-called Temples in my youth. I once met the Duchess of Devonshire there...."

It was, Michael thought, time to tune out of the conversation and concentrate on matters of more immediate interest: Cecilia and the last fugitive remnants of the lunch. He had already eaten his fair share, but the indisposition of so many of his fellow diners had ensured that there was food in abundance still available, and he still felt ravenous. He continued to satisfy that particular appetite, while making quite certain that he paid due attention to the love of his life as he did so, at least with his gaze.

They don't even know that I'm a hero, he thought. *They haven't the slightest idea. To most of them, I'm still just the fool who's painting the Folly. Except that they won't think me quite as much of a fool as I seemed before, once they know that I'm going to marry Cecilia. What wiser step could any man take?*

He waited until the picnic was over, however, before he and Cecilia sought and found an opportunity to catch Lord Langstrade apart from the crowd. "My lord," he aid, without beating about the bush, "might I have the honor of asking for your daughter's hand in marriage?"

Lord Langstrade still seemed a trifle confused by his experience of being stored in a phantom bronze head while displaced from his body. "You're the third person to ask me that today, sir," he replied, a trifle gruffly, "and it's not yet two o'clock. Best get the business over and done with for good, I suppose, if Cecilia's agreeable. Are you, my dear?"

"I wish you would allow me to accept Mr. Laurel's proposal, Father," Cecilia said, with all due delicacy.

"I suppose I ought to ask Emily first," the Earl said, glancing in the direction of his wife, who was chatting with the Monticarlos and the rejuvenated Dr. Carp. "She'll want to know what your prospects are, I dare say."

"I'm not rich, as you know, Milord," Michael said, "but I have some ability in my vocation. What's more—and I think Mr Hope would agree with me on this point—I now have the utmost confidence in the future, and the prospects of progress."

"That's good enough for me," Langstrade proclaimed. "Cecilia and I will square Emily, between us—but you'd better make yourself scarce while we do that."

"I have to get back to my painting, in any case," Michael said.

"I didn't, by any chance, leave my walking-stick by your easel when I came to see you this morning, did I?" Langstrade asked. "I seem to have mislaid it, today of all days." He shot Michael an enquiring glance, as if to make sure that Michael still knew why he had said *today of all days*.

Michael nodded. "It's safe, Milord," he said, "and I'm fully aware of how much the instrument means to you. If you care to come and pick it up later this afternoon, I'll have it ready for you."

"Excellent," said the Earl. "In that case, I think all's well with the world." There was just a hint of uncertainty in his voice.

"So do I, Milord," Michael said, without the slightest suggestion of unsteadiness. "So do I."

As Michael began to walk away in the direction of the Keep, however, Quentin Hope hurried to intercept him, and to fall into step with him.

"Forgive me if I'm being indiscreet, Laurel," he said, "but did you just ask Lord Langstrade if you might marry his daughter?"

"I did," Michael confirmed.

Hope swallowed hard before saying: "And what was his answer?"

"He said that he would have to consult his wife, but that he foresaw no difficulty, in view of the fact that the request was in accordance with Cecilia's wishes."

"Oh," said Hope. "Right. You know, I suppose, that I made a similar request earlier this morning?"

"Yes," Michael confirmed.

"Escott got in even before me, the treacherous swine," Hope commented, resentfully, but was quick to add: "That's not the point, though. I wanted to congratulate you, and assure you that there are no hard feelings—on my part, at least. I hate clichés, so I won't say that the best man won, but I wish you every happiness, quite sincerely."

"That's very gentlemanly of you," Michael said, "and I thank you kindly. I've learned a lot this weekend, Mr. Hope, and a lot of the credit for that is due to you. I like your philosophy."

"And why should you not, since it has elegance and intelligence, as well as optimism?" said Hope, beaming broadly—but the smile quivered slightly as he seemed to remember another reason why he had taken the trouble to run after the artist. "By the by, Laurel, I had a very strange dream last night. You were in it, briefly, although I'm not sure why, as you had no actual contribution to make to it."

"Did I not, Mr. Hope?" said Michael, blithely. "I'm sorry for that."

"I dreamed that I went back in time to some strangely distant past, and that I was able to speak to Edward Kelley through the medium of the notorious black stone. He took me for an angel, and was so avid for guidance that I was able to give him a long lecture on the substance of the revolution that his master's secret college was fated to bring about. I even threw in the elements of Marlstone's theory of time, with a few addenda of my own. It was foolishly narcissistic, I admit, to imagine myself the maker of the scientific revolution rather than merely its beneficiary, but I have to confess that it was not the first time I had imagined making such a speech. I had it, so to speak, already prepared. Indeed, while I was in the dream, I was haunted by the notion that the entire purpose of my life had been to compose, prepare and deliver that missive. I usually forget my dreams almost as soon as I wake, but this one lingered."

"I believe that we all had strange dreams last night, Mr. Hope," Michael told him. "Signor Monticarlo's concert had excited us more than we supposed, and Dr. Carp's *séance* had disturbed us more than we pretended. When we set off into the Maze, not so much in quest of ghosts as in the determination to play the role of ghosts ourselves, were we not setting ourselves up to experience strange dreams?"

"I suppose we were," Hope said, tentatively. "I suffered further today—I've lost nearly two hours from the continuity of my consciousness, and had a frightful nightmare: the same one that Escott insisted on relating to me full before we finally went to bed last night. That man has been such a blight on my life…but I believe that his malice rebounded this time, for he suffered a recurrence himself."

"So it seems," Michael admitted.

"I was sitting next to Lady Phythian at lunch," Hope continued, "and she told me that she did see a ghost in the Maze last night— and that you would confirm that she was telling the truth."

"That's true," Michael said. "Lady Phythian did see a ghost in the Maze last night, and I can confirm that she is telling the truth. If ever she has difficulty, in future, in persuading anyone of her sincerity when she tells the story of the Langstrade ghosts, I shall be ready and willing to endorse her account. She is an authentic ghost-seer."

"Right," said Hope. Then, seemingly tiring of beating around the bush, he bit the bullet, and said: "It *was* a dream, wasn't it. You and I didn't *really* go back in time together, to change history by educating the secret college? It really was just an idle narcissistic fancy?"

Michael barely hesitated before replying: "You should not underestimate the significance of dreams, Mr. Hope. Narcissistic your fancy might have been, but it was certainly not idle. You really were prepared to make that speech, to change history. No one else could have done it—no one, at least, who was a guest at the Hall last night. There *is* a sense in which your whole life has been a preparation for the substance of that dream, just as you will live the remainder of your years working tirelessly, both imaginatively and intellectually, for the cause of future progress. It was and is a very fine dream, Mr. Hope, and I beg you to maintain it, for all our sakes."

Hope paused momentarily for reflection, and then said: "Thank you for that, Laurel; it's good of you to reassure me. I feel more in need of reassurance now than I usually do, perhaps because I woke up in the Keep in such dire confusion that I don't even remember going in, and have no idea why I had a shotgun by my side. Do you happen to know whether I fired it?"

"Twice," Michel confirmed.

"Harmlessly, I hope?"

"Quite harmlessly, as luck would have it."

"Good," Hope said, dully—as if he would have liked to ask for further details, but did not dare. He sighed theatrically. "Sometimes, Laurel," he said, sadly, "I wonder if I might actually be the giddy fool that people often take me for. Do you know Voltaire's *Candide*?"

"No," Michel admitted.

"It features a character named Dr. Pangloss—a Leibnizian who has taken a slightly excessive moral from the great philosopher's *Theodicy*, and keeps insisting, in the face of all the disasters heaped upon his world and his friends by the author—war, famine, pestilence, rape, and so on—that everything is for the best in the best of all possible worlds. Most readers take him for a perfect imbecile, as Voltaire doubtless intended him to seem, but I always had a certain sympathy for the man, and felt that the author was stacking the deck against him unfairly. After all, even if we don't live in *quite* the best of all possible worlds, it's by no means as black as gloom-mongers like Escott insist on painting it, is it? If people think me a Dr. Pangloss, I'm not prepared to be ashamed of it, even if it does make me out to be foolish. After all, if we can't believe that there are good things in life, and that they might become even better, then there isn't much prospect of them becoming better, is there?"

"You're absolutely right, Mr. Hope," Michael assured him, serenely. "For me, I must admit, at present, this *is* the best of all possible worlds—and I can't see the slightest reason to doubt it, to regret it, or to be ashamed of my joyful conviction."

"You're a good man, Laurel," Hope said, as they reached the entrance to the Maze. He was evidently feeling much better. "I wish you the best of luck with your painting…and everything else."

"Thank you," Michael said, and left him at the entrance.

When he arrived in the center, the first thing he did was to recover the two separated parts of Lord Langstrade's forgotten swordstick from the grass and the stone floor of the Keep, and reunite them. He propped the stick against the frame of the easel, and then took up his palette again. He was, however, interrupted before he could complete his preparation to begin painting—not, as he had expected, by Lord Langstrade, but by James Escott.

"Sorry to disturb you, Laurel," the thin man said, in all seeming sincerity, "but I feel that I owe you an apology."

"Not at all," Michael said. "I have no complaint against you for asking Lord Langstrade for Cecilia's hand. Nor has Mr. Hope, although he might feel obliged to sulk for while. By the time we all catch the train on Tuesday morning, everything will be back to normal, and you'll be arguing to your hearts' content."

"That's very fair of you," Escott judged. "I couldn't help feeing guilty, though. I had a dream in which you saved me from a fate worse than death—and then I tried to beat you to the punch with Langstrade, having at least suspected that you were head over heels. I was punished for it, mind—sent back to the hellish prison before the morning was half way through. I'm not quite sure how the second nightmare ended, but I had a vague feeling that you might have pulled me out of that one too. Funny how guilt works. Anyhow, I thought it best to apologize, just in case there was a hint of rancor in your heart."

"None whatsoever," Michael assured him.

"If I weren't such a curmudgeon," Escott remarked, with a sigh, "I dare say I'd have pleasant dreams, as others seem capable of doing, but I just can't see the world in the same kindly light as Hope. I can always see the things that might go wrong. I was perfectly ready to believe the somniloquist's dire prediction that a catastrophe was inevitable if Marlstone's time machine worked, even though I was perfectly certain that it couldn't and wouldn't work, and in spite of the fact that I don't have an atom of faith in the oracular prowess of Mesmerists' marionettes. The problem is, of course, that things *can* always go wrong, even with the best-laid plans. No matter how cleverly things are arranged and adapted, they're always at the mercy of chance, malevolence and the unintended consequences of our actions. There's no way things can ever be finally settled and perfected, no matter how hard we try. Leibniz was right, you see— even an omnipotent and omnibenevolent God couldn't contrive a universe in which evil is impossible, because the raw materials of creation simply don't permit it. Every time we avoid one catastrophe, or contrive an improvement in the world's circumstances, there's another catastrophe waiting around the corner, threatening not only to wipe out our new achievements but all the advantages we inherited. That's just the way things are."

"I can't deny it," Michael admitted, in a cheerful tone that was quite unfitted to the admission.

"No," Escott, observed, "but at least *you* can defy it, for now. You're in love, and Cecilia loves you in return. You're happy—on top of the world. Make the most of every minute, Laurel—don't waste a second."

"The present moment is all there is, Mr. Escott," Michael told him, absent-mindedly. "The past is gone, no more than a vast collection of phantoms, and the future is still a dream…from which, as you say, the threat of nightmare can never be conclusively banished, any more than the prospect of every success. But all there actually is, *is*. Time never really was, and is never really past. Only brazen heads and the inventors of time machines think otherwise."

Escott said nothing to that, but contented himself with watching as Michael, having scrupulously loaded his palette, set about applying paint to his canvas, with minute care. After a few more minutes, the cadaverous figure turned to go away, but Michael barely caught a glimpse of the other's retreating back from the corner of his eye.

"At any rate," the painter murmured to himself, having already forgotten what he had just said, "there's no point in talking to me about such weighty matters. Like Signor Monticarlo, I'm just an artist. If there's anything that needs to be said, my work will speak for me."

ABOUT THE AUTHOR

BRIAN STABLEFORD was born in Yorkshire in 1948. He taught at the University of Reading for several years, but is now a full-time writer. He has written many science fiction and fantasy novels, including *The Empire of Fear, The Werewolves of London, Year Zero, The Curse of the Coral Bride*, and *The Stones of Camelot*. Collections of his short stories include *Sexual Chemistry: Sardonic Tales of the Genetic Revolution, Designer Genes: Tales of the Biotech Revolution*, and *Sheena and Other Gothic Tales*. He has written numerous nonfiction books, including *Scientific Romance in Britain, 1890-1950, Glorious Perversity: The Decline and Fall of Literary Decadence*, and *Science Fact and Science Fiction: An Encyclopedia*. He has contributed hundreds of biographical and critical entries to reference books, including both editions of *The Encyclopedia of Science Fiction* and several editions of the library guide, *Anatomy of Wonder*. He has also translated numerous novels from the French language, including several by the feuilletonist Paul Féval and various classics of French scientific romance.